Praise for Keith Melton's *The Zero Dog War*

"Melton has a strong writing voice that is hard not to love."

~ *Anna's Book Blog*

"Keith Melton writes an absurd mix of heavy-duty action and hilarious quips...I cannot wait for more books in the 'Zero Dog Missions' series."

~ *Alpha Reader*

"Urban Fantasy meets hilarious sarcasm at its best...I had high expectations and *The Zero Dog War* didn't fail to deliver."

~ *Book Lovers, Inc.*

"Mr. Melton entertains his readers with wit, humor, and a whole bunch of kick-ass. It just doesn't get any better than this. I was hooked from page one... The action is exhilarating and the humor is laugh-out-loud."

~ *BookWenches*

"The plot is brilliant; we get a lot of very random and interesting things happening throughout the book, lots of excellent explosions and fight scenes..."

~ *BaffledBooks*

"...a hilarious tongue in cheek satire that pokes fun at the supernatural in a fast-paced, action-packed storyline."

~ *Smexybooks*

Look for these titles by

Keith Melton

Now Available:

Nightfall Wolf Clans Series

Run, Wolf

Zero Dog Missions Series

The Zero Dog War

Nightfall Syndicate Series

Blood Vice

Ghost Soldiers

The Zero Dog War

Keith Melton

Samhain Publishing, Ltd.
11821 Mason Montgomery Road, 4B
Cincinnati, OH 45249
www.samhainpublishing.com

The Zero Dog War

Print ISBN: 978-1-60928-403-9
Digital ISBN: 978-1-60928-364-3

Editing by Sasha Knight
Cover by Kanaxa

First Samhain Publishing, Ltd. electronic publication: February 2011
First Samhain Publishing, Ltd. print publication: January 2012

Dedication

For the Scribbling Ninjas: Alisha Rai, Bree and Donna of the Moira Rogers duo, and sometimes Vivian Arend, our friend to the north. Here's to all the chaos we've caused and have yet to cause in the years of running amok to come.

Also, for my editor, Sasha Knight, who makes books tighter, faster, stronger, and never once accused me of using mind-altering illegal substances.

"I am so clever that sometimes I don't understand a single word of what I am saying." Oscar Wilde

"Humor is the sense of the Absurd which is despair refusing to take itself seriously." Arland Ussher

"L33t haxxor pwnage of lame weaksauce n00bs!!11! DIAF kkthx!" Gavin Carter, Epic Mob Raid Leader

"...Mercenaries do nothing but damage." Machiavelli, *The Prince*

Absurd: adj. So clearly untrue or unreasonable as to be laughable or ridiculous.

Pretentious: adj. Defining common terms for the audience as if they didn't already know.

Warnings:

Do Not Operate Heavy Machinery While Reading This Book

This Product is Not Food

Product Does Not Give User Superpowers

This book has been clearly marked Parody and Satire. Read at your own risk. Humor quotient is not guaranteed. This book is not FDA approved.

This book does not contain sparkly vampires.

Chapter Zero: Napalm after Noon

Mercenary Wing Rv6-4 "Zero Dogs"
TastyTech Foods Corp
NE 181st Avenue, Portland, Oregon
1417 Hours PST April 7th

The first bullet is always free.

That's the motto of the Zero Dog mercenaries. After the first bullet, the charges come fast and steep because, while we aren't the best, we're certainly in the top ten, and you had to pay for quality. I should know. I run this chickenshit outfit and my name's on all the invoices: Captain Andrea Walker, Pyromancer. My job description included burning everything from bad guys to bunkers into charred toast and getting my people home with all their pieces in the proper order.

Oh, and getting paid.

The Zero Dogs had deployed near a Portland-area industrial park just off I-84, close enough to the Columbia River to smell the water, but not see it. We'd been contracted to deal with a radical fringe element deemed a clear and present danger to the private-label packaging industry. Negotiating with food-industry terrorists could be tricky, so here I stood in the turret of our M2A3 Warhammer Bradley Fighting Vehicle, peering along the barrel of the chain gun and wishing I had some more coffee.

It was gonna be one of those days.

I keyed my mike. "Tiffany, you're clear. Get in the air and give me a good lookdown."

"Roger wilco, Captain." Behind the cover of the Bradley, my scout, Tiffany Sparx, spread her black wings and took to the air. She swung overhead, and I turned to watch her fly, a curvy shape against the low cloud ceiling. Tiffany was a succubus. Even decked out in flak jacket, sky camo fatigues and wearing a helmet with a side-mounted camera, she drew whistles and cheers from the SWAT team guys stationed behind the perimeter barricades.

Tiffany's voice, sultry and silken, came over my headset. "Captain, they're *whistling* at me, over."

"Don't worry, I'll singe their jockstraps later." I kept my own voice reassuring and very open to interpretation on whether or not I was kidding. "Focus on the mission. You're my eyes in the sky, girl. Out."

I watched as she swung back in a slow arc, her wings massive, bat-like, pounding the air with hard strokes as she picked up speed and altitude. My insides felt as if they were frozen solid, and my heart beat hard enough to shatter them. I hated sending Tiffany over hot zones. That damn flak jacket wouldn't stop much more than shrapnel, but heavier armor would mean too much weight to fly. Still, she had a job to do, and I wanted a lookdown view on the plant before I decided which side to assault. I pulled down our modified Helmet Mounted Display System visor that fed me real-time information and images from the camera on Tiffany's helmet.

"How long, Captain?" Gavin asked over the com. He gunned the Bradley's engine, underlining his impatience with a diesel roar, and a cloud of black diesel exhaust billowed out on the right side of my turret. "My jockeys are riding up my crack, over."

"Be patient. Cut the chatter. Out." I mentally reviewed my mission assets as I scanned through Tiffany's feed.

Gavin Carter, at the Bradley's controls, could drive anything and drive it well, including the ill-fated prototype armor-plated Urban Assault Solo Segway design with the rather unfortunate acronym of UASS. He was registered as a Class 2 empath, yet flaunted the social skills of a tree frog, a sarcastic streak as wide as an aircraft carrier, and a heap of artistic pretension to boot.

I had Hanzo Sorenson, our medic, on the weapons systems—a damn sight better than letting him sneak around with his katana and Band-Aids. His real name was Austin, and he was as white as freshly bleached socks, but he'd had his name legally changed to Hanzo in honor of some legendary ninja. The fact that we had our medic on guns was another example of how desperately shorthanded we'd been for the last six months.

I'd claimed the commander's spot atop the turret. In the back I had my quick deployment team, led by my second-in-command, Sergeant Nathan Genna, ubiquitously known as Sarge, whose issues revolved around being a demon and having lost his key for the elevator to heaven, our werewolf, Rafe Lupo, the horniest bastard I'd ever seen and always on the prowl for his destined mate, and our summoner mage, Mia Tanaka, who—thanks to the fact she surrounded herself with chittering death pets from another dimension—smelled like wet fur most of the time. Only Stefan Dalca, our vampire, wasn't present because the lazy, delicate-skinned bastard wasn't available for the day shift.

At first blush it might not seem like a lot of punch, but for destruction, we were pretty damn Sierra Hotel badass. And we needed to be shit-hot badass, because a few hours ago four heavily armed dark elves had broken into TastyTech Foods Corp, a canning plant well northeast of downtown. Due to a union strike, economic recession and a plant slowdown, nobody had been working at the time except for the custodian, who'd called the cops. The first cruiser on the scene had been shot up by assault rifles and then disintegrated by a spell that rusted all the metal down to dust. No casualties, but the cops had pulled back and called in SWAT. Once SWAT learned of the dark magic involved, they doubled back and called in the Zero Dogs. We had an independent contractor agreement with the city for handling thaumaturgical threats. The dark elves had holed themselves up with automatic weapons, defensive spells, and made bomb threats by singing them over the phone in haunting, maudlin and overly complex Elvish verse to the SWAT team negotiator.

A typical, everyday, willy-nilly clusterfuck of righteous proportions in other words.

"I can't go on this mission, Captain," Rafe said over the com, interrupting my brooding thoughts.

"Shut up, Rafe," Mia answered. "You already said that twice. We all know your fun needle went off the scale ten minutes ago."

I heard his low growl. He hadn't shifted yet—he'd do it right before the assault—but like mustard stains, wolf traits bled through. Thank God he was housebroken.

"And I *mean* it," Rafe said. "I happen to agree with what these guys are doing. They're threatening to destroy processed food that's been leached of every bit of nutrition, loaded down with high fructose corn syrup and—"

I cut him off. "I don't care if they make radioactive Twinkies. Keep this goddamn channel clear of chatter."

Good images of the canning plant started to stream across my HUD display as Tiffany circled. I had building blueprints from the city, of course, but I needed to see how their spell defenses were set. Two massive decay spells glowed with black auras in my display, one near the roof access and one near a group of A/C ducts. That meant no topside assault, because I didn't have a spell sapper. Note to self: Put a job ad in the paper for one, post haste.

"I've got a hostile on the roof, Captain," Tiffany said.

I zoomed the camera in on the tiny figure that jumped out

from behind an A/C unit. A dark elf in urban camo, holding an AK-47 instead of a trusty longbow which never missed, even at three thousand meters in hurricane winds, as he glared up at Tiffany. I zoomed in still closer, cursing the unsteady image. He had those noble elven features, so beautiful you wanted to blacken one of his eyes just for the pleasure of making his face asymmetrical. The dark elf sported long, narrow ears that would shame Spock, and smooth gray skin. He had pure white hair tied back from his head held with golden bangles, creepy pale eyes, and a chin I could only describe as an arrogant, jutting monstrosity. Full disclosure: I loathed elves with the heat of a thousand burning suns.

He lifted the assault rifle and sighted in on Tiffany. The HUD view in my visor swung wildly as Tiffany saw the threat and peeled away, twisting and swooping through the air. The *crack, crack, crack* of rifle fire echoed down the street.

"I can't get close enough to charm him, over," Tiffany said.

"Pull back and stay out of range." My heart thudded with a rapid, dull punch. I had to force my breathing to remain even. I took it personally when bad guys shot at my people. *Very* personally. "We're going in, hard and hot."

Gavin snickered, and werewolf Rafe said, "That's exactly what I told Cindy last night."

"You two miscreants not hear the captain?" Sarge's bass-heavy voice rumbled in my ear. "Cut the chatter and that's an order."

I smirked at the ringing silence that followed Sarge's words. There were times I loved that demon. Too bad for my currently anemic love life that he was gay. I keyed the mike again. "All right, people, let's roll out. Attack plan Theta."

The diesel engine roared and the Bradley lurched forward, treads crunching on the asphalt as the fighting vehicle rounded the corner of the cinderblock wall, bringing the plant into view. The building stood two stories high, painted off-white, surrounded by an eight-foot chain-link fence, and baking in a concrete frying pan devoid of trees, shade and minimal landscaping.

"Which one is plan Theta, again?" Gavin asked over the com.

Hanzo keyed in. "It is the approach of silence, like wind above the water. The slide through shadows, as the fog creeps in from the ocean on the quiet feet of monkeys."

"Yeah, because Bradleys are so like ninjas," Gavin replied. "Or monkeys."

Mai sounded her usual serene self when she added, "I thought it was the Shattered Jewel Attack. But with ferrets and tear gas—"

"No, no," Rafe interrupted. "It's simple. You run on first down, throw on third. Start with Plan Theta, end with Plan Napalm Everything. You guys didn't read the manual? It even has pictures."

"Goddammit!" So much for cutting the chatter. When we got back to base I'd hand out some hardcore attack plan memorization as well as a heaping cupful of weeping and gnashing of teeth. "Blow a hole in the wall and drive the Bradley through."

"Affirmative, Big Mama One," Gavin said, and then muttered, "Why didn't you just say so in the first place?" He gunned the engine again and angled across the street, straight toward the plant's closest wall while I debated the best way to kill him later.

We used the Warhammer version of the Bradley Fighting Vehicle, with the Javelin missile system instead of the TOW IIs for its fire-and-forget capability. The boys had painted the Bradley black, added an image of a snarling pit bull on the turret, and covered the back end with bumper stickers. Among them: *Keep honking, I'm reloading.* A large green sticker that read: *A Gun Nut is Someone Who Doesn't Own One.* And my personal favorite: *Jesus Loves You. Everybody Else Thinks You're An Asshole.* Mia had painted a bright pink peace sign on the front armor. Her version of a joke. The wind snapped and fluttered the edges of our Japanese warlord banner (Hanzo's idea) displaying our Rv6-4 insignia, black long sword on a beige field with an inverted crimson chevron.

The Bradley rumbled over the curb, antennae swinging, spewing diesel fumes in clouds of black smoke like a dragon after a bucket of habañero-and-garlic-flavored chicken wings. The dark elf on the roof ran to the edge and began to fire at the Bradley. I ducked inside and slammed the hatch. A couple rounds zinged off the armor. I killed the video feed and peered out the view port, watching as the guy deluded himself that 7.62mm ammo would do anything more than make scuff marks I'd have to clean off later with a magic eraser.

"Suppress that guy," I ordered. For a moment I wanted to grab the hand station joystick and use the weapon systems to do it myself, payback for his potshots at Tiffany, but I held the urge in check and left it to Hanzo.

The turret swung and the Bushmaster 25mm chain gun angled upward. "Target acquired," Hanzo said. "Engaging target."

The dark elf seemed to realize he was attempting the equivalent of poking a rhino in the balls with an electric cattle prod. He ducked back behind the raised roof ledge. Too late. The chain gun spat tungsten APFSDS-T rounds and that section of roof disappeared in a billowing cloud of brown dust and debris. And since APFSDS-T stood for Armor-Piercing Fin-Stabilized Discarding Sabot with Tracer—a long acronym to say depleted uranium death dart not made by Nerf—I knew the bastard was going to feel it in the morning.

"That's gonna leave a mark," Gavin confirmed.

"Prepare for assault," I said. "Weapons free."

We crashed through the chain-link fence, crushing it beneath our treads. The turret moved again. I glanced at my tactical display and the image relayed to me by gunner Hanzo's Integrated Sight Unit. At less than a hundred meters this would be pretty much point-blank. We'd be charging into our own shrapnel and right through the smoke, but the Bradley could take the dings.

"Target acquired," Hanzo said. "One away."

A Javelin missile roared out of the launcher in a cloud of white smoke and hit the nearside wall. I felt the explosion vibrate up through the metal floor of the fighting vehicle. Shrapnel and debris shot across the pavement, some of it *tinging* off our armor, and smoke billowed out in a roiling black mass. A second later another Javelin launched and slammed into the damaged wall, blowing the gap wider.

We bore down on the jagged opening, what grunts called a mouse hole, at thirty-plus miles an hour. The Bradley crashed through the debris, rocking hard to the right as one of the treads bit into a pile of rubble and scrap metal, and we plunged through the roiling gray smoke. There were no hostages and the surrounding streets and businesses had been shut down and evacuated, so we didn't need to worry about crushing some poor civilian.

Gavin smashed the Bradley through some kind of stainless-steel-shrouded conveyor belt, and a section went skidding across the work floor with a tortured groan of metal. The destroyed conveyor was empty, and the dispensers and racks of the flanking machines stood silent and bare. Their metal panels gleamed with spots of reflected fluorescent light.

I threw open the top hatch and climbed halfway out, ready to help suppress fire with flame of my own. I could smell metal, machine oil and some other chemical stink as I searched for targets to suppress. The Bradley's rear hydraulic ramp descended with a whine.

A dark elf stood near one of the canning machines and pallets of cardboard. His rifle barrel swung toward me. I thrust out my hand, calling on my fire magic and directing the extremely flammable vapor I'd summoned in a psychic-controlled flow toward the elf, less than a second before I sparked flame and watched my fire race along the vapor column toward him.

He shrieked and hurled himself out of the way of the fire stream an instant before it incinerated the stacks of unfolded cardboard boxes. He half-scooted, half-crawled behind the cover of the canning machine, screaming Elvish words. The room flared with yellow-orange firelight as the cardboard on the pallets burned.

Rafe leapt off the ramp edge before it had dropped halfway. He'd shifted into his werewolf form, an intimidating hybrid of wolf and man, his slavering wolf jaws too full of teeth, complete with blazing yellow eyes and long claws. Behind him came Sarge, our muscle-bound demon sporting a huge fucking gun, skin the color of an eggplant and looking like a stuntman who'd wandered away from a Terminator movie. His red pupils glowed like laser pointers, and his irises were as black as the barrel of a M4 carbine at midnight. Mia Tanaka brought up the rear, a slim shape in blue and yellow summoner robes wrinkled beneath her Kevlar vest, one dark strand of hair hanging out of her black helmet with a goddamn daisy painted on the front. A dozen ferret-like creatures with glowing red eyes flanked her and filled the air with high-pitched squeaking.

Assault team deployed. Time to kick ass.

One of the dark elves popped out from behind a file cabinet and opened fire with some kind of bullpup rifle, maybe a SAR 21 or QBZ-95. Rafe leapt toward him, taking the bullets without slowing. He howled with glee a moment before falling on the dark elf.

"Hey, wait, arrest that guy!" I shouted.

"Too late," Sarge informed me. The sounds of Rafe's bad table manners echoed through the office. The other dark elf who'd dodged my fire stream now sprayed bullets at us as he retreated. Sarge dropped him with a single headshot.

I saw the last dark elf and I froze, my breath catching in my throat. He was wrapped in a vest covered with explosives, standing in front of two spill-containment caddies with 55-gallon drums of acetone inside. About a million and a half red diamond flammable stickers were pasted everywhere, and because nobody on SWAT had bothered to inform me the place had hazardous materials stored inside, I'd just lit a merry cardboard bonfire.

Oh shit.

"*Nuru heren huo!*" the dark elf screamed, holding his hand over a classic red-button detonator switch.

"Everybody out!" I yelled. "Fall back!"

I slammed the hatch down. Sarge, Rafe and Mai and terrified demon ferrets piled into the back of the Bradley. The ramp came up, the hydraulics whining in a halfhearted machine scream.

"Get us out of here!" Through the Commander's Independent Viewer, I could see the dark elf threatening us with the detonator, his thumb over the switch. We couldn't light him up because of the flammable material. If he was determined to suicide himself, none of us could stop him. Few individuals scored as high on the bat-shit-crazy scale as a creature that strapped itself with explosives.

The engine rumbled and whined as Gavin reversed out of the hole in the wall, treads spitting chunks of concrete and plaster. He clipped the shattered edge of the hole and more of the wall came clattering down on the chassis with dull thuds. I clung to the metal support bar as we jounced around. My muscles trembled with all the adrenaline sizzling in my veins. Smoke curled out of the hole we'd blasted, and the inside glowed orange and yellow, making me think of a Jack-o'-lantern with a bullet hole in its forehead.

The explosion tore the world with a *ka-whump* that rocked the Bradley with a powerful shock wave. Shrapnel pinged off the armor. A roiling cloud of black smoke swept toward us with a fireball at its heart and then surged over us. I heard someone cussing over the com and realized it was me. Larger chunks of debris came crashing down, hitting topside with resounding metal *clongs* and *clangs* as if wrenches had started to rain from the heavens instead of frogs.

Gavin kept backing up, and seconds later we were free of the smoke cloud. He continued reversing out of the parking lot as fast as the Bradley would go. He accidentally backed over a parked Geo Metro and it crumpled like a soda can beneath a boot heel. Spectators cheered from behind the distant police barricades.

“FISHDO,” I said over the com. A very utilitarian acronym meaning *Fuck It, Shit Happens Drive On.*

“FISHDO, copy,” Gavin answered.

He finally stopped near the southern police perimeter which sealed off the street. My ears were still ringing from the explosion, and I could feel the tightness across my chest, the tremble of my muscles as reaction set in.

“Everybody all right?” I called out.

One by one, everybody checked in, including Tiffany, who sounded beside herself with relief, almost sobbing over the mike. Things must’ve looked bad from the air.

I switched radio frequencies. “SWAT, this is Zero Dog One. Targets neutralized. Send in the hose jockeys, over.”

“Neutralized?” some guy’s voice came back over the headset, sparking with either outrage or jealousy. “You fucking nuked that place.”

I keyed off without responding. Some people loved to wallow in the melodrama.

Patrolmen moved the barriers and let police cars through to escort the advancing fire trucks. The place burned with a furious intensity, sending up a huge twisting column of black smoke. The firefighters swarmed around, within minutes dumping streams of water onto the flames.

We hung around the Bradley and watched the festivities, waiting for a liaison from the mayor’s office to sign off on the contract work order and take our carbon copies. Gavin sat on the Bradley's front end as he sipped an energy drink and chewed a candy bar. Tiffany wrapped herself in her wings and stared over the top of them at the fire with wide, unblinking cat's eyes. Rafe had shifted back to human form and strutted around naked, showing off all his tattoos.

"Rafe," I said, "get some clothes on."

"What if my destined mate walks past? She won't recognize me if I hide the wang."

Sarge eyed him. "I suggest you do as the captain asks. Otherwise, I'll be forced to strip down and shame your earthworm."

"You guys are disgusting," Tiffany said, but I noticed she cast a surreptitious glance at Rafe's bare ass.

Hanzo walked over from the other side of the Bradley, having escaped his gunner position. He gripped a smoking piece of metal in one gloved hand, his black ninja pajamas and white face streaked with ashes. The hilt and grip of a katana poked up over his shoulder with the sheath strapped to his back over the red cross identifying him as a medic. This certainly qualified as a violation of the Geneva Convention rule about medics not being used in an offensive capacity. *Our* reality-challenged medic believed he was the reincarnated soul of a 14th-century ninja from the Iga Province during the Kamakura period.

"Captain," Hanzo said. "My sword cries to me its vengeance is appeased. Those dark elves died like warriors. Like snow throwing itself from the clouds to perish upon the mountains. I have a haiku I'd like to read—"

I held up a hand. "Hanzo. Don't." Between haiku and naked werewolves, my head threatened to explode. Honestly, I could see the countdown in my mind's eye. An egg timer on a bundle of dynamite, ticking away. "Can we please *try* and appear professional? At least until we get paid?"

"Look, Captain." Mia pointed across the street. A ferret had curled itself up on her shoulder. The rest she'd sent back to the dimension they'd come from. "The TV people."

Sure enough, news cameras and crew had lined up along the barricades, busy filming the still-naked Rafe. Rafe grinned and began to run through his selection of Mr. Universe poses.

Blessed Bitch of the Apocalypse, redeem us all with fire. Things couldn't get worse.

A black SUV zoomed past the barriers and slid to a stop near us with a serenade of chirping tires. The door flew open and out came four men, all in suits, all looking like veteran bureaucrats of the file-cabinet wars and cubical trenches. Two of them had digital cameras and began taking pictures. I recognized the guy who power walked over to us. Norville Ford. He had a piece of paper in his hand and jerked it around like a conductor who'd consumed far too much caffeine.

"You blew up that plant!" Norville yelled. "The jobs! The tax revenue lost!" He looked at Rafe and his voice screeched with the dulcet harmonies of a rake on a chalkboard. "And that's indecent exposure!"

What the hell had I been thinking when I'd said things couldn't get worse? God must hate me more than I'd suspected. I cleared my throat and tried on my shiniest smile. "Hi there, Norville—"

Norville locked in on me and didn't just invade my personal space—no, he blitzkrieged right into my face. His eyes were wild, outraged, and he screamed intermixed gibberish about the fire and naked Rafe. A bit of his spittle landed on my cheek.

I took a deep breath and leaned toward him, which he hadn't expected. He drew back and his rapid-fire word assault died off.

"SWAT called *us* in," I told him. "At no time were we warned that the elves had strapped *explosives* to their bodies and were standing next to *flammable* materials. It makes a difference, you know, in how we approach a problem." I leaned in even closer, doing my shark-grin thing, and pointed my finger in his face. "*They* blew the place up. We didn't. No good guys got hurt."

"Of course not," he snapped. "That's why we sent *you*

instead of SWAT. If you inept circus freaks got hurt, nobody would care. I didn't want city employees in danger. Imagine the lawsuits." He looked back at the fire and his fingers twitched. "But you weren't supposed to burn it down!"

I held up the contract copies. "Speaking of which, can you sign this? We still need to be paid."

His face flushed red. Then purple. Part of me wondered if he'd spontaneously combust in front of the TV cameras. Then he went very, very still. I didn't like the cold smile that curled on his lips like a dying worm. Didn't like it at all.

"We're going to have to deduct damages from the fees owed you." He glanced at the burning building, and then swept a hand around at all the cops and firefighters. "You may even have to reimburse the city for all this." His grin grew positively Grinch-esque. "Union employees on overtime."

"Dammit! You can't—"

"Oh I assure you I very much *can*. And, Ms. Walker, the city's contract with the Zero Dog Mercenaries is *terminated* as of *now* for flagrant and willful breach and destruction of significant Portland cultural and economic landmarks. I think you'll find a clause in section J, paragraph three that deals with just such an eventuality."

Oh shit. We could not afford to lose this client—our only current client, steady revenue stream and paycheck source for the foreseeable cloudy-gray Oregon future.

Norville took a moment to revel in the panic he must've seen in my eyes. Then he turned and marched back to the SUV, followed by his scurrying, paper-shoveling lackeys. I watched them drive off and somehow resisted the urge to light their tires on fire. Burning bridges. I was all about that, thank you very much.

"What now, Captain?" Mai asked. I glanced back and found everyone staring at me. All those eyes. Waiting for me to make things right.

I forced a grin on my face even though my facial muscles

felt like plastic. "I'm thirsty. Let's go get some beers." General cheers erupted all around, even if they sounded a trifle forced. "And, Rafe, put some clothes on, dammit."

I climbed onto the Bradley and scrambled up the turret to the top hatch, my heart thudding dully. We weren't getting paid. We'd probably end up *owing* money. Our expenses had spiraled out of control in the last few weeks. Our single biggest and currently only client had just metaphorically torn up our contract and pissed on it for good measure. No wonder the acid in my stomach felt as if it sloshed around like dirty water in a mop bucket.

We rolled out past the police barriers. A crowd of people pushed up against the barricades, taking pictures with their cell phones and pointing. All the news channels had shown up, KATU, KOIN, KGW, and they tracked us with their cameras. I smiled and did my beauty-queen wave from atop the turret as they filmed. Probably looked dramatic against the backdrop of the burning building.

I'd started to drop back inside the turret and shut the hatch when I saw him, and for a moment all my newfound money troubles blinked away into nothing.

A man stood away from the crowd, leaning against a police cruiser while he watched me, but he was no cop. Military. Had to be. And not just some run-of-the-mill grunt, either. He wore black fatigues, combat boots and sported a M9 Beretta in a shoulder holster. His dog tags glinted against his wide chest. Tall. Good-looking. Sandy-brown hair, cut very short. The Bradley passed within a half dozen feet of him and the guy never looked away from me. He was cut, hard muscles sculpted in all the right places, scars on his lower biceps. Clean-shaven. Looked like he could wrestle crocodiles and turn them into matching handbag and gator-skin boot sets. A real hard case, giving me the evaluation eye.

We locked gazes until the Bradley rumbled past him. He never smiled, but neither did the look on his face seem aggressive or antagonistic. It had been...interested. Intensely interested. So who was he? Competition? A prospective client, please God? A grunt on leave who liked caterpillar treads? Some psycho stalker?

I glanced backward and caught a last glimpse of him ducking under the police barriers and disappearing into the crowd.

What the hell had that been about? I tried to shake it off. I had more important things to worry about, all of them related to money and the sudden dismaying lack thereof. Still...his face lingered in my mind, like drifts of ashes after a fire.

Chapter One:
Mercenary Angst in the Age of Reason

Mercenary Wing Rv6-4 "Zero Dogs"
The Zero Dog Compound
NW Hilltop Drive, Portland, Oregon
1045 Hours PST April 10th

There are moments when I wish I'd been born Amish. This was one of those times.

Three days after the TastyTech Food Corp fiasco and subsequent loss of the city of Portland as a client, I sat hunched over my too-small particleboard desk, my head in one hand, my fingers hunched into a claw on top of the keyboard number pad. On the computer screen, QuickBooks gleefully informed me I couldn't code 25mm depleted uranium shells as a receivable.

I suppressed the urge to melt the computer down to slag, but then I'd end up scraping the bloody thing off the desktop with an industrial-grade spatula. Four hours of bean counting and while none of our books lined up, the news they did give was grim. Add any more financial stress to my already seething cauldron of anxiety and people around here should really count it lucky I didn't start more fires.

The good news: we weren't going bankrupt this week. The bad news: at this burn-through rate we'd be bankrupt in roughly twenty-eight days unless we scored a high-paying gig.

Chapter 7 stuff, no reorganizing, just total liquidation. In this economy, few clients would pay top dollar for mercenary paranormal assault teams. Not when you could hire an entire army of pookas for less than the cost of re-tiling your bathroom or putting in that bidet you always wanted. Pixies came even cheaper by the dozen.

I stood up and stretched, trying to work out the kinks in my neck. The initial bass drum beats of a headache throbbed at my temples, and I could feel that internal percussionist in my head warming up for the kettledrums. Sunlight poured from the window in a blazing white square across the carpet, falling across the top of my bookcase and my cactus in its ceramic sombrero pot. The room's warmth made me sluggish. I yearned to lie down in that pool of sunlight like a cat and nap the rest of the day away. But no, I had to lead the Light Brigade. The time had come to slouch into the valley of death and spread the misery.

The house was quiet. Strange. Usually the air resonated with shouting, the crash of things breaking, drunken singing, weird animal sounds, and enough general commotion to qualify us for a reality television show. The more I thought about it, the more whoring ourselves out to reality TV seemed a viable possibility...

The phone rang. I snatched the cordless off the base, eager for any reason to take my thoughts off the dark cloud of bad news. "Merc World. All your chaos needs. Sale on spatulas and cluster bombs, today only."

A long pause gestated on the other end, long enough for me to regret saying what had seemed so damn witty at the time. Impulse control. I made a mental note to lease some. I'd been expecting a call from those idiots in Merc Wing Lk12, hence my snark. If I lost a potential client due to spontaneous unprofessionalism, I'd have to commit seppuku with a butter knife.

"May I please speak to Captain Andrea K. Walker?" a man finally asked.

"Speaking." Beautiful. My full name. Had to be a bill collector. Almost as bad as losing a client.

"Captain." The voice sounded older but still silky smooth. I amended my guess to politician. Probably seeking campaign donations. "I represent a certain government agency with very deep pockets. I'd like to discuss a very lucrative contract with you. In person."

So much for my psychic powers. I spun back to my desk and managed to topple a dozen manila folders full of crumpled receipts when I grabbed my schedule calendar. I immediately switched to my competent leader routine, making my voice a bit deeper and talking in complete sentences. "I'm certainly interested. When would be a good time for you?"

"One hour from now would be ideal," the man said. "Can that be managed?"

I had no idea the last time anyone had cleaned the client conference room—hell, I was fuzzy on the last time we'd even *used* the damn thing—but as surely as an OCD Pandora opened boxes, I wasn't about to let this whale off the line. "An hour is absolutely fine."

"Perfect. I'll be sending an agent directly to you. He will carry credentials, but he may arrive before me. Is this a problem?"

"Not at all," I lied. It meant I'd have to babysit the chump personally since I didn't trust any of my misfits to uphold our pristine image of professionalism, sad as that might be. "I look forward to it."

"Good." Dial tone followed, the flat line of telephone calls.

So who said the universe didn't randomly hand out miracles to the undeserving? I did a little hell-yeah dance in my office because no one else could see me. I set the phone down and hammered the intercom button. A crackle of distortion blared over the speakers installed throughout the house. "Listen up, people. We got clients coming in. So let's not scare them off like last time."

Twenty minutes later, I thumped down the stairs into the main living area. I had on my full dress uniform, dark gray coat, light gray trousers with black piping, gray cap, fruit salad—a choice bit of jargon referring to my assorted ribbons and medals—and captain bars on my chest and sleeve. I'd taken the time to spiffy up, forced my hair into some kind of order, put on fresh deodorant but skipped the perfume. There were no good floral scents that complemented my image as a soldier of fortune.

As usual, the living room bore a close resemblance to the aftermath of a natural gas explosion. A huge HD television, a mess of stereo and surround-sound equipment, video-game consoles and a nightmare tangle of cords dominated one wall. Through the picture window I could see the sloping front lawn, hedges, trees and wide swaths of green grass complete with a bomb crater where Gavin had exploded munitions in some half-assed practical joke. The rest of the room was strewn with takeout containers, pizza boxes, empty cans, bottles, coffee mugs, a replica of a *LOTR* sword thrust through the drywall, a pair of Scooby-Doo boxer shorts I prayed were clean, and a plastic hula girl upside down in the fake potted palm we'd strung with multicolored Christmas lights.

All of which reminded me, we *really* needed a housekeeper. Our last housekeeping company had fired us as their client within three months, and I couldn't find the heart to blame them. I also couldn't find the money to pay a new cleaning company. *Le impasse.*

Rafe sprawled on the L-shaped sofa. Next to him slept our huge mutant housecat, Squeegee, who took up the rest of the couch. *Rafe Lupo* certainly wasn't the name he'd been born with. According to his file, he'd had it changed from Jim Thatcher after he'd been bitten by a lycanthrope dogcatcher in Scranton, PA. Good-looking enough, but covered in tattoos, so a girl had to really love ink. Rafe also qualified as a total man slut, trolling through club after club and trying to bang anything female and of legal age that smiled in his general direction. He seemed to see me more as his den mother than anything else, which made me exempt from his attentions, even though I was only a few years older. Honestly, I didn't know whether to be relieved or insulted.

Squeegee was our calico cat, all scattershot white, brown, black and rust colors. Oh, and she weighed close to three hundred and twenty pounds. We'd found her in Thailand, enslaved to a smuggler kingpin we hunted down. She was larger than most dire wolves, and when she purred she sounded like an idling Harley Davidson.

I loomed over Squeegee and counted off points on my fingers. "A thousand dollars in Friskies cat chow. Two dump-truck loads of beach sand for kitty litter *this month alone*. And I found a hairball the size of a basketball in the bathroom. Remind me *exactly* why we keep you around, your highness?"

Squeegee rolled on her back, the couch giving a pained groan, and she curled her huge paws in the air, doing her best to look like three hundred pounds of adorable kitten. One eye cracked open, regarded me briefly and then closed again when she saw I was not charmed.

Rafe grinned. "C'mon, Captain, relax. She's a chick magnet when I take her to the park."

Squeegee purred and he scratched her head.

I turned on Rafe. "And *you*. I want you home before two a.m. on weeknights. Stop walking through the house naked. And since your New Year's resolution to attempt thinking with something other than your dick has been a colossal failure, at least *try* and maintain decorum—and finally, don't have your girlfriends call our business line anymore."

Rafe's smile widened, God help me, becoming positively wolfish, and I had to resist the urge to singe his eyebrows. Only one thing really bothered me about werewolves—their eyebrows. Hell, I even liked some of Rafe's body art (though some of it, like the full-color tattoo of Dogs Shooting Pool on his back, made me want to gouge out my eyes with salad tongs). But those eyebrows appeared as if fuzzy yellow caterpillars had fallen asleep over his eyes. I knew he plucked them, though he vehemently denied it. I also could see them growing back with a vengeance. They were the Chia Pet of eye fur. Pluck all you want, he'll grow more.

I pinned him with my evil eye and cranked my flaming-ire knob to eleven. "*Also*. We buy our beef in bulk for a reason. I don't want you sneaking in receipts for that goddamn butcher shop down the road. That meat costs twice as much, and you eat more than anybody here."

A look of horror flitted over Rafe's face. "That other stuff is full of hormones and steroids. It's genetically modified clone beef. A cancer study—"

"*Enough*." Give Rafe an opening and he'd go forever about how processed food was slowly killing everyone born after 1945. Life could be depressing enough without worrying about how Twinkies had spackled my large intestine. "No more free-range beef. And forget about the organic vegetables. I'm serious, Rafe. We're going down to ramen noodles and sugar-free Jell-O before the month is out."

He kept silent for a moment, staring at Squeegee. Then he looked back at me and gave me his best wolf grin. Must be the wolf grin that got those club-hopping women to drop their panties because it sure as hell couldn't be his eyebrows.

"I've got something to take your mind off your woes, Captain," he said. "Did I show you my new tattoo?"

"Is it any more disturbing than when you had *Joystick* tattooed across your stomach in Gothic script with an arrow pointing toward your crotch?"

He scowled. "Hey, I got that at Mardi Gras."

And that explained exactly nothing. "I don't have time for body art—I have an important client meeting in less than an hour. Which reminds me. Don't let them in through the house. When they page us over the gate intercom, send them around the side driveway to the conference-room door." We had an external conference room entrance to avoid having a client slog through a drift of Chinese takeout boxes or see something that would make them take their business elsewhere, such as Rafe doing naked yoga.

Rafe saluted and went back to watching *Buffy the Vampire Slayer* on the widescreen. Squeegee began to snore.

I continued toward the conference room, checking my dress uniform to make sure I hadn't picked up any stray cat hair. Still looked good, and I'd always loved the way I looked in full dress uniform. Long legs let me cut a striking figure with the right outfit. Wrong outfit and I looked like a stork, or worse, a flamingo with attitude.

A few of the windows were open along the backside of the house, looking out on our training grounds, and a slight breeze blew in the smells of grass and evergreen trees. I lingered near the windows, inhaling deeply. Worry had twisted my stomach into loops of kinked hose. This meeting *had* to come off perfectly, and it'd be a razor edge to walk. I couldn't appear desperate, but couldn't seem standoffish either. And, as usual, it was all up to me.

Sometimes being the boss really sucked.

Now, if I were Amish, for instance, I could reconnect to the land, wear a kapp, make beautiful blankets, slow down and cut myself free from my worldly worries. Free from the crushing weight of responsibility and the iron chains of leadership.

Yeah...who was I fooling? Time to put on the big-girl panties and suck it up. Something told me the Amish wouldn't be pleased to welcome an unrepentant pyromancer into their ranks—blind subservience went down with me about as well as nitroglycerin in a paint mixer—and last of all, I wouldn't get to play with the grenade launchers anymore. Clearly the Amish career path remained out of the question.

I shook my head and pushed open the door to the conference room, an Englisher with a mission, but sure as hell not one from God.

The conference room stretched along the ground floor of the house's north side, with a large, east-facing window providing a killer view of downtown Portland. As if meetings weren't dreary enough, the architect had decided to torment us with the views during After Action Reports and phone conferences.

I waited alone for the intercom call from the gate, musing about this agent the mysterious telephone guy had spoken of. Probably some skinny, paper-juggling bureaucrat who'd never seen a lick of action. Oh well. This job could still save our asses—at least for a while. Dealing with the government meant nearly everything was deductible, reimbursable, or over-chargeable. I almost started to salivate and had to remind myself to hold steady, not seem too eager. I rocked back in one uncomfortable chair and put my feet up on the table, striving for cool, calm and nonchalant.

A man walked into the room. Not just any random male either. It was the same man I'd seen on the street three days ago following the TastyTech disaster. The cut, drool-worthy pistol-guy. He strolled through the doorway and destroyed my nonchalance as thoroughly as if he'd shoved a grenade into a termite mound. I flinched and reached out to summon my magic. The temperature in the room started to rise by degrees. Never surprise a pyromancer. We'll sear your jockey shorts off first and apologize later.

Then the man smiled. Simple as that. One damned smile that animated his face from strong jaw to green eyes, and that hard-case sniper-eyed military-look softened into something that yanked at all my nerve endings and made my stomach do a lazy flip, not in fear, but with a low-grade desire dripping through my veins like warm molasses. At that moment, everything finally clicked into place inside my brain. *This* had to be the guy our mysterious client had mentioned on the phone. He'd been scoping us out on our last job. Sizing us up. He must've liked what he'd seen...though maybe that alone should've set off warning bells. After all, we'd bollocksed that job but good, didn't get paid, and Rafe had been naked at the time.

The guy was just as impressive as I remembered, human (as far as I could tell), dressed in fatigues, an olive green T-shirt and jump boots. Nothing screams hot to me like paratrooper jump boots. It's like a leather jacket—it sweats all kinds of sexy. I shivered, despite my heat-rising skills, and then I felt my face flush, as if I'd been caught staring at his crotch. Which I decidedly did *not* do. Nor did I stare at his pecs. Or at the way those shoulders bulged against his T-shirt. Or his damn-hot military-cut hair that certainly *wasn't* making my fingers twitch with the need to run themselves through the bristles. Nope. None of that.

All right I'm lying.

I stopped rocking back in my chair and thumped the chrome legs back on solid ground before I toppled over and completed my humiliation. I pushed out of the chair, irritation dousing my initial firework explosion of drooling lust. Goddamn it, who'd let him in? There'd been no intercom call and no doorbell.

"Sorry to barge in," the man said, keeping his distance. Of course, he had a smooth baritone that seemed to vibrate right through me. "The gate was open."

"I'm sorry, what?"

"I said, the gate was open."

The gate. Open. Holy flaming monkey shit, someday I'd kill somebody for incompetence, and no jury would ever convict me. "Who let you inside the house?"

"The gentleman with lots of tattoos, who prefers public nudity."

Rafe. I should've known. Rafe and security procedures knew each other about as well as virgins and labor pains. "Ah. Well, then...welcome to Zero Dog Compound." I tried on a smile that didn't quite fit. "Are you the agent our prospective client mentioned?"

He nodded once and kept a grin on his face as he walked toward me. I could've sworn his eyes glinted with something...either humor or pure evil, I wasn't sure which, and either way they were intense—dark green with flecks of gold—piercing. Eyes that noticed too much. Despite my body's initial flood of reaction, I started to think I didn't like the guy. He smiled too much and I suspected his easy confidence would rub my fur the wrong way in roughly five minutes.

"I'm Captain Jake Sanders, US Army Special Forces, Operational Detachments Alpha 2nd Special Forces Group out of Fort Bragg. Good to be a part of this." He held out his large hand.

I looked at his hand and slowly took it. His skin felt warm against mine. I loved warm things. It was a particular weakness of mine. Rough calluses covered his palm and fingers—shooter's calluses, I guessed—either that or he really loved to jerk off. I snorted at my own crude joke and he lifted one eyebrow in silent question, his damn smile faltering a bit. His grip on my hand was firm, not crushing. A lot of macho guys liked to impress me with their toughness by breaking my fingers. He gave my hand two brisk pumps and released it. A stray, traitorous image flashed through my mind—him running his hand up my neck. Tracing a soft circle behind my ear...

Enough. I yanked both hormones and emotions back into line. There was professionalism to maintain here. I represented the entire team. And damn him for making me feel this way.

"I'm Captain Andrea Walker, Merc Wing Rv6-4. A pleasure."

"The pleasure's mine, Captain Walker."

Now it was my eyebrow's turn to arch. Was he being a smart-ass or coming on to me or had I overreacted? Hard to tell because he kept smiling at me, and when a man is smiling, it meant he either wanted something or he did something he doesn't want you to know about. Either way, I didn't like it.

I retreated toward the safety of my chair, still fighting my traitorous hormone and endorphin invasion. I couldn't afford to turn into a drooling eggplant at the sight of some good-looking bastard in uniform. And what the hell was it about men in uniform, anyway? Some kind of biological booby trap.

"Please sit down." I gestured at a chair positioned along the middle of the table. His gaze swung from my chair at the head of the table to the chair at the opposite end. I couldn't help a tiny smirk. An Alpha Dog, eh? Wanted to have the dominant table position. Too bad I got it first. I settled into my seat, making sure my full dress uniform displayed me to my best advantage.

He hesitated, and then took a chair close to mine, not the one I'd indicated, but not one opposite me at the other end of the table either. I fought the urge to draw farther away as he sat down. It was a little unnerving to be this close to him. Distracting.

The intercom buzzed. Sarge's deep voice rumbled over the line. "Captain. I have a visitor here. He has an appointment."

I pushed the button. "Thank you, Sergeant. Please escort him to our conference room."

"Copy that. On our way now. Out."

An uncomfortable silence spread between us while we waited. I concentrated on not scaring off the cake-filled goodness of a government contract and silently prayed Sarge would bring our prospective client around the side of the house instead of taking the direct route through the wreckage inside. Army poster boy Captain Jake Sanders kept interfering with my attempts to keep calm. Not a subtle interference either—more like cranking a stove burner from high to jet-engine-on-afterburner. Sonuvabitch.

Sarge brought the client around the side way and up to the outside glass door, thank God for stupid favors. The man he escorted was old but looked spry—appeared, in fact, to resemble one of those bankers from the *Mary Poppins* movie that get all bent after a run on their bank. He wore a gray twill suit with a vest and a striped gray and black tie. A gray bar of mustache spread across his upper lip, and deep lines scored the skin around his mouth and eyes. His briefcase swung in his hand, back and forth in impatient little arcs.

Sarge escorted the man inside, didn't salute me, and stared at Captain Sanders as only a six-foot-four demon with red pupils and jet-black irises could do. Captain Sanders's face remained impassive, but I got the feeling the two of them eyed each other like tigers, comparing biceps sizes or crotch bulges or something. Men. I loved them, but I swore God built them stupider every year.

A long, uncomfortable pause drew out, in which I could hear the wall clock humming. I stood, but before I could speak, Sarge nodded to me...and then winked. He left before I could melt his boot heels. I knew that goddamn wink. He was telling me to *go for it.* As if I'd throw myself on a Green Beret. Everybody knew the SEALs could kick their asses.

I introduced myself to the old man, and his slightly pensive, unhappy look softened.

"Ah, yes. Captain Walker." He placed his briefcase on the table and settled into the chair at the opposite end of the table. "I'm William Harker. Delightful to make your acquaintance. Shall we get down to business?"

"By all means."

"Excellent." Harker cleared his throat. "The Department of Homeland Security Office of Intelligence and Analysis, working with other governmental agencies, has identified a developing threat to the security of the United States. I represent the Office of Operations Coordination and Planning. OPS is interested in contracting with Merc Wing Rv6-4 for certain services to be determined at an immediate future date, pending contract acceptance. Details of the services required and information on the developing situation is classified and will only be shared following your signature on a legally binding nondisclosure form. Your security clearance has already been evaluated."

"Great, but that's all a little vague—"

Harker raised a hand. I stopped, fighting annoyance at being interrupted. He ran a finger along the top of his briefcase, and then popped open the gold clasps. "Please, let me lay out all the compensation details before you decide. I have a contract here for your services, exclusively, for a time period of not more than one year. There will be a bonus of three percent of total offer paid if you complete your task within two weeks." He gave me a prim smile. "We'd like this wrapped up as soon as possible."

"How much are we discussing in terms of remuneration?" Yes, I always asked about the money before I asked about the job. Enough money and you could ask us to invade the moon for all I cared. *Ask*. Didn't mean I'd accept, though. I'd turned down high-paying jobs where the risk to my people was too high and the odds too long. Everybody loved money, but it meant little if you weren't around to enjoy it.

Of course, I also liked to eat and I had plenty of hungry mouths to keep fed, so that had to be factored into the equation as well.

Harker folded his hands. "Twenty-five million dollars. However, your own operating expenses must be deducted from the stipend."

I nodded, not quite trusting myself to speak. If we could do this job with minimal cost—which, like the apocalypse, might actually happen some day—twenty-five million could keep us running smoothly for at least a year, maybe two, if we were careful and didn't have to pay any lawsuits.

"I suppose you might be wondering about Article 47 of the Geneva Convention's Protocol 1 or perhaps UN resolution 44/34," Harker said, although I'd been doing nothing of the kind. "The restrictive conventions forbidding government use of mercenaries in armed conflict."

"Ah, yes."

"I assure you, Rv6-4 and the Hellfrost Mercenary Group is

classified as a private security force under your registration, and regardless, exceptions are made in times of extreme circumstances." Harker opened his briefcase and took out a sheaf of papers. He leaned forward and slid them across the table to me. "Please sign this nondisclosure form. Once signed, I'll allow Captain Sanders to fill in the details."

I scanned it quickly. All the usual stuff. Promises of lawsuits, incarceration and ritual dismemberment if I shared any classified or proprietary information. I snagged a pen and scrawled my signature on all the necessary lines while they watched in silence.

When I finished, Captain Sanders leaned toward me, his eyes intent. "There's been a RCT outbreak." He paused for effect. "A Reanimated Corpse Threat..." Yet another pause for effect. "*Zombies.*"

I stared at him. With all the buildup I'd expected something a trifle more dramatic. Like cyborg dragons or Godzilla on crack. Hell, a rampaging horde of menopausal lemmings would be more of a challenge. We'd done zombie duty before in Nogales, supporting the Yao Mercs, and "head duty"—the jargon term for zombie headshot kills—was gory, distasteful and mostly boring. It might sound strange to the uninitiated, but there were only so many times you could headshot a walking corpse, or light it on fire, or smash it with a mace before the law of diminishing returns kicked in. Still, as a professional, I wasn't about to let my disappointment show. Shit, hadn't I just been salivating at the prospect of all that income? And now I learned it'd be a cakewalk. The bonus would definitely be ours.

Sanders continued. "A necromancer established himself in a Portland business district two months ago. Since then, he's raised a considerable force of the undead. Three weeks ago he began shipping more of the living dead from Idaho, where we think he had his origins. I don't need to tell you this is a serious charge of interstate zombie trafficking. Since his arrival, he's attacked two financial institutions with a quick deploy force of RCTs, both well-known commercial banks."

I grinned. "So, for customers, instead of a run *on* the bank, it was a run *away* from the bank, right?"

Crickets. Blank stares from both of them, and not even a laugh track to save me.

Everybody's a fucking critic.

Harker cleared his throat. "The necromancer seems to be planning something large scale and requires more financing. We wish to disrupt those plans."

"So, basically, we're talking potential Zombie Apocalypse here. You need the Zero Dogs to make sure the dead stay dead. Help them out by ventilating their skulls with high-velocity projectiles." A wistful smile crept across my face. "Light some things on fire."

"We're hoping for a modicum of discretion as well."

I nodded and lied through my teeth. "We're known for discretion."

"The situation is delicate." Harker tapped one finger on his briefcase. "The zombies appear to be contained at the moment, but the target is hardened. We're afraid dropping bunker-buster munitions may allow some zombies to escape into the general populace. So precision is required."

"You're in luck, because we're also known for precision." I made a gun with my hand and aimed it at Captain Sanders. "Like a laser." He raised an eyebrow at me. Lucky for him, I refused to be embarrassed by my actions, no matter what.

Harker nodded. "You may be wondering why DHS doesn't handle this with Department of Defense resources."

I'd been wondering nothing of the sort. In fact, I didn't give a flying fuck at a rolling donut. Clients had all kinds of reasons for wanting to employ Paranormal Action Teams, not all of them strictly *legal* in the strictly *law-abiding* way. I figured they wanted a result but didn't want to risk exposure. Hellfrost Mercenary Groups had to sign Oxford Dictionary-sized confidentiality agreements. Things still leaked out, but not as often as one might think when dealing with soldiers of fortune.

Mercs had a rather Darwinian way of policing themselves...and people had been known to get disappeared for running their mouths to the press.

Harker flicked his hand as if brushing away a fly. “Frankly, this is a small-time concern. More of an annoyance really. Our primary strike teams are busy in Brownsville and in Ithaca. Dealing with infestations of gnomes and a group of militant fairies controlled by an extraterrestrial fungus, respectively, and we’d like this particular situation handled immediately, before it develops into a media circus.”

I nodded, sympathizing with their asset-allocation problems. Gnomes could be utter bastards, and I loathed their pointy red hats with a passion. Of course, it was a twenty-five-million-dollar small-time concern, but who were we kidding? This was the government. The fountain of perpetual money. “I’m definitely interested, Mr. Harker. I think you’ll find our service contract quite to your liking. We can start prepping an operation right away.”

Harker leaned back and folded his hands into a steeple before his chin. “Magnificent. There is one other small condition, however.”

Beautiful. I liked added conditions about as much as I liked stapling my tongue to sandpaper, but I kept my smile in place. “Name it.”

“You must accept Captain Sanders onto your team.”

I nearly choked. I cleared my throat to cover the reaction and ended up sounding more like Squeegee hacking up a fur ball. Neither of them seemed fooled. Sanders stared at me, his face impassive, but his gaze rapier-sharp.

God must hate me. I didn’t even know where to begin my bitching. An officer of the same rank would provoke a constant power struggle. An outsider who didn’t know our methods and the peculiar balance of power, position and respect among mercs would be even worse. In terms of both personal and team performance, Spec Force Sanders would be a cinderblock on an iron chain around my neck. Things would be even worse since I'd already felt that soft explosion of physical attraction, misguided as it might've been. All perfect reasons to refuse.

"I'm afraid that's not part of protocol," I said.

"A contract such as this...protocols can be adjusted."

"I would love to, Mr. Harker," I lied again, "but we work alone. Maintaining the integrity of our fighting team. We're like German precision machinery."

Captain Sanders gave me a tight smile. "I assure you, Captain Walker, you won't find me a drag on your team's performance."

"No offense, *Captain* Sanders, but Paranormal Action Teams don't bring unenhanced humans with us into the fray. It's company policy."

Harker shut his briefcase, and the clasps *snicked* into place. He smiled at me like a grandfather. A very powerful, very potentially scary grandfather. "Captain Sanders is part of an elite Special Forces group. His detachment concentrates on paranormal threats within the United States and abroad. He's quite capable of taking care of himself in any situation. You may be surprised to find him a considerable asset."

"Maybe he can shoot a pistol, but we'll be going up against dark, forbidden magic." I looked at Sanders. "Again, not to be insulting, but maybe you'd better sit this one out."

His eyes glinted, and his jaw muscles tightened. It seemed my last comment got under his skin a little. Good. He glanced at Harker. "With your permission?"

"If you must."

Captain Sanders stood from his seat and pushed the chairs out of the way. "If you think I can't handle myself, Captain Walker, I'll give you a chance to prove it. Try and hit me. Hard as you can." He raised his hand like a Boy Scout swearing an oath. "On my honor, I promise I won't touch you back."

For a moment I fell into stunned silence. Oh God the machismo, and the arrogance—practically a chunky milkshake of male ego. Hell yeah, I was tempted to knock him on his ass and enjoy every minute of it, but I didn't want to get my dress uniform dirty. "Interesting proposition. I assume you don't mean hit you with a stream of fire."

He shrugged, as if dodging fireballs were an everyday occurrence. "Your file says you have martial-arts training. I'm sure you have a couple favorite moves. Show them to me."

Still, I hesitated. Something twitched my antennae. I didn't like how Sanders acted—far too nonchalant for my taste. It wouldn't pay to be provoked into something stupid, and his confidence said he was either as intelligent as pond scum or he had something up his sleeve.

I bet on something up his sleeve. "I've trained in multiple styles. Kenpo, judo, aikido, shotokan."

"I don't mean to brag," he replied, "but I do Tai Chi and watch Bruce Lee movies. Oh, and *The Three Stooges*."

Perfect. A smart-ass on top of it all. "Very amusing, Captain Sanders. But unlike certain other members of my species who carry their egos in their ball sacks, I don't need to prove anything."

Mr. Harker favored me with an even stare. "I recommend you do as he requests, Captain, or you take him onto your team untested and like it. Otherwise we shall find another wing of the Hellfrost Group with which to deal."

Beautiful. I didn't see any easy way out of this, and the only thing I hated more than being interrupted was getting backed into a corner. I slowly stood and walked toward him. I didn't want to hurt him—despite all my fire breathing. He kept still, no longer smiling, watching me with a disconcerting intensity. He didn't strike up a defensive stance. He merely faced me, his hands loose at his side.

Best to make this quick. I pivoted, turning my hips over as I shot out my right leg in a vicious sidekick, putting all my force and precision into striking at his midriff with the outside edge of my foot.

My foot struck an invisible barrier six inches in front of where I'd aimed. Pain shot from my foot up my leg as if I'd kicked a steel wall with all my strength. The ribbons on my chest jingled and clacked together. I stumbled backward, unable to kick through my target, as all that deflected force came rebounding at me.

Jake watched me, still not moving, his mouth set in a grim line.

I closed in once more. Drove my boot down toward his foot. No impact—blocked again—but I anticipated it and swung a back-fist at his head. My fist smacked another invisible barrier six inches from his jaw and bounced off, making a meaty slapping sound.

A string of curses blasted out of me, oaths so profane they'd blister Teflon off a frying pan. I hopped back out of range, but true to his word, Captain Sanders never raised a hand.

What an idiot I was. I should've seen it right away, but the standard Special Forces graphic on his shirtsleeve—the black heater shield with the white diagonal—had thrown me into believing he was a Norm. Too late I sensed the slight tingle of magic after he'd actively tapped his powers. My skin felt too hot, too tight, and the undersides of my shirt grew damp as I stalked back to my seat and sat, crossed my legs, and pinned Mr. Harker with my best *not amused* glare. "What are his abilities?"

"He's a barrier mage. A walking shield wall. A talent I believe you will find extremely useful in fulfilling contractual obligations. Also, he's an excellent officer, well-versed in combat tactics, counter insurgency, violent creature suppression, and will advise you on how Homeland Security would like you to proceed, should there be any larger questions of strategy involved."

Five years ago I would've calmly suggested they screw a light socket and leave me be. Now I had responsibilities. People counted on me. And all those damn bills...we bled red ink from a thousand cuts. "Fine. He's on the team for this mission. But *I* give the orders here. If he doesn't like that, he can ship himself back to Fort Bragg and file a complaint in triplicate."

Captain Sanders said nothing, but a ghost of a smile lingered on his lips. I didn't drop my gaze—keeping up the challenge.

"You will be commanding officer for your people in the field," Harker said. "Captain Sanders will remain under control of Special Operations Command."

"Fine. He can tag along, make sure we uphold the deal. He can even play a bit. But my price just went up to twenty-seven million."

"The offer is twenty-five. That will not change."

So much for bluffing my way to an easy two million more. "Fine. Anything else?"

Mr. Harker opened his case again and withdrew a small mountain of paperwork. "These forms will have to be completed, but you may do so at your leisure. Rest assured you will not be paid in full until they are." He snapped shut his briefcase again. "Everything else has been settled satisfactorily according to government requirements."

"I look forward to working with you, Captain Walker," Sanders said. "What time should I move my gear in?"

"You'll be living on site?" I don't know what terrified me more, having him on the team, or having him in constant close contact.

"We might have to do a rapid deploy," he said. "Don't worry, I pack light."

No way out now. "Then...I'll need to schedule a team meeting tonight. 2030 Hours, after our vamp is up. You can haul your stuff in this afternoon."

"Excellent," Harker said. "Captain Sanders can provide a detailed briefing for your entire team. He'll be keeping me informed of progress throughout the mission. You'll be paid in full when the threat is completely neutralized...and provided the relevant paperwork is completed." He stood and walked toward the side door, the briefcase in his hand rocking like a ship in stormy water. Captain Sanders stood and again offered his hand to me. I hesitated, and then shook it. His skin still felt deliciously warm, much to my dismay.

This was going to be such a problem.

Chapter Two: Charge of the Undead Brigade

Undead Army of the Unrighteous Order of the Falling Dark
EZ Pantry Convenience Store
SE 12th Street, Portland, Oregon
1:06 p.m. PST April 10th

Necromancer Jeremiah Hansen sat in the driver's seat of the yellow school bus with his zombie horde. He wore a Mariners hat, red and black flannel and hiking boots, and sported a devil goatee to jack up the evil quotient in his publicist photos. Just another average denizen of the Pacific Northwest driving a bus full of undead people.

The bus stank like a morgue low on formaldehyde. Jeremiah made sure he only breathed through his mouth. Even though he was a necromancer, the smell of dead flesh didn't exactly make his mouth water. He glanced in the wide overhead mirror at the seats behind him. Every seat was crammed three deep with zombies...except in the case of zombies of larger girth, which were two to a seat. And the undead Samoan guy, who took up the entire bench by himself. Jeremiah also had the aisle packed full of zombies, which was not ideal, since they'd rattled around like crazy the entire trip, stumbling and falling and moaning as he'd driven from his factory lair, skirting downtown and crossing Hawthorne Bridge during lunch hour.

Jeremiah looked at his watch and chewed his lower lip as

his heart beat faster in anticipation. His skin felt tight, like vacuum-sealed plastic wrap, and he wished he'd downed less coffee. The big moment had arrived, a turning point in his career toward achieving Zombie Overlord status. After this, he'd be able to make an offer to the top candidate of his resume call on the online job board. He really needed someone still living to help him run his expanding commercial enterprise. Zombies were great for grunt work and for eating the bodies of competitors. Finesse, however, they did not have...and they weren't known for their scintillating conversation skills either.

As if to prove him right, a zombie moaned behind him in one of the front seats, and he glanced at her in the mirror. She'd been beautiful in life, noble features, stunning blonde hair that was falling out in clumps, vivid eyes...or eye, since one of them was now missing after a crow had pecked it out. A great body...well, her skin seemed rather gray and greenish in places, and prone to lividity...but she had great tits. Too bad he wasn't into the whole necrophilia freak show like some of those other perved-out necromancers.

He sighed. When he was rich and successful, he'd get himself a nice living girl. Yeah, someone intelligent (but not more intelligent than him) and able to help him in his quest for market domination. Someone beautiful, of course, who didn't reek of decay but smelled more like waffles, and *loyal.* She had to be a hundred and fifteen percent loyal. That's all he wanted. Oh, and someone with great tatas, because, let's just face it, woman tits were God's way of rewarding men for being created first. Those feminist necromancers could take their burial-shroud-burning ways and their bumper stickers that read: *A woman needs a man like a corpse needs Viagra* and shove them.

More zombies moaned. He mused on whether or not he could teach them traveling songs, "Ninety-Nine Bottles of Beer" or "Kumbayah" or something. Or maybe he could teach them to moan in chorus and take them on the road, maybe Carnegie Hall and the Vienna Corpse Choir. Could be big.

Nah, who was he kidding? Better to stick with something

simple, like monopolizing the gelatin-manufacturing industry.

The zombies stared out the windows with their flat, empty eyes at the people strolling by and the cars driving past, which is why he'd kept the windows closed and locked. The smell was one thing, but hungry zombie moaning was hard to ignore. He'd been parked on the one-way street for the last half hour, waiting for the Safe Steele armored car to arrive and restock the ATM at the convenience store. He'd parked past the intersection, just beyond the chain-link fence that bordered the edge of the store's parking lot—out of direct view of the counter clerk, but attracting his share of curious stares all the same.

He glanced at his watch again and drummed his hands on the large steering wheel. He didn't want the zombies loose until the armored car arrived, what with the constant moaning, slouching and staggering, the grabby-grabby, and the all-around attracting negative attention. So he was forced to keep them on the bus with him and suffer in the stink. His little electric fan didn't move enough air. Next time he'd rivet eighteen hundred air fresheners into the metal ceiling.

Finally, he caught sight of the gray and white armored car rumbling up the street. It pulled into the parking lot of the EZ Pantry convenience store and sat there with its diesel engine idling.

Showtime.

Jeremiah turned on the bus's flashing red lights and pulled the door lever. After disabling the alarm, he'd rigged the lever with a system of pulleys so that yanking the lever also opened the emergency exit at the back. He concentrated. In his mind he could feel the cool, sleek silver cords of his necromancy magic controlling the hundred zombie pseudo-consciousnesses around him. He started to prod them to stand and shuffle toward the exits. He could even see through their dead eyes if he chose—not something he enjoyed, especially when they were eating.

Outside in the parking lot, two guards climbed out of the

armored truck and walked toward the back. One of them glanced at the bus and frowned. Jeremiah raised a hand in a casual wave and the guard gave him a puzzled look, but turned back to his work. The first guard swung the heavy rear door open. The second guard scanned the street and the storefront for threats.

Jeremiah's first zombie, some dude in a tattered business suit, walked to the edge of the highest bus step and toppled forward, thumping against the side of the door as he fell. He ended up sprawled on the sidewalk, making sounds like a man having his appendix removed with a garden trowel. The next zombie took the steps with more grace, but the third zombie got caught staring out the front window at the guards and licking his lips, missed a step and crashed into the second, leaving Jeremiah with a pile of groaning zombies just outside the door. He cursed to himself and got up to help direct traffic. Zombies were already plunging through the emergency exit and off the back end of the bus, bouncing off each other and making a moaning, slavering mess.

He pushed his way down the steps, accidentally stepping on businessman zombie's face on his way out. Street traffic was light, but a few cars had stopped for the bus's flashing reds. An old lady who could barely see over the wheel stared at the zombies disembarking from the bus with wide, disbelieving eyes. A few pedestrians and a cyclist had also stopped to stare, well out of eating range, lucky for them. The security guards glared at him, as if *he* were responsible for the disorderly exit, instead of a bunch of coordination-impaired walking dead people.

"Don't worry, everybody!" Jeremiah yelled. "Just tourists from Canada! Had a little too much to drink. Ha. Ha. Maybe a little food poisoning." One zombie's arm fell off its shoulder joint with a wet, tearing sound and a thud. "And some minor skin problems," he added quickly. "A few cases of scurvy. Nothing serious. Nothing to see here."

A long moment of silence spun out, in which he could hear

the rumbling idle of the armored car's diesel engine, some birds far off in the trees, the dulcet tones of a hip-hop artist rapping about drive-by shootings, the low-power beep of somebody's cell phone, traffic rushing past on Morrison, a road crew using a jackhammer a couple blocks away. And then the pristine silence shattered into screams and running footsteps as the pedestrians decamped en masse. The traffic stopped by the bus's flashing red lights tried to back up, speed past and generally ensnared itself into a gridlock tangle of steel-bodied knots like a mammoth stuck in tar without a moist towelette.

Or something like that.

The dead continued to shuffle off the bus toward the armored car, most of them managing to stay upright, which made him almost proud. One of the security guards drew his pistol. The other one stared, openmouthed, at the first row of zombies. Jeremiah pulled out a stopwatch from his pocket and clicked it. They didn't have much time. He had to split his attention between the truck and the bus still disgorging his minions, lest any of his zombies wander off and attack some hapless civilian. Feeding would only slow them down.

"Halt!" the armed guard shouted.

The zombies moaned at him, jaws gnashing in anticipation of living flesh. A pistol shot cracked through the air, echoing down the street. One of the zombies—a dead guy in a Red Sox jersey and paisley boxer shorts—staggered backward with a hole in his chest. The zombie grunted, paused, and then continued his shuffling lurch toward the guard, moaning with the same murderous rage as a Beantowner who'd witnessed a Yankees fan pissing on Fenway's home plate.

"Minimum ain't worth this shit!" The second guard sprinted away across the parking lot, his hat flying off and landing on the asphalt. One of the zombies snatched up his hat and chewed on it before tossing it away rumpled and stained with drool.

The other guard fired two more rounds, blowing off one

zombie's ring finger and then clipping the EZ Pantry sign pole. He backed up several steps as the zombies closed on him in a relentless wave before he turned and ran off, screaming like a gamer on the release day of a Resident Evil sequel.

No one remained to stand in the way of looting, pillaging and larceny by Jeremiah's zombie army. The undead encircled the armored car, except for the Samoan zombie, who'd lurched off toward an old lady. The old lady flailed at him with a handbag the size of Rhode Island.

"Get back here." Jeremiah used his power to yank on the ethereal silver cord linking him to his undead minion. The Samoan jerked and trembled, fighting him, but Jeremiah's control was stronger. "Don't give me that look. She'd taste like cheap beef jerky anyway."

Samoan zombie remained sullen, but rejoined the shambling undead charge.

Now came the hard part. He used his eldritch powers to compel his zombies to file inside and begin to empty the truck. They flailed their way into the back, careening off each other, grabbing sacks of money and shuffling back out. He directed them to carry the sacks in two hands to avoid spills, but one zombie fumbled a sack anyway and a flood of loose change bounced down the street.

For the *coup de grace* came the challenge that separated the masters of the undead from the two-bit Vegas Voodoo priests. He had to keep the line moving from the truck back to the bus to deposit the cash, and precision direction of this many zombies while keeping them from attacking the living was much harder than it looked on TV. Sweat beaded on his forehead. The tension made his bowels feel loose and hot, which was probably too much information, but there you go.

Eleven minutes and forty-six seconds later and it was over. He directed the last of the shuffling zombie horde back up the steps of the bus and into their seats while stopping the first zombie on the bus from walking all the way to the back exit and falling out again.

He glanced at the drifts of moneybags strewn about the aisle, less than he'd expected, but still a decent haul. There'd been a few losses, like the dropped coins, and he'd noticed one zombie actually *eating* handfuls of coins by the sound of breaking teeth, before he'd managed to put an end to it.

He settled himself into the bus's driver seat just as he heard distant sirens. He pulled the lever, popped the switch, and the door folded shut, catching one hapless zombie half in, half out of the back door, who gave a surprised and dismayed moan. Then he pulled away into the street and floored it. The diesel engine roared, back end pumping out noxious fumes, and within what seemed like a minute and a half the bus reached thirty-five miles an hour. He turned onto Stark Street headed west, back to the lair to count his swag.

All in all, not a bad day for an evil overlord of the dead. Certainly not pretty, but effective enough.

And this was just the beginning.

Chapter Three: The Zero Dog Crib

Mercenary Wing Rv6-4 "Zero Dogs"
The Zero Dog Compound
Second floor, South wing
1330 Hours PST April 10th

The more I thought about the Captain Jake Sanders thing, the more I didn't like it. He was an unknown factor, and I didn't like the unknown. No commander did. The unknown could get your people killed.

Besides, I had a bad feeling having Sanders around might negatively affect my performance. That initial flash bang of attraction had unnerved me, had kicked the legs out from under my confidence a bit, and that was dangerous heading into a mission—especially heading into a mission against the cannibalistic undead. Not that I had much choice. We were in no position to dictate terms to this particular client, and that fact also made me edgy.

First thing first. I had to get with Sarge and discuss developments. If I could count on anyone to give me the straight dope, it was Sergeant Nathan Genna.

Finding him in the untidy vastness of Zero Dog Compound was another story. I walked the length of the house searching all three floors, the tower, the library, the dojo and the kitchen before Rafe bothered to inform me Sarge had gone to our underground shooting range.

Let me take a moment and tell you a little bit about Zero Dog Mercenary Wing Rv6-4. Technically we're not a wing, as in squadron, though we do have a V-22 Osprey painted black and white we call Chilly Willie. We were currently under strength, totaling only eight people on the roster, and I use the term *people* extremely loosely. Most were handpicked by me, and that's why I always felt this crushing weight of responsibility for each of them. Our Tooth to Tail ratio—the ratio of war-fighting types, ground-pounders and trigger-pullers to non-war fighting types, medics, mechanics and such—ran something like eighty-twenty, with only the medic Hanzo and Gavin in the second category.

The Zero Dogs belong to the larger Hellfrost Mercenary Group...something of a mother Union that sets rules, collects fees, administers fines for minor violations, comes down hard on war crimes. No Merc Wing or PAT could operate legally without being part of the mother group.

I'd been team leader for four years, following the retirement of Captain Mackey Black. Stupidest thing I'd ever done—take control and responsibility for this group of misfits and rejects—but I guess maybe I'd come to love it too, and that's all the dewy-eyed sentiment I cared to spill.

The Zero Dog Merc Wing's motto was *The First Bullet is Always Free*. We chose that motto only after our lawyer rejected *Kill 'Em All and Steal Their Fillings* as a possible cause of future legal trouble. Our unofficial insignia had a super-deformed pit bull with vampire fangs, red eyes, one paw grasping a lightning bolt, the other holding an olive branch on fire. That's what you get when you hire a Hello Kitty-obsessed college kid to do your graphic-design work. Our real insignia was a black long sword on a beige field with an inverted red chevron. That banner fluttered on the lightning rod atop the house that made up our living quarters.

The Zero Dog Compound was eleven acres of training ground located in the Tualatin Mountains—a group of forested hills, really, though we did have a stunning view of downtown Portland, the Willamette River and far to the southeast, a snowcapped Mt. Hood. We had no immediate neighbors, but if I stood on the perimeter wall and looked down I could see the top of the Pittock Mansion a ways off through the trees. Regardless, the Zero Dogs were not beloved due to the copious amounts of noise we generated. We bunked in a massive eighteen thousand square foot main house complete with dojo, gym, billiard room, porticos, gun range, infirmary, breakfast nook and Jacuzzi. The landscaping bill alone was atrocious. The electric bill made me want to swallow rusty staples.

Each member of the team had a suite of rooms. Sarge and I had the largest rooms with the best views since rank had its privileges. Other rooms included the conference room, a massive kitchen with two sets of double wall ovens, two Sub-Zero fridges and a walk-in freezer for sides of meat and stored blood, and a weight-lifting room. A gnome-proof walk-in pantry, three river-stone-fronted fireplaces, a great room with twenty-foot ceilings and wood beams carved from Dryad deadwood, a small theater that might or might not be haunted, our own vending machine that dispensed energy drinks, chai tea, soda and miniature sample bottles of booze, in that order. A turret-tower library which held all kinds of media. A detached six-car garage that had been converted for our Bradley, a launch pad for the V-22 Osprey, an underground firing range, a brig and an armory.

Not a bad place to call home.

It was just really, really hard to pay for.

Chapter Four: Happiness is a New Gun

Mercenary Wing Rv6-4 "Zero Dogs"
The Zero Dog Compound
Lower Level Shooting Range
1342 Hours PST April 10th

I found Sarge at one of the gun stands toward the far end of the shooting range. He held an oddly shaped rifle in his arms. I watched through the soundproof glass, approving of his intense focus as he stared along the weapon's sight. The gun didn't have a barrel, just three long antennae-like rods jutting out beyond the stock. He squeezed the trigger and a bolt of lightning arced through the air with a loud *crack* I could hear even through the soundproofing. The lightning obliterated the dark silhouette target. Only a tiny piece survived, dangling from the clip, its edges burning.

Holeeeeee shit. I wanted to play with that too.

I slipped on ear protectors and safety glasses, entered the range and walked toward Sarge. Fallen angel color pallets seemed limited to black and sometimes red, and Sarge held true to the pattern, dressed in a black T-shirt so tight that his biceps seemed poised to burst his sleeves, black cargo pants and combat boots with a perfect shine. He wasn't handsome so much as striking, with a shock of dark hair, short and unruly, and reddish-purple-colored skin. Some people called him a demon, lashing the term at him like an insult. Sarge had always preferred the term Paradise-challenged, though I had no idea why. To me, the term Paradise-challenged applied to politicians, lobbyists, bank CEOs and certain church leaders who preached one thing while merrily lying, cheating and stealing from the devout. Demons ranked last on a list like that.

Sarge had told me three things the day I brought him onto the team. The first: he'd been bounced out of Heaven for speaking his mind. The second: he was gay. The third: he liked to blow shit up. The first I found surprising—I'd thought they'd be less draconian in the afterlife, but apparently things weren't as rosy as they claimed in the brochure. The second was peachy with me, though I'd known a few women who would've sold their soul to win a bronco ride with him. The third, well, *that* was my kind of attitude. I'd hired him on the spot. A year later I'd promoted him to Sergeant. The rest, as they say in the clichés, was history.

He sensed me coming and glanced my way, and then set the long, strange-looking weapon down on the table, careful to keep the dangerous end pointed downrange. No salutes, of course. We were mercs, not soldiers. I only enforced absolute discipline in hot situations, when the blood and the bullets got intimate and didn't respect each other in the morning.

He pulled off his ear protection. "You like my little friend?"

"What. The. Fuck. *Is* that thing?"

He grinned. "MK203 ARC rifle. A friend with the Hollow Point Mercs sent it over to try out." He swung off the bench and stood. I wasn't short for a woman by any measurement standard, but Sarge towered over me by at least eight inches. This close, his skin had delicate gradients of red-purple and violet, like a fading sunset. His eyes, however, had the old black iris, red pupil thing going on that terrified small dogs and Jehovah's Witnesses. He waved a hand at the strange rifle. "Care to try?"

I wanted to. I really did. Except I knew what would happen.

Sarge and I would be in here all afternoon and night vaporizing targets and I'd miss the meeting, the accounts would never get done, and Captain Jake Sanders might just kill our contract. With no money rolling in, it'd only be a matter of time before some vendor got pissed and I'd end up short on shotgun shells or Stefan's red vintage from the blood bank and I'd have a genuine crisis on my hands. Oh, and we'd get our asses evicted too. There was that.

"Love to. Can't." I leaned against the wall. "We've got problems. And then we have *complications* for our problems. Finally, we have a solution, but with our luck it'll end up being the worst of the problems."

He seemed unfazed by my cryptic predictions. "Fill me in."

"A new job, just in time. Unfortunately, we picked up some kind of Special Forces barnacle who's gonna be advising us on how to kill zombies. As if we need help. So we have to call a meeting and get briefed by the magical Green Beret. Likely a BOHICA adventure, but we need the business." BOHICA was an acronym meaning Bend Over, Here It Comes Again, and honestly, who couldn't relate to that once or twice or, in my case, three hundred and six times in their life?

He rubbed his chin, fingers rasping against his stubble. "Meetings never go well."

Last meeting, Mai had gotten bored and summoned a bunch of Death Chibi Bunnies, who'd managed to eat all the donuts and chew the hell out of the couch before she'd shoved them back into their alternate universe. One of our cushions had gone missing—I knew it was in a digestive tract somewhere—and the couch still had teeth marks and a drool stain on the back.

Although, honestly, the drool stain could've been Rafe's.

"This meeting will be different," I lied.

"Mmm. So what's the first problem?"

"Money."

"When isn't money a problem?"

Touché. "It's shoving its way to the absolute top of the list. As in, we'll soon be forced into rolling drunks, selling our own blood, and returning bottles and cans to keep the doors open."

"That government guy I brought in today. What agency was he with?"

"Homeland Security—from one of their octopus-tentacle offshoots." I shrugged. "I took the job. Had to." While mercs might run looser ships in downtime, the right to accept or reject a job offer always fell to the captain. The weight of command and all that good stuff. "Twenty-five million."

Sarge looked at the lightning gun. "A lot of money. Makes me think the job is going to be slogging through a lot of hell."

"Nah, it's pure cake. A zombie kill hunt. Some necromancer's running loose, transporting zombies across state lines or some stupid-ass thing. Our people can cut through zombies like a chainsaw through cream cheese."

"Easy. Unless there are too many of them."

"We can take them. This is nothing like that situation with the rocket launcher and the damn witch house walking around on chicken legs."

He stayed quiet for a moment. I hadn't expected a lot of dancing-naked-in-the-street-style rejoicing because Sarge stayed reserved at the best of times. On second thought, maybe his reticence had more to do with my pessimistic conversation opening. Note to self: work on motivational skills.

"There's something you're not saying, Captain." He crossed his arms and cocked his head at me. "It's that guy. The Green Beret. He smelled of magic. You smelled of...desire."

As a hardened mercenary, I was beyond things like blushing or blanching. "Yeah, and apparently when that yeti busted your nose last summer, it stayed busted. And *you* were the one dropping those damn winks."

He shrugged. With his massive shoulders, the shrug made me think of a shelf of ice falling off a cliff into the Antarctic. "It's just good to see you interested again. The last time we talked about your love life you were crying into a shot glass of tequila at—"

"Let's focus on the *issues*," I said. "Our new Special Forces comrade is going to brief us at 2030 hours. I want you to keep an eye open. This whole thing seems a bit too fall-into-our-lap easy." Maybe I just mistrusted the benign hand of providence. With one hand it giveth, with the other it stabbeth you in the face.

"Guess we have some work ahead." Sarge paused and looked back at the ARC rifle. "I'll bring the gun."

I hurried off to round up the last of our usual suspects and let them know about tonight's briefing. I'd already told Rafe and Mai in the course of my search for Sarge. He'd promised to take care of informing Stefan, who was still asleep, and our medic, Hanzo. It was up to me to find Tiffany and Gavin.

Tiffany answered the door dressed in what I could only describe as a shapeless purple, yellow and red frock, which complemented her about as well as a circus tent draped over a Lamborghini. Her wings were neatly folded behind her, and she favored me with a shy smile.

I grinned back. "You have a moment, Tif?"

As a succubus, she had vertical slit pupils like a cat—which was either cool or creepy depending on which side of the monster kink scale you fell on—and her irises were deep blue. Her gaze dropped from mine and contemplated my boot tips before she nodded and let me in. She had long, jet-black hair cascading past her shoulders in a careless tousle. I'd have bet all my ill-gotten filthy lucre she didn't have to spend hours at the mirror and hundreds of dollars in hair-care products getting it that way either. Damn succubus genes. Her skin was pale and lustrous, a cousin to vampire skin but warm, and a succubus wouldn't incinerate in sunlight, which made her more useful than my slacker vamp Stefan, who collected a paycheck sleeping in his bloody coffin half the time. She had flawless features. Perfect cupid-bow lips. And if she weren't so damn shy, I'd secretly hate her to death.

Tiffany turned and walked to a stool with alluring grace. Her hips swung side to side in a seductive saunter...beneath the frock. I knew from experience she wasn't consciously aware of it, since there sure as hell weren't any men in the room, and I wasn't into women in that way. I'd called her on it once and she'd been mortified, claimed it was all unconscious body language, the way her programming worked.

I closed the door behind me. I don't know what people think a succubus's room should look like—heart-shaped beds and mirrors on the ceiling, maybe. Statues of people screwing. Vibrating chairs and whatever. Tiffany's rooms were decorated in some kind of ad hoc minimalist style, unadorned chairs, few decorations and neutral colors. In one corner stood a gray, granite pedestal holding a single translucent jade vase with a bright red crystal rose, which was about it for the opulence.

Tiffany sat on the stool, adjusting her frock to make sure it covered her ankles, and folded her wings so she could sit comfortably. I slouched in a slat-back chair across from her and watched her for a moment, not saying anything. She fidgeted on the stool and pulled her knees up to her chest, but at least she didn't wrap herself up in her wings like she did when she wanted to avoid all scrutiny.

When Tiffany had first been reassigned to me from those idiots in Merc Wing Pvb6-25 aka the Salt Lake City-based Scarlet Mushrooms, I'd been pissed enough to spit fire after reading her psych evals. What did I need a *repressed* succubus for? The entire concept was absurd. The whole point of a succubus was using a target's sexual lusts against it, feeding on the erotic and using sexual energy to make the succubus more powerful. They had certain charm spells that could hypnotize weak-minded creatures, typically males—and that's a thoroughly redundant correlation if I've ever heard one. Every succubus or incubus I'd ever seen in action had reveled in their body, in their sexuality, in their power of pleasure. In contrast,

Tiffany kept herself in baggy, unappealing clothes, seemed to flinch away from the male gaze, kept quiet and to herself much of the time and was still unsuccessful in suppressing the allure of her sex magic.

Yet, after spending ten minutes with her, my inner big sister had taken the reins. I'd set down the laws with the other mercs (out of her hearing range, of course), especially with that scumbag vamp Stefan and horndog Rafe, making it crystal clear if I found anyone putting the moves on Tiffany, macking, gaming, pimping, acting like a player, circling her like a shark, staring at her ass, or in any other way making her uncomfortable or harassed, I'd start imprinting my boot on some backsides with extreme prejudice. I had deeply mixed feelings about the power of the male gaze, but in my book, if sex made her uncomfortable, then I'd do what I could to make her happy. Though a part of me still wished she'd learn to love herself for who she was, both inside and out. I wasn't big into shame. If shame were a physical thing, I'd burn it down to ash and then piss on it...but that's just me.

"What's up, Captain?" Tiffany kept her voice low, but it still came out throaty and sexy, something one would expect to hear after dialing certain 900 numbers shown on late-night television.

"How you holding up? You've been kind of quiet since the TastyTech job."

She gave a soft smile. "I'm okay, thanks. Sorry I couldn't get that guy on the roof. And...sorry the building blew up."

"Forget about it. Not your fault." I smiled to show I meant it. "Anyway, we got a briefing at 2030 hours. A major new job's in the pipe."

"I'll be there. Sure. What kind of job?"

"It's no big deal. Cannibal corpses knocking over banks or something." I shrugged and gave her a conspiratorial grin. "You know me. Any excuse to light some stuff on fire before we're done."

She giggled, yes, *giggled.* “Captain, you’re terrible. Remember when we went to that nightclub? And that guy with the comb-over kept hitting on me?”

“Good times,” I said. We both fell silent. Maybe six months ago I’d managed to drag Tiffany to a club on ladies’ night. Big, *big*, oh-so-huge mistake. Tiffany wore something modest. I’d been the one slinking around in what felt like ten-inch fuck-me shoes, but she’d earned all the lustful stares, provoking venomous vibes from a good many of the club’s patrons of the female persuasion. From the instant we’d walked in, she’d had all the males locked on her like guided missiles. Nobody paid me any attention, and I’m not exactly tenderized hamburger.

Tiffany had seemed to sense she was the object of everyone’s attention and she’d hated it. I’d almost convinced her to join me on the dance floor to lose ourselves in the pounding music when the sharks had circled in. And what a range of sharks—everything from just-turned-twenty-one college studdite to Mr. Comb-over who drove a Corvette. All of them hitting on her. The comb-over guy had been the worst. The second time he’d invaded her personal space I’d lit his knuckle hair on fire. But comb-over guy hadn’t been dissuaded. When the house DJ spun a slower dance number, Mr. Comb-over had come back up to Tiffany, put a hand on her hip and tried to urge her out onto the floor. That time I lit another batch of short and curlies on fire. Mr. Comb-over had squealed like a raccoon getting a rectal exam and dumped his White Russian on his crotch. And so ended our first ladies’ night out.

Like I said, good times.

Tiffany met my eyes and just as quickly glanced away. “I did like the music. And the dancing... We should go out again...sometime.”

“Count on it. We’ll find some smoking-hot guys...” I paused, thinking, “maybe a couple of firefighters, and we’ll drink too much, party too late, and wake up hung over.”

“Just so the firefighter doesn’t have a comb-over. And I

don't know about getting drunk—"

"Trust me, it makes dancing easier." I cleared my throat. "Don't be late for the briefing. Oh, and before I forget, you did good work last time out. I'm glad you're on the team."

"Thanks, Captain." Real pleasure shone in her eyes. It made her look so damn innocent I wanted to find the nearest cherub and kick it in the balls, just because.

"All right then." I pushed myself out of the chair and made my way over to the door, my mood gray-scaling down toward black. Wishing I could make her that happy more often. Wondering why I didn't.

"Captain?" Her voice was hesitant, little more than a curious whisper. I glanced back with eyebrows raised in silent question.

"Your scent..." She lifted her nose, delicately sniffing the air. "There's a man...a mage. You're attracted to him. *Really* attracted. I can smell your—"

"Thank you, that's enough, carry on, see you at eight thirty, or 2030 hours as we say in the business. Ha-ha." I retreated out the door and pulled it closed before I could learn anything else I didn't want to know. So much for tactful discretion. Thank God Rafe the werewolf had been too busy scarfing down a garlic-heavy chicken dish to scent anything off me when I'd told him about the meeting.

Still, if Tiffany didn't keep that little secret quiet, I'd drag my prudish succubus kicking and screaming into a Victoria's Secret buying binge as revenge. Or take her to the Thunder from Down Under male review. The image put a grin on my face, and I walked off down the hall with a new bounce in my step, decidedly not thinking of Special Forces Captain Sanders dancing on stage like an over-muscled idiot.

All right. Another lie. But the image amused the hell out of me and right about then I could use the yuks.

I double-timed it up the stairs off the foyer, thumping my way toward Gavin's rooms. I wanted nothing more than to get this over with ASAP, and I'd just raced up to the second-floor landing when I rounded the banister and crashed right into Captain Sanders. For one moment all I could think about was muscles and the smell of gun oil...until I realized he held me steady, his large hands on my upper arms. I shoved back from him, and he let me go. I could feel my skin grow blazing hot.

"Excuse me." I stepped farther away. He'd come early. I hadn't expected him until tonight. Something else to deal with, and my list already floweth over.

He smiled, but he had a way of looking at me that made me feel as if I were the focal point of the universe, as if he waited for every word I might chose to speak. I didn't like it. The word *disconcerting* sprang to mind.

"I'm sorry," he said. "I should've been more careful. I was looking for you."

"I'll let you know when I find me."

He cocked an eyebrow, but his smile didn't falter. I took a deep breath and willed my heart to airbrake back to a normal speed. A muscle in my cheek might've twitched with my effort to suppress my stupid schoolgirl-crush reactions. I clamped down even tighter. I had a job to do and a team to run. I sure as hell wouldn't allow this distraction to endanger either.

"I wondered if we could sit down together and go over a few tactical scenarios before the briefing," he said. "Make sure we're on the same page."

"I'm still tracking down my people." I glanced at my watch. "And I'm scheduled out until about...eight twenty-five. And hey, that's when your briefing starts. How unfortunate."

His smile slipped a notch. "Maybe afterwards—"

"Look, Captain Sanders—"

"Call me Jake. Save syllables."

"Fine. *Jake*. I'm busy running a team, *Jake*. Not a lot of time to attend your little *tête-à-tête*." Hail, and all witness Captain Andrea Walker behaving like an ass—yet, I couldn't stop now. Inertia was a horrible thing.

He didn't seem daunted as the wattage on his smile dialed back up to blazing. "May I call you Andrea? In private, of course."

God. Damn. It. Men, you let them pick up the ball and they ran off the field with it, yelling how they'd won. "I'm more comfortable with Captain Walker, *Jake*, thank you."

"All right, Captain Walker."

We stood so close, with no one else around. My skin felt afire, flushed, and sweat dampened my armpits. The urge to drop my gaze from his eyes pulled at me like an iron chain, but I refused to look away. Dominance games? I could play them all week, and he'd soon find out if he didn't stand down. I stepped back from him again, putting even more distance between us. Any farther and I'd fall down the stairs—but I still didn't blink, so point to me.

He didn't pursue. "I'm confident we can map out some strategies to maximize our team assets."

"*Our* team assets? Look, *Jake*, those are my people. Mine. I'm responsible for them, for keeping them safe and getting them back here every night after we go out and bust our asses, blowing shit up. I call the shots. I'm the only Captain Ahab around here. You can dispense advice when I damn well decide I need the input of a magical Green Beret."

Something flared in his eyes—either anger or respect—before the professional detachment slammed back down. Anger I could understand, but respect would only vex me more. I didn't need his damn respect.

"I didn't mean to violate protocols," he said in a smooth, calm voice. "I just want to make certain we mesh together well. That our leadership styles are fully integrated to avoid any splintering of command."

Mesh together well. That conjured up some distracting images. Oh, he did vex me something awful, the bastard. "We can fully integrate if you listen to my orders. When we're hot, I'm calling the shots."

"Understood. I'm here to support and advise. My only goal is to achieve our mission objectives."

"Then I suggest you stay out of my way. I'm driving this truck." I walked around him, careful not to touch him again, and continued up the next set of stairs, willing my fists to remain unclenched and my jaw muscles to cease and desist from grinding my teeth to powder.

He called after me. "One last thing, Captain Walker."

I glanced down. He had his game face on—a hard-as-steel, raptor-eyed, chew-dynamite-and-spit-out-nitroglycerin look which appeared pretty damn impressive. "What?"

"I meant what I said about achieving mission objectives. I'll do whatever I have to. There are lives to save."

I swallowed my cheeky comment and gave him the benefit of a nod, despite my smoldering irritation. As if I didn't know there were civvy lives at stake. Who'd he think he was dealing with? Backwater hicks?

I spun on my heel and took the stairs two at a time, eager to be away from him. God help me, this might just be the hardest damn job I'd ever done.

My skin still burned from my run-in with Captain Sanders—and no, I wouldn't start calling him Jake—and my stomach still practiced sailor's knots with my guts. I was so flustered I walked right past Gavin's door before realizing it. Men. Problems. The lament of the double-X chromosome for half a million years.

Gavin Carter, driver, pilot and wannabe novelist. He was also technically an empath—or at least that's what his file claimed. I'd never seen any evidence of it and figured he'd copied it from *Star Trek* to pad his resume.

I hammered on the door. Six months ago he'd had his music cranked so loud he couldn't hear my knocks, and I'd made the mistake of opening the door and wandering inside, only to discover Gavin absorbed in some good old-fashioned naked web-cam cavorting. The kind that involves rapid motion of the right hand while staring at jerky web video, pun definitely intended. I still had nightmares.

"Come in, goddamn it!" Gavin yelled.

I took a deep breath, prayed for mercy to the gods of decency, and stepped inside.

His walls were covered with NASCAR posters and framed pictures of jet fighters and scantily clad women. The furniture reminded me of the mismatched junk from my stint in a college dorm. The place smelled of stale garlic and beer, and all the blinds were shut, which I took as an ominous sign.

I peeked around the corner into his office. Gavin sat slumped in his leather chair in front of a computer and focused on the screen. Oh God. Not again.

He heard me gasp and whipped around, then frowned when he recognized me. "For God's sake, Captain. Let it go, will you? I'm writing. Totally innocent."

I hazarded a few steps closer. "Mandatory briefing tonight at 2030 hours."

"Mandatory? Somebody die or something? I have an epic mob guild raid scheduled for then."

"This is real-world serious, not computer-game stuff. A new job, capping zombies. I expect your ass there and you on your best behavior."

Most of the time I felt bad for Gavin. He wasn't fugly or anything, but he appeared plain put up against someone like that bastard Captain *Jake* Sanders. Oh, and empathy or not, his people skills were about as finely developed as lead Play-Doh.

"All right, I'll be there. But you owe me."

"Yeah, right. Send me a bill." I glanced at his screen. "What are you writing?"

He covered the screen with his hands. "It's not ready yet."

"Give me a break, here," I said. "For once I'm interested.

Don't play like you're shy. I know you too well."

"Fine. It's probably just the best thing I've ever written. A novel about a shape-shifting Himalayan Long-Haired Bovine, commonly known as a yak. There's some kung fu, a vampire samurai, some hot spanking monkey sex, true love and a happily ever after. Some ninja aliens too, as the bad guys. It's gonna sell gazillions." He grinned. "I'll buy you a Porsche when I'm rich."

I raised an eyebrow. "Big market for that kind of book?"

"There will be."

I began to back out of the room. Slowly. So the crazy person wouldn't attack me. Never show fear. Never let them smell your sweat. And never, ever, turn your back. "About that briefing. It's required. So. See you at 2030 hours. Big job ahead, lots of money. Come early or Squeegee will steal your seat on the couch. That is all. Carry on."

I exfiltrated out of there as fast as I could. Some days it just didn't pay to crawl out of bed. Or skip the Thorazine.

Chapter Five:
SNAFU Briefing, Baby

Mercenary Wing Rv6-4 "Zero Dogs"
The Zero Dog Compound
1st Floor Great Room
2031 Hours PST April 10th

Captain Sanders turned out to be more of a problem than I thought.

He stood at ease near the wall in our great room, next to the projected image of a grungy building. Problem was, my mind kept drifting off the mission-briefing details and onto stupid, inconsequential things. Like how warm his skin had been when I'd shaken his hand. Those intense eyes. How well he filled out his fatigues. Bankruptcy. Yeah. Bankruptcy tended to crush the desire like a boot heel on a cockroach. I was tired, but that was no damn excuse, and my unprofessional thoughts made me furious. I had responsibilities, and I couldn't let my people down just because I felt a little horny. I wouldn't shirk my duty for anyone, and especially not for some FNG Army eightball. Fucking New Guys, they should come with a product warning or something.

The projector hummed, connected by a USB to Sanders's laptop. The rest of the Zero Dogs had gathered around in a wide semicircle, deployed as follows:

Rafe lounged on the couch, Squeegee on his lap—or rather

Squeegee's massive feline head on his lap, an ear idly turning to follow the sounds. Tiffany sat in a recliner, knees drawn up to her chin. Mai had ringed herself with small summoned creatures—things that resembled Guinea Pigs with glowing neon purple eyes and which probably had acid for blood. Hanzo, no matter how badly he might've wanted to sit next to her, didn't risk getting too close to those furry little bastards, despite his legendary ninja skills.

Stefan slouched against the far wall, arms folded, his noble features set in a grim scowl. Nothing new there. The lazy vamp liked to tell people he was some kind of Romanian aristocrat who'd once hobnobbed with the king of Hungary, but I knew better. He was merely some rich kid from the Hamptons who'd been bitten at Woodstock during the age of peace and love, when he'd been rebelling against his parents. He didn't sparkle, either. Only fairies sparkled, and mostly when you lit them on fire.

Gavin sat on the little bit of couch free of Squeegee's limbs, toying with one of those maddening intelligence games—figure out how to detach these two twisted nails and win absolutely nothing.

Sarge stood in the doorway to the hall, hands in his pockets, massive shoulders almost filling the entry from wall to wall. The dim light made his skin appear a dusky eggplant purple. He'd also been quiet so far.

As for me, I'd claimed my leather recliner—the back of which hung in shredded tatters thanks to Squeegee's claws—legs crossed, trying to watch the slideshow and not the presenter. Trying to convince myself Sanders didn't present a threat. Not doing a very good job of it.

Our new Green Beret cut straight to the chase. "I'm Captain Sanders, US Army, Special Forces. I've been assigned as a Force Multiplier to the Zero Dogs for this operation."

Nods all around. A good start, but I wondered how long it would last. We could go from zero to clusterfuck in less than five point two seconds.

Sanders raised the control for the projector. "Here's what we know." He flipped to a new PowerPoint slide. A color shot of a plain, unassuming man in his mid-thirties, close-shaven goatee, brown eyes, brown hair, fleshy face but not quite overweight. To me he looked more like a manager at a Blockbuster Video chain. "On March 4th, this man, Jeremiah Hansen, a necromancer of the Unrighteous Order of the Falling Dark, transported a group of between fifty and seventy-five RCTs to First Federal Bank in Beaverton—"

"Did you say the dude's name is Jeremiah?" Gavin interrupted. "Talk about epic villain name fail."

Rafe shook his head. "Yeah, it's even worse than Gavin."

"Fuck you, fleabag."

"I don't do guys. Call Sarge over. Gotta warn you though, I suspect he's got better taste."

"Leave me out of this, Rafe," Sarge rumbled. "Or I'll kick your mangy ass."

Mai raised her slender hand as if she were in school. She'd worn blue and yellow summoner's robes, with a pattern of falling leaves down the sides. All her demon Guinea Pigs cocked their heads up at her in adoration when she started to speak. "Captain Sanders, I'm not familiar with the term RCT."

"Noobcake City, here," Gavin said with disgust. "RCT is an acronym for Reanimated Corpse Threat."

Hanzo stood up slowly, staring at Gavin with narrowed eyes. "Apologize to Ms. Tanaka before I decide to NKYITF. An acronym for Ninja Kick You in the Face."

"Big talk from a sawbones Band-Aid pusher. Newsflash, otaku head. You're no Bruce Lee. You're not even Asian. Now, shut the fuck up before I go crunchy on your ass and run you down with the Bradley."

"You *will* rue this day the next time you bleed, *kono yarou.*"

Sarge's voice snarled out of the back. "Shut your fucking

holes, *both* of you. I've got some goddamned acronyms for you, you fucking POG POS REMFs."

Roughly translated: Person Other than Grunt, Piece of Shit, Rear-Echelon Motherfuckers. Ah, *esprit de corps*. We had it in such abundance it leaked down our legs. Still, I couldn't help but yawn for Jake's benefit, feigning boredom, flaunting my acting skills, eager to see the Green Beret squirm.

Poor Captain Sanders watched as his briefing died a premature goat-rope death, glancing from speaker to speaker like a tennis match attendee, with his face a mask of dismay. Finally, he looked at me. I shrugged and tried to hide my smile, but didn't do a very good job of it. Hell, he *wanted* to be here. Even asked me to attack him for the honor of joining up. Could I help it if I'd found a more effective way to plant my foot in his ass?

After all, these were mercs, not toe-the-line, into-the-breach-without-a-bitch, salute-and-keep-your-mouth-shut soldiers. Free of hot zones, opinions were like assholes, they all stank, and mercs loved to show them off. Only in firefights did we maintain professional-soldier status. Well, other merc wings maintained that status. I just did the best I could with what God had seen fit to torment me. Still...I'd made my point. Time to get down to business, get this done so I could go drink something with high alcohol content. I cleared my throat to get everyone's attention.

Rafe, the very soul of helpfulness, said, "You guys are making the captain cough up a lung."

I ignored him. "I suggest we all pay better attention to Captain Sanders. Less collateral damage when you guys actually comprehend our mission objectives."

"Thank you, Andrea." Sanders nodded at me, and I went very still, feeling as if my skin had turned to ice and started to crack. Did that bastard just call me by my first name in front of my team? Sonuva*bitch*. But before I could channel my outrage, Sanders pushed on with his briefing and I had to bite my tongue. Oh shit we were gonna have such a talk later.

"Jeremiah Hansen," he said, "controlling his RCTs, advanced in force through the Beaverton bank's front doors." He clicked through several stills from the bank cameras showing a diverse menagerie of zombies swarming into the lobby. He clicked on a video file and four different views of the bank interior came up, a long string of numbers counting off on the screen bottom. No sound, but I watched the bank tellers and a few customers react with terror as the undead tide swarmed toward them.

Sanders continued. "Luckily, a quick-thinking bank teller rallied the customers and her coworkers and locked everyone in the bank vault, where they remained safe until rescued by SWAT."

On the screen, the teller in question sprayed a zombie with mace. The zombie sneezed and one of its eyeballs fell out. The zombie grabbed at her, and she slammed one of those chain-connected pens into its other eye socket. Needless to say, the chain broke too. *You go, girl.* It was like watching Wonder Woman without the star-spangled panties.

"Despite the teller's heroics, the bank and depositors suffered monetary losses of about fifty thousand dollars, judging by FDIC and insurance records."

"On March 12th, Hansen struck again at a Chasing bank in the Northwest District. His forces engaged just as the bank opened for business, and there were no customers inside. However, the bank manager, Felix Fisk, was eaten by the RTCs." The slideshow displayed grim pictures of a Very Mustachioed Rich Man (or VMRM because acronyms are as addicting as popping bubble wrap) in a perfectly cut suit flailing around as a circle of zombies closed around him. Blood spray doused the zombies when they ripped into him, but the blood appeared more like maple syrup on the black-and-white camera feeds. I winced. How long before *that* clip showed up on the internet?

"The zombies didn't touch the three tellers, who barricaded themselves in a break room, but on this occasion they compromised the vault despite a time lock. This engagement netted him over a hundred thousand dollars. The newest attack took place today at around thirteen hundred hours. I was just briefed on it. The necromancer hit an armored car at one of its scheduled ATM refill stops."

"Small-time stuff," Sarge said. "This guy's not causing much mayhem."

"Not yet. His real goal is this." Captain Sanders clicked forward to a slide featuring an industrial building. "We have information he's now incorporated and ramping up operations."

"Manufacturing bio weapons?" Mia asked. Her pet demon Guinea Pig-things had curled up around her like drifts of furry snowballs.

"Gelatin."

Silence.

"I thought I heard gelatin," Gavin said. "But that can't be right, because that's what I'd expect to hear if I was smoking weed, and I'm clearly not smoking weed."

"Gelatin is correct. His factory focuses on the manufacture of powdered gelatin products. He's using the living dead as a labor force, allowing him to run operations for twenty-four hours a day and skirt all OSHA regulations and labor laws, destabilizing the market."

Hanzo frowned. "I believe in the sanctity of the free market. In Japan, business is war. As Sun Tzu said, 'All war is deception.' Deception is the ninja way."

"Sun Tzu was Chinese, you fucking poseur," Gavin said.

Rafe scratched at his chin. "Free markets? I only believe in free porn."

I could see Captain Sanders's jaws tightening, could almost hear his teeth grinding together from across the room. If he hadn't just called me by my first name, I'd have felt some amount of chagrin at how my people behaved. Now I just wanted to yank his chain. Smear off some of that military spit and polish. Show him how we did it merc-style.

But two seconds later I did a hard mental one-eighty turn. This wasn't about a pissing contest with Jake. If we lost this client, we'd be screwed. I'd pushed things far enough. Time to grow up and get back on track.

"Zombie containment and destruction is standard protocol," I said. "But I get the impression the government's even more concerned about the economic angle to this."

Sanders nodded. "Leaving aside implications of widespread zombie infection, the Zombeconomy, as it's sometimes called—"

"I'm not sure I can say Zombeconomy with a straight face," Mai warned, and Rafe snorted laughter. Squeegee the mutant cat rolled on her back, furry belly up, and farted. All Mai's pets scrambled to their feet and squeaked in outrage.

"God, that smells like lighter fluid," Gavin said.

Captain Sanders scanned the room with his best Special Forces hard-ass stare. I also made scary faces at my troops. God, what had I started, letting them off their leashes? I swallowed and my throat made a dry click. Visions of vanishing government money danced through my head.

"Zombification has grim implications for workers in Mexico and China," Captain Sanders said. "A Harvard business analyst predicts it could collapse the low-wage, high-hour labor market. If the concept of using a zombie work force spreads, the garment industry could be wiped out. It's not outside the realm of possibility that the phenomenon known as zombie creep will bleed into the US marketplace. First with low-pay, low-prestige jobs, and then working its way up to higher-pay, low-prestige jobs such as used-car salesmen." He paused, his face grim. "If his business model succeeds, we're looking at the collapse of current free-market capitalism for all non-zombie entities."

"What, no credit-default swaps?" Gavin said. "No hedge-fund implosion? No sub-prime mortgages offered in an orgy of greed and predatory lending?" He glanced at Rafe and whispered, “The Mayans predicted all of this. Here’s a hint: buy gold and stock up on toilet paper.”

Captain Sanders cleared his throat. “This threat, viewed in the long term, may be more serious than any of those. While Wall Street investors might view zombie creep and the resulting free labor in a positive light, I’m afraid our analysts predict long-term consequences for the American electorate, including widespread unemployment, being eaten, the breakdown of society, the decay of traditional family values and an exponentially expanding zombie apocalypse. To name just a few.”

“This is interesting and all.” Rafe made a spectacular show of yawning. “But we’ve done zombies before. Just airdrop me into that plant and I’ll sort out your RCT problem.” He grinned and winked. “Maybe afterwards you can hook me up with some hot Army tank girls.”

“Yeah, right, furball,” Gavin said. “What do zombies taste like?”

“Zombies taste like chicken.” Rafe paused and considered. “Maybe a little rubbery.”

“An assault won’t be easy,” Sanders warned. “This is a hardened target. Internal defenses. A hostile work force that doubles as a security apparatus. Our mission is essentially a decapitation strike. Neutralize Jeremiah Hansen first, and then defeat the zombie horde in detail. Once the command and control is degraded, we’ll find the zombies no longer able to act in concert. We roll up the flanks and incinerate the facility.”

“Possibility of collateral damage?” Sarge still leaned against the wall, arms folded, with his black and red eyes locked on Sanders.

“High. Our Rules of Engagement give us restricted operating parameters. We go in with weapons tight. Check your targets. This is a built-up commercial and light-industrial environment, which means there will be civvies. So keep sharp.” He clicked forward a couple of slides to a satellite photo of the plant. "I'll be working to set up a training regimen to master our assault tactics."

For once my people stayed professional enough not to groan at the extra work. Strangely unexpected. Most of the time I had to herd Gavin, Rafe and Hanzo around as if they were two years old and needed naps. "I assume we'll be drawing up an assault plan?" I asked. "Together, I mean."

Out of the corner of my eye I saw Rafe nudge Gavin and grin, but I ignored them. My people, unruly as they could be, were not going to get hurt on this mission due to someone else's half-assed, Sir Douglas Haig-esque frontal assault strategy à la the Battle of the Somme. So Sanders had damn well better include me in the mission planning.

"I have several options I'd be happy to review with you in detail," he said carefully, and then addressed the group again. "First phase will be training and planning. When both Captain Walker and I feel the Zero Dogs are prepared, we'll recon in force. Information gained at that time will determine our final assault."

Sarge spoke up. "Clearly there's no time crunch if we have opportunity to train."

"Not completely accurate, Sergeant. Because available assets are low, DHS decided to use Special Forces to bring in a private contractor force to accomplish this objective. Under ideal circumstances it would be handled immediately. However, while the long-term implications of zombie creep are grave—"

Gavin snorted.

"—Necromancer Hansen seems to be focused on the economic advantages of his RCT labor force instead of initiating widespread havoc. The necromancer's approach, should it remain consistent, gives us a small window for training, therefore increasing our predicted success ratio. So, in answer to your question, it *is* important. It's National Security level, let there be no doubt."

"It's important enough for them to pay us well," I said. "End of the day, that's why we're all here. So I suggest we keep it frosty, keep it sharp, get some rest and hit the ground tomorrow with our boots on and big girl panties duct-taped in place. *Capiche*?"

Nods all around. Even from my troublemakers. Joy. "Good. I'll see you all tomorrow. Bright and early." I looked at Stefan. "We'll set up a specific regimen for you. One you can work on at night." He nodded, bowed, faded back into the shadows and vanished. Vampires. Always with the showy, showy.

Everyone got up and wandered off in different directions, some toward the kitchen, the rest headed off to their rooms. Sarge and I waited until the last of them filed out.

I meant to talk with Sarge, but as soon as I started toward him, Captain Sanders called out to me. "Captain Walker, I'd like a moment. In private."

My heart rate sped up, the undersides of my armpits grew damp, but I fought back against my reaction, whatever had triggered it, fight, flight or fuck response. Flesh was stupid, a stupid pleasure/pain box plugged into a part of the brain more reptilian than anything else. I could hold the line against hormones, pheromones, electrolytes and dopamine. No slave to emotion and response was I. And something told me I wouldn't like what Jake Sanders had to say, anyway.

"Let's talk outside then." I glanced at Sarge. "I'll catch up with you later."

I led Captain Sanders down the corridor past the huge Tuscany-style kitchen and out the glass doors that opened onto our decking. Our deck looked out on the training grounds behind the house and the distant, dark shape of the V22 parked on the landing pad. A tall line of evergreen trees formed a barrier beyond the last set of bunkers and the half-demolished group of out buildings we used for urban-assault training. The air smelled of pine needles, and a warm, gentle breeze brought the distant sound of traffic from West Burnside Street.

We walked across the deck with me in the lead, my footsteps heavy, resounding. He followed at a distance, moving with the quiet grace of a phantom cat. When I came to the porch rail, I turned to face him down.

He stood a half dozen feet away, his hands shoved in the pockets of his fatigues. He stared out over the training ground, brow furrowed, clenching his jaw. For a moment part of me admired his profile. Hard jawline. The short military haircut that looked as if the killer from the *Friday the 13th* movies had attacked his hair with a weed whacker...

He took a deep breath and slowly let it out. "I'm killing this mission."

My heart did a *Titanic* and sank all the way into my guts. I swallowed and my throat made a clicking noise, but I couldn't seem to speak. Then the fire streamed through my veins. "You don't have that authority. My client is Mr. Harker and Homeland Security. You're just along for the ride, pal."

He leaned toward me. "I damn well *do* have that authority. If I don't like what I see, I yank the plug. Somebody else does the job."

"Why the hell would you do that? You haven't even seen us in action yet."

"I did, remember? I saw you tangle with those idiot terrorist dark elves and burn down the building."

Shit. In my ire, I'd forgotten. "That guy was a suicide bomber. Not our fault the place exploded."

Captain Sanders didn't answer.

My fists clenched. "You really don't think we can fucking do this? You think we're a bunch of civvies with guns, don't you?"

He shrugged. "A step up maybe. Militia stuff."

"Well, fuck you, John Wayne."

He scowled. "I've never in my life seen such a sorry bunch of soldiers—mercs, *condottieri*, whatever. That can be traced directly back to you."

"You waltz in here and criticize my command? You've got some shiny brass balls."

"What command?" he asked. "I don't see any command. I see a team flailing around in need of leadership. That briefing was the worst, most disjointed, most *interrupted* briefing I've ever given, constantly usurped by a bunch of bickering adolescents. How do you people even function in the field?"

"This isn't the lock-step army. These people are warriors first, not soldiers first. You don't have the first clue about it."

"I think I do. The clue tells me the Zero Dogs have no discipline. And that goes straight to the top."

I flushed cold, and then burned hot again. The air around me started to grow warmer. "You bastard. You fumble one little briefing with a bunch of free-thinking mercs and now you're crying like a bitch. If DHS dumps us, it'll be because of your whiny ass, not any lack of skill on our part."

"I don't see anything here." He shook his head and glanced away. When he looked back at me, his eyes flashed, as if my people personally offended him. "The place is a pigsty. No order. No discipline. Barely any command structure, and what's there doesn't work—"

"If you keep insulting my leadership abilities, there's going to be one serious goddamn problem in about two seconds."

He shrugged again. "If you people fight in the field like you behaved at my briefing, then I'm surprised any of you've managed to stay alive this long. Guess God loves fools, drunks and soldiers of fortune."

I leaned toward him, into his personal space, and glared up at him with my head cocked as if I were an instant from clamping my teeth on his throat. "Listen and listen good. We have our issues. I've never seen a squad that doesn't. But on the field, when things are live and hot and it's fucking go time, you better believe we carve up bad guy flank steak and serve it with sauce. You *understand* me? I took these guys to Mogadishu after a Xanna demon out to poison the fucking

World Tree. Just on a bounty hunt. Just to help out in a part of the world that makes our sewers look like a decent hotel. In two weeks we cut that thing to shreds and shipped our client its flaming heart in a glass jar."

He watched me. "I was briefed on your exploits."

"Then you know when there are asses requiring boot prints, the Zero Dogs get to work wearing the steel toes. We ain't pretty, we ain't shiny, but we get it done."

There. That was all I had. If he still wanted to kill our involvement, I couldn't stop him. I hated him having so much damn power over us, and especially over me. It made my insides churn like an off-balance washing machine.

For a long moment there was only silence. He stared off at the iron fence surrounding the compound. "All right." He waved a hand, but kept his scowl. "I'll hold judgment. You guys aren't quiet professionals, but we'll see what you can do with me around."

Outrage burned furnace-hot inside me. I simply could. Not. *Believe*. This. Man. "Maybe next time you shouldn't goose step in here with preconceived notions of how things get done."

"Maybe. And maybe the guy who recommended the great Captain Andrea Walker shouldn't have put you on such a pedestal."

I opened my mouth. Closed it again. Somebody put *me* on a pedestal? Oddly touching...and yet how dare Sanders imply, in the same goddamn breath, that I didn't deserve to be on one?

Jake's face softened into a smile. "Yeah. You come highly recommended—and right now that's the only reason I'm holding off killing this mission. That and your little impassioned speech a second ago."

My heart pounded too hard. I didn't think I could say anything without acid and more fireworks. The silence stretched out and at the same time sharpened in intensity.

His smile slowly spread wider. "So why don't we sit down and sketch out some training plans, come up with a forward operating scheme." He paused. "This needs to go off perfectly."

"This is cake."

"That's the spirit." He swept a hand toward the sliding door. "After you."

I marched back inside, trying not to let my anxiety show, although to Rafe's nose I no doubt reeked of worry. A close call, no denying it. I'd avoided a wreck, averted losing the contract, but several other dangerous obstacles loomed on the horizon, speeding ever closer. For example, would Captain Sanders opt for a power grab and try to run this show himself? Maybe even trying it in the name of discipline or the old favorite, National Security? My people would back me, I felt a hundred percent on that, but it'd leave the mission a smoking ruin.

Sanders hadn't been kidding. Everything about this job needed to come off perfectly, for so many reasons.

The long day finally showed signs of winding down, but I remained keyed up, my nerves still sizzling from the strategy session with Captain Sanders I'd just left—and not in a good way. Just me and him and a million pins and needles, while his words about our professionalism, about *my* leadership, smoldered in my marrow. We'd come up with some good approaches, and we'd synched on most issues, but the tension in the room had me feeling as if I'd chugged six double-shot espressos in a row.

Even though my body ached from brittle exhaustion, I knew I'd have a hell of a time falling asleep. The irony. I pressed my thumb to the scanner pad and unlocked the door to my third-floor suite. The smells of cinnamon and baked goods lingered in the air from an early morning run to the bakery, since I certainly had no time to bake while running this three-ring circus. I shut the door, leaned against it and closed my eyes. My neck and shoulder muscles felt hard and tight, and the first throb of a headache ghosted from my temples to my hairline.

The question remained. Could I trust Captain Sanders? If so, how far?

Despite the earlier hostilities, we'd managed to act professional during the planning session. I'd even decided to let drop the issue of Sanders using my first name during the briefing. But that certainly didn't mean I trusted him or forgave the slight. Not at all. He had too much power, too much control over our future. Captain Sanders was a threat. Maybe in more ways than one.

I kicked off my boots, peeled off my socks and chucked them across the room, and scrunched my toes in the deep carpeting. The air from the vents felt blessedly cool on my skin. I lingered for a moment with my eyes still closed, working on deep breathing and imagining my stress transforming into tiny dust motes and drifting away like pollen on the wind. It helped a little, and I walked through my hall flipping on more lights, headed toward the kitchen.

So what would it be? A beer? I had a few bottles of Black Strap Stout in the fridge, but decided I wasn't in the mood. Tonight demanded something with more fire. My bottle of Chivas lurked in the cabinet over the microwave. The scotch went down smooth and warm, spreading its heat out through my body. I took the glass with me back into the living room, glanced around, and started to pace in front of the large picture window. During daylight the window gave a great view of Mt. Hood, but now the darkness seemed to huddle against the glass. I shut the blinds to block it out.

I paced again as a stray thought pushed into my mind. What would Captain Sanders think of my little favorite space? Would he think it too *unprofessional*? I'd decorated in a style I liked to call *warm eclectic*, but which Sarge always referred to with a smirk as *random psychotic*. Comfy couches, fat candles on wrought-iron holders, colorful fabrics for texture, silks, velvets and a river-stone fireplace. I'd covered the walls with old English tapestries and Toulouse-Lautrec prints. An intricately detailed rapier and dagger set with silver and gold inlay leaned on a stand in the corner.

Anyway, who cared what Sanders would think? Stupid, irrelevant question and a patently idiotic line of thought. Jesus, I had to get a grip. I had so many more important things to worry about. If he hated my decor, I'd merely stab him with the dagger.

Dammit. Still thinking of him.

I wheeled around, nearly sloshing Chivas out of my glass, and stomped toward the French doors leading to my balcony. Night air and quiet. They had to keep me from replaying earlier conversations in my head and coming up with wittier replies, right?

The night was calm, cool and dry, a kind I didn't see enough of here in Oregon. It only took a few minutes to admit the night air and quiet had no effect. My thoughts still churned, and I could hear Jake's voice, harsh with scorn, in my mind. I leaned against the railing, gently swirling my scotch. Was he right? *Was* I incompetent as a commander? Were things in my unit really as bad as he'd claimed? I stood so close to the situation that maybe I couldn't see how chaotic they'd become.

Bullshit. We did job after job and did it well. Except for that last one with the dark elves where we'd lost the plant. I took another sip—more of a gulp—and focused on the warmth sliding down my throat.

Should I hang up the proverbial jockstrap?

Like hell.

So should I put the boot heel down? Demand more discipline in noncombat situations?

Everything in me said no. Yeah, we were chaotic, disorganized, at time fractious, and often we behaved more like a dysfunctional family than a squad of professional warriors. Despite those things, we had real cohesion when we deployed to the field—a unity I was afraid to endanger. I'd helped rebuild the Zero Dogs on a foundation of trust and mutual respect, not some constantly enforced chain of command. Hell, I lived, ate and fraternized with my troops—not something officers in the mainline army often did—and what's more, I *liked* it. I wasn't going to change. Not for him, not to impress him, not to placate him.

Captain Jake Sanders would just have to man up and deal with us. I hadn't lost anybody since I'd taken the reins, and a wise woman didn't fix what wasn't busted. I wouldn't let an outsider march in here and impose some military discipline code on warriors who hated that system. And that was that.

I pushed my hair back from my face and stared out at the night, again trying to calm down. No moon tonight, just an expanse of stars and the dark shape of Mt. Hood on the horizon.

Calm.

I took another sip of Chivas and slowly exhaled, smelling the alcohol on my breath.

Focus on nothing.

I wasn't drunk at all, but the tightness in my neck and shoulders started to fade, and I congratulated myself on heading off the impending headache. Crickets chirped, the faint Doppler hiss and rumble of traffic drifted up from the far-off streets, and the trees rustled in the breeze. A divine slice of peace and quiet—a Valhalla for the average gun-toting, flame-throwing nature girl—now only if I could finish unwinding enough to enjoy it.

A door opened somewhere below me, and I glanced down over the railing, more by reflex than anything else. Captain Sanders walked along one of the lower decks. I jerked back so he wouldn't see me leaning over the rail. Goddammit, I hadn't realized Sanders had been set up with rooms a level below mine. He talked into a cell phone in a low, urgent voice. I leaned forward again, straining to hear him, but the rustle of the breeze swelled in the treetops and obscured his words. I bit back a curse. For a moment I considered climbing down and sneaking closer through the shadows. Then again, shadowy sneaking was more a Hanzo the Deluded Shinobi thing to do. With my luck I'd end up in the infirmary with a broken ankle and facing embarrassing questions.

Sanders paced back and forth along the decking, head down, staring at the ground as he talked, all his body language telling me he spoke about something intense. Was the bastard telling Harker we were a bunch of incompetents, despite reassuring me he'd hold off? Damn I wished I could get closer... I leaned farther out and finally caught a few words when he turned back toward me.

"...uneven in some areas..." Sanders said. I missed the next string of words but he finished with, "...still meet the objectives."

My heart punched my rib cage and my pulse throbbed in my temples. My mouth felt dry, my throat parched, my tongue like sandpaper. I leaned out as far as I dared...

He turned away and I missed more of the conversation. He started to pace back toward me and then paused. I stared at his face, not breathing, trying to read his expression in the darkness.

"Only if there's no other option," he said, his voice louder than before. "Those kinds of changes might not be necessary."

I couldn't speak, couldn't breathe. My fingers loosely held the glass. Any less strength and it would've fallen and shattered on the deck below.

"At this point I believe we'll be ready in time, sir," he continued. I lost a bit more when the breeze stirred again, but caught bits of the end, "...Walker shares my assessment...early to promise success but..." More words lost. He paused, listening. "Thank you for going with me on this, sir."

He snapped the cell phone closed and slipped it into his pocket. My gaze never left him as he stood at the railing, staring out over the grounds. I forced my breath out and dragged in another. Had he been talking to Harker or to some other high-ranking pencil pusher from DHS? And what was the *other option* Sanders seemed to dismiss? I didn't like the sound of it.

Not at all.

The stupidest, most disturbing thing about the whole situation had to be the fact I could still feel an attraction to him simmering inside me, defying my will and better judgment. It had grown so intermixed with my wariness, my animosity and my wish to hold judgment and give him a chance, that all together they twisted my stomach into balloon animals. Part of me viewed him like a lioness staring at a strange lion, evaluating his every action with the cold interest of a rival hunter—but I didn't know if it was a hunter in search of a compatible mate, or a hunter stalking another who had wandered into its territory and threatened the food supply. Maybe both. Hell, no *maybe* about it. Definitely.

Sanders finally seemed to feel my gaze burning holes in his back. He glanced around, and then looked up at my balcony. I drew back out of sight, wishing I'd thought to turn off all my interior lights. Too late now, but I didn't think he'd seen me. A few seconds later I heard the whoosh and click of a door below me.

When I peeked again, he was gone.

Chapter Six:
A Few Evil Men

Undead Army, Human Resources Division
Peet's Coffee & Tea
NE Broadway, Portland, Oregon
7:45 a.m. PST April 11th

Overlord Jeremiah Hansen, Necromancer of the Unrighteous Order of the Falling Dark, wasn't a coffee lover. He crossed his legs and sipped from his recycled paper coffee cup filled with a dark, bitter mixture he hadn't been able to save with either cream or three packets of sugar substitute. He burned his lip, bit down on a curse, and did his best not to appear vexed in front of the man he had yet to interview.

A corner coffeehouse wasn't his choice of meeting places, although they did have excellent scones. Filling his second-in-command position had turned out to be more of a challenge than he'd expected, and he loathed this human resources crapola. The exhilaration of yesterday's armored-car heist had already evaporated. The fact that he hated the taste of coffee didn't help either, and these chairs outside the coffee shop put his ass cheeks in a coma.

The man on the opposite side of the iron table, Blake Delaney, took a sip of his tea and managed to appear entirely too cool and collected. He had a face full of angles, like a geometry lesson gone horribly awry, and a thin body lost in his suit. The suit appeared expensive, maybe silk, probably from some big-name designer. Showoff. Jeremiah wore only chinos and a University of Oregon hoodie with a faded chocolate stain on the front.

He shifted, suddenly uncomfortable. Blake Delaney gave off such an air of utter competence, accented with a slight fragrance of generalized contempt, that Jeremiah felt a bit self-conscious. He never felt self-conscious around his zombies.

Blake cleared his throat, scowled into his tea and then tapped a gold cufflink. “The absolute first thing you must realize is my services are highly sought among those who seek to rule the world, and therefore, are quite dear.”

“Money’s not an issue.” Not with yesterday’s armored-car haul. A bit of seed money remained from the first couple of banks he’d knocked over with his zombie horde, as well as some cash from diamonds and gold he’d fenced in Idaho. He didn’t feel the least bit guilty about the robberies either. He’d needed the start-up capital. Don’t blame him because he’d come up with a novel way of withdrawing it. It was quintessentially American to think outside the box.

Blake gave him a tight smile. “Your pardon, I beg to differ. Money is *always* an issue.”

Jeremiah played with his cup, spinning the heat shield around and around. “How much did you have in mind?”

Blake named a figure. Overlord Jeremiah did his best not to crush his cup with a convulsive squeeze and spill coffee all over the pigeons hopping around their table searching for crumbs. Good God Almighty the man was right. Money *was* an issue. He could pay that kind of fee for what...maybe six months? Outrageous. Yet, if he couldn’t get his startup off the ground in six months, he wasn’t really worthy of the title, was he?

“Done,” he finally answered, although his voice came out a little strangled.

Blake nodded, but his face never changed from his studied

indifference. "I have a few other terms and conditions."

"I'm not in the habit of granting terms and conditions." Zombies didn't require them. Hell, zombies weren't even articulate.

"I'm afraid these terms and conditions must be met in order to procure my services, Mr. Hansen."

The man sounded like a damn lawyer. Never a good sign. "Name them."

"First and foremost, you must change your name. Jeremiah Hansen does not inspire terror."

"So what do you suggest instead?" Not that he hadn't heard that crap about his name ever since kindergarten or anything. Still, he busied himself imagining Blake dangling by a chain over a zombie pit. Maybe *that* would inspire some fucking terror.

"We'll focus group some possibilities and come up with something appropriate. My second condition is I must be allowed to manage your detail work without interference." He picked up Jeremiah's prospectus for his company, Bokor Gelzonbi Foods. "This claims you have over four hundred zombies in employment..."

"Four hundred and counting." Jeremiah's tone skated into defensive. "I'm acquiring more all the time."

"Hmm. And, according to this, you are endowed with necromancy magics, specifically a reanimator skill set, specializing in the undead, *vis-à-vis*, zombies."

"More voodoo theme than the chaos of *Night of the Living Dead*, if that helps. Although they do like to eat people if you don't watch them."

"I see. And, as referenced here, you wish to use an army of zombies within your factory to undercut the competition on wages, benefits and insurance, as well as other overhead costs, such as heating and lighting?"

"I know, it's fucking brilliant. Zombies work twenty-three hours a day without complaint. No unions. No health insurance or even sick days. No OSHA. No carpel tunnel—hell, no worker-comp claims. Give them a little training on pushing buttons à la Pavlov and we're good to go."

"Twenty-three hours? Why twenty-*three*, may I ask?"

"One hour for side activities—feeding, staring at the sun, watching old episodes of *Three's Company*. We also do a little chant to keep up morale—well, more of an organized series of moans than a chant, really. Want to hear it? It's better than Walmart's."

"No. No, I don't." Blake peered back at the prospectus and paged forward. "And, as delineated in paragraph 2C of Section 17, you wish to use said zombies in the manufacture of food products, specifically Type A powdered gelatin?"

"We have several flavors and application types available. I'm considering calling it Zello. You know, zombie plus Jell-O, but there might be trademark issues." He waved a contemptuous hand. "Lawyers would get involved."

"Zello. Charming. We'll work on it. So, according to the mission statement, our long-term goal is an attempt at...*Localized world domination through the manufacture of collagen-derived gelling agents*? I believe you lost me there, Mr. Hansen."

"Basically, we aim to follow the approach to world domination used by certain computer software and operating system manufacturers. It's rather a slow creeping sort of domination, you know, to avoid antitrust laws. My catch phrase is: *Start Local. Infect Global.*"

"Cute. And what, pray tell, do you feed your *employees*? I assume they require sustenance? Brains?"

Jeremiah shrugged. "Pineapple-strawberry-flavored sugar-free gelatin. I mix in cremation ashes and some medical waste. They seem happy."

"Hmm. And as a list of assets in this addendum, you have listed a factory on Holgate Boulevard."

"I prefer the term secret lair, actually."

"Actually, I do not."

Jeremiah cleared his throat. This guy had better be as good as his resume claimed. Otherwise, he'd find himself and his condescending demeanor upside down in a vat of lime gelatin really goddamn quickly. "Yeah, I purchased the factory site in full, thanks to some earlier funding opportunities in Idaho. I've done extensive remodeling and have more in mind." He drew in a breath to tell about his plans for secret underground chambers and the sauna, but Blake cut him off.

"Ah. You procured this factory through capital acquired in several...bank robberies and armored-car heists?"

"Exactly." He grinned. "It takes a bit of concentration, but I can maintain collective control of my minions—"

"Another requirement of my employment. You cannot use the term *minion* in any capacity."

"That's outrageous!" Jeremiah shouted. The pigeons took flight with a dismayed whirring of wings. Several more coffee-toting customers glanced their way.

Blake sat there with his legs crossed, his hands folded and his face impassive.

Jeremiah took a steadying breath. "All right, fine. Anything else?"

"I will notify you of further terms as they arise or as the situation permits."

"Remind me exactly who is hiring who here?"

"I assume you mean *whom*?" Blake gave him a tight smile. "Mr. Hansen, my expertise is such that the market prizes me very highly. Are you familiar with the Rise of the Mole People? I ran that project from inception to completion. The sentient tofu scare that decimated the tofu market? My fingerprints were all over that incident. The gigantic tapeworm which destroyed a slum in Bangladesh, clearing the way for development of the Hasher Chemical plant by my clients? Yes, I'm certain you get my point."

Jeremiah kept silent. That rampaging tapeworm *had* been

pretty damn impressive...except he would've sent the thing after trial lawyers instead of wasting it on poor people.

Blake nodded, licked a finger and again picked up the prospectus. "Please continue. I believe you were telling of your sudden influx of capital?"

"Yeah." But it wasn't the same now. He felt kind of deflated. "I'll give you the abbreviated version: zombies, bank heist, pandemonium. I cleared a bunch of money and valuables from the safety-deposit boxes and safe at one bank, though a few zombies lost teeth chewing on the lockboxes."

"Hmm. Other losses or depreciations?"

Jeremiah shrugged. "A few zombies got stuck in the safe, and the cops shot down a dozen or so. A couple got run over by the bus."

"Bus?"

"The safest and most efficient way to haul the undead. Zombies might drive better than people from California, but I wouldn't want to be in the passenger seat when either one's at the wheel." He waited for laughter or even a smile. Nothing. Talk about cold fucking fish sticks—the guy was just about freezer burned. "Actually, *I* drive the bus."

"I see." Blake looked over the report again, tapping his nail against his front teeth. "Well, Mr. Hansen, I *can* say I'm intrigued. I think there are several good opportunities worthy of pursuit here. I'm willing to offer you my services, provided you deposit half my yearly fee in this Swiss Bank account." He handed Jeremiah a business card with a gold-embossed account number. "The rest will be expected upon completion of the project. We can discuss stock options and my health-care benefits at some other time. Before the papers are signed, of course."

A turning point. Paying Blake Delaney would eat up a bunch of his liquid cash, but Delaney seemed to know his stuff, especially cyclopean tapeworms. Maybe he could leverage some capital, a derivative perhaps...maybe loan out some of his zombie minions—no, zombie *associates*—to open up other revenue streams. Birthday parties. Traffic flaggers at construction sites. Fast-food drive-thru employees. Well, something would certainly come up. He was an accomplished necromancer after all. Dead was his business...and business was good.

"I think that can be arranged," Jeremiah answered with a smile. He tried his best to make it an evil smile, although Blake didn't seem impressed.

"Now..." Blake rubbed his hands together. "First on the agenda, let's select you a new name. A moniker suitable of your soon-to-be notorious prestige. Hmm. How about Skuld Le Mort?"

Jeremiah closed his eyes, raised his cup and chugged lukewarm coffee, wishing it were Johnnie Walker Red. Apparently it would be a long day ahead, and he had a feeling he'd need something a helluva lot stronger than coffee to get through it if he had to go by the name Skuld Le Mort.

Chapter Seven: We Were Mercs Once…and Stupid

Mercenary Wing Rv6-4 "Zero Dogs"
The Zero Dog Compound
Outdoor Training Grounds
1032 Hours PST April 13th

The Zero Dogs trained in rain, sleet, snow and wind, but not without a dump-truck load of bitching and moaning. In Portland, we had rain. Lots of rain. Today was no different.

I yawned, trying to turn away and hide it behind my hand. The morning rain had died off to a spitting mist, the kind that kept you damp but didn't have the balls to soak you through. Rain. God, I hated it, especially how it blanketed the world in gray. Good thing I lived in the Pacific Northwest—Portland saw forty inches of rain a year, but it was a very misty, gray and depressing rain. The rain equivalent of watching art-house films after losing a job and having a well-loved goldfish die.

Captain Sanders stood next to me, scanning the three multilevel buildings at the corner of the training grounds through high-powered binoculars. The buildings were large but shoddy, mostly just framework with the Tyvek house wrap still visible, designed to simulate urban close-combat assault without costing a lot of money. The building on the far right had a scattering of bullet holes riddling its side and scorch marks from a fire started by a certain person who would remain anonymous.

Mai and her horde of summoned attack pets were Red Team for this assault. She'd summoned squirrels this time—or what resembled squirrels, anyway, despite their vampire fangs, wicked claws, jet-black fur and eyes the color of copper pennies. The sound of squeaks and chittering drifted across the no man's land that separated us from the buildings. Mai was the main target for this exercise, playing the role of the necromancer, and her Death Pet squirrels were designated as zombie targets, despite being fuzzy, chattering and very small.

Hey, we worked with what we had here.

The heroic Blue Team had the role of assault force, led by Jake and our unflappable hero, Captain Andrea Walker, currently referring to herself in the third person, whose dark hair had frizzed something awful in the damp air. Thank God for helmets. We'd paused behind an embankment a hundred or so meters south of the obstacle course to recon the objective. This exercise revolved around meshing our operating style with Jake's information on the target's capabilities, working out kinks, and smoothing over rough patches in the command structure. Oh, and keep a snowball from melting in Hell's hot fires. Nothing too challenging for our third day of training.

"One hostile visible," Jake said. "Building two, second-floor stairs."

He handed me the binoculars and I looked for myself. The black squirrel sat on the top railing, grasping its crimson tail in two tiny paws as its head rotated from side to side, scanning for us. I searched the rest of the building roofs and windows for other lookouts but saw nothing.

"I could send Tiffany in," I said. "She could charm that little bastard, bring him to us. I mount a tiny camera on him. Use him to scout the inside and feed us live images."

Jake shook his head. "Not enough time, and he'll be missed. Besides, your succubus won't be able to charm zombies."

Damn. In my haste to sound strategic, I'd forgotten that Mai's pets represented the necromancer's zombie army with both its plusses and minuses. And that idea had been damn good too.

Gavin leaned back against the Bradley and laughed. "Yeah, not much for a succubus to work on when it comes to zombies. Not a lot of lift in the old piston once you lose blood pressure. Probably why you don't see a lot of zombie porn on the interwebz."

No. I was *not* going to acknowledge that statement. In fact, he was lucky I didn't have his tongue ripped out with red-hot pincers.

"Tiffany, come here," I said into the comlink. Tiffany hurried over, keeping low and moving with quiet steps, her wings folded behind her back. She leaned in close and stared at me with her wide, slit-pupil eyes. She had full gear on, but both Gavin and Jake's heads swiveled and their gazes locked on her. The wash of her sex aura swept across me. The effect was muted somewhat on females who weren't of the lesbian persuasion, but still, it remained a little suffocating. "Whoa, tone it down a notch, 'kay?"

Tiffany blushed and gave me an apologetic smile. I felt the strength of her aura lessen enough so that she wasn't pulling in the gaze of every male organism in a hundred-foot radius.

"All right." I set my hand on her shoulder. "I want you to use cover to sweep around to the west. Keep low, out of sight. I need you to recon the west and north approaches. If we have a better assault line, I want to use it."

"Affirmative, Captain." She turned and ran off, long legs pumping. After a dozen steps she unfolded her wings and soared along just above the ground, the tips of her wings kissing the dirt when she flapped them. She wove in and out of the strand of trees fronting a rise in the ground level.

I glanced at Jake, trying to be nonchalant about it. He'd resumed scanning the target, although I noticed a muscle twitching in his jaw. Point for him. Most men couldn't help but stare at her ass as she retreated. Although...he'd better not be gay. I bit down on my tongue and silently cursed myself. So what if he was gay? Nothing wrong with that. Why would I care? And what the fuck was I doing thinking about it during a training op?

I resolved to ask Sarge about him later, in secret.

"I say we use a pincer movement," I told Jake. "You lead a strike with the Bradley. Get everybody's attention on it while I circle around their flank with a secondary assault team. Back door them. Make it really uncomfortable."

He shook his head. "It'll diminish our firepower. Up against a real zombie wave, that could be a problem."

"You're kidding right? Since when could a zombie chew through a Bradley?"

A tight smile curled on his lips. "You might be surprised what a couple hundred zombies can do. Especially prodded on by a determined necromancer."

"Doesn't matter. You'll be shooting at them and not sitting still, yeah? I assume you can manage to keep their attention. We'll cut into them from the west, set up a crossfire and slice them to pieces."

"Captain," Hanzo interrupted. He wore his ninja blacks, a hood with his lower face covered by cloth, a katana slung on his back, and bright red medic crosses on his chest and shoulders. "As a follower of the Way of Stealth, my skills would allow me to infiltrate the target area and execute a decapitation strike at our mortal enemy, ensuring total victory. Without a head, the chicken flails."

"No."

"But—"

"You're the medic. Now get your healer-ass back in the Bradley and work the guns."

Hanzo hesitated, and I could see how hard he struggled not to argue. At last he bowed and went slinking off, head down.

God, I hated it when men pouted. Jake watched me with a cocked eyebrow and his quirk of a smile. I knew what he was thinking. I could hear it in my mind as clearly as if he were a telepath.

I cut him off with a gesture before he could get the words out. "Yeah I know. Medic on the weapon systems. But we're multitaskers with overlapping roles." Also, I was short-handed in the extreme. Not something I wanted to admit, especially to him, though only a card-carrying imbecile wouldn't have noticed it already.

His smirk wouldn't die. "You're a hard-ass, Captain Walker. What about his ninja role?"

Annoyed, I reached up and turned off the hot mike. "Let's put it this way, Captain Sanders. I have more ninja skills in one heel of my Jimmy Choos than Hanzo has in his entire repertoire—no matter how many times he watches *Ninja Brothers of Blood.*"

"What the hell is a Jimmy Choo?"

"A fancy shoe. Never mind."

He glanced down at my combat boots. "To be honest, I can't see you wearing them."

My ire flared like a supernova. What the hell did that mean? Some kind of I *can't be feminine and wear combat boots* backhanded insult? I had half a mind to show the bastard how I made expensive shoes look good, and not the other way around...except that I'd sold them three months ago to help pay for an order of incendiary shotgun ammo.

"Forget about the damn shoes," I snapped. And he'd had the balls to bitch about *his* briefing getting derailed? "Point is, Hanzo's a top-grade healer. Under no circumstances are his deluded fantasies to be encouraged. It's bad enough the Hellfrost Group has no uniform code for medics except for that damn red cross."

He raised his hands in a placating gesture, amusement still on his face. "A hot-button issue."

"*All* my issues are hot-button issues. So let's just focus on the mission."

Tiffany's voice crackled over the com. "No visual contact on approach." Succubus eyes were like hawk eyes, they could focus in with perfect clarity on distant targets, making her a scout par excellence. "No lookouts on the west or north sides. No sign of hostiles, over."

"Roger that." I turned and smiled at Jake—and yeah, I'd taken to thinking of him as Jake in my head with disturbing regularity, despite my vows to never do so. "We try my plan." I keyed on the mike again, issued the relevant commands and received a flurry of affirmatives. The Bradley rumbled when Gavin started it up.

Jake stood with his hands on his hips and jerked his chin toward the Bradley. "So it looks like I get the commander's seat this time."

God, the man delighted in provoking me.

"Don't get used to it." I motioned Rafe and Sarge over to me. They came in from their picket positions covering our flanks. "Let's move out." We'd meet up with Tiffany prior to entry and go in hot.

I started off, crouched to keep low to the ground. I glanced back, because I've always believed Lot's wife got screwed for her curiosity, and I could've sworn Jake stared at my ass as I moved away from him. He glanced away at once, but I'd have played Vegas odds I was right. Well, well, well. Wasn't *that* interesting?

It took less than three minutes, using cover, to flank the target buildings. We hurried along the tree stand, past an unused bunker, and swung around to the west, where we'd meet up with Tiffany. The ground was wet but firm, since it hadn't rained hard enough to make good mud. We took cover behind the rusting frame of a '68 Cutlass station wagon and a pile of broken cinderblocks. I checked the target again with binoculars. Since the outbuildings were arranged in a line west to east, only one outside wall faced us now. It had two windows, both without glass, and through them I could see the framework of the interior walls swallowed in gloom, drowned in the shadows of a gray rainy day. No guards stood anywhere in view.

"Better shift, Rafe," I said. I keyed the mike as Rafe yanked off his cammies with disquieting enthusiasm. Clearly the man had missed his calling as a male stripper. He shifted into werewolf form and picked up his paintball gun again. I decided not to tell him how stupid he looked as a huge werewolf clutching the tiny paintball gun in his clawed hands because I couldn't exactly have him eating Mai's pets during a training mission. "Check your weapons."

We looked over the paintball guns, ensuring a ball sat in the chamber. We used paintball instead of laser combat simulation systems because...well, because it was cheaper. I knew a guy at the paintball place, and he hooked me up with some great deals. Normally paintballs were for shooting people, who were idiots, and not animals, but we made exceptions for the unnerving creatures Mai summoned.

"Blue Team Two stand by," I said over the radio. "Blue Team One ready?" I looked at them and got nods all around. "Go. Go. *Go*!"

I stood and ran toward the house, paintball gun up and sweeping left to right as the rest of the team followed on my heels. We made it to the building and spread out along the wall, keeping watch on our sectors of fire. I crept to the corner and used a small mirror mounted on a rod to peer around the edge and check for hostiles. Nothing.

"Blue Team One in place," I confirmed over the mike. "Blue Team Two, begin your assault."

The Bradley's engine roared and grew louder as it came around the embankment, speeding toward the buildings, but from this angle I could only hear it, not see it. The air filled with chittering as the Death squirrels rallied. I checked around the corner again with the mirror. This time I caught sight of a lone black squirrel running in circles at the bottom of a doorway.

"Engaging," Jake said over the com. "Check your targets." I heard the understated *thup thup thup* of paintball guns followed by enraged squeaking.

I used hand signals to alert my team we were going in. The single Death squirrel guarding the back never had a chance. I swung out and capped him with a bright blue blob of paint. He tumbled over, his tail flopping. Then he rolled back to his feet and favored me with an evil copper eye. Still, he was technically dead and out of the engagement.

We stacked against the wall and prepared for a dynamic entry into the building. Sarge covered me as I gathered energy for my spell. The energy coursed through me, humming in my bones, warming my body as if a sphere of fire floated in my chest. I signaled, and Rafe kicked in the door and dodged to the side, pressing his back against the outside wall.

"Eyes!" I yelled.

Sarge, Rafe and Tiffany turned their heads away from the doorway to protect themselves from the blinding light. I focused my concentration down to a pinpoint and flashed off a super-amplified pulse of light inside the room, high enough up that it wouldn't hurt anybody. I glanced aside at the last instant, still shielded by the wall, and saw the flare paint a brilliant white column on the ground in the shape of the doorway. The spell might not produce concussion or sound assault, but it was as blinding as a hundred simultaneous lightning strikes.

Sarge charged through the entry as soon as the flash vanished. Rafe followed on his heels, covering a supporting sector, and Tiffany and I brought up the rear. We had to clear the entrance immediately, one of the most dangerous bottlenecks, where we'd be silhouetted against the gray daylight and highly visible from inside the building.

We quickly cleared the corners, found no hostiles, formed up and advanced deeper inside. I made a mental note for the

After Action Report about our good muzzle control—nobody swept anyone's head with a gun barrel—and our smooth dispersal, but had the uneasy feeling I'd just jinxed us by thinking about it.

We swept through the rest of the building, clearing room after room. No Mai and no other "zombies". Outside, the high-pitched chattering and the hiss and splat of paintballs intensified. I risked a look past the doorway. The Bradley had drawn fifty or so squirrels out of cover and engaged them.

I signaled, and my team advanced out of the building. We opened fire on the squirrels running around the Bradley, setting up a vicious crossfire. Dozens of squirrels went tumbling with blue paint splotches covering their fur. Soon there were no enemy targets left to engage.

"All right," I said over the com. "Blue Team One form up. Let's go. Blue Team Two, cover us, over."

"Roger that, out."

We swept toward the second building. I stopped at the doorway and crouched down, ready for another dynamic entry. Sarge and Rafe both covered me as I gathered energy for another flash spell. I set it off, just like last time, and we charged inside with the same deployment as before.

Four squirrels stumbled around the central room in a light-addled daze. In seconds they were covered with paintball splatter. We fully advanced into the large central room, which spanned fifty feet across easy and had three interior doorways, one at each wall.

Mai appeared in the east doorway, dressed in black, wearing a dark cloak with the hood up and a paintball face mask decorated with kanji symbols. A mass of black squirrels surrounded her. More squirrels filled the other doorways—a furry black carpet of them. Mai swept up an arm and pointed toward me. The squirrels surged forward in a chittering wave from all three sides.

We opened fire. I shot three paintballs at Mai's head, but

the squirrel surge rose up like a barrier and a couple furry creatures took the hits instead. The front line pressed too close, and I had to adjust my fire to the nearest threats. For a moment we held them off with accurate, concentrated fire.

I emptied my hopper and Rafe, Sarge and Tiffany covered me while I reloaded. Paint layered the walls and floor in vibrant splatters. Then Rafe went down under a swarm of battle-cry squeaking furballs on our right flank. The air sang with the pop and hiss of paintballs, the nonstop chittering and Mai's maniacal laughter.

We laid down suppressing fire in each sector, but the squirrels still pressed forward in a relentless banzai charge.

"Fall back!" I yelled over the radio. "Blue Team One fall back to the Bradley."

We retreated steadily backward behind a hail of cover fire, but before we reached the entry door, Jake, Gavin and Hanzo pushed in behind us and opened up with supporting fire.

The squirrel charge withered and broke up under the new assault. Before Mai could escape, I sighted in on her and shot three times. A squirrel launched itself in the air, taking one paintball, but too few squirrels remained to block them all. I hit her with two paintballs, one in the chest, the other on her face mask. She raised her hand and called, "I'm out!"

The remaining pets stopped their charge and swarmed back in a huge furry sea to tumble and play at Mai's feet. Mai pushed back her hood, pulled off her face mask and began to tickle them and coo over their paintball-splatter wounds. The scene drowned in cloying cuteness...and yet the show didn't come with an airsick bag.

"Primary target neutralized," Sarge confirmed, still carrying a paintball gun in each hand. "Mission accomplished."

"Exercise over." I yanked off my face mask and wiped the sweat from my forehead and cheeks. Damn. Things had gone dicey at the end. "Good job, people. Mai, what was up with the deranged laughter?"

She smiled and shrugged. “Don’t all dark lords do evil laughter? I was just trying to simulate our experience.” She lifted a spattered mostly blue squirrel and kissed it on the nose, getting paint on her lips.

Disgusting. “Yeah, well, leave off next time, it gives me the creeps. And stop kissing those things. You’ll get a disease.”

Rafe shifted back to human form and stood there naked. “How many pets did you summon anyway?” Dozens of teeth marks covered him, fading fast as his werewolf healing abilities kicked in. “Looked like thousands.”

“Only a couple hundred or so. I wanted it to be realistic, like a true zombie horde.”

I glared at bare-assed Rafe. “Didn’t I tell you to start packing some boxers on these missions?”

“But, Captain, where can I put them when I shift?”

“I don’t care. Wear them on your head if you have to.” I turned back to Mai. “Nice work taking him down. You almost had us.”

“You did such a good job, Mai.” Tiffany clapped her hands, beaming a thousand-watt smile. “It was so *thrilling*.”

Anyone else and I’d have thought they were trying for ironic or mocking, but I could tell from the pleasure shining on her face that she was sincere. It made me strangely happy. “We all did a good job.”

“Except for Rafe,” Gavin said, leaning against one of the wall struts. “Who ended up zombie chow.”

“Yeah, well, I might have gotten eaten, but it felt damn kinky with all those little furry things running all over my body. And the love bites.” He shuddered (I strove not to notice something else flopping around) and growled, and wiggled his eyebrows in a most absurdly obscene way. “I think I’m in love.”

“Rafe,” I warned, “too much information. Hanzo, get over here and finish healing his bites. And bring a blanket, I think he’s in shock. Mai, send your pets home. I don’t want to have to feed them. Gavin, go put away the Bradley before we burn up all the diesel."

"Hey, Captain," Gavin said. "We could roast the squirrels and save on food— *Yow*!" Gavin twisted around to stare down at his ass. A black squirrel dangled from one cheek, biting through his fatigues. "One of those little buggers bit me!"

Mai snapped her fingers and the squirrel detached and scampered to her. She picked it up and touched her nose to its tiny twitching nose. "Oh, now you're going to need mouthwash, little heart. How many times do I have to tell you? Don't bite things you'd never eat."

"Hey, thanks, Mai." Gavin held his injured ass cheek. "The love is much appreciated."

"Enough chatter." Sarge's frown turned his chiseled face and jaw into something dark and forbidding—a mix of Easter Island statue and escaped nightmare from a Goya painting. "You heard the captain. Hard chargers back to base camp. Clean up and double-time it. After Action Report in thirty minutes. Now *move*."

The troops scattered. A moving carpet of fur followed Mai toward a clearing where she could teleport her Death Pets back to their home dimension. A curious person might wonder where they came from. I was decidedly not curious—not about that anyway. The rest of the Zero Dogs filed toward the Bradley parked outside.

Jake stood near the west doorway. He'd been quiet the whole time. I gritted my teeth and fought back a sudden nervous twinge. I didn't want him talking over me, but too quiet made me uneasy.

"Walk back with me?" I jerked my head in the direction of the door.

A slow smile spread across his face. "My pleasure."

I had the immediate stomach-drop feeling I'd made a horrible mistake, and it started to rain.

Captain Sanders and I stood in the drizzle, watching as

everyone else piled in or on the Bradley. Mai ran out from the tree line alone, her hood up, water beading on the fabric and running down the edges, making me wish I had a cloak of my own. I'd always hated the sound of rain tapping on my helmet. Damn rain. I'd already considered reneging on my offer to walk with him, but I didn't want to look like I carried the wussy gene somewhere in my DNA.

Sarge paused before raising the ramp. "Coming, Captain?"

"Nah, I'll walk back. I want to go over some things with Captain Sanders."

Sarge glanced at the gray, dripping sky and smiled. When he smiled it changed his face again. It lost the forbidding aspect and became downright striking in an otherworldly way, like some twilight-skinned warrior who'd wandered out of Valhalla. I waited in dread for another wink, like in the conference room meeting with Harker, but he just gave Jake a half salute. Jake returned the half salute and added a half smile. Something passed between them, leaving me to feel left out, as if they'd been talking about me with group telepathy and I'd been disconnected from the party line.

Our black Bradley took off toward the garages with its antennas swinging and the banner dangling in a sopping wet bunch. A belch of diesel fumes flavored the air in its wake. With the rumble of the engine gone it seemed very quiet. We began to walk side by side toward the distant house. I cut him a sidelong glance. "So what was that all about?"

He raised his eyebrows but didn't answer.

"Don't play dumb with me. That bromance look between you. That brothers-in-arms thing. Some kind of male-bonding moment? Or something else?"

He looked at me as if I'd escaped from a mental institution or a live children's show. "I don't know."

I stared at him.

He shrugged. "He handles himself like a professional. That's all."

"Don't take this the wrong way, and I know I could get in trouble for asking, but you're not gay, are you? I mean, there's no problem if you are, Sarge's gay and I love him to death. But I'm only looking out for him. He's involved in a long-term relationship with a wonderful guy, and I don't think Shawn would appreciate the flirting."

He watched me, again not answering.

Irritation flooded through me in a hot surge. "Let me ask it another way, before I have to break out my interpretive shadow-puppet routine, 'kay? I'm not trying to be a CB'er, but on the DL, I don't think Shawn, Sarge's SO, would appreciate the competition."

"What the hell kind of acronyms are those?"

"Cock Blocker. Down Low. Significant Other. Try and keep up here. Someday you'll have to merge with the fast traffic on the intelligence freeway."

A grin spread across his face. "Don't worry, I'm not gay."

"Oh. Because I thought..."

His eyebrows lifted again and he tilted his head, regarding me, seeming to revel in my discomfort. Hell, it had been an honest question, though I'd been out of line, and part of me damn well knew it.

"I think you're reading a little too much into this, Captain Walker...maybe on purpose?"

Me purposefully reading too much into something? The man had to be a conspiracy theorist. I cleared my throat. "So. You're not gay then." I felt like fidgeting and clamped down on the urge. "So...you don't have a problem with gay people, do you? I mean, because *I* have a problem with people who have a problem with gay people."

"Not at all."

"I mean, with don't ask, don't tell, and a bunch of testosterone, sometimes people get a little prejudiced—a little, you know, as if I'm offending your manhood."

He grinned wider than ever. The bastard was clearly enjoying himself. "My *manhood* is just fine, thank you."

Heat crept up my neck to my cheeks. Don't blush, don't blush, *don't blush, goddammit.*

"Ah. That's good to hear," I said. "I mean, not that I care. Not that I wondered about your manhood at all, either as a concept or otherwise. So...how about that training exercise? I think we pretty much ripped shit up." I tried to laugh and ended up sounding like a drowning peacock.

He was merciful enough to finally let me off the hook. "Not bad."

"High praise coming from you."

"Still, there are definite areas to improve. Your people are good, react quickly, take orders well—in the field anyway. But there's a lesson to be learned here."

"And what's that?" I couldn't keep the edge out of my voice. We passed beneath a canopy of interlaced evergreen branches, and our boots whispered over the fallen needles. The sharp scent of pine and wet earth lingered around us. I took a deep breath, fighting to keep myself calm and steady as she goes.

"You're lucky Blue Team Two came in to back you up," he said. "Otherwise you would've lost more than just Rafe."

"Lucky?" I kicked a pinecone and it bounced off the sandbags and into a cluster of mushrooms. "Hardly. That was the plan, remember? I asked you to cover me. Besides, we'd already gained the upper hand."

He snorted. "So that's why your team was in full retreat. You must be one of those rare, wily commanders who, gaining advantage, prefers to withdraw instead of advance. Admit it. Without reinforcements you guys would've been meat."

"I love armchair generals. You didn't happen to notice we used *paintball* guns on squeaking hairballs that move a helluva lot *faster* than zombies. Don't tell me it's a one-to-one simulation. Rafe couldn't cut loose, and I didn't even use any fire."

"True—"

"Of course, it's true." I straightened a little and forced my fists to unclench. I could see most of the house now, beyond the backyard and the obstacle course. Why the hell had I ever agreed to walk with this nimrod in the first place?

"It's true as far as it goes," he continued. "But this was a useful exercise even if we're just simulating zombies. That's their strength, the unending push. You can slaughter a hundred of them and they'll keep coming, even as your machine gun barrels overheat, the action jams and you run short on ammo. It's both their greatest strength and their weakness. Up close, we're at a disadvantage." He frowned and looked off eastward toward the city. "That's why this assault will be tricky. We get bunched up in his factory and it's going to be wall-to-wall undead in three seconds. We have to keep nimble, keep moving, keep escape routes clear at all times. And we can't dilute our firepower."

"Thanks for the lecture, General Sherman," I said through gritted teeth. "But you might remember this isn't the first zombie kill job we've ever done."

"I know you did some work against RCTs outside Nogales. But you were part of a larger merc group, and the area was scrub desert, with clear lines of sight. This'll be in-your-face, whites-of-their-rotting-eyes, urban combat, and I want you and your people prepared for it."

"Point taken." I tried not to sound grudging and again failed. "We'll focus on similar training scenarios from inside. Good enough?"

He seemed thrown off by my concession. "Yeah, Captain Walker. Good enough."

The silence spreading between us seemed to bother him more than me, and he broke it first. "I want us to work together smoothly. I'm here to make the Zero Dogs more effective, not less."

"Yeah? What is it those Navy squids say? A ship can't have

two captains. I clawed my way up to this rank, busting my ass twice as hard as anyone else. And I have to work three times as hard to maintain it. So excuse me if I ain't thrilled to have some John Wayne and his snot-colored beret horning in on my command."

We walked another dozen steps in silence. The sun shone through a thin layer in the overcast sky for a moment, a disk of muted smoky yellow, before the slate-gray clouds thickened again and it vanished. I was wet and tired and wishing more than ever I'd taken a ride back on the Bradley when I'd had the chance.

We'd come up to the tier at the lower yard before he spoke again. "It's clear your people trust you. In fact, I'm far more impressed right now than after the first briefing. I may have been wrong to call you on it before I recognized how things go here."

I opened my mouth. Shut it again. That must have taken some spine to say, even if he *had* tagged on a qualifying "may".

He continued. "Nothing's more important than the mission, Captain Walker. It's my job to help you achieve our objectives, no matter what. I'll do everything in my power to make it happen, and if you're able to get it done and get it done right, then I'll back you up all the way to the black gates of Hell."

"Fair enough." *Just keep out of my way, then*, I thought but didn't say. The time had come to be diplomatic. Not my default setting by any means. "Go ahead and call me Andrea. In private."

His smile warmed his eyes. God, you'd have thought I'd just promised him a free lap dance and a cold beer.

"I'm Jake, then." He held out his hand again.

I looked at it and arched an eyebrow. "Haven't we already done this once?"

"Yeah, but afterward you tried to kick my ass."

"You provoked me. Over and over again."

"I know," he said. "Pulling the tiger's tail. But admit it—

since you thought I was a no-talent scrub, I had something to prove."

I didn't know how I felt about him being right, or even half-right. Admitting it seemed like the first step down a long road where I might come to like him, even after our little confrontations. Not to mention the phone conversation I'd half overheard.

I reached out and shook his hand. Again, the warmth of his skin made my heart rev faster. Either he was some kind of cyborg with an industrial-sized space heater hidden inside, or my sensitivity to him buried the needle. Of the two choices I preferred to believe he was an evil cyborg who'd betray us at some crucial moment. It made life easier.

I broke contact first and glanced at the house. "Now, let's get the hell out of the rain."

"By all means," he said, smiling and sweeping a hand toward the house, "after you."

And as long as it stayed that way, I told myself, I might let him stick around. A few things still worried me though. He had far too much practice being charming. Also, he smiled too much—and even if I liked his smile, it was the mark of a man used to getting what he wanted, one way or another.

Chapter Eight:
The Jungle

Undead Army of the Unrighteous Order of the Falling Dark
Bokor Gelzonbi Foods Manufacturing Plant
SE Holgate Boulevard, Portland, Oregon
3:49 p.m. PST April 13th

Overlord Ctephakrillu, formerly known as Jeremiah Hansen, walked along the metal catwalk running above the manufacturing floor with his hands folded behind his back. Beside him walked Blake Delaney, his new second-in-command. Blake carried a PDA and noted information in it as the overlord took him on a tour of the lair—no, the *facility*. He kept trying to sneak looks at what Blake was writing, or emailing, or clicking and dragging or whatever, but Blake favored him with such an intense frown that he gave it up.

They both wore white lab coats, plastic hairnets, beard covers, safety glasses and slip-resistant shoes as per OSHA safety regulations 1910.133 and 1910.136 and FDA 21 CFR 110.10(b)(1) and (6). Beneath them, the zombie workforce went about its business, some of them entirely without shoes or even pants. In fact, all the zombies gathered from various morgues worked without the benefit of clothing—a fact he planned to strive mightily on keeping from the general public. The facility hummed and clanked and whirred with the business of making gelatin for the world.

They both paused on the section of catwalk spanning a huge vat of lime-flavored powder. Overlord Ctephakrillu looked down into its unnaturally green depths.

"I don't think my name's working out," he said. "It's too...I don't know, Lovecraftian. I never could pronounce those goddamn names without breaking my tongue."

Blake frowned. "I see." He searched through screens on his PDA. "We focus tested a few more which earned positive results in the evil world-ruler category. Last names with descriptions are big right now. How about Sven Dreadmouth?"

"Er..."

"Norz Frostbane?"

"Hmm."

"Two that scored very well with the twelve-to-eighteen male demographic—Knobz Ironstones and Bludkurl Wang."

"No." He thought about it some more. "Really, *no.* I thought I'd go back to Overlord Hansen. You know, original gangsta, old-school stuff."

Blake managed to appear appalled and amused at the same time, like a man who'd found a dead clown floating in his soup. "I suppose I still can't convince you to add a Dark Lord in there somewhere?"

"I'd rather not. It's been done to death." Strange. For a man who insisted on calling the lair a facility, banned the word *minions*, and sometimes referred to zombies as re-purposed life-challenged resources, Blake had some hang up on Jeremiah's name. The stupider, the better, it seemed.

"Overlord Hansen certainly has...originality going for it." Blake touched his stylus to his chin. "I do understand your reluctance at adopting one of these titles. However, there are certain tropes, certain *expectations,* in the field that must be addressed."

"If I can't refer to my manufacturing plant as a lair, then I don't need a stupid name." He crossed his arms.

Blake frowned. "There's always a bit of disconnect between operational language and PR speak. However, I suppose Overlord Hansen will have to do for now, until poll results start coming back in. We'll have to remain nimble though. In light of potential negative reaction, we'll hold a press conference and announce a new title and corporate logo."

Score one for the boss. Time for round two. Jeremiah started to walk along the catwalk again. Somehow, moving made it easier to bring the next bit up. Maybe because he wouldn't have to look right into Blake's eyes when he said it. "So, I was thinking."

"Ah," Blake said.

Jeremiah glanced at him and hurried on. He felt like a grammar-school kid asking a sadistic teacher for permission to use the restroom.

"I have some more ideas for the lair—I mean for the *facility*." If the smile on his face felt any more sheepish, he'd be choking on wool. He hated it, but for all Blake's talents, he seemed to suck Jeremiah's Iron Fist Ruler Mojo right out of the room. "Um. I think we could really do with some bodyguards for me. Some living ones, anyway. Preferably females. In fact, I thought maybe sex ninjas."

Blake stopped. With a slow pivot, he turned toward the railing and stared down at the manufacturing floor. Jeremiah joined him, his heart pounding away and his mouth dry as dust. They both stared at a zombie who pushed a large green button over and over again with a finger missing two joints.

"I'm not certain I heard you correctly," Blake said. "Did you perhaps say *sex* ninjas?"

"Exactly. I was thinking maybe some beautiful lady ninjas, we put them in distracting outfits, something with G-strings, lots of cleavage, possibly even a nipple slip now and then, for the fans. Maybe mix up the outfits according to rank. One rank could be leather. The next up could have...maybe garters and stuff, or French-maid ninjas even. Another, I think...a nurse style. You know, with ninja swords and martial arts, of course."

"Oh, of course."

Silence.

"So what do you say?" Jeremiah pressed. "I'm kind of tired of looking at decaying people."

"With all due respect, I don't think nurse sex ninjas fit into our action plan at this point in time. The cost of upkeep alone would strain our operating budget. Furthermore, any attempt to codify the inclusion of sex ninjas would simply remain a distraction and ultimately diminish our collaborative efforts. While I may encourage the use of dramatic names to titillate public discourse, every other element of our operation must be thoroughly professional. So, no. Can't be done at this time."

Shit. He'd had his heart set on the sex ninjas. This overlord stuff wasn't always all it was cracked up to be when you had glorified bean counters running around smacking great ideas with the NO stick. Still, this was why he paid Blake an obscene amount of money. He'd help make Jeremiah's vision a reality in as cheap a manner as possible, while attracting wheelbarrows of cash once they went publicly traded. Mark his words, though. When he achieved billionaire status he'd damn well score himself some sex ninjas.

Blake seemed to sense his disappointment. "However, I'm relatively pleased with the layout of your facility. I think, with some minor adjustments, we can count on this as a fully optimized plant, operating at peak efficiency, and ready to repel any threats to your industry dominance."

Jeremiah motioned toward the end of the catwalk and a small air vent above the access door. "I made sure all the air ducts are only a foot square, too small for a person to crawl through..." He allowed himself a smirk. "Except for the main duct...which holds a few little surprises. I can flood it with gelatin at will. I lost a poisonous dart frog in there. I also had a motion-tracking, movement-activated Advanced Artificial Intelligence-controlled Browning .50 caliber heavy machine gun mounted on a reinforced frame with a prototype down-recoil system. And, after all that, the air duct leads to a dead end."

"A kill box in other words." Blake gave him a grim nod. "Always a respectable choice."

Jeremiah puffed his chest out a little bit. He was about to ask what was most impressive, the gelatin trap or the AI machine-gun, when Blake spoke again.

"I also recommend a variety of small-scale but highly effective methods to amplify security. Motion detectors. Overlapping camera positions. Retinal scans. Independent power generators and a redundant power grid. Both may increase overhead but should stop power failure of everything short of an electromagnetic pulse."

"That's great. I also thought maybe we could get some more traps. Crushing walls. Floors that fall away onto spikes. Or bottomless pits. Um. Swinging axe blades. A mine-cart level."

Silence stretched for a long, uncomfortable moment while Blake tapped a finger against his teeth. "While those things may, at first, seem like they would increase overall security, I can assure you maintenance and upkeep would be prohibitive. There are other low-hanging fruit we might pick to better our endeavor. Also, I've never read data on a single adversary actually being crushed by crushing walls. Quite frankly, I'm at a loss of what to say regarding the mine-cart suggestion. Life is not a video game."

Obviously not, if he couldn't get some good sex ninjas. "Well, just bouncing some ideas around. Trying to think outside the box. To...modify our objective paradigm to incorporate...uh, market-tested methods of best practices free from...um, holistic group-think."

Blake stared at him with his cold Jack the Ripper Project Manager eyes. Jeremiah felt his cheeks flush. The zombies voiced uneasy moans and shuffled at their workstations. He took a deep breath, calming them again, and they returned to their prosaic thoughts of button pushing and consumption of human flesh.

"Usually I would encourage that," Blake said after a long, painful moment. "Usually." He started to walk again. "Let us continue our review. I have a few more standard questions to address. There are no super devices on site containing self-destruct mechanisms, are there? Any tiny weak points, any fatal flaws or isolated energy ports that some enterprising young individual hostile to our cause might seek to exploit?"

"Nope. This was a bread factory once. Now it makes gelatin."

"Ah. Perfect. Do you, perchance, have prison cells for hostages?"

"No. I feed everybody to the zombies right away. That door-to-door guy selling citrus cleaning solution and magazine subscriptions? Yeah, I threw him to the zombies." The bastard had deserved it too. Interrupting at a crucial moment when Jeremiah had been watching *Dancing with the Stars*. Honest to God, only an industrial grade asshat would willfully ignore a sign that said: *No Soliciting. Violators Will Be Eaten.*

Blake noted something on his PDA. "Excellent. Excellent. Now that security questions have been addressed, perhaps you might give me an overview of your process flow."

Jeremiah led Blake down the metal stairwell and toward the loading dock. His zombies turned their heads to stare at Blake, and he could feel their hungry speculation through the ethereal silver cords of his necromancy magic. He quickly set them back to their tasks among the hum, roar, slosh and rattle of the stainless-steel machinery.

He pointed toward the loading dock. "Pretty straightforward. I take delivery of pork skins on the dock."

"Pork skins?"

"Yeah. For collagen. We buy them from slaughterhouses already stripped of hair and fat. People love bacon, and people love gelatin desserts. Who knew they both came from the same animal? It's like divine providence."

"I now regret knowing." Blake gestured. "But please proceed."

"Next, I have a highly trained zombie crew transfer the pork skins into the cold-wash sprayer." Jeremiah gestured to a large machine fed by conveyor and connected to so many pipes and cables it reminded him of a shiny upside-down squid. The machine hissed and gurgled as a zombie in a Motörhead T-shirt loaded the thin, evenly cut, whitish-pink skins onto the conveyor.

Jeremiah directed Blake's gaze to another series of huge stainless vats. All the zombies around the vats stared unblinking at a light display with green and red bulbs. "The cleaned pork skins get soaked in hydrochloric acid for a few hours. After which the light turns red, the team here unloads and moves them into another wash cycle—"

Blake stopped and peered at the zombies watching the wash cycle's green light. "These undead personnel assets appear significantly degraded."

The skin of the zombies was a ravaged and mottled red and gray. Their clothes hung in disintegrating tatters on their bodies. A metal sign on a nearby load-bearing pillar dangled askew and had so many small pits in the surface the words couldn't be read.

"We had a few low-grade acid spills," Jeremiah said. "And we have some issues with acidic mist. Actually, I wouldn't get too close if I were you." He hurried Blake farther down the production line.

Blake noted something else in his PDA. "Then we aren't ISO 9000 certified, I take it?"

"Are you fucking kidding me?"

"Indeed. I suppose we must save a good deal on personal protective equipment."

"*Exactly*. Now after another wash, the skins are ready for extraction. We use three cycles to maximize production time for each batch. Cycles have different pH and temperatures, et cetera." He pointed to a thin zombie chewing on a pen, his lips, mouth and chin stained with blue ink. The zombie clutched a clipboard in one hand. "That guy notes down batch numbers when he isn't busy eating his writing utensils."

"Seems as if there must be a good deal of process variation," Blake said. "Do you use any statistical process controls? Control charts? Deming philosophy? Even, God forbid, Six Sigma?"

"I'm lucky I can get my zombies to push buttons and follow simple directions. Fancy stuff like that might work for the Japanese, but in case you haven't been paying attention, Bokor Gelzonbi Industries relies on cheap, unskilled labor to mitigate the cost of fuckups."

"Ah."

Shit, how could the man condense a mountain of disapproval into one simple syllable?

"Anyway, where was I?" Jeremiah continued. "The gelatin in process is filtered, deionized, yadda-yadda, and then extruded." He brought Blake to the part of the manufacturing floor where six huge stainless-steel pipes pushed out noodle-like strings of yellow gelatin onto a metal-mesh conveyor belt. The belt led through a series of partially enclosed chambers. "The extruded gelatin is dried—I use an hour cycle to increase throughput—and then ground down to fine particulate. Which is the part of the process where most of our accidents—"

"'Unfortunate industrial challenges' sounds better," Blake suggested.

"I guess if you call a zombie being pulled into a grinder and turned into a fine powder a *challenge*, then that works."

"Do we conduct quality tests?"

"No. I forge results and grease palms."

Blake nodded, his face thoughtful. "While it's clear we have some challenges to address, I'd say, with some planning and some focus, we'll soon be ready to impose our will upon the gelatin market. The invisible hand will be forced to pause before us, open in supplication."

"Er...exactly." That sounded like something *he* should say as the Evil Overlord, not the number-two guy. He'd have to keep an eye on Blake and make sure more thunder wasn't stolen. Make sure the guy wasn't in his lighting, stealing the scene.

They walked toward the break room. Several insanely cheery motivational posters hung on the wall next to a mess of bulletins about Federal minimum wage and the Family Leave Act. All in all, Jeremiah thought the tour had gone rather well. Well, except for the lack of alluring ninjas of the feminine persuasion, that was.

Blake gave him a needle-thin smile. "So, how well do you play golf?"

Chapter Nine:
A Few Good Mercenaries

Mercenary Wing Rv6-4 "Zero Dogs"
Zero Dog Compound
North Wing Stairwell 3rd Floor Landing
1846 Hours PST April 13th

The heavenly smells of stir-fry drifted through the house. My stomach grumbled, sounding like an outboard motor drowning in four-stroke engine oil. I followed the scent down the stairs, toward the large dining room. Mai's voice announcing dinner over the intercom had cut my shower short, although most of the time I was an empty-the-hot-water-heater kind of girl. I'd thrown on some cargo pants, a long-sleeve shirt with the word *Pyromania* in fiery letters on the front, and boots. Jump boots, not anything with heels. What the outfit lacked in feminine style it more than made up for in comfort and utility.

Besides, I wasn't about to start dressing to impress Jake.

The After Action Report following our training exercise had been long and detailed, with both Jake and I going over what the teams had done right, what goals we achieved and what could use work. We presented a unified command front, but I took the lead, doing most of the talking, and he seemed cool with that. I felt proud of my people. I thought we'd handled ourselves well overall, but I focused on the challenges Jake had mentioned, how splitting our forces had diminished our firepower in close quarters. I took the blame for the call, of course, but I made it sound as if I'd been the one to recognize the potential problem first and I didn't feel guilty in the least about doing so. Jake didn't protest and didn't even seem to notice. Which annoyed me. No man should be that easy to get along with or sport that much self-control.

I hadn't seen him since the AAR. I'd been locked down in the office, poring over the accounts. The initial payment for the mission had gone through. After I'd indulged in a little happy cha-cha-cha in my chair, I'd used the payment to gain some breathing room with our vendors, setting aside a healthy chunk for rent and other overhead. Next, I'd obsessed over the cost of diesel fuel. Drank strong coffee. Obsessed over the cost of paintballs. Drank tea, English breakfast, so hot it almost burned my mouth, just the way I liked it. Obsessed over food costs. Considered drinking something alcoholic, but had behaved like a big, responsible girl and hadn't.

I finished double-timing it down the last of the stairs, on my way across the tile floor and hall toward the main dining room. My heart beat faster, and not from the stairs. All right, I might have left something out earlier when I'd been vowing never to impress Jake. Despite the clothes, I'd prettied myself up just the tiniest bit. Light makeup, doing my best to make it look *au naturel.* He'd probably never notice. But just in case...

Damn, talk about stupid. What the hell was I doing? He was a problem. He'd been a problem since he arrived. My mission was to get the job done, get him gone and get on with life.

Well...maybe, just maybe, he might be fun too. If he weren't working with me on this mission, that was—and let's tell the truth and screw the devil—if he weren't an outsider, a possible threat to my people and my command, it'd be a no-brainer. Because every so often I caught that vibe from him, an intense regard, the focus that made me feel like a piece of art in the center of a gallery, displayed in the perfect lighting. A feeling I found both exhilarating and teetering on the edge of terrifying.

The whole crew had converged on the dining room and were already well into the business of dishing out food. Nobody stood on ceremony here. Come late to dinner and you had table scraps—if that. The table stretched nearly the length of the room, a long marble slab which could seat twenty easy. Everybody clustered around the far end near Jake.

"It's the captain." Gavin raised his beer to me in mock salute. "Mai cooked, which means something edible tonight."

Mai grinned. One of her pets had draped itself around her shoulders like some weird mink stole. In fact, the thing looked suspiciously like an ermine. Except pink and white, with an all-too-expressive face and three strange sets of folded purple wings appearing as soft as velvet. The more I thought about it, the more my gag reflex and I didn't want to know if she let her summoned pets help with the cooking.

We rotated through cooks (since the last one had quit after Rafe, in werewolf form, had chased him around the yard, terrorizing him for serving something loaded with soybean oil, trans fats and high fructose corn syrup). Mai ranked as the best cook out of all of us, and cooking on a large scale demanded a certain amount of talent and planning. My cooking skills scored in the mediocre-to-poor range, though I thought my meatloaf always turned out decent. I tended to over-spice things. Oh, and burn them. Go figure.

I took my seat at the head of the table, Sarge on my left, Jake on my right. I didn't feel as uncomfortable having Jake this close as I'd felt during our client meeting—a disturbing change.

"Wine?" Jake indicated a bottle with a fancy gold and black label.

What kind of commando drank wine? Still, in an attempt to be diplomatic, I made a show of smiling and nodding, although I'd always thought wine tasted more like fermented elf piss. Don't ask how I knew about elf piss. The long and horrible story didn't have a happily ever after.

He filled my glass while I speculated whether I could get away with accidentally knocking it over so I wouldn't have to drink it. Sarge passed me one of the serving bowls filled with stir-fry, and I loaded up. The furnace must have fuel, so I grabbed a fork and shoveled it in.

Tiffany's quiet, smoky voice broke through the conversation, surprising me because she usually stayed so reserved, and when Tiffany spoke, people listened. Mostly men, but whatever. "Captain Sanders, may I ask when we'll go after the necromancer?"

Jake smiled at her and rasped a hand across a cheek dark with stubble. I watched him like a Catholic nun at a junior high dance for any sign of flirting. Tiffany—I loved her to death, but if she pulled this guy's attention off me, I'd sew her into a burka and sell her to a convent. The strength of my reaction gave me pause for a second, and then I dismissed it. Yeah, Captain Sanders was growing on me. So fucking what?

Don't answer that.

Jake kept silent for a long moment, swirling his red wine in his glass. I started to think he wouldn't answer, which began to rub my fur the wrong way. I'd never been one for keeping information from the grunts. Hell, I'd been a line animal myself for too long. Double hell, I was *still* a line animal.

At last, Jake answered. "When? Soon. A couple more days perfecting our offensive capabilities and we'll timeline an assault. Then Captain Walker will give the final go order."

"What if the necromancer makes a move before then?" Mai asked, as she fed snow peas to her alien ermine. "Will we quick-deploy?"

Mai had directed her question at Jake, but I answered before he could. "We have multiple assault scenarios planned out." Mai glanced at me and seemed a trifle miffed. I started to feel unloved. "If we need to stop him right away, we have a contingency plan for just that purpose."

Stefan the vampire stood up and lifted his glass. "To us

renown, to us the glory bring. Thus we may free the Zero Dogs of war."

"Hear, hear," Rafe said and raised his glass. From the smell of it, he'd just toasted the Zero Dogs with açaí berry juice in a double shot glass. He wore his favorite T-shirt, the one with three disembodied wolf heads howling at the moon—a piece of clothing he'd once, to my amazed horror, told me had gotten him laid dozens of times.

Everyone else lifted various drinks in a toast, and I did too, not wanting to bring bad luck on us, though premature celebration made me skittish.

Stefan kept standing. He'd dressed in coat and tails, with his hair raked back from his forehead and shiny with something I assumed wasn't frying-pan grease. He sipped from his glass, which didn't hold wine, no matter how dark red the liquid might be. Looking at the contents of his wineglass killed what little desire I had to finish my own. I had blood shipped in from a blood bank in Beverly Hills, at Stefan's expense, coded by donor details and year. Something a trifle disturbing about the bouquet of your warm inner red suddenly turned into a product's selling point or a wine-tasting joke.

Everybody continued to look at Stefan, and he reveled in the attention. His pupils glowed a mellow red, lighter than the blood in his glass. "Although," he continued, "I've raised my objection to the term *Dog* in our moniker on several occasions, since it conjures images of flea-bitten curs slinking through the gutters, and I say that only as an aside."

Gavin laughed. "You hear that, Rafe? He's talking about you and your personal flea circus."

Rafe glowered. His myriad tattoos added to his dangerous predator air—an air diminished more than a little by the açaí berry juice. "Hey, Gavin, you're supposed to be an empath. What am I feeling right now?"

"You're feeling sorry for yourself because you're an idiot."

"No. That's not it."

"You're feeling a burning desire to hump Sarge's leg."

Rafe growled deep in his throat. "You know, for an empath you can really be an asshole."

"My work here is done. Get my punch card, it's time to clock out."

"Enough, you two." Must I ever be the den mother for kindergarteners? Could they not *for two seconds* act like professionals and not embarrass me in front of Jake? "Until we get a green light, I want us to stay in top shape, and that includes refraining from pointless bickering. I emailed each of you dossiers on necromancy and zombie plagues. Read them and memorize them."

"Know thy enemy," Hanzo said, stroking his smooth chin. "Know thyself. And you will never be defeated. So says the great Sun Tzu."

Had he been weaned on reruns of *Kung Fu* or had he just been dropped on his head as a small child? Probably both.

The ermine squeaked, and Mai let it lap out of her wineglass. "Remember that fight we had in Shenyang? Against that outbreak of yaomo monkeys? We were neck deep in screeching monkey demons and some Chinese government official showed up and wanted to quarantine Gavin for the swine flu."

"Good times," Rafe said, grinning.

Good times, my ass. But I kept my mouth shut and poured more hot mustard on my plate. Two years back we'd been reserve support for a Hellfrost Group detachment backing up the Ministry of State Security's demon suppression wing. Lots and lots of money, but murderous paperwork, passport problems and bureaucratic political nightmares abounded. And Rafe barely avoided arrest for tattooing *Free Tibet* on his forearm.

"What about you, Captain Sanders?" Sarge asked in his deep bass rumble. "Don't like to talk business at the table?"

Jake shrugged and pushed his food around with his fork.

"Don't believe in trotting out the glory days to impress others."

"A worthy sentiment," Stefan said. "I never mention the glory I earned in Vlad Tepes's Night Attack, or as we say in the homeland, *Atacul de noapte.*"

"The captain is too reserved," Mai chided. Her ermine let out a chirrup, as if in agreement. "We're curious."

"Yeah." I gave in to the devil on my shoulder. "Tell us about the good old days. Don't be shy. We're all friends here."

"Except for me." Gavin raised his beer bottle in another mock salute. "I hate you all equally."

Rafe snorted, berry juice spraying from his nose. He grinned and wiped his face with the back of his hand. The flower vase now contained dead roses speckled with purplish spots.

Jake gave us a small, wary smile. He shifted a little, stared down at his plate for a moment and then looked straight at me. "What do you want to hear? War stories?"

Although he'd been looking right at me, it seemed everyone felt the need to chime in.

Tiffany's slit eyes glowed. "Ooh. Something exciting!"

"Something hardcore," Sarge suggested. "Guns. Magic. Certain death."

Rafe nodded. "Yeah, what Sarge said. Needs hot chicks though. There should be far more melons to sausage. A three-to-one ratio at least."

"Guys," Mai said. "This isn't story hour. He isn't making it up for you."

"Spoken truly, Mai." Hanzo gave Mai such a look of puppy-love worship that I almost heaved up my stir-fry. I hoped to God I never appeared that desperate. I caught myself glancing at Jake and heat crept up my chest and neck.

"I could tell a tale or two," Stefan said, and smiled so as to show a glimpse of fang. "Of murder and treachery in the old country, and how the proud Dalca family spared an entire seaside peasant village from assault by drunken mermaids."

Gavin sneered. "Nobody asked to hear that stupid story again, Stefan. Better yet, if we're gonna rehash stupid stories, tell them how we used your hair grease to fry those crawdads we caught when we almost starved to death in the bayou hunting that fucking cybernetic goblin wizard with the nose shaped like a can opener. Now *that's* a story."

Stefan's fist clenched. "Lies, you worthless hack. You purveyor of filth and sentence fragments. Peddler of poor grammar and misused semicolons, be warned. I can smell your blood from here."

"And I can smell your Brylcreem, you blood-sucking freak," Gavin shot back, half-rising from his seat. "Why don't you go put on a shirt with frilly cuffs and mismanage an exotic nightclub? And don't forget the goddamned glitter, so you sparkle in the midday sun...right before you burst into *flames*."

I stood up at the same time as Sarge. Tiffany wrapped her dragon-like wings around her body, covering her face up to her eyes. Mai's alien ermine made a flurry of outraged sounds—think squeaky dog toy being devoured by an alligator.

"Enough, dammit," I snapped. "Gavin, stop being such a prick and ease down. Stefan, you can tell your drunken mermaid story later." I glared around at everyone involved, skipping Jake. "Let's try and behave like professionals, especially in front of guests." I made air quote marks around the word professionals. "Otherwise, no dessert for anybody."

My words on dessert sliced through the building tension with the finality of Alexander the Great severing the Gordian knot.

"Yes, Mom." Gavin grinned and sat down again.

I gave him a flat stare. Must. Keep. Temper. In. Check.

Rafe cut in. "Don't worry, Captain. You're a total MILF. Mammal I'd Like to Fuck."

I hovered two seconds from nuclear explosion when Jake began to speak.

"All right," he said, his voice restrained. "I'll tell you about the time I air-dropped into a Belize jungle to help take down a nightmare that had crawled out of the depths of the Great Blue Hole."

All heads turned to him. It fell so quiet I could hear the A/C whooshing through the vents and the muted hum from the lights in the copper and iron chandelier. I slowly sat back down and picked up my fork.

"What's a Great Blue Hole?" Tiffany's eyes widened and she leaned toward him. "Is it like the Bermuda Triangle?"

"No," Jake answered. "It's an underwater sinkhole. From the air it looks like a huge blue circle. And it's deep. JSOC sent me as a force multiplier for a team of Belize commandos, training, support, that kind of thing. We went into the jungle to check out a report that a village had disappeared. We found the village empty. Everyone, gone. Even the chickens were nowhere to be found. We'd found a Roanoke Colony of the rainforest."

"What happened then?" Tiffany clutched at the edges of her wings.

"We tried to solve the mystery—"

"Like Scooby-Doo," Gavin suggested.

"—and we found huge trails of slime inside the villager huts and covering the dirt paths. The place stank like pineapple and brine. The unit commander came to me to talk about following the trail into the jungle, and then something massive crashed out of the deep rainforest shade. Bright yellow. Huge, shapeless, translucent and quivering. It had no eyes, but rippled and wobbled as it moved toward us. At first I thought it some kind of giant amoeba, but it never stopped its slow, disturbing jiggle..." He paused and gulped down the last of his wine. He snatched one of the beer bottles out of Gavin's Seahawks ice chest (Gavin being too lazy to walk the seventy feet back to the kitchen refrigerator to get more beer). A breathless silence hung in the room.

Jake's eyes stared unseeing into the distance. He took a

swig of beer, and I wondered how the hell I'd ended up stuck with wine.

"The reek of pineapples and low tide poured off the monster. The Belize commandos opened up with assault rifles, but the bullets just lodged inside with no effect, as if they were shooting into ballistic gelatin. The creature rolled over the top of one commando, trapping him in its gelatinous core, drowning him in yellow goo."

"How did you triumph?" Hanzo asked.

"We started to pull back, but the thing absorbed another commando." Jake gave a half shrug. "I went in after him before he could get sucked into its core. Hacked my way into its cool, yielding surface with my bayonet, dragged the commando back out and shoved an incendiary grenade into the hole I'd cut."

Sarge grunted. "Nice."

"Yeah. Incinerated a good chunk of that wobbling bastard. The rest of it tried to jiggle its way back to the ocean, smoking and bubbling and losing pieces along the way, but I called in an airstrike. Two F-15s dropped a bunch of Mark 77s and napalmed it down to ashes." Jake took a long drink from his beer. "From that day forward, whenever I see a gelatin dessert, I douse it with lighter fluid and send it back to hell."

A long moment of quiet drew out. I could think of nothing witty to say. What kind of iron will did it take to cut your way into a man-eating blob and rescue some grunt you didn't even know? And then incendiary grenades... I shuddered a little in pleasure and then threw a guilty glance around the table to make sure nobody had noticed.

"Sweet," Gavin said. "A carnivorous jelly from the black depths of the sea. Where's *Mystery Science Theater 3000* when you need it?"

Rafe snorted. "I preferred *Elvira.* More impressive mammaries. She stirred all kinds of tingly feelings within my furry loins."

"Rafe, please," I said. "Not everything in this world is about your dick."

"That's not what she said."

"How fast can you heal third-degree burns, Rafe? Fast? Hold on then, because this is gonna hurt you a helluva lot more than it's gonna hurt me."

Tiffany broke in before I could make good on my threat. "Is that why you took this mission, Captain Sanders? You want to kill this necromancer for making gelatin?"

Jake gave another shrug but didn't look at any of us. "Gelatin and zombies. The goddamn end of the world."

"Speaking of the end of the world," Rafe said. "Here's a fun fact. You can starve to death eating gelatin. It has zero essential amino acids."

The conversation turned to other topics, but I didn't join in. I kept busy shoveling food in, replaying Jake's story in my mind. Maybe...just maybe I'd been wrong about him. A guy like that wouldn't be interested in deposing me and seizing the reins. A guy like that, a guy who would follow you *inside* a monster and then blow the fucker up, well, that was a helluva guy to have around.

Jake caught me looking at him once. He held my gaze, and I didn't glance away.

I might have smiled and nodded my respect.

He might have smiled and nodded back.

I walked back alone to my room after dinner, feeling like I'd eaten too much and not giving a damn. Running footsteps pounded the tile behind me, and I wheeled around to face them. By habit, I reached out to touch my magic and shifted into a fighting stance.

Hanzo rounded the corner at a full run. He saw me, and his eyes flared wide. He drew up short, sliding to a stop on the tile just out of kicking range. Ninja delusions or not, there were no flies on that boy. I slowly dropped my guard. Releasing the power I'd summoned was more difficult, since it always felt as if I lost something, became less substantial, less *alive* when I let it go.

"What's up, Hanzo? Ultimate Fighting Championship on TV or something?" I tried to appear interested, but right now I just couldn't muster any excitement about watching men beat the shit out of each other. I felt damn exhausted. Just being in the room with Jake made me feel all DEFCON 1. Him and his damn story. And even if I *had* liked it, it'd gone on too long.

"A moment of your time, Captain. If you would do me the honor."

"This isn't about turning the med center into a tearoom again, is it? Because my answer is still no. You can perform tea ceremonies on your own time and dime."

He shook his head. "No, this isn't about *chanoyu.* I have a solution to the problem which stands before us indomitable, like Mount Fuji swathed in morning mist."

"All right. Look. No offense. You know I love you. You know you're a vital part of this team, and you know I don't want to crush your dreams. But would you stop talking like some half-assed samurai movie? Just talk normally around me. There's no one else here to impress."

"But I like talking that way."

Time to hand out the hard truths. "I hate to tell you this, but you sound like a white guy with a very shallow concept of pseudo-Confucius speak. It gets old. Really fast."

"All right then. I see." He swallowed. Opened his mouth and closed it again. He tried to smile and failed, and turned to walk away.

Ah crap. A surge of guilt swept through me like a flash flood. I reached out and touched his arm before he could get more than a step away. He stopped and looked back.

"What was your solution, Hanzo? You didn't tell me."

"Do you really want to hear it?" he asked. "I thought—"

"Of course I want to hear it. I just don't want to hear it in mangled haiku."

"You'll love it. Listen, you mentioned we had all these costs. Why don't we just do this mission the easy way?"

Oh God. Here it comes. "What's the easy way?"

He grinned. "Let me use my ninjitsu skills. I'll infiltrate that factory at night. Find where the necromancer's sleeping, use the thing where you drip poison down a dangling waxed string into his mouth. I then escape through the shadows, and an easy job is complete. No headaches for you." He paused. "Maybe a bonus for me."

I took a deep breath. Counted to ten. Let the air out in a slow, steady exhale. "No."

Surprise flashed across his face. "But it's perfect. Ninjas are flawless assassins."

I took another deep breath, counted to twenty and again let it out. "What about all the zombies? This job is as much about pest control as taking down the necromancer."

"I'll have my katana and my shuriken. You'll be able to walk across the Columbia River on the zombie heads my blade will sever."

Looked like the respite from ninja-speak only lasted for thirty-second intervals. "Hanzo, I think the time has come to let go of the ninja thing. What's it been? Three years since you started it? When was the last time you actually hit something with a shuriken?"

"What are you saying?" His voice cracked on the last word. I felt like a total ass, but I was determined to make a clean cut here. This ninja delusion had grown dangerous.

"I'm saying that you're on this team as a healer...and you work the main gun on the Bradley, but just until we up our roster a bit, so never mind that. You're the best healer I've ever seen. We've never lost one of our injured—and that's *directly* related to you. So why can't you be happy with what you are?"

"Maybe because I don't like what I am."

I blinked. Hanzo looked away, jaw clenched, and stared at one of the art prints on the wall. I reached out and touched his shoulder again. "We don't get to choose our talents. We have to go with what we're given."

"Easy for you to say. You're a walking flamethrower. I have to heal people—people that *other* people break. It's the warriors that get all the respect, all the love."

"You're wrong. I want to live in a world with more healers and fewer people running around breaking each other."

His hand slashed downward in dismissal, and his scowl deepened. "Like that will ever happen. I can be a master ninja if I keep trying. It's all about training, and I have the iron will—just the same as you." He took a steadying breath. "Besides, Mai likes ninjas."

News to me. Mai seemed more fascinated with furry things sporting pink noses and lots of teeth. "How do you know that?"

"I, uh, overheard her talking on the phone once. And anyway, *everybody* loves ninjas. Nobody ever messes with a shinobi. *Women* love ninjas. They're like cowboys with swords."

Some pop-psych book claimed men and women came from different planets, and I wasn't going to make Uranus jokes about the guys. The whole idea stank like cow manure in the sun. Men and women came from different *dimensions*. I didn't know how to reintroduce Hanzo to reality, so I ignored his cowboy/ninja comparison before my mind melted into a puddle of microwaved cheese.

"Tell you what," I said, keeping my voice soft. "You want more attention from Mai, right?"

"Yeah."

"So stop trying to sound like you're some half-assed Asian philosopher, stop hanging out at the Japanese Gardens hoping she'll notice and ask to go, stop drinking green tea when you think she might be looking, stop collecting ornamental fans and talking about cherry blossoms, and just *be yourself*. See where that gets you."

"It doesn't get me anywhere, Captain. That's the problem."

I sighed. "Don't worry about it now. But you *will* go in with the rest of the team, *not* solo. Bring your katana, I don't care, because I know I can count on you to patch people up when we're inside and going live and the blood's flowing down the floor drains." I squeezed his shoulder. "We're a team, and you're a vital part of it. So enough of this solo talk."

"All right." He managed a weak smile. "I'll think about what you said. You're missing an opportunity—"

I opened my mouth to interrupt, but he hurried on.

"—but I see where you're coming from. Thanks, Captain."

He turned again and started to leave, but I called out after him. "Hey, Hanzo. One more thing."

He paused and looked back.

"What do you think about the new guy? Captain Sanders."

"He's not ninja..." He paused and rubbed a thumb over his lower lip. "But I think he just might be samurai."

Back to the whiskey. The Chivas burned a little going down, but I loved the lazy warmth spreading throughout my body once it hit my stomach. I leaned against my balcony rail, swirling my glass so the ice cubes rattled, enjoying the quiet and the cool air. The rain had left off for now, and the sky, while not cloudless, had huge gaps in the cloud cover, so I held hope the celestial water faucet would remain off for a few hours. I'd had to sluice off water droplets from the rail before resting against it, but the metal remained cold and wet. I'd glanced over the rail to the lower levels more than once, hoping to catch another glimpse of Jake, but the balconies stayed empty.

A few stars shone through the gaps in the clouds, bright enough to be seen through the Portland light pollution. Crickets chirped and the sound of distant traffic murmured far off, joined by a fire-truck siren and dogs howling in sympathy. The air smelled of pine, and the scent of stir-fry lingered in my clothes.

Motion caught my eye. Two people moved through the shadows down near a stand of black cottonwoods, close to the low wall separating the backyard from the training grounds. There was no mistaking Sarge's massive shape, despite the darkness. He had his arm around someone else, and when they moved out of deeper shadow and into the slanting light from one of the security lamps, I recognized Shawn. They walked a few more steps and stopped. Sarge leaned up against the wall, and Shawn pressed against him. The sound of their voices drifted to me—Sarge's deep rumble and Shawn's mellower baritone.

I watched for a few more seconds, my chin resting on my arms as I leaned against the rail, but when they kissed, guilt nipped at me for spying. I threw back the rest of my drink and went inside, closing the door behind me. The soft strains of Beethoven's "Moonlight Sonata" drifted through my apartment. I set my glass on the table, lay down on the couch and laced my hands behind my head.

My apartment seemed too large, too empty, and I felt as if I were nothing more than a shadow flitting across the ruins of a coliseum. I concentrated and lit all the candlewicks at once with a flex of power. Real shadows did a slow, undulating dance on the ceiling.

Thoughts chased themselves through my mind, sliding against one another, moving too fast to focus on any single one for long. The mission. The money. The risk. All of them interwoven with Jake, his smile, his eyes. From Jake back to my annoyance at his distraction, at *allowing* myself to be distracted when my people were headed into a dangerous situation, and then circling back to the mission again. Sarge and Shawn. The heat between them, flames which sometimes burned slow and steady, and sometimes spread like a brush fire, but never sputtered out and died like all my other loves had. Guttering. Flickering. Consuming what little fuel remained, until nothing was left but cold ashes, and no choice but for each of us to go our separate ways.

Was Jake worth the risk? Because it was risk, greater than just a quick hot fling where I could enjoy myself and not worry about consequences. It was a risk not merely to my heart, but also to my command and to my people. The other issue—*time*. The mission could be over soon, hell, tomorrow if we got the green light. Then he'd go back to Fort Bragg or wherever and that would be the end.

I had a responsibility to my team that outweighed my personal life. Could I give my people my best if I were constantly distracted by my growing feelings for Jake? What if he ended up injured? Captured? Would I put the mission at risk to save him? Safer never to find out. Duty first. Always.

I turned on my side and stared at a delicate tongue of candle flame. The music seemed to pour over me, each note starker, more harrowing than the last. Sleep would probably be a long time coming tonight.

And about that, I was finally right.

Chapter Ten:
Battle on Green Fields

Undead Army of the Unrighteous Order of the Falling Dark
Riverside Golf and Country Club, Hole #10
Northeast 33rd Drive, Portland, Oregon
9:34 a.m. PST April 14th

Golfing sucked.

Necromancer Jeremiah Hansen turned to Blake with a three iron clutched in both hands like a broadsword.

"Golfing sucks," he said. His zombie caddy moaned in agreement.

"It's a gentleman's game." Blake fixed him with one of those disapproving Catholic-nun looks that made him feel as if he'd failed miserably at the whole Evil Corporate Villain thing. "It is a *businessman's* game. More deals are sealed here than in the boardroom or conference room. Fail to become halfway competent at it and you'll find your career suffering a slow descent into irrelevance."

Irrelevance? Hitting a tiny ball into a distant hole seemed pretty fucking irrelevant to him. Jeremiah gritted his teeth, clenched his jaw and peered down at his golf ball. He'd bought a bunch of Titleist Pro V1 golf balls, since according to the package they sailed the farthest, but he'd already lost four of the damn things in the pond on hole eight. No doubt the Pro

Shop dredged the lake daily and resold the balls to suckers like him. What a fucking racket.

The ball sat in the rough, looking smug, mocking him with its pristine white dimples. Jeremiah stepped up to it and settled his feet on either side, determined to smack the living hell out of it. He concentrated, visualizing his swing, visualizing the clubface hitting at the perfect angle—

Something rasped behind him, over and over again, like sandpaper on a rubber hose. He slowly raised his head and stared at his caddy.

His caddy was a zombie, some young guy wearing a rather worn polo shirt and wrinkled yellow slacks. Polo zombie stared at another group of golfers and licked his lips again. The rasping turned out to be the sound of his gray, mottled tongue scraping over his gray, mottled lips.

Jeremiah yanked on the silver necromancy cord to get the zombie's attention. Polo zombie turned back to him, smiled and pulled the putter half out of the golf bag and offered it up. Jeremiah might be new to this sadistic game, but he was pretty goddamn sure you didn't use a fucking putter in the rough a hundred and twenty yards from the hole.

Zombie caddies sucked too.

At least Blake had to endure an equally inept zombie caddy. His caddy wore a button-down shirt with a picture of a dancing anthropomorphic hotdog, bright red Hawaiian-style shorts and an orange plastic visor askew on his head. Did nobody die and reanimate in *normal* clothes anymore?

At least the zombies he'd chosen didn't show any visible wounds or bloodstains or teeth marks, though the sunlight made their grayish skin and sunken, bruised eyes rather noticeable. Maybe he'd suggest makeup next time, although who in their right mind would want to apply that shit to a zombie? Still, zombie caddies were better than paying a living caddy, who'd expect a tip and would no doubt secretly mock all Jeremiah's whiffs and divots and mulligans. He just had to keep a tight hold on the control cords to ensure his zombies didn't wander off and eat somebody in the sand traps.

Jeremiah settled down again and set his clubface near the ball half-hiding in the grass. He concentrated. Eye on the ball. He was still water in a mountain valley. Serene. He could do this.

No, he couldn't. He'd shank it or slice it or top the damn thing and drive the ball farther into the wet ground. He glanced at Blake. "Game doesn't do much to foster serenity and mental well-being does it?"

Blake shrugged. "It's golf."

"It's sadomasochism." Jeremiah swung the club back, careful not to bend his arm, trying to contort himself into proper form. The club cut down, hissing through the air. He pivoted, swinging his hips over. The club bit deep. He powered through. A chunk of grass and dirt went sailing through the air.

"Fore!" he yelled. The divot thumped on the fairway ten feet away. The ball still sat untouched on the rough. A huge gouge marred the earth—a dark scar, practically a Grand Canyon for ants. Shit.

Blake cleared his throat. "I don't believe you're required to yell fore unless someone is in danger of being hit."

"Somebody *is* in danger of being hit. With my golf club. Over and over again."

On his second try, Jeremiah managed to connect with the ball. It caught air, slicing to the right, and landed on the very edge of the fairway about forty yards from the pin. Just like he'd planned.

Sort of.

Next, they walked forward to Blake's ball, which sat in the center of the fairway as a result of his flawless drive.

"We're supposed to be talking about business out here?" Jeremiah asked as Blake bypassed his zombie caddy's offer of a three wood and selected a seven iron. "So let's talk business."

"Very well. Will we make deadline for shipping to our distributor? I seem to recall mention of various issues with the supply chain."

"I resolved those issues on Monday. A truck should be here tomorrow to pick up the first shipment. All the paperwork's perfect."

"Excellent." Blake settled himself beside his golf ball, drew the club back in a perfect arc and swung forward again, sending the ball sailing through the air. It landed on the green a dozen feet from the hole. Jeremiah struggled not to appear either vexed or impressed. He yanked his Blazers hat lower to better hide any lingering trace...such as his eyelid twitch.

Blake handed his club back to his caddy. "The good news is we've seen no hint of law-enforcement interest in our operation."

"How do you know that?"

"My contacts claim the US Special Forces teams tasked with handling supernatural infestations and paranormal threats to public safety are all busy with various other hotspots. If we can shift from obtaining funds through high-risk heists and settle on steady income through legitimate business ventures, then we can continue to operate below the radar until our long-term goals are achieved—"

A ball bounced along the fairway a dozen feet from them. Jeremiah looked back. Some morons had teed up behind them and hit without even a courtesy shout of *fore*.

"If I get nailed with a golf ball," Jeremiah warned, "somebody's going to end up lunch."

Blake turned to peer at the other golfing party, cold annoyance on his face. The fat guy in a cap that should've been banned for plaid violations waved a hand at them, mouthed sorry and laughed.

"Some people have no etiquette," Blake said. "Such people can be purged at a later date."

It took three more strokes for Jeremiah to get on the green

after he put the ball into a sand trap. He took a drop, rules be damned, and in only four putts managed to get the ball into the hole. Hallelujah. He missed the fake castles and windmills and tunnels of miniature golf, which even had arcade games and racecars. Real golf only had those carts. And sand traps, but you couldn't even drive the carts into the sand traps. No comparison.

Jeremiah had just shoved in the tee on hole eleven when the party behind them caught up.

"Sorry about the close call," the fat guy in the bad hat said. He looked askance at Jeremiah's caddy and then glanced at his Rolex. "We're kinda in a hurry. Can we play through?"

"No," Jeremiah answered, reminding himself not to feed the other golfers to his zombies. Bad form, old boy.

Still, he took his damn time setting up. So much so that the woman with the blue-tinged hair started to heave dramatic sighs and shuffle and shift her feet. He could feel the pull from the zombies, their temptation to sink their teeth into all the warm flesh nearby. Polo zombie started to drool, staining the front of his shirt.

"Hey, buddy, you all right?" some other old guy in plaid pants and ugly shoes asked polo zombie. "You look like shit."

"Don't talk to him," Jeremiah said. "He'll chew on your spleen."

They stared at Jeremiah as if he were rabid coyote running amok on the putting green.

Jeremiah pointed at them with his club. "Yeah, I'm crazy. So what? I was sane when I drove in here. So don't fuck with me or I swear to everything unholy I'll feed you to my employee of the month."

The group started to edge away from him, fear shining in their eyes.

"Perhaps we should leave?" Blake suggested. "We can hire a golf pro to improve your skills in a more private setting. Tax deductible business expense, after all."

"Hold on, watch this." Jeremiah faced off on the ball with his driver and swung back. The driver head cut the air like the tip of an arrow. He brought all his power and dexterity to bear, aiming for that one little sweet spot on the little white ball. The clubface hit with a satisfying *WHACK*!

The ball rolled along the fairway for sixteen feet and came to a stop. He'd clipped the top of it with the bottom of the clubface. He'd also shattered his little red tee. Oh sweet fucking Zombie God of America did he ever hate this goddamn game.

Somebody in the waiting group of golfers, who now stood a safe distance away, gave a loud snicker. Somebody else cursed and muttered how at this rate they'd be here all day. Jeremiah's fists clenched on the driver's grip, visions of total zombie apocalypse floating in his head.

He took a deep, steadying breath.

"Let's call it a day and grab some beers," he said to Blake. "And get me a real pro. I want to fucking *own* this game by next week. No sport makes a fool out of a Necromancer of the Unrighteous Order of the Falling Dark."

"I shall attend to it." Blake's face remained impassive.

They climbed into their golf carts, the zombies still a little stiff and uncoordinated trying to settle in the passenger seats, and zipped away down the path. What a colossal waste of time. At least driving the carts was fun. The fresh air felt great too. Next time he'd do better, and that was a promise.

Until then, he had some gelatin to inflict upon the world.

Chapter Eleven: The Zombie Hunter

Mercenary Wing Rv6-4 "Zero Dogs"
The Zero Dog Compound
Shooting Range
1110 Hours PST April 15th

Training exercises dominated the morning, starting with a quick round of physical training, then a detailed walkthrough with the teams on effective small-unit tactics versus Reanimated Corpse Threats. I'd finished up kenpo and judo training an hour ago, and then headed out alone for a mile run along our track before stopping to chug Gatorade and wolf down a couple of bananas. I wasn't due for another round of simulated urban assault training with the crew and Jake until this afternoon, so I checked out a pistol from the armory and headed downstairs to the range, hoping to clear my head with a little precision shooting.

I'd been off focus the entire morning, just enough to frustrate me. Thinking too much, that had always been my problem. Nothing had changed, yet I still found myself thinking about the mission, thinking about my people and thinking about Jake with a relentless persistence. All these thoughts careened off one another like billiard balls clacking around on some mental pool table until I thought I might just go mad.

The shooting range was empty, as I'd hoped. I grabbed ear

protection, safety glasses and flipped the switch that turned on the red light outside the door, letting people know the range was occupied and live rounds in use.

I might be something of a walking flamethrower—and the Beretta I'd brought couldn't compare to loosing streams of flame and hurling fireballs—but the very act of shooting never failed to calm me. The focus required for grouping shots on the human-silhouette targets always drowned out the cacophony in my head, no matter what had caused it. I could use that right now.

My favorite firing station sat at the far end of the range. Once there, I pushed the button and brought forward several hanging targets, arranging them at different distances. The cool moving air from the exhaust fans raised gooseflesh on my arms. Without thinking, I heated the air around my skin until I felt warm again. I set out the ten clips I'd loaded, arranging them in a line in front of me. Next, I slipped the magazine into the M9 Beretta 9mm and chambered a round. I flipped off the safety, drew down on the nearest target and started to fire.

Four empty clips later I cleared the pistol, set it down and pushed the button to bring in the targets. I took them down from the clips and checked the groupings.

"Not bad," Jake said behind me.

I jumped, despite my ear protection dampening sounds, and jerked my head around to glare at him. How long had he been watching?

He flashed me that mischievous grin and walked closer, staring over my shoulder at the targets. "Groupings all within three, three and a half inches of each other." He pointed at a shot I'd pulled, putting a hole in the silhouette's outer shoulder. "Except this guy. The statistical outlier?"

I yanked off my ear protection. "Cut me some slack. I just shoot to tap into the Zen of it. I need something dead, I charbroil it."

"One thing I love about you," he said. "Extremely direct.

Like a bullet."

"I don't have time to waste sugarcoating things or talking in circles. People count on me being clear."

His eyebrows rose. "And so prickly sometimes."

"Why not? That was one of those comments that can go either way—compliment or insult."

"And you chose to see it as an insult. Admit it. I just burn your tater tots and chafe like beach sand, don't I?" He smirked and held out a hand for the pistol. "May I have a go?"

I picked it up, double-checked the safety and thrust it out to him pistol butt first. "Going to show off a bit? Trying to impress me, or just trying to show how much better you are?"

My words poured out with far more acid than I'd intended. Why did I feel such a pull toward him when we seemed to grind against each other like two saw blades?

He looked at me and something flickered in his eyes. He waved off the pistol. "You know, you're right. I *was* just trying to impress you." He cocked his head. "Sometimes it's unnerving talking to somebody so direct."

I didn't know what to say to that, so I ignored it. "Why'd you come down here, anyway?"

"I wanted to see you."

"So now you're trying for direct?" The challenge ran rampant in my voice. "How far do you want to go? Why, *exactly*, did you want to see me?"

His grin faltered, but his gaze grew more intense. "Maybe I enjoy being around you."

I snorted. "That's the most tofu statement I've ever heard."

"Tofu statement?"

"Bland. White. Tasteless. Floats in miso soup." I shook my head. "You look at me that way, and then you say something so...passionless."

"Look at you like what?"

"Like you want to come over here and tear these clothes off

me."

He looked away. "You're *too* damn direct."

"Yeah? Fuck you. That's who I am. Get used to it. But you know what, forget that. I can be tactful. I do it with my people all the time—especially all their deluded foibles—but with you, I don't bother. I assumed you were a big boy and could handle it."

"That right?" He leaned forward, settled a fist gently around the front of my jumpsuit, just above my breasts, and pulled me slowly but irresistibly toward him. Did I say irresistibly? Not quite. I knew six different ways to break that hold, one of which would leave him with broken fingers, one with a broken wrist. But I didn't protest as he lowered his face to mine. His lips pressed against mine. Warm. I opened my mouth and kissed him back. He took my ferocity and gave it back. He pulled me closer so that my body pressed against him.

I broke the kiss first, pushing back on his chest with gentle force.

He touched my face. "Your skin is so warm."

I stepped away from him, now uncertain, and turned back to the table with the Beretta and the clips. I put my hand on the cool surface, feeling my muscles tremble, my heart beating hard.

"What's wrong?" he asked.

"This is stupid." I glanced back at him and saw something in his face. Hurt? Anger? Maybe frustration. That's what I felt now. "This isn't going to go anywhere."

"Why? There's something between us. We both know it."

"There's no happy ending here. We finish this and you're gone. Back to gung-ho army land. We can pretend all we want, but you're not part of this team. Our worlds only overlap at the edges. Their centers don't touch."

"People make happy endings all the time, goddamn it." His face was fierce as his words lashed against me.

"Yeah, *other* people. I'm not a cock tease. Neither am I a quick tumble and tickle-fuck or whatever stupid slang you guys have for it. You want some honesty? All right. Sure, I'm attracted to you. Have been since I first saw you on the street before we even met. But you know what? It doesn't *matter.*"

"Explain that."

"It doesn't matter because I'm more than the sum of my parts. I'm not a slave to hormones. You make all the right noises. You give me all the right looks. And next week, when all the zombies are dead, you'll get new marching orders and it'll be 'nice to know ya, text me sometime.'"

"I don't operate that way."

"I have three brothers. I know the game."

He kept silent, so I charged on. Nothing could stop me once I got all four tires on the road and the engine revved.

"And I've been around the block a couple times. If we keep hands off, I get the chance to demand your respect, whether or not you want to give it. We get down and dirty and all of a sudden you think you're in charge. You own me. A guy shoves his dick in something and all of a sudden he thinks he gets the right to determine its future. I worked damn hard to claw my way up to where I am now. These people depend on me. *Me.* Captain Andrea Walker. Not you. You're not part of this team, and soon you'll be gone, and if something breaks, then I have to pick up the pieces."

"It seems you know everything about me already." His tone was bitter. "Including how I'll act. Your file didn't say you were psychic."

"Who needs psychic powers? I overheard you on the phone that first night. Yeah, I did, so don't look surprised. I watched how you handled that first briefing. You've always considered us a bunch of scrubs, a step up from civilians maybe, but not much. Undisciplined pirates motivated by greed. Admit it."

"All right. First night here maybe I acted like a bit of an ass."

"You acted like a full-on raving, balls-to-the-wall ass clown."

He scowled and said nothing.

"In fact," I continued, "now that I think about it, you acted like an overbearing, vise-clamp-sphinctered, know-it-all ass king of America." I paused dramatically. "I was quite taken aback."

"You done?"

"That's a stupid thing to ask a woman."

"Look, maybe I was wrong," he said. "And the more I see of you in action, the more I think I might've been." He shrugged. "I won't lie to you. I can't be sure until I've seen you guys go hot and fought alongside you. Respect is earned in this business."

"No shit. But you threatened to kill our role in this mission once already. I had to force you to back off. You think that makes me trust you?"

For a long time he didn't answer.

He finally said, "Maybe I came in here with too much Green Beret can-do. Too many rigid expectations. If that's the case, then the fault is mine. But make no mistake, I want us to win."

"Then we should focus on winning," I said. "Nothing else. Because if we fall into each other, we'll be compromising everything. I won't do that to my people."

"I didn't expect anything less."

We stared at each other. My skin felt too tight, shrink-wrapped over my bones. My heart thudded along, and a sharp ache zigzagged up my jawline where I clenched my teeth. The exhaust fans hummed in the walls, but aside from that, the silence held steady. I could either burn this bridge or help repair it. Choice was mine.

Slowly, I held out the pistol again as a rather ironic peace offering. "All right. I feel like I went over the edge into flamethrower mode a little. So why don't you show me how it's done, cowboy?"

He grinned. Repair it was. It seemed one of the best ways to a man's heart was to ask him to show off and pretend to be wowed. Still, I remained more amused than annoyed.

We put on our ear protection again. He inserted a fresh magazine, worked the slide, thumbed the safety off and took up position in the classic Weaver stance. He popped off shot after shot, firing in a controlled yet rapid fusillade until the slide came back. He hit the button and the target moved forward. He pulled it down and handed it to me. Two holes. Both large. One of them dead center of forehead and I could see where the following rounds had enlarged the edges. Same with the second, heart shots, all in such a tight cluster it appeared as if one huge caliber bullet had ripped through the paper.

Okay, forget that part about pretending to be wowed. "I think that's even better than Sarge."

"I grew up target shooting. Puts me in another world. Just me, the gun and the target."

Pretty much how I felt about it, except that he was a helluva lot better at it. "You picked the right job then. Would've sucked to have gone into human resources or accounting."

He laughed, engaged the safety and set the pistol down. "What about you? Tell me something about the captain of the Zero Dogs not in your dossier."

"I'm boring. I hate to talk about myself, because, if you watch closely, you can see the exact moment the other person's eyes glaze over."

"C'mon. Give me a break here. You can be very determined when you want to be elusive."

I frowned and shifted. "All right, fine. There's nothing exciting. I'm the only daughter in a big family. Three older brothers. From Illinois, and the rest of the family still lives there. See? Yawn festival."

"Why'd you become a mercenary? Were you a soldier before?"

"No. All my brothers are military. So in a wild fit of

rebellion, I headed straight from West Point to a job with the Hellfrost Merc group." I left out the part about being expelled from West Point, since it'd been one huge misunderstanding. If he'd seen my file, he knew it already. "Been clawing my way up ever since." I shrugged. "There's a lot of prejudice against pyromancers."

He cocked his head. "How so?"

"People think we're little better than deranged firebugs."

"Is that bad?"

"Stop with the flattery. What about you?"

"College at UNLV. Into the Army to pay for it. Ended up liking it. Did some time with the Rangers. Ended up transferring into Special Forces. Did bodyguard detail for US government VIPs in Iraq. Among other things."

"I bet the shields come in handy," I said.

"Saved my ass when we first met, didn't they?"

"Tell you what. Let's make a deal. You fill me in on the secrets to impeccable shooting. I'll show you a bit of my dark martial arts knowledge."

"Deal." He grinned. His grins took the edge off him. Made him seem less like a hyper-trained soldier and more like an impish boy. I liked those grins, but I'd never tell. "Look at us. First-date stuff in a firing range."

"What would Mother say?"

"Maybe she'd say we're better cut out for each other than you realize."

I said nothing and looked away down the range.

"Ah," he said. "More of that command stuff getting in our way."

"We've known each other less than a week. Let's be real."

"Let's be real then. I'm not a complex man. I'll tell you everything you need to know in under five minutes. A lightning briefing."

I snorted. "Go for it."

"I want to keep people safe. Nothing more complicated than that. I want to carve out a slice of the world that can be as free from the violence, the suffering and despair as I can. Yeah. I'm a starry-eyed idealist with a pistol."

"Maybe," I said. "But if nobody ever tries it, there'll never be hope for it."

"I've never failed a mission. I won't let this be the first, either. I'll do whatever it takes to stop that necromancer. So I understand you. Very well, in fact. This isn't about us. It's about duty."

Duty. That about summed it up.

The PA system speaker overhead crackled. Gavin's voice blasted over the com. "Captain to the bridge. The Klingons are attacking!" He cut off and the gentle strains of Muzak started to bleed through. The elevator-music version of Metallica's "Kill 'Em All". I was surrounded by comedians.

I walked past Jake toward the range exit, grateful for the chance to escape.

"Hey," he called before I'd gone ten feet.

I glanced back.

He leaned against one of the shooting-station walls, his arms folded across his chest. "When this is over. I'll have something else to prove to you. Like how I don't love 'em and leave 'em, as you want to believe. And I damn well mean to prove it, Captain Walker. Prove it so well, you'll never forget."

Dozens of witty and caustic replies flashed through my mind, but I held my tongue. *Bit* my tongue to keep it from running on its own. Only when I felt certain I had it cowed did I risk an answer. "Better train up, Captain Sanders. I'm no easy opponent."

"No. No, you're not."

"And you can start proving it by cleaning my pistol."

I walked out on him. I could feel his gaze burning on me as I left, but I didn't look back. My lips still tingled from our kiss. I smiled a little. My good mood lasted until I reached the top of the stairs, where the weight of duty crushed down on me again, heavier than ever.

Chapter Twelve:
The Jungle Part II (Or Eating the Man Who Moved Your Cheese)

Undead Army of the Unrighteous Order of the Falling Dark
Bokor Gelzonbi Manufacturing Facility
SE Holgate Boulevard, Portland, Oregon
2:45 p.m. PST April 15th

Supreme Zombie Commander Jeremiah Hansen surveyed his domain with a jaundiced eye. Running a start-up company was hard, the way teaching cats to march in step was hard. Zombies continually had to be brought back to task. They remained easy to distract, prone to zoning out, and ever ready for a lunch break. Time to face facts. His factory had become a disorganized, underproductive mess since he'd gone full-scale production. He really, really needed a Master Scheduler.

Or Darth Vader.

Speaking of Darth Vader, Blake Delaney, his right-hand man, was out of the office today, trying to round up a respectable mage to build them a golem to help with the loading and unloading of freight. Of course, a golem would cost an arm and a leg and a left testicle, so Jeremiah would likely have to knock over another bank to pay for it.

Perhaps he needed a Controller as well.

With Blake gone, it fell to Jeremiah to crack the whip and

oversee the timely completion of production orders. Along with a Master Scheduler and a Controller, he needed a foreman or floor manager. Maybe a foreman in an armored power suit, like Iron Man, to protect him from hungry zombies. Hell, if they went that far, Jeremiah wanted a power suit for himself, something uber-cool...and a kick-ass gun. It was nothing but a travesty he didn't already own a good gun or a Sentient Sword of Soul Drinking or something. He didn't even have a wand made out of Dryad dermis with a dodo feather inside. How lame was that?

Jeremiah grabbed a clipboard and pen and headed down the catwalk stairs to the production floor. After only a few minutes of creative rearrangement, he pulled three zombies off the packaging line to work the grinding mills. To increase throughput and reduce production time, Jeremiah had linked several shredders, crushers and massive stainless-steel rolling pins that turned the extracted gelatin into a fine granulated powder. However, the lack of guards and auto stops meant every so often a zombie operator ended up pulled into the machinery and also turned into powder. He'd lost another one this morning, so now he'd try the union thing and have three operators instead of just one. With zombies, redundancy came cheap. Downtime, however, was an entirely different kettle of fish.

He stood off to the side of the machine with his zombie trio. Two of them were tall males, one older, bald, with a walrus-like face and wearing a battered tracksuit, the other looked college age, pasty, sagging skin, dull piggy eyes, wearing a bloodstained button-down shirt. The third zombie was a woman, thick limbs, rather hunched forward and missing her lower lip. She kept staring at Jeremiah's mouth, which unnerved him. He got the impression that she wanted to kiss him, and maybe tear off a flap of his own lip in the process.

"You guys are on the grinders today," he told them. "I don't want a lot of problems this time. A while ago one of you drones got sucked into the teeth and ended up in the gelatin, and I don't want it to happen again. Workplace accidents are the bane of productivity, *comprende*?"

The zombies stared at him in their unnerving zombie way—faces blank, but deep in their listless eyes, a spark of undying hunger. He made certain he kept a tight mental grip on the cords binding them to his will.

It took twenty minutes of good old necromancer focus to get his three trainees up to speed on what buttons to push, how to regulate throughput speeds and clear jams. He watched them work, his mind running over better ways to automate the process, identify the slow down and snag points, and engineer out the flaws. He just about had everything up and running smoothly enough with his trainees to risk leaving them alone when the bell at the loading dock clamored. All the zombies in the factory paused and looked around as if God had started performing interpretive hand puppetry in the clouds. One of the newly trained zombies—walrus-face, in fact—left a hand dangling too close to the grinder and it ripped off his entire arm. Walrus-face stared at his shoulder, his mouth making a dull O of surprise.

Beautiful. "Get back to work, people!" he yelled. "This shop isn't union. No breaks."

General discontented moaning broke out, but lacked the articulate and inspired bitching of normal workplaces. One zombie lost his balance staring at the overhead fluorescent lights and fell over with a surprised grunt. Jeremiah sighed.

The loading-dock bell rang again, and the same exact thing happened. Another zombie, staring upward and searching for the noise, ran right into one of the waist-high barriers he'd installed to direct undead traffic flow. The zombie toppled over the barrier and crashed to the linoleum tiles. He heard a bone snap even over the machinery noise.

Jeremiah hurried to the loading dock before anything else could go wrong, glancing at the clock on the wall. The damn truck was early. Four zombies stood in the loading dock, all staring unblinking at the bell above the steel door. Clearly, zombies had a slacking off-to-work ratio worse than teenagers with cell phones.

He shooed them back into the factory before he opened the steel exit door. The driver was a short, wiry guy with a mullet, dust-smeared jeans and cowboy boots worn down at the heels. He held a clipboard in a hand decorated with wiry black knuckle hairs and scowled at Jeremiah.

"Got a pick-up order for ten pallets of freight. Sign here." He shoved the clipboard at Jeremiah.

Jeremiah signed and handed back the clipboard.

The driver flipped the top sheet to reveal a new pink sheet full of miniscule text and long chains of numbers. "And here."

Jeremiah signed there.

"Initial here."

Jeremiah initialed.

The guy flipped to a yellow page. "Initial here, here and here. Sign here."

Jeremiah pulled off a triple-twist initial with a half-gainer signature.

The guy flipped to a white page. "Signature and printed name here on the X."

Jeremiah suppressed the urge to attack the shipping company with zombies. He signed and printed his name.

The driver tucked the clipboard beneath his arm. "All right, show me what dock you want and I'll back her in. Hope you got your own pallet jacks cuz I don't do loading-unloading." He chewed on a thumbnail and spit out a chunk. "It ain't in the contract."

It took two hours of herding zombies in and out of the truck and one forklift accident (one of the forks impaled the torso of a greasy-haired zombie sporting several bite wounds and a bit of fungus growing on his jowls) before they finished loading. At last, he shut all the bay doors, herded the zombies away from the docks again and went out to let the driver know they'd finished.

The driver pulled the semi-trailer forward and sealed up the truck. He wrote down the control number on the seal and handed Jeremiah a wad of paperwork. "Lucky you guys didn't damage the truck. Sounded like you didn't have a fucking clue what you were doing."

Jeremiah took a deep breath. First rule of effective leadership: Don't kill people you couldn't easily replace. He needed the guy to drive the truck, so Mullet-Face got a free pass. Though maybe he could get himself a driver of his own—a vampire maybe? Somebody the zombies wouldn't go after, anyway. He was probably opening himself up to a HR nightmare, since he'd always heard zombies bitterly envied their undead cousins, the way a garden slug envied a sea cucumber.

Finally, the truck rumbled off with Bokor Gelzonbi's first-ever shipment of gelatin to the distributor hub. Jeremiah had just started across the dock on his way back to his office when the damned bell clanged again with its strident, obnoxious clamor. All zombie work production stopped as they looked toward the sound. He stomped back to the steel door and opened it. A large, bald guy stood there wearing a Harley T-shirt. He frowned and glanced at a clipboard whose bottom edge appeared to have been chewed by a dog.

"Got a delivery for Bokor Gelzonbi Foods, care of J. Hansen. Two hundred and ten frozen sides of beef. You guys'll have to unload—that damn 'frigerator truck gives me freezer burn. Oh, almost forgot." He thrust the clipboard at Jeremiah. "You gotta sign for it first."

Chapter Thirteen: Apocalypse Tomorrow

Mercenary Wing Rv6-4 "Zero Dogs"
The Zero Dog Compound
Office
1939 Hours PST April 15th

I finally got the chance to put my boots up on my desk and steal a few minutes for myself after another full day of training. We'd finished a second simulated assault on the training grounds, with Mai again filling the role of necromancer and her pets playing zombies. This time things had gone with flawless precision—practically the synchronized swimming version of a full-frontal military assault. I hated to admit Jake had been right, but when we pushed into the buildings with two teams in close support we hammered back the press of tiny, furry faux-zombies without losing any people.

At least Jake had been professional enough not to appear smug.

After that, I'd ordered pizza delivery for the crew, snagged a few pieces for myself, and escaped to the office to check my email and procrastinate about crunching numbers for the upcoming live-fire mission by playing solitaire. But after losing my seventh straight hand, I powered down the computer and reached over to click off the desk lamp. In the darkness, the slashes of moonlight fell across my sombrero cactus pot and across one of my legs. The hush in the office seemed very deep, though I could hear faint music from the hallway. I turned the blinds so I could see out into the yard and took a moment to stare into the night. I felt restless. Uneasy. Yet I couldn't say why. I shook my head and trooped back downstairs. Maybe company and laughter would drive off my disquiet.

Music drifted down from the hallway PA system speakers mounted in the ceiling—Bob Marley's "Buffalo Soldier". We had a year-long free subscription to a satellite music service, and any time we used the PA, some glitch allowed a flood of random commercial-free music over the speakers and would continue until someone reset the control switch. One time the damn thing had come on of its own accord at two in the morning, blasting Frank Sinatra's "Very Good Year" into the darkness of the house. The hair on the back of my neck had stood straight up and gooseflesh had writhed on my arms. If Frankie's voice echoing down empty, shadow-filled hallways in the middle of the night didn't creep a person out, that person had nerves of titanium.

When I reached the first-floor landing, the walls trembled with a sudden bass rumble, and gunshots and screams filled the air, drowning out Bob Marley. My heart lurched. I reached for my magic before realization crashed home. The gunshots, screams and moans came from Gavin's contribution to our training schedule, namely, watching every zombie movie ever created to get a feel for our opponent. The rest of the crew had been game and agreed to start with the classic *Night of the Living Dead*, but after that things had grown a little heated. Rafe and Gavin had started to argue whether the zombies from *Dawn of the Dead* held the mantle of true shambling undead or if the "Braaaaains" zombies from *Return of the Living Dead* held more pop-culture appeal. About that time I'd pulled up stakes and headed for my office.

Glass shattered in the television room as I walked toward it. I frowned and walked faster. That had sounded *real.* A flurry of shouting filled the air, followed by a blast of high-pitched screeching that made me grit my teeth. What the hell was going on? I couldn't leave for five damn minutes—

A silver monkey jumped onto the doorjamb and launched itself off again. Actually, it only resembled a monkey in passing, but it had thick silver fur, an unnaturally long tail, and a wizened, pale face with creepy jade eyes and a lizard tongue. Ear-splitting shrieks blared out of its mouth as it scurried past me and rocketed up the stairs.

Gavin crashed through the doorway after the strange creature. He gripped the replica *Lord of the Rings* sword in one hand so tightly his knuckles were white. "Stop that monkey!"

The sad state of affairs I lived with every day meant I didn't find requests for monkey chasing the least bit surreal. Still, I'd be damned if I'd run after one of Mai's pets. Filthy thing probably had weird microscopic bugs, and I wouldn't touch the monkey with a twelve-foot pike unless somebody autoclaved it first.

Mai charged in, right on Gavin's heels. Her summoner robes billowed out behind her in folds of yellow silk. Her dark hair had slipped free of her barrettes and stuck out in spiky tufts, and her brown eyes shone with wild desperation. "Don't you stab him. *Don't you touch him*!"

I held up my hands. "Whoa! Whoa, people. What the hell's going on?"

Gavin and Mai slid to a halt in front of me. I suppose I should've been grateful Gavin hadn't inadvertently stabbed me in the process of stopping. The silver monkey swung along the stairwell railing. It hung upside down and whooped at us.

The bottom of the main stairwell began to fill up with people following the commotion. Everyone stared at the monkey. I caught sight of Jake, who leaned against the wall with a beer in one hand and a grin on his face.

I scowled at him. "A little help, maybe?"

His grin only widened. "Wouldn't want to interfere with your command."

I was still trying to come up with a suitable retort when Mai spoke. "Gavin provoked my pet, Captain."

"I didn't do anything—"

"Don't lie. Every time a zombie came on screen you'd point at my tiny friend and yell, 'Thar she blows me. Zombie monkey off the starboard bow.' *Every* time."

"That monkey's a mouth-breather with squinty eyes. And he ate all the popcorn."

"Enough," I said. "Gavin, put that sword down and try acting like a man—"

A cell-phone ring interrupted me. Everyone went phone fishing to find out whose had gone off. Jake came up the big winner. He flipped open his phone, glanced at it and paused. I saw his mouth tighten, and his face turn all business. He hurried out of the room without another word.

"What are we going to do about that monkey?" Rafe asked. Mai's demon monkey still hung upside down from the balustrade by its feet, peering at us with wide alien eyes and sticking out its lizard tongue in defiance.

"Mai, send that thing home. I'm sure it's not housebroken, and I'll take the carpet-cleaning bill out of your salary."

"Yes, Captain." Mai stepped to the side and began to chant a string of strange, liquid-sounding words. A breath of wind pushed against me, stirring through my hair. A spark appeared, floating in midair. The spark flared outward into a shining ring and expanded into a portal hovering unsupported in the air. Through the portal I could see an alien jungle of strange white plants, ridges of red ground veined with gold streaks, and waterfalls of a silver liquid, maybe mercury.

The alien monkey made purring sounds. Gavin lurched forward while the rest of us peered at the alien world. He seized the monkey by the back of the neck and flung it toward the portal. The demon monkey sailed past my face, screeching its outrage all the way into the portal, which snapped closed behind it and vanished.

The descending quiet struck me as a step short of ominous. The intermixed smell of popcorn, bananas and ammonia reached my nose and I grimaced. God, that was foul.

"That little bastard crapped on me!" Gavin yelled. Sure enough, the smell came from greenish-purple goo spattered across his right leg from the knee down and the top of his shoe.

"You deserved it." Mai folded her arms and glared at him. "You manhandled him and you deserved it."

"Few people deserve to be shit on by a monkey..." Rafe said, "but you're one of them, Gavin."

"Hey, dog breath, blow it out your ass with a brass tuba."

Satan's sizzling goat balls, I just couldn't stand it anymore.

"Gavin," I snapped, "leave Mai's pets alone or next time I'll let them eat you. Mai, stick to furry monsters with a sunnier disposition, will you? Cut me some slack here people. I'm out of antacid."

I'd just finished shooing everyone (except Gavin, who had to go change his pants) back to the movie still sending out scary music, groans, screams and the occasional gunshot when Jake walked up to me. I'd never seen him look more serious, and my stomach did a slow twist and flop in my gut.

"Captain Walker," he said. "I need to talk with you. Immediately."

Formal again. Before I could say anything, he turned and headed down the hall leading to the kitchen and the back deck. I followed behind, my stomach feeling as though it were a water balloon sloshing acid from side to side. Outside, the air held a touch of fading winter bite. I shivered and heated the air around my skin. I hated the cold.

Jake started to walk, and I fell into step beside him. The suspense shredded my nerves like a cheese grater. I had to chew on the inside of my cheek to hold a flurry of questions in check.

We walked down toward the large garage bays on the west side of the compound. The buildings were locked up tight and the windows dark. I thought he might want to review the Bradley's combat readiness, but he walked on past the buildings, toward the hangar where Chilly Willie the V22 Osprey lived. The sight of the hangar made me frown. We were still paying back the loan on the hangar's construction. The Osprey we didn't even own—we rented it month to month from the Hellfrost Merc Group.

I couldn't stand it anymore. I pulled up short and turned toward him. "What the hell's this all about?"

He hesitated and stared off at the hangar. "Can we use that Osprey in an assault?"

"Not unless you want to take your life in your hands. We don't have a mechanic. Haven't had one for six months since Merkle went crazy. Certifiable crazy, not just the normal crazy you see around here."

Jake didn't laugh, which bothered me more than a little. "Do I even want to know?"

I waved a dismissive hand. "Convinced he was secret royalty. Believed his parents were killed by an evil sorcerer. Gave his two weeks and went trekking off to find some Object of Power."

"You still have a pilot though?"

"Gavin has his wings and he's fully certified on it. Hanzo could copilot in a pinch, but that leaves us short a medic."

"Do you take heavy losses on operations?"

"I've never lost anybody in four years. Before I took over as captain, we lost a few. One time an ogre ended up head-shot with an antitank missile on an op in west L.A. Why? What's this all about?"

Jake glanced at me again but ignored my questions. "An ogre?"

"He was a real hard charger. Not exactly housebroken, but he was highly skilled at opening jars with stuck lids and killing weird bugs. It was a shame, but shit happens."

"Yeah." Another hesitation. "You guys are seriously understaffed. I just wondered about the churn."

"You brought me out here to talk about turnover? I wasn't born with a lot of patience, Jake, so why don't you tell me the real reason we're out here? Who called you?"

Again, he didn't answer right away, but instead stared back at the house. I felt a scream of frustration building while alarm bells and air-raid sirens sang "Apocalypse in D Minor" inside my head. My teeth clamped together so hard my jaw muscles started to ache. If he were just trying to fucking manipulate me...

"Orders from Homeland Security," he said. "I just got the call. We go live tomorrow with the assault."

"And you didn't tell me that *first*?" Goddamn it. I knew I'd been wrong to let him slobber all over me in the shooting range. Men. You give them an inch and they break the goddamn ruler.

He shrugged, and I could've happily kicked him in the shin. "I needed to gather my thoughts."

"Must have been a daunting prospect. So don't stop now. Give me details."

"The Oregon State Police, under orders from the Governor and backed up by a National Guard unit, stopped a semi-trailer on I-84 headed toward Boise. The truck had come from the Bokor Gelzonbi Foods plant. The Department of Defense and DHS decided to move on it. The truck and driver were quarantined for possible exposure to RCTs. The CDC's onsite lab tests determined the powdered gelatin had traces of human DNA—maybe some zombie fell into the machinery, or maybe something else. Word just came down the pipe to DHS to terminate this problem before a nationwide recall of every box of gelatin hits stores and further undermines consumer trust in the Food and Drug Administration."

Ugh. Chalk up lime-gelatin shooters as something else I'd never look at the same way again. "And our orders?"

"We're to deploy tomorrow and neutralize their production

capability, exterminate all zombies, and kill or capture Necromancer Jeremiah Hansen. I didn't say anything inside because I wanted to set it up with you. Let you drive the pre-op briefings and be the front man on this."

"Mighty kind of you. Since I *am* the front woman on this." I paced back and forth, thoughts flashing through my mind like lightning. "I'll need a check on the Bradley first thing tomorrow morning. Same with the equipment and ammo. Also, we'll have to settle on the best assault plan based on recent satellite photos and new estimates on the number of hostiles." I looked at him again. "I want to call in Sarge on this and sit down to review our operation plan. Will we have a real-time satellite lookdown during the op?"

"Not real time, but a spy sat passes over the plant tomorrow morning and the NSA has orders to send over the images."

"It'll have to be good enough. I want nothing left to chance. This goes off flawlessly."

"That's why I'm here," he said, nodding. "To make sure it happens with perfection."

I stopped and looked at him. "I'm sure you didn't mean to sound as arrogant as you just did."

He only smiled. "You guys weren't half-bad before I got here. Now you're better."

"Not half-bad, eh? Damning with faint praise, are you?" I could feel anger start to smolder.

He shrugged and seemed a little confused by my building anger. "You aren't quiet professionals. But not many are."

"You do this shit on purpose, don't you? Again you're implying my people are half-assers. Not like the big bad Special Forces cowboys. *They're* consummate professionals."

"How come every time I talk to you, the words come out wrong?"

"Oh, I don't know. Maybe because you're choosing the *wrong words*? No, that can't be it."

He took a deep breath. "You're protective of your people. I admire that."

I opened my mouth to give a smart-ass answer and managed to bite it back. Barely. Using sheer unadulterated-steel willpower. Silence was the only way I'd avoid a stream of colorful profanity.

Jake looked out at the sprawling city lights. "It's hard, isn't it? Leading people. Being the one in charge, responsible for everything."

I stared at the outline of his face against the harsh white glow of the halogen security lights and still didn't answer.

"For me," he said, "every time I've got people in a firefight, it's like my heart's in my mouth and if I dare bite down I'll bite right through it. All of them counting on me to make the right choice. Depending on me to get them home again."

I touched his arm, my fingers on his skin. He glanced at me, smiled and shook his head.

"Your skin is so warm," he said. "The second thing I noticed about you."

I bit off a snide quip before it could escape my mouth. After a moment I settled on something nonchalant, though I could feel my pulse beating so hard I could've tap danced to it. "What was the first thing?"

He laughed and shook his head again. I started to draw my hand away, but he reached out and caught it with one of his. And I let him.

"I know you see me as an unwanted complication. A problem, maybe even a threat. Perhaps I deserve it, the way DHS dumped me onto your team. But you need to know, I want this mission to succeed. I'll do whatever I have to. I'm not here to make your life difficult, Andrea."

Why was it when he said my name, my heart began to beat harder? Look at the hardcore mercenary captain now. One romantic starlit walk down to the aircraft hangars and she turned into a great big sentimental soft-serve ice-cream cone.

And then she referred to herself in the third person. I laughed aloud at my own joke. He cocked his head, a quirk of a smile still on his lips and a question in his eyes.

I withdrew my hand from his and waved his unasked question off. “Nothing. Just the voices in my head.”

“You hear voices?”

“Let’s not talk about them now. It feeds their ego.”

He looked at me as if uncertain how serious I was.

“Oh, for God’s sake, I’m kidding,” I said. “You’re killing my routine.”

His face grew grim. “Then I apologize for saving the world from your comedy.”

I laughed, and he grinned. A gentle quiet fell between us. I shifted, trying to find something useful for my hands to do.

“All right,” I finally said. “No more sniping over who’s the better soldier. Let’s declare a fresh ceasefire since we have more important things to go over. Seeing this mission safely in the bag, for one.”

He nodded once. “Let’s get it on.”

“I hope you mean that figuratively because I’m busy right now planning to stave off a zombie uprising.”

“Pencil me in for later, then.” He grinned again, but it seemed more reflex than anything, as if his mind had already turned to the mission, where mine should’ve been. “I’ll go set up in the conference room. Bring Sarge and we’ll plan how to save the world.”

He turned and hurried toward the house. I didn’t follow, not yet, instead watching him go. I could feel the frown on my face, feel the groaning ache of a tension headache beginning behind my eyes. His words on leadership...well, they’d struck a chord with me, but I didn’t have time for Captain Sanders, dammit.

Tomorrow this ended, one way or another.

Chapter Fourteen: All Zombies Must Die!

Mercenary Wing Rv6-4 "Zero Dogs"
Bokor Gelzonbi Manufacturing Facility
SE Holgate Boulevard, Portland, Oregon
1110 Hours PST April 16th

Go time.

The Bradley Fighting Vehicle raced down the street toward the Bokor Gelzonbi factory, engine roaring and our banner fluttering in the wind. The only thing missing was a bugle sounding *charge* or maybe "Ride of the Valkyries" theme music, although Mussorgsky's "Night on Bald Mountain" might've fit the Zero Dogs better.

"Objective in sight," Gavin said over the com. "Hold on to your pantyhose. We're going in."

No fence surrounded the factory, which boded well for the speed of our initial assault. The building stretched across a wide lot, two stories high in back, with white outer walls topped by black metal awnings. Large glass windows wrapped around the entire front side, and the street-facing grounds had been landscaped with well-manicured grass, bushes and evergreen trees. The loading dock dominated the building's back end, which was a massive two-story rectangle of white cinderblock broken only by a few narrow reinforced windows and two diamond-plate stairwells that lead to swipe-card-controlled steel doors.

Last night Jake, Sarge and I had narrowed it down to two plans. In the first plan we blew a mousehole in the west side of the building—an expanse of wall with no windows—drove the Bradley through and deployed, repeating the tactics used in our last major assault. The second plan involved using the Bradley as heavy fire support and zombie suppression while the team penetrated the factory, hunted down Necromancer Hansen and destroyed the zombies. We'd settled on option two because I didn't want the Bradley tied down and unable to provide rapid-fire support or facilitate a rapid retreat, should the situation demand it.

"Lock and load, people," I said. "Weapons tight until we get inside. Let's get this done and go for ice cream."

"Roger that," Sarge said, and a chorus of affirmatives echoed through my headset.

The building appeared empty. No sign of hostiles on the rooftop or at the doors. Only one car sat in the lot—a high-end Audi. A huge yellow school bus was parked at the opposite end of the building.

The Bradley roared toward the factory. I braced myself in the commander position atop the turret, hatch open, wind on my face and a smear of dead bug on my visor. We jumped a curb, crushed a shrub and approached at an angle to the loading bays. Twenty feet from the wall, Gavin turned us so the Bradley's backend faced the building. The turret swiveled to cover the steel bay doors.

Sarge slammed down the ramp and charged onto the asphalt, his Heckler & Koch MP10 submachine gun locked against his shoulder. He swept the parking lot with the barrel as he advanced. He ran slightly hunched over, looking like a tank with a very tiny gun, though I knew he'd chosen the weapon for its minimal recoil and almost nonexistent barrel climb. In other words, it'd be excellent for headshots in close-quarters battle. Rafe loped along behind him, already in werewolf form, followed by Jake and Mai with a horde of ferrets surging around her ankles. I swapped helmets, climbed out of the turret and hopped off the backend. The ramp clanged under my boots. Hanzo came up beside me, dressed all in black with a red cross on his chest. He gripped his katana in one hand, and his healing aura flared in a sapphire nimbus around the other hand.

"Kill 'em all, Captain!" Tiffany yelled over the com. I found it a little startling to hear such a sultry voice, a voice made to purr in the sunlight and sigh in the moonlight, say something as unsexy as *kill 'em all.* Kind of like having the soothing voice of the GPS computer in a car say, "You drive like an asshole. Have a nice day."

I glanced over my shoulder in time to see Tiffany give me a thumbs-up from inside the Bradley. She raised the ramp, and the Bradley sat buttoned up tight, our ace in the hole against the zombie zerg. A moment later the turret turned and the barrel of the chain gun pointed toward the door we planned to breach. Tiffany was on the guns instead of scouting since Hanzo had deployed with us. While we didn't need a ninja (or even a delusional ninja-wannabe), we very well might need a medic.

We advanced toward the building in a line, Sarge on point, followed by Jake, me, Rafe, Hanzo and Mai with her horde of pets, each of us covering our Area of Responsibility, searching for hostile targets. Once I had to grit my teeth against skeeving out when Mai's carpet of blue and silver ferret-looking creatures brushed my shins. Mai pulled them back with a gesture so none of us accidentally stepped on one of the things with their too-large eyes and twitching pink noses.

We reached the building and stacked up single file against the wall. Sarge had the entry covered with his MP10, Jake covered the front of the team with his pistol and shielding, and because the rest of the team lacked ranged offensive power, I covered the rear sector. I focused on controlling my breathing, keeping my heart rate slow and steady, even as adrenaline sizzled through my veins. As much as part of me hated the risk to my people, especially on entry when we'd all be charging through the death funnel at the doorway, another part of me loved this shit. Wallowed in the rush. Reveled in the stark challenge of life and instant death.

The steel access door stood at the top of a concrete incline, next to a battered loading bay door and a section of black railing. Sarge hurried up the ramp, and the rest of us followed close behind. No muzzle sweeping of friendly targets. We moved nice and tight. Even Mai's pets stayed out from underfoot and made no sound.

Sarge signaled us to halt at the top of the ramp, and we took up defensive positions. He swung past the closed door to the opposite side of the threshold. Jake took the other side, with me pressed close beside him, a hand on his shoulder and the rest of the team parallel to the wall behind me.

Sarge slung his MP10 and faced the door. For a moment nothing visible happened, but I sensed the crackle of raw energy as he summoned spell fuel. He reached out with his index finger and began to trace a design on the gray steel door. Power hummed in the air. Where he touched the metal with his finger, dark purple lines etched deep into the steel, glowing with faint light and giving off wisps of black smoke.

Jake and I covered Sarge while he worked the spell, and Hanzo and Mai covered sectors facing out into the empty parking lot, giving us one hundred eighty degrees of cover with the wall at our backs. The spell design took less than ten seconds to complete, and when finished, resembled a group of sharp-angled hieroglyphs bordering the edge of a circle. Lines of power, still glowing purple, radiated from its center, and smoke curled from several places.

"Fire in the hole!" Sarge pressed back against the wall, unslinging his MP10 again.

The spell-drawing glowed brighter and the hum intensified, revving up to a jet-engine scream. The door imploded, crumpling like aluminum foil with a wretched screech that made my ears want to do a double Van Gogh and cut themselves off. A drift of sparks fell to the concrete like cherry blossoms on fire. A basketball-sized chunk of metal hit the floor with a *clunk*. The air smelled as if somebody had stuck a hot straightening iron into a bucket of molasses.

My turn. I conjured my own spell, forging highly flammable vapor into—

"Dammit, Rafe," I snapped. "Stop panting down my vest with your dog breath."

"Sorry, Captain." It could be a challenge to understand Rafe in werewolf form, with all the growls and howls and such, but no one could miss those sad puppy-dog eyes.

A hungry, curious moan echoed from inside the dock. Shit, no time to waste.

I super-condensed the concentrated sphere of magefire and lobbed it into the open doorway. "One, two, three! Cover!"

Everyone turned away and shielded their eyes. The ball of magefire exploded in a dazzling burst of light brighter than three flash bangs, but without the concussive effect. "Go, go, *go!*" I yelled.

During an assault, the doorway was known as the fatal funnel—the chokepoint where the incoming team had the greatest chance of taking fire. We'd trained around Jake's skills, and point, or number-one status, switched to him. He pushed straight into the room with the shimmer of his barrier curved out in front of him. Sarge swept around the threshold and moved to the right, clearing the hard corner. I moved through and to the left as soon as he vacated the doorway. The flat report of pistol shots rang out, followed by the single-shot pop of the MP10 on semi-auto. I flinched a little at the first shot, but I didn't glance outside my tight AOR, which was the hard corner to the left. A blood-spattered male zombie staggered and bumped against the wall in my sector, blinded by my flash spell. I cut loose with a stream of fire, slamming the zombie off the cinderblock wall with the force of the magefire. I swept back, searching for new targets to engage as Sarge and I ran the walls.

The rest of the team cleared the entryway. A brief, violent cacophony of gunshots filled the air, mixed with surprised moans and crackling flames. The dock stank like charred bacon and decaying flesh.

Nine zombie corpses lay strewn about the cement floor, most with neat headshots. One still smoldered in a haze of greasy black smoke, my doing. Two had been torn to pieces by Rafe's teeth and claws, and Sarge swept along behind him, putting bullets through the skulls of the chewed undead. One shot, one kill, and making sure dead stayed dead.

A stumbling mass of fur moaned piteously in the far corner, near a forklift flipped on its side. It took me a moment to recognize a zombie beneath the full assault of Mai's ferret horde. The ferrets seemed to drool some kind of corrosive saliva, because the zombie began to smoke and dissolve, filling the air with the smell of burned hotdogs. The loading dock's aroma-fest of meat dishes was enough to make a person a born-again vegetarian.

"Clear!" Jake called out.

"Clear!" I answered, and the rest of the Zero Dogs rattled off the status of their sectors, all clear. An ominous quiet descended in the wake of the shooting fury.

The loading dock was perhaps a hundred feet long by a hundred and fifty feet wide. Stacks of pallets leaned against the far wall. Several pushcarts had piles of what looked like thin, flat squares of meat on them. I tried not to imagine what that meat might be. Three large metal bins sat near a huge roll of plastic wrap and a neon green pallet jack. Scarred stripes of red tape marked the cement. Clipboards hung from screws in the cinderblock, next to the chains of the loading bay doors. Another zombie floundered out of a small receiving office and wobbled toward us in a drunken zigzag.

A shot cracked through the air, followed by the chime of a brass shell casing bouncing off the cement. Jake dropped the last zombie with a perfect shot—center of forehead at sixty feet, be still my beating heart. My ears were still ringing from the gunfire. Spent shell casings littered the floor like gun-battle confetti.

A wide blue internal roll-down door sealed off the loading dock from the shipping warehouse and manufacturing floor. We stacked again and approached it. Jake took point, leading with the shimmer of his barrier in front and his pistol out as he swept hazard spots and obstacles. Sarge followed on his right, sweeping the cone of his sector, and I had Jake's left side. Heat distortion warped the air around me. Rafe brought up the center. Congealed zombie blood stained his fur up to his elbows, a stark reminder that watching a werewolf attack was not for the faint of heart. Mai followed Rafe with her carpet of ferrets undulating along the cement beside her. Hanzo brought up the rear with his katana. He had his ninja mask up and all I could see were his eyes—the exultant, shining eyes of a teenager who had just *borrowed* the keys to the Corvette.

The roll door whirred upward when we drew close, triggered by a motion sensor. Our team pushed beyond the loading dock into a warehouse filled with shelves of gelatin boxes. Ready-to-ship plastic-wrapped pallets of gelatin boxes sat in rows near the dock entrance.

A skinny zombie with serious decay issues slumped behind a gray metal desk and stared at the psychedelic screen saver on a computer monitor. His bloodshot eyes rolled in their sockets and locked onto Jake. The zombie began to stand, gnashing his teeth. Jake dropped him with a single shot. The zombie fell back into the swivel chair, head thrown back, just another rotting worker sleeping through his shift and never mind the brain splatter on the wall.

Two female zombies stared at us with dull, dead eyes. Foamy saliva ran down their chins. They lurched toward us, moaning with an eagerness I always found disturbing.

"I got 'em," I said. "Going hot."

Mai and Rafe knew enough to give me space. Hanging too close to a pyromancer could result in singed fur and eyebrows. I conjured magefire and cut loose, sending a thick stream of flames roaring across the warehouse into the closest zombie, knocking it back into the second RCT. They burned like kerosene-soaked sausages in the seventh circle of Hell. I would've felt terrible about scorching them had they been living, sentient beings who could feel pain. Zombies didn't count, because A) They were already dead and B) They tended to eat people. I was all for alternate lifestyles, but I drew the line at cannibalism.

Evidently there'd been no smoke detectors on the dock, but here the sprinkler system went off, spraying down sheets of water. A shrill alarm blared. The sound stabbed in my ear like an ice pick, making me want to duct tape a pillow over my head to drown it out. In no time we were soaked.

"Nice one, Captain," Rafe growled. Water streamed off his fur, and he looked both wet and miserable.

"It's only a little mist." I laughed to show how little I minded the water, but nobody joined me. Ingrates. I could burn right through the spray if necessary, but doing so would make a lot of steam and visibility would suffer. "All right, enough playing in the sprinklers. Move out."

We'd barely started to advance when the water shut off all at once—an eerie event, because the necromancer had to be behind it. Zombies wouldn't turn off a sprinkler system unless directed to do so. Which meant someone watched us. I searched for spell traps, but didn't see any—which made me more nervous, not less.

"Cameras." Mai pointed to dark hemispheres mounted on long poles dropping down from the ceiling.

"Fry 'em," I said.

Sarge began to put neat three-shot groupings into each camera housing. Bits of plastic rained down like polycarbonate tears from the gods. No more visuals for the bad guys. The only things I wanted Necromancer Hansen to hear were Rafe's bad table manners, Mai's squeaking ferrets and our gunshots getting closer and closer as we dropped, dissolved and chewed our way through his zombies.

"All right, move out," I ordered. "Keep frosty. Keep moving. Clear those corners, people."

We advanced again, moving out of shipping onto the manufacturing floor, headed toward the door that, according to the blueprints, led to the front offices. Huge, mysterious stainless-steel machines loomed on either side, fed by pipes and conveyors and wiring. Zombies worked the machines, maybe twenty RCTs total. They turned toward us, sniffing the air. One short zombie in black socks and sandals took a step toward us, slipped on the water pooling on the tile and slid into a support column. Jake and Sarge began to shoot, dropping the undead with a merciless precision almost frightening to behold. Rafe charged at a cluster of zombies in his AOR, and Mai sent her alien ferrets to support him. A fat male zombie wearing a tiny yellow bib with a lobster on it came at me, pinching his fingers to thumbs as if he had lobster claws.

I incinerated his head for him.

The fight was brutal but short. We burned, shredded and shot our way through them until the bodies of the re-killed undead littered the floor in every direction. Sarge and Jake switched out clips with mechanical precision. I had to once again admit we were pretty damn Sierra Hotel badass.

"All right, nice work," I said. "Form up and let's tear this place apart. I want to be home in time for dinner. And who's up for Jell-O shots?"

The resounding silence told me no one was. I smiled anyway.

Spoilsports.

Chapter Fifteen: Executive-esque Decisions

Undead Army of the Unrighteous Order of the Falling Dark
Office of the Zombie Overlord
SE Holgate Boulevard, Portland, Oregon
11:28 a.m. PST April 16th

General Manager slash CEO slash CFO of Bokor Gelzonbi Foods Jeremiah Hansen sat in his leather executive chair, leaning forward, elbows on his knees and his hands steepled in front of his face as he watched the video monitors. The invaders had just destroyed most of the cameras, but as part of the security apparatus, he'd paid a huge chunk of change to have hidden fiberoptic cameras installed, so he still had a decent view of the carnage on the manufacturing floor. His zombies hadn't exactly shown Viking berserker fury in destroying these intruders. In fact, his zombie security team on the dock hadn't shown much competence at all. Yet, Jeremiah still held a few unplayed cards...

He used the silver cord connection to direct another group of zombies into the fray. Every time those soldiers out there terminated a zombie, the severed cord snapped back to him. It didn't hurt, but his collection of cut puppetmaster strings had started to grow at an alarming rate. This would be a nightmare of costs and equipment loss, not to mention the havoc it'd play with the schedule. The water damage would be atrocious. God, the *costs*. He didn't even want to think about what the water had done to his batches of gelatin, to say nothing of the stuff already boxed up and waiting to be shipped.

Son of a bitch.

He knew those soldiers, whoever they were, wanted him and probably wanted him dead. They'd been cutting their way through his zombies toward the offices since they'd blown their way in. His throat clamped so tight it felt as if somebody had wrapped a tourniquet around his neck. Still, he wouldn't flee, pissing his pants and running away from the first serious fight of his career. Not yet, anyway. Necromancers were known for bringing the devious and bringing it by the bucket load.

Blake walked into the office. He halted in front of Jeremiah's desk and consulted his PDA. "We're being attacked by a mercenary team. They're part of the Hellfrost Group. A source of mine indicated they're acting on behalf of the Federal Government. Most likely the Department of Defense or Homeland Security."

How the hell had Blake found that out? He opened his mouth to ask, but stopped himself. It didn't matter. That was the kind of shit he paid Blake for anyway. Of course it would've been nice to have some actual *notice* they were going to be attacked.

Jeremiah turned back to the monitors. "Looks like they have a six-foot dog eating my zombies. And a horde of weasels or...something. Not to mention the demon. And...is that a ninja?"

"These mercenary teams are often a conglomerate of differing creatures. Their diversity is their greatest strength."

"That's encouraging, since we only have zombies." Whose idea had it been to forego the sex ninjas? Oh yeah. Blake's. Disciplinary action might be in order. Disciplinary action with extreme prejudice.

A burst of flames filled the view from one camera, turning the image bright white for a long moment. When the camera lens recovered from the flare, he saw the fire had come from the hands of a woman—and he'd bet two hundred zombie foreskins, a prime currency during Biblical times, that she hid a great shape under all that assault armor. He moved his wireless mouse, clicking and dragging a box, zooming in on her.

He was right. Her face was pretty, even if it didn't quite reach the level of angelic beauty—especially since she happened to be soaking wet and kept baring her teeth like a wolf. Her eyes though...he had a thing for women who could do a hard-ass stare. Dirty Harry with tatas. Yeah, that flipped a few of his switches, big time.

"Who *is* that woman?" he asked, right before she turned toward another group of zombies and thrust out her hand. A stream of fire shot out and engulfed them and a few more severed cords snapped back to him. Damn. Really fucking cool. "How does she do that?"

"I don't have that information...yet. She appears to be some kind of fire mage." Blake did inscrutable things on his PDA screen with his stylus. "Pyromancers construct a kind of flammable energy they can manipulate by a version of telekinesis. They ignite the substance—"

"Yeah, that's great," he said, staring at her. God, she was awesome. Of course she'd come here to kill him, which put a bit of a damper on his hard-on.

He zoomed the camera out again, and then closed his eyes and directed another horde of zombies to their position. "Too bad they didn't try and come in through the ventilation ducts..."

He hadn't expected a full-out assault without a probe or infiltration of some sort. That broke the rules in a most egregious way. It also might've been nice to have some crushing walls right about now. Maybe a collapsing floor booby trap. Or a Tyrannosaurus Rex with an antitank gun mounted on its head.

Blake moved around the desk and glanced from monitor to monitor. "Mmm. They do seem extremely competent." He sighed. "This was not unforeseen, but still, our insurance policy doesn't cover mercenary assaults. We'll need more undead assets to replace our losses. The water damage from the sprinklers will be horrendous. Assuming that, with the sprinklers down, the plant doesn't burn to the ground during our altercation."

"Don't worry," Jeremiah said. "We can rebuild—bigger, better, faster, and with an arcade. As for them..." he waved a hand at the screen, "...I have a surprise."

Blake Delany turned to look at him. Jeremiah smiled, and with one click of his wireless mouse, killed all the lights.

"I hope they can glow in the dark."

Chapter Sixteen:
A Bridge So Not Far Enough

Mercenary Wing Rv6-4 "Zero Dogs"
Bokor Gelzonbi Foods
Manufacturing floor
1134 Hours PST April 16th

"Steady, Zero Dogs," I said over the comlink. "Nobody's afraid of the dark."

"Gavin is," Rafe volunteered, a little off mike because his com headset hung battered and askew on his werewolf head. He went through headsets at a dismaying rate, as fast as tissues during hay-fever season.

"I heard that, you mange-riddled flea-circus freak show."

"Keep this channel clear," Sarge said, thunder in his voice.

The darkness wasn't total. A dingy, weak light filtered in through a few soaped-over windows. Moans echoed all around us. The shuffle of feet dragging on concrete drifted down the rows between storage shelves. Sarge clicked on his MP10's flashlight. Jake turned on his pistol's laser sight. I lit the cardboard in the metal recycling bin on fire. Smoke billowed out and coiled along the roof, but the flames threw almost as much light as the grimy windows.

The zombie horde attacked, pouring through two double doors onto the manufacturing floor and slouching out of the rows of damp, ready-to-ship product. More zombies appeared behind us, lurching in from the direction of the loading dock. We tightened formation and faced outward at every approaching threat. Outside, the chain gun began to spit 25mm ammo in sharp, loud bursts.

Shit. What was Gavin up against? We couldn't risk getting cut off from our rolling armor. I lobbed two firebombs at the horde before I backed off and keyed the mike. "Gavin. What's your status, over?"

"A couple of zombies came out a side door, sniffing around. We Swiss cheesed 'em. What's your status, over?"

"We're busy. Out." Damn, was the necromancer already scouting our positions? Did we miss a camera?

Sarge changed out clips and opened fire on single shot, dropping zombies by the score. More RCTs filed in, some of them tripping over the felled zombies, making an absolute marching disaster fresh out of a Keystone Cops film.

Jake held out a hand. His brow furrowed, and the muscles in his arms stood out rock hard. A slight shimmer appeared in the air at the double doorway leading into the manufacturing floor. The advancing zombies ran face first into an invisible barrier. Some of them hit so hard they broke noses and damaged dental work. A few of the undead seemed to catch on and started to pound on the barrier with their fists.

Mai swept a hand at the zombies closing in from behind. Her corrosive-drool ferrets raced off like a chittering bear rug and began to piranha zombies down. I sent arcs of fire snaking across the warehouse, lashing them against the zombies coming out of the stacks. If any burning zombie got too close before being consumed, Hanzo would leap forward and hack off its flaming head with a sweep of his katana. The air stank of burning hair, smokeless powder, and, God help us all, fried pork skins.

"I can't hold them forever." Sweat beaded on Jake's forehead and his arm started to waver. More and more zombies hammered at his barrier.

I scanned for our objective in the dim light while the Zero Dogs wailed on the zombies. *There.* The gray metal door leading into the front office area. A red light in an iron cage flashed above the doorjamb, casting bloody light across a half dozen safety signs tacked to the wall. *Eye protection required beyond this point. Hairnet and gown required on manufacturing floor.* A sign that warned people if they stole a fellow employee's lunch, they'd be banned from the break room for the length of their employment.

"Zero Dogs, follow me!" I shouted over the gunfire and moans. "We're late for our status meeting!"

We withdrew in formation toward the door, but as we did, Jake's barrier started to falter. Zombies pushed past its edges, only to be dropped by headshots. Rafe ripped into any zombies who closed with us, showing what savagery and canines could do against walking corpses.

I reached the door first and yanked on the handle, but it didn't budge. "Sarge! Door!"

He slung the MP10 and began to work the same breach spell he'd used before. I backed up to give him room and covered him.

"Barrier's down." Jake sagged against a snaking metal track of rollers—some kind of treadmill designed for sliding things along. His face streamed with sweat and his breath rasped in and out of his mouth.

The zombies flooded into the gloom, spreading out as they advanced, forming a wall of rotting flesh. Mai pointed, directing her ferrets to attack, but I raised a hand and she called them off. I concentrated, fighting off the weariness seeping into my muscles like acid eating away my strength. I sent a wall of flames blazing along the floor. Steam hissed upward from the wet tile. Bright orange-red firelight painted everything and threw dancing shadows along the walls and the steel roof beams. The zombies threw up their arms to shield their faces from the heat while they moaned in dismay. More zombies crashed into them from behind, shoving them forward into the fire. The rest of the zombie horde marched over the top of its burning front line and continued toward us undeterred.

"*Shit.* Hurry up, Sarge."

"Got it."

The door imploded with a grinding shriek and more sparks cascaded down like handfuls of burning tic tacs. The fluorescent panel lights were on in the hallway and cold white light poured out around us into the shipping area. Sarge lifted his MP10, squatted down and used a mirror to peek around the corner. "Clear."

Jake slapped another clip in his pistol and chambered a round. He began to pick off zombies with headshots as they closed in. Mai had pulled the ferrets back in a loose arc around us. One of them perched on Rafe's wolf head, squeaking at the zombies.

I closed my eyes for a second, fighting to recall the plant's layout, a memory which felt fish-slippery in my mind. My brief exhilaration had fled and left a gaping hole inside me—a hole filled with rising dread. We'd already downed over a hundred zombies, but they kept on coming. Jake's intel had put the number of RCTs at around a hundred, tops. Even allowing for a few truckloads of undead reinforcements, we seemed to face overwhelming numbers. Some Intel bastard had fucked up big time. I didn't know why I felt surprised. Bad intel was business as usual for war fighters.

No choice but to push on and fight our way out. Sarge went first, hunkered down but moving with quick steps into the hall. The MP10 looked like a toy in his large hands. I followed him, resting a hand on his shoulder, ready to sling fire.

Mai hurried behind me with Hanzo at her side and the swarm of ferrets lined against the far wall to avoid our boots. "That's a lot of zombies," she whispered, glancing behind her.

Hanzo leaned one arm against the wall. Gloopy zombie

blood smeared along the katana's blade. "The undead don't seem to fear ninjas."

A loud metallic crash shook the walls and made me flinch. Several more crashing and smashing sounds came from behind us inside the factory, followed by a flurry of pistol shots. Rafe jumped through the doorway and into the hall with us. Blood spattered his muzzle and beaded on his gray fur.

"Where's Captain Sanders?" Panic flared inside me with a white-hot fire of its own.

"Here." Jake stepped into the hall, reloading yet again. "Rafe tipped a few of those shelves over. Should slow them, but not for long."

No time to wallow in relief seeing him safe and sound. We still had a paycheck to earn. I moved back to the doorway and peered into the firelight, smoke and gloom. Toppled shelving had crushed several zombies in a tangle of steel struts, wooden shelves and boxes of gelatin. More zombies climbed over the shelves toward me, hunched and scrambling in jerky motions like spiders dying from pesticide. I glanced at what I had to work with for fuel, and then lit the closest shelves on fire. Hopefully it would make them hesitate...if they just didn't push each other through the flames like before.

I spun back to my team. "Stack up and move out."

We advanced up the hall in formation and pushed into the cubicle farm in the main office. Sounds had a muffled, flat quality—as if the atmosphere of violence, suffocating dread and flagrant Human Resources abuses smothered the sound waves. I could barely hear the moans behind us or the angry crackle and roar of the fire. Blinking lights flashed on a phone at the nearest cubicle—messages that would never be answered. A fluorescent light flickered and buzzed, one end of the tube swirling with what looked like gaseous light.

"I smell dead people," Rafe said, and punctuated his sentence with a growl—an idling chainsaw rumble able to lift the hair on anything alive.

I tried to will my heartbeat to slow but had no luck. This room was a nightmare of blind spots and far too many places to hide. "Keep sharp. Clear the area and lock it down."

We moved deeper into the cube farm, tightening up while still maintaining our formation and fields of fire.

A man stepped into view at the far office, across the maze of cubicles. He stood in a rectangular window with the vertical blinds drawn up and stared at me with open curiosity. Necromancer Jeremiah Hansen. I recognized his dark goatee and meaty face from the dossier photo and briefings. With his slacks, white dress shirt and askew tie, he better resembled a young, slightly frazzled accountant than a dedicated force for evil.

"Primary target at eleven o'clock!" I yelled, pointing. "Drop him!"

Jake and Sarge opened fire. 9mm and 10mm rounds ripped into the glass and left a cluster of white craters, but the window didn't shatter. Fifteen or so shots grouped around his head and chest in big, milky blotches. Bullet-resistant glass. Too much for the caliber of bullets we had on hand. The man hadn't even flinched.

Jeremiah stepped to the side of the marred section of glass and looked right at me again. He shrugged and smiled. The look on his face seemed more *Isn't this just one of those completely FUBAR Mondays at the office?* and not *Die, you mercenary scum!*

For a long moment nobody moved. The quiet descended in a soundless snowfall.

A cubical wall toppled over with a bang and a thud. Hungry, pained moaning filled the air in surround sound. Zombies staggered to their feet, rising off the floor, falling out of the supply closets, climbing from beneath cubicle desks, pouring out of the conference room until the office swarmed with enough zombies to rival Walmart on Black Friday. They started toward us in a shuffling mass. The necromancer had held them back, waiting to spring this trap. More moaning echoed down the hall behind us, growing louder and closer—the second horde, sealing off our escape.

Oh shit.

I keyed the mike. "Zero Dogs, we're buggin' out! Fall back in defensive formation to the reception area. Bring the Bradley around front. *Now!*"

Sarge and Jake opened fire as we retreated. Jake had his free hand thrust out, fingers splayed, as he swung one of his barriers around and slammed it into the undead, hammering them back. Zombies appeared behind us in the hall. Rafe turned and leapt at them, slashing and tearing with jaws and claws. He seized one zombie and hurled it into the drywall so hard I heard bones shatter and studs crack twenty feet away. More zombies pressed in around him, grabbing and biting, but he shrugged off their attacks, ignoring the damage.

The necromancer still watched us through the bullet-riddled glass. Another man, cadaverous-looking, with slicked back hair and cold, dark eyes, leaned in close to the necromancer and said something in his ear. The necromancer nodded and stepped away from the window.

Dammit.

The office had filled with a nightmare blitz of sound—gunshots, moans, collapsing cubical walls and toppling file cabinets, Rafe ripping things apart, and wild, frenzied ferret chittering. My breath rasped in and out of my mouth as if I'd just sprinted a mile, and my tongue felt like a dry lakebed. Several of the overhead panel lights flickered and buzzed, giving part of the huge room a frenetic twitch between gloom and harsh light.

Zombies dropped left and right, but more kept coming as we retreated toward the reception area. I caught sight of the Bradley through the windows. It sped around the corner and jumped the curb. The treads shredded tracks through the grass and shrubs as Gavin raced toward the front doors.

"Short on ammo." Sarge slapped another clip into the

submachine gun and pulled back the bolt.

Mai sent her ferrets on sweeping sorties against the oncoming zombie tide. The zombies began falling on the demon-ferrets and trying to eat them. Soon our right flank became a chaotic, tumbling and writhing mass of teeth, claws and smoking flesh dissolved by acidic ferret drool. Mai Tanaka's eyes blazed with the fury of an akuma straight out of myth.

Two zombies pushed over another cubicle wall and lunged toward Hanzo. He slashed with the katana and severed the head of a female zombie wearing spandex and a mud-stained bike helmet. The zombie head rolled along the carpet and came to rest next to a paper recycle bin. Her gaze remained locked on Hanzo and her teeth gnashed together.

The second zombie closed on Hanzo too quickly, forcing him to stab with the katana instead of slash, and he ran the blade through its body. The zombie, dressed like a hospital orderly, pulled itself forward along the blade with its jaws gaping to take a chunk out of Hanzo's neck. Hanzo struggled with it, cursing. I lifted my hand to risk a fire spell but a group of Mai's ferrets swarmed over the zombie and stripped it down to the bone.

Shit. Shit. *Shit.* I lanced out with precise streams of fire but couldn't cut loose until we were ready to exit, and the relentless press of zombies intensified. Their moans filled the air, the song of the undead, punctuated by bursts from the MP10 and Jake's pistol. Somewhere, a phone started to ring.

Rafe howled in pain. Zombies swarmed around him, biting and grabbing at him. He slammed another zombie into the wall so hard it crushed the drywall to dust. He drove his clawed fingertips into another zombie's eye sockets and tore off its head like a 'roid-raging bodybuilder heaving a bowling ball out of its case. But another huge zombie grabbed his legs, and a half dozen clamped onto him like leeches, tearing at him, dragging him down. Rafe disappeared under a writhing wall of undead.

Time seemed to distort, and sound traveled up the register

until it screamed in a high-pitched whine. My teeth clamped together so hard pain shot up my jaws. I had to check the urge to run to Rafe and start ripping zombies off him with my bare hands.

"Get behind me!" I stepped toward the approaching zombies with my arms at my side and my palms alight with flames that did not sear my skin.

Mai and Hanzo ran past me toward the reception area. Jake halted at my side with his automatic up and steadied in two hands. He shot round after round into the writhing ball of zombies piled on Rafe. Several zombies fell away, the tops of their heads blown off.

"I can't get a barrier around him." Jake ejected a spent clip and slapped in another. "Last one."

"Get out!" I yelled. "I'm gonna burn it all!"

Jake didn't move.

I killed the fire around my hands and shoved him toward the reception desks. If he stayed this close, he'd be burned. "Get to the Bradley. Make sure the rest of them get out."

"I'm not leaving you." He opened fire, punctuating his words with gunshots.

Goddammit. I had no more time to deal with Jake, but an idea exploded into my mind that might save him from ending up in the emergency ward with third-degree burns, or worse.

Glass shattered behind me, but I didn't turn. I drew in all the power I could handle and focused my concentration down to a pinprick. The closest zombie—an old lady with pinkish hair and a tattered floral-print dress—had staggered within two meters. She opened her mouth and I saw she had no teeth, only grayish gums. Must have had dentures and lost them. Oh, the beautiful irony.

I summoned and dispersed an expanding flood of flammable vapor, buffeting it against the zombies. I waited until it suffused the entire center of the office with fuel, like a propane leak filling a room. Jake cursed beside me. I risked one last look at Rafe. He still struggled to fight his way free, but more zombies threw themselves on top of him.

"We're clear," Sarge said over the com. "Pull out, Captain."

"Not without Rafe. Jake, put your barrier up."

He lowered his pistol without question and thrust out his free hand. A shimmering barrier wall opened right in front of us.

I tapped my power and lit a spark. The world exploded into a red-white sun of fire and light with a colossal *WHUMP* that should've knocked me flat with its shock wave, but didn't because of Jake's barrier, though Jake stumbled backward and barely managed to keep from falling. Every zombie in the room and the hallway went flying, hurled away by the expanding shock wave, along with chairs and staplers and every manner of debris. All the windows blew out in one catastrophic crash of breaking glass. Burning papers blew around like fiery leaves in a windstorm.

The ceiling burned in a roiling corona of flame. The sprinkler system didn't come on at all. The explosion had destroyed it. A deep roar filled my ears, a sound like a crowd screaming at a football stadium, and it took me a second to realize it was the raging voice of the fire, closer and louder than I'd ever heard it.

I dropped low and so did Jake, both of us pressing close to the ground. Flames spread everywhere. Burning ceiling panels started to fall. Thick, black and gray smoke filled the office, curling around the edges of the barrier. We began to cough, and I couldn't seem to get enough air into my lungs. I crawled toward Rafe through the smoke, avoiding piles of burning wreckage. Rafe pushed himself up on all fours and looked at me. Burns covered his back and the side of his face where fire had seared away his fur, leaving pink, angry flesh. The zombies piled on top of him now lay in scattered drifts, some stirring with weak, convulsive movements, many of them burning.

Fatigue clutched at me, making my arms and legs feel

leaden and unresponsive. I bared my teeth and kept my breaths shallow to avoid coughing as I crawled toward Rafe. The smoke was too thick. More of it swept in along the sides of Jake's barrier. An old-style computer monitor exploded nearby with the sound of a firecracker shoved into a coffee can filled with glass.

Rafe dragged himself toward us through the gray and black haze. We finally reached him. This far into the inferno the air blazed like Hell on broil setting. My Kevlar armor smoked, my uniform felt like an electric burner pressed against my skin, and I was glad of my helmet. Pyromancy raised my skin's resistance to fire, but my hair could still burn, and so could my clothing. Jake had it worse, but he said nothing and never fell behind or flinched back.

Jake and I grabbed Rafe at the same time. Together we dragged him away from the flames. Frantic moans echoed behind us in the smoke, and that goddamn phone still rang somewhere, punctuated by a strident, pulsing fire alarm.

Jake's barrier dropped. I couldn't stop coughing enough to ask why. The smoke enveloped us, disorienting me as I tried to lead us out. I coughed almost continually. I was damn near exhausted from the spell and from half-pulling, half-dragging Rafe along, though Jake supported most of his weight. Maybe standing in the middle of my biggest firestorm hadn't been the best idea I'd ever had.

Panic had started to fill me like cold, black water when a massive, dark shape crashed through the window frame to my left with a loud, grinding crunch, causing the few remaining shards of glass to fall with a musical tinkle I heard even over the fire's roar. It was our Bradley, less than ten feet away. It backed out, leaving a gaping wound where there'd once been wall and window frame. I dragged Rafe toward it.

"We're coming out!" I shouted over the com. "Hold your fire!"

No replies. A strange buzzing came from my earpiece.

Maybe my helmet had melted in the heat. I glanced at Jake and tapped my helmet near the ear. Jake repeated the call over his mike. I saw his lips moving, but I still couldn't hear him over the radio.

We stumbled out the hole the Bradley had smashed. Nobody shot us, which would've been a particularly bad end to an already Fucked Up Beyond All Recognition day. My lungs filled with blessedly clean, blessedly smoke-free air. My armor and fatigues still smoked. Rafe reeked of burned wolf hair. Jake and I got his arms around our shoulders and carried him toward the Bradley, which was good, because I'd started to flag. My firebomb had tapped me out, not to mention our baby crawl through the smoky throat of an incinerator.

"Hanzo!" I yelled. "Rafe needs a medic *now*!"

Hanzo appeared beside me as if he'd materialized from the concrete. Maybe his ninja-medic skills were better than I'd appreciated, or the explosion, heat and smoke still had me loopy and disoriented. He took Rafe from me and, with Jake, hurried the injured werewolf up the Bradley's ramp. They laid Rafe down and Hanzo began to work on him, his hands glowing blue with his healing aura as he moved them above the bites and the burns. I crossed my arms over my chest as waves of nausea swept through me. Those burns...*I'd* done that to Rafe. Me. I'd been desperate. I couldn't think of any other choice that would force the zombies off our backs long enough to escape. Still...

Jake slipped an arm around me, and I let him do it. Streaks of ashes striped his jaw. He stank of smoke, but so did I, and right now I could not care less. I leaned against him. A dim part of me started to protest that I couldn't appear weak in front of everybody, but I shut that voice down at once. It felt good having him hold me. I felt steadier with him near me. If anyone made any snide comments, I'd remind them I'd just walked out of the lower intestine of Hell, right before I punched them in the face.

Sarge stood atop the Bradley's turret. He'd changed

weapons and now held the ARC lightning rifle we'd played with on the shooting range. He sighted into the smoke billowing out of the gap smashed into the wall and the broken windows. The plant's roof had caught fire. Flames had swallowed the entire front of the building.

"Let's pull back, Captain," Sarge said. I heard him with my ears, not my earpiece. I pulled off my helmet and almost laughed. I'd been right. The helmet was scorched and half-melted on one side, the headset destroyed. I flung it away.

"Move back a hundred feet," I ordered. "Keep the guns on the front of the building. Shoot anything that comes out."

The Bradley backed up, dragging the lowered ramp along the blacktop. Jake helped me follow along behind while Mai covered our retreat with her ferret army.

The chain gun started to spit rounds. I glanced back in time to see several burning zombies blown to shreds.

"We didn't get the necromancer." My words sounded ragged and hoarse. My throat burned, and every syllable rewarded me with pain. "That bastard got away."

Jake glanced at me, his face grim. "He might've died in the fire."

I didn't answer. He'd escaped with the other guy I'd seen. I could *feel* it.

"We should disable the bus and the car we saw earlier—" The chain gun roared again and drowned out my voice. More burning zombies staggered out of the gap into our kill zone and were disintegrated by the Bradley's main gun.

Jake leaned in close and yelled in my ear to be heard over the gunfire. "If you send the Bradley, the zombies might break through into the neighborhood."

Dammit. Keeping the undead from breaking loose and shambling amok was the highest priority now that we'd lost sight of the necromancer and since I'd neutralized the plant by converting it into an insurance adjustor's nightmare. I would've sent Tiffany aloft to scout for the vehicles, but she was on guns now, and Hanzo had his hands full healing Rafe. The understaffed thing had circled back to bite us in the ass, big time. All of which meant if the necromancer made it to the vehicles at the back of the plant, he had free rein to escape, since he was safely out of our line of sight. "Shit."

"We neutralized his manufacturing capacity." Jake put a hand on my shoulder, but I couldn't feel it because of my body armor. "We seriously degraded his zombie assets. Even if he survived, he won't be able to start up again anytime soon."

"For how long? He'll go back to robbing banks for funds. People will still be in danger. Face it. We had our chance and lost it."

Jake looked at me but didn't reply.

A huge column of black smoke snaked up into the sky. Ashes drifted down in flurries like snow. The stink of smoke and a sickly sweet chemical reek filled the air. In the distance, police and fire truck sirens sang their warbling cry. Across the street, a few spectators milled around, taking pictures with cell-phone cameras and gaping at the fire.

"We better get the cops to seal the place off," I said. "What about the fire department? They're gonna want to fight the fire. It's in their DNA."

"We'll let the place burn to the ground. CDC orders. Decontamination by incineration."

I wiped a hand across my face. It came away sweaty and streaked with grime. I'm sure I smelled just as appealing. "Shit. What a clusterfuck."

The chain gun roared again, followed by the ear-splitting crack of the ARC rifle as Sarge dropped zombies by exploding their heads with lightning bolts.

I leaned toward Jake, coming into kissing distance, and grabbed his helmet microphone. "Hey, Tiffany, how about using the goddamn machine gun instead of disintegrating zombies with the chain gun? Each of those chain-gun rounds cost more than Rafe's weekly grocery bill." Talk about overkill. Next she'd be dropping fuel-air explosives.

"Roger that, Captain, sorry," Tiffany replied, sounding a trifle sheepish.

Cop cars started to arrive. I saw the first cop's eyes bug out at the sight of the Bradley and the inferno which had once been a perfectly respectable manufacturing plant. The cop would probably need new jockey shorts.

"I'd better go take care of the official end," Jake said. "You all right?"

"I'm fine."

I moved away from him to prove it. My legs felt rubbery, my mouth tasted like I'd been licking the inside of a chimney for the last half an hour and I reeked of smoke. Oh, and my head pounded with a dull, monotonous thud. Other than that, it was just another great day in my blissful and serene existence. I should've been a Buddhist.

Jake watched me for a second longer, as if afraid I'd fall over as soon as he let me go. I concentrated on ignoring him. After a moment, he turned and hurried toward the cops with his pistol holstered and his ID out, shouting that this was a government operation and no one should interfere.

I went to check on Rafe. He'd changed back into human form and lay on the metal floor in the back of the Bradley. Hanzo crouched next to him, frowning in concentration as he patched Rafe up with his healing powers. I could feel the strong thrum of magic. Rafe grinned at me, still missing a patch of hair from his scalp, but the skin had healed clean. Thank God for werewolf genes and healer spells.

I tried to grin back. "Hey, somebody ruined your haircut."

"Chicks dig injured guys, Captain. Wait till you see how much action I score out of this, since my dick still works. Wanna see?"

"No. That's all right. Really." I was more relieved than disgusted, but he really should come with a warning label. I started back down the ramp. The Bradley troop compartment was too crowded, and I didn't want to get in Hanzo's way.

"Hey, Captain," Rafe called.

I looked back.

"Thanks," he said softly.

I smiled, nodded and turned away. My throat tightened, making it painful to swallow. I'd started to blink rapidly too. Goddamn smoke. Always stinging my eyes.

Another explosion at the rear of the building boomed like thunder, echoing back from the surrounding streets like an artillery barrage. I stood a few feet from the Bradley and watched the flames consume Bokor Gelzonbi Foods. The firefighters set up their hoses, but only stared at the fire, holding off at our orders.

Would we get paid for this since there'd been no confirmed necromancer kill? I tried to remember the exact language of our contract and couldn't. My mind was filled with images of the yellow-orange blaze of fire, of burning corpses and Rafe crawling toward me in the smoke. It would be a nightmare identifying the necromancer anyway, with all those crispy zombie bodies. But maybe we'd get lucky.

Lucky. Who was I kidding?

Mai walked up to me. She had only one ferret left with her—she'd already ported the others back to their home world on Planet Furry Demon or whatever.

"Captain," she said. "The bus is gone."

Chapter Seventeen: To Hell and Back, On A Bus

Diminished Undead Army in Asset-Relocation Program
Zombie School Bus
SE Powell Boulevard, Portland, Oregon
12:06 p.m. PST April 16th

Deposed Necromancer of the Unrighteous Order of the Falling Dark Jeremiah Hansen drove the school bus down the street at precisely the speed limit. Blake sat in the first seat of the opposite row, his hands wrapped over the top of his briefcase like a gargoyle clutching a rainspout. The slightest frown marred his usual bland expression as he stared out the front window.

Jeremiah glanced at the tall side mirror. He could still see the massive column of smoke twisting up into the clouds a mile or so behind him. What a completely fucktastic epic disaster. All his work, all his dreams, literally up in smoke.

A zombie moaned in one of the back rows. Jeremiah glanced in the wide overhead mirror before he coasted to a stop at a traffic light. Less than fifty zombies remained. One of them, a Hispanic guy in a muscle shirt, still smoldered, and the white smoke rose off him like steam from boiling noodles. The air inside the bus smelled of burned hair, smoke, and strangely, BBQ pork. He wanted to open all the windows but couldn't risk stopping and didn't quite want to risk ordering Blake to do it.

Blake had been silent since they'd escaped. Disturbing.

Sirens warbled in the distance. He came to another intersection and scanned for cops. A block farther south a fire truck rushed past. The traffic light turned green, and Jeremiah proceeded through the intersection in a responsible fashion.

Blake leaned toward him, raising his voice to be heard over the diesel engine. "How soon might we acquire new undead assets?"

"I don't know." His hands tightened on the wide steering wheel. It'd taken him a long time to gather all those zombies and now most of them had been cremated. Story of his life. A sip of success, and then the sweetness stolen away. "Depends on the local death rate, how many funeral parlors and hospitals we could get to. I don't think I can get another zombie shipment from Idaho. It'd take forever to ship them from Mexico."

"We managed to extract fifty-three undead, by my count. I suggest our first move might be to secure a place to lay low, as they say."

No shit. He wasn't exactly on his way to the local Hooters for hot wings and hot pants. The term *furious* summed his feelings up nicely. Now throw in the words *alarmed* and *discouraged* and pick out a prize. He yearned for vengeance...but wreaking maniacal revenge with only fifty zombies would be a serious trial and tribulation.

"I have a couple of storage garages I rent at Sam's Secure Shacks," Jeremiah finally replied. "We could ditch the zombies inside. Abandon the bus somewhere."

"At this stage I'm hesitant to lose one of our biggest assets. Transportation is a requirement. Even transportation such as this."

"Good point."

"We have access to funds, I assume?"

"Yeah." He had access to some of his stolen money, squirreled away in safety-deposit boxes, although a good deal of the rest had metamorphosed into ash when the plant burned.

That damn woman. Sure, she'd looked smoking hot—what he could see of her outside of her helmet and all that armor, anyway. But she'd had those eyes, the fiery gaze of some pissed-off dragon. Not somebody he wanted hunting him.

Instead, he'd rather hunt her. Since she'd been the one who'd destroyed his manufacturing venture beyond salvage, he intended to extract some fair market value for watching his dreams burn. If he could turn all of those mercenaries into zombies...not the werewolf, that wouldn't work because they were immune to his death magic, but the others, that pretty fire girl and that Clint Eastwood-squinting hard-ass guy with the pistol. The demon would have to go, of course. But the Asian woman had been a summoner, so maybe he could get a bonus. A sub-army of undead summoner monsters. An interesting prospect. With zombies like that—*paranormal* zombies—maybe he'd been setting his sights too low with the gelatin thing. Maybe he needed to rule a city. A small one at first, so he could get the gist of it without bankrupting Los Angeles or turning it into a smoking heap in his first week. *More* of a smoking heap, that was.

From there...well, what if he managed to lobby for the right for zombies to vote? An intriguing idea. Establish an undead voting block. They'd be lax on the FDA, EPA and indifferent to the SEIU and other unions...but knowing zombies, they'd be antagonistic about the Second Amendment and gun rights, which meant no NRA support. What about social programs? Were zombies pinko Santa Claus-esque socialists? Nah, they didn't strike him that way. On the flip side, though, zombies weren't likely to be pro-military either. So how would the Moral Majority take them? Did the Bible say anything specific about cannibalism? He was pretty sure it wasn't specifically in the Ten Commandments, the only thing they ever seemed concerned about anyway.

He opened his mouth to tell Blake about the new zombie voting demographic idea, but before he spoke something tripped all kinds of alarms in his skull. His necromancer magic swirled around him in a silver and black aura, making it next to impossible to drive in a straight line.

He could see something...something across the web of psychic connection he shared with his undead minions. One of the zombies—no, one zombie *head*—was still active. In fact, those damn mercenaries had it. Apparently, they'd decided to tote it around in a plastic grocery bag. He could hear the rumble of a large diesel engine. He concentrated harder and heard the sound of a man's voice across the telepathic link.

"Did you see the captain go nuclear?" a male voice said. "She, like, *exploded* the building. It was the most awesome thing I've ever seen."

"And did you see?" a female voice answered, smooth and delicious and sexy. Jeremiah immediately got hard. "Captain Sanders refused to leave her side, even when she told him to."

"Yeah," the male voice replied, "and he's lucky she didn't bite his head off and do the Charleston on his body for ignoring her."

What the hell was this? *Days of our Lives*? He dimmed the connection so he could focus on driving and avoid ramming the bus up the tailpipe of a Volkswagon. Still, this had turned into a beautiful stroke of luck. A zombie head was better than a tracking beacon for a person of Jeremiah's particular skills. Those mercenaries had been damn unnerving. He'd thrown everything at them, shot every barrel, and even when it seemed he might win, they'd managed to blow up the best gelatin manufacturing plant this side of the Rocky Mountains. Now he'd make them pay. Pay *extreme* restitution.

He glanced at Blake and smiled. "I think I have a plan."

And, of course, it involved zombies. Sometimes he even amazed himself.

Chapter Eighteen: Gods and Generals and Zombies

Mercenary Wing Rv6-4 "Zero Dogs"
Zero Dog Compound
Garage
2041 Hours PST April 16th

The Zero Dogs got home well after dark. I should've been tired, but instead I felt as if I'd downed half a dozen energy drinks with coffee chasers. Things had broken down along these lines:

Rafe's wounds healed over, and Hanzo patched up all Rafe's burns and bites. He treated the rest of the assault team for smoke inhalation and minor injuries. I had to admit, when he wasn't running around in black pajamas waving his stupid sword, Hanzo was a damn fine healer. I only wished he realized it. Or maybe I just wished he'd finally accept it.

The Bokor Gelzonbi Foods manufacturing plant burned to the ground. Only a section of the south wall still stood, scorched black and sprouting broken steel girders and rebar. When the police commissioner learned there'd been zombies inside, he sent in HazMat teams with the firefighters digging out hot spots and spraying down the smoking rubble. The heat had been so intense that body identification would remain an iffy prospect.

Worse, a witness had positively identified Necromancer

Hansen and a bunch of zombies fleeing the scene in a school bus. The police put out a BOLO on the bus, but the cops didn't have a bus number or plate number, and the necromancer had a large head start.

Finally, Norville Ford from city hall had shown up in his government-black SUV foaming at the mouth about how we'd pay for the damage to the property, for the cost of the fire and police response, for the cost of cleanup, city-worker overtime, paperwork handling and on and on.

Then Jake went and impressed me without even pulling out his gun or stripping down to his jockeys. He'd taken Norville aside, one hand on his back, bent close and had spoken in a low, calm voice so I couldn't quite make out the words, although I'd have sold a kidney to eavesdrop. A couple minutes later, Jake had strolled back to me and Norville had abandoned the scene. I hadn't asked Jake what he'd said, and he hadn't volunteered, despite his cat-who-ate-the-canary smirk.

We'd rolled out long after the sun had gone down, detouring through the Taco Bell drive thru to grab dinner because everyone was starving. Rafe didn't even complain about all the saturated fat, trans fat, sodium, butylated hydroxyanisole, sodium nitrite and monosodium glutamate in the fast food. At the pick-up window, the girl's eyes had bugged out when the Bradley had rolled up. I'd had to climb down from the turret to get the food...all three hundred dollars of it.

Now, hours later, I had a tension headache and pain all through my shoulders. I'd been in the garage for the last twenty minutes going over the supplies. I'd showered the moment we got in, but despite washing my hair three times and standing in the hot water for half an hour I could still smell the lingering stink of smoke.

"I've been looking for you, Andrea," Jake said behind me.

I jerked, my pen skating across the clipboard. I spun around, heart pounding, annoyed with myself at the effect he had on me, even though I was bone-weary. I fought to keep irritation out of my voice and failed. "I'm gonna staple a bell to your forehead," I snarled. "What do you need?"

He shook his head. The shadows had gathered in deep pools inside the garage with only a few overhead spot fluorescents on. Half his face was lost in darkness. The smells of oil, iron and lingering diesel fumes filled the air.

He shoved his hands in the pockets of his black fatigues. "What do *you* need?"

I glanced around. "There an echo?"

"A rough day. What can I do to help?"

"I'm almost done." I turned away, and then looked back over my shoulder. "But...thanks."

He shrugged, but didn't leave. I went back to counting the remaining ammo Tiffany had unloaded from the Bradley's Bushmaster chain gun, trying to calculate how much it would cost to replenish it. Using the chain gun on zombies had been complete overkill, and now our bank account would feel the pain. The price of diesel fuel already had my stomach in knots. At least she hadn't fired any of the Javelins.

I noted numbers for a few minutes more. After I recounted the same ammo box for the third time I had to stop and admit I couldn't focus with Jake this close. My thoughts kept circling back to him, and whenever he made the slightest sound, I wanted to look at him.

I sighed, capped the pen and set the clipboard on an engine stand. "I can't concentrate."

"You look stressed."

"And they say men don't have any powers of intuition. Obviously they're present, but like their brain, underutilized."

A grin. "You're lucky I'm not easily offended."

"And you're lucky you're a barrier mage and I can't just bounce you and your incredible inflatable ego out of here."

"So prickly." He cocked his head. "Why is that?"

I looked away, staring at engine parts. "I'm not comfortable answering—"

"I thought maybe things had changed after what happened earlier, but you keep right on trying to insult me away. The constant sniping about men. Am I a threat?"

"Hardly."

"So why the hate?"

"I don't hate men. I love them to death. They're just exasperating." I thought for a moment. "And easy to make fun of."

"Ah."

"Look. I'm just teasing. Don't get your testicles in a knot."

"How about I start *teasing* back?"

I didn't answer right away. While everyone had to admit I was pretty fucking high-larry-us most of the time, I wondered how many PMS, toilet seat or shopaholic jokes I could take before going DEFCON 1. "All right. You made your point. I'll be nice."

"I don't want nice." He moved toward me, taking unhurried steps. His eyes never left mine. They burned with a quiet intensity, like a predator...or a lover. He came very close to me, his face now fully revealed in the yellow light. A hard face, with hard eyes, yet I noticed something else in them now. Something that made my stomach flutter.

He moved even closer.

"Don't," I warned.

"Why?"

"I'm...taking inventory and I'll lose count."

"Don't worry about it." He moved around behind me. I started to face him, but he placed his hands on my shoulders. I immediately tensed, but forced myself to relax. That I'd even let him get this close spoke volumes.

He began to massage my back and neck, rubbing his thumbs against my muscles and helping them unclench. I tried to keep my eyes open and swallowed a sigh. A distant, and quite frankly minority part of me wanted to tell him to take his hands off. But Mother said never turn down a good back rub, so for a while I let everything go and enjoyed it.

"I'm exhausted," I finally said. I stepped away from him and his touch I'd been enjoying too much. "I can't deal with this now."

"I want you," he said, and I could hear it in his voice. I opened my mouth to pop off with something wiseass but he held up his hands. "I can see you want me too. It's in your eyes."

"You're an arrogant bastard."

"Am I? I was trying to be direct. Like you. Thought you'd appreciate it."

I didn't answer.

"We're adults. We're attracted to one another." He touched my hand. Not possessively, but with an almost hesitant grace, as if seeking invitation to touch me more. "Haven't I proven I'm not a threat?"

"I can't deal with you. We already talked about this."

He watched me, his head tilted, waiting me out.

"I have responsibilities. People are counting on me. You blow in here, upset all the routines. Hover on the edge of compromising my command. And you expect us to hook up?"

"I want to see if this spark between us leads anywhere."

"I know all about sparks and fire and the burning-searing-inferno metaphors. Talk to somebody other than a pyromancer."

"I can use any metaphor you'd like," he said. "Or none at all."

I had to stop this now. *Had* to. I couldn't take it. Couldn't take lowering my defenses and letting him charge all over me and leave me a smoking, looted ruin.

I waved a dismissive hand at him. "Look, I have duties. We're gonna be done here—likely this necromancer guy is halfway to Mexico by now, planning to wear sombreros, drink tequila and play in a mariachi band—and you're gonna leave and I'll still have to deal with everything. I believe in making a clean cut. A *pre*-cut in this case."

Jake nodded. Yet he leaned toward me, holding my gaze, and kissed me. His lips felt soft and warm on mine. My traitorous lips opened in response. Second time he'd kissed me. Second time I'd ignored my own protests about why we wouldn't ever work.

I let him break the kiss after a long, far-too-short amount of time.

"That doesn't change anything," I said.

He smiled. "It's a start. And that's all I ask."

He turned and walked off. I watched him leave, part of me wishing he'd come back.

But he didn't.

My apartment echoed as I stalked through it. The place seemed eerily empty and joyless. I poured myself a glass of scotch—the amount of amber liquid in the bottle had grown noticeably lower since *he* had arrived—and sipped it as I paced around the room, looking at the art on my walls and thinking about Jake.

Annoying. Vexing that I should be saddled with him—making me think about him when I should've been thinking about the ongoing manhunt for Jeremiah Hansen. This was exactly what I'd feared would happen. Jake was in the way of me doing my job like a professional, dammit.

Fatigue leached away my energy and made my thoughts random and confused, but I felt too restless to sleep. I slipped on shoes and abandoned my room. I wandered through the house like a ghost, half-hoping I'd run into Jake again in some secluded hallway, half-irritated with myself for even nursing such a stupid, trite fantasy.

I passed by the laundry room on my way to the kitchen and noticed Stefan inside. He leaned against one of the huge industrial front-loader washers and stared at something out of my line of sight. I hadn't talked to Stefan yet tonight, so my scotch and I paid him a little visit.

He glanced up at me and frowned before turning his attention back to the object on a sorting table—the zombie head Sarge had collected and brought back to the house. The severed head sat in the round white laundry basket I'd left in here a couple days ago. I approached it with caution, as if sneaking up on an alligator, and peered over the top. Bringing the head back with us hadn't been my idea, but Sarge believed there might be a way to trace the silver cords of death magic from the zombie head back to the necromancer. Jake had agreed. I'd finally gone along, not wanting to lose any chance at a lead, but really, *really* loathing the thought of an undead cranium wrapped in a plastic shopping bag within a ten-mile radius of me.

"Stefan." I tried keeping my tone even, calm, Zen-like. "Why do you have a zombie head in the laundry room? Or do I not want to know?"

He stroked his right fang, still staring down at the head. The zombie head had belonged to a guy with a long shaggy haircut in fashionable—if somewhat greasy—disarray, a close-cropped beard and filmy blue eyes. Those eyes had rolled in their sockets and locked on me the moment I peered over the edge of the basket. His mouth dropped open and his tongue lolled out. The zombie closed his teeth on his tongue and began to chew on it, which qualified as the most unnerving thing I'd seen in at least an hour and a half.

"Gavin gave me this...*thing* to watch. He made some disparaging comment about the undead watching the undead." Stefan's face betrayed his disgust. "Never a man mind that vampires are not even distant cousins to zombies. It's an egregious insult."

"Mmm. So why are you in the *laundry* room? And why is a zombie head in *my* laundry basket. A basket that has, on occasion, held my lingerie?" Now I'd have to send the basket to the incinerator. No way I'd ever use it again.

"Because I needed to wash my whites, and I very well can't have this head rolling off when I turn my back."

"That's a great image," I replied. "A bowling-ball zombie head tumbling down the hallway. Thanks, I'll sleep better."

He rolled his eyes and showed me a little fang—unconscious vampire body language. I wondered if he'd had that widow's peak before he became a vampire, or if it were just some kind of genetic side effect.

"All irrelevant buffoonery aside," he said. "I see you warm bloods have been up to no end of mischief without me. A fortunate thing I'm on salary."

"We managed to burn down another building, if that's what you mean."

"I assume that was your doing, Captain."

I favored him with a mysterious smile and took another sip of scotch.

"So where is the necromancer now, may I ask?"

"Nobody knows. The cops have an APB out on the school bus. We'll see if anything turns up."

"A school bus. Villains a hundred years ago wouldn't be caught dead or *un*dead in such a vulgar, unstylish contraption. Things have truly gone to the curs of late."

"Alas for the good old days. But maybe this zombie head will lead us back to our target. Sarge says there's some kind of invisible cord or something still attached."

"The web of the necromancer. A crude, yet effective magic. I'm surprised Sarge knew of it."

I sighed. Having a vampire around for night ops was a terrific plus, but dealing with *this* particular vampire and his Nova Scotia-sized ego could try my patience. "Let me know if the zombie says anything important while you're washing your jockstrap, will you, Stefan? And for Heaven's sake, keep that unsanitary thing out of the kitchen. Now that I think of it, keep your jockstrap out of the kitchen too."

I left him to his emo brooding and went looking for Sarge. I wanted to discuss our plans for the zombie head—namely my suggestion we light it on fire and have done with it.

Sometimes our house seemed cramped and small, with everybody tripping over each other and sneaking the last slice of pizza or putting the milk back in the fridge empty. Other times the place seemed cavernous, a lonely, haunted manse with me as a specter, drifting down empty hallways. Drinking scotch whiskey. While the song "American Pie" played through the PA speakers. Go figure.

Mai and Tiffany lounged in the main living area. That damn replica sword had been rammed back into the wall. Somebody had hung an umbrella on the hilt. I definitely needed to hire another cleaning agency post-haste.

They both stopped talking as soon as I walked in, setting off all sorts of internal alarms inside my skull. Nothing screamed guilty like sudden, uncomfortable silence when one's superior officer showed up unannounced. I put my hands on my hips and arched an eyebrow. "So who wants to come out with it first?"

Tiffany showed me only wide-eyed innocence...a difficult trick for a face that was a Renaissance artist's wet dream (barring perhaps the slit pupils, which might get said artist in trouble with certain prominent religious institutions and goat-advocacy groups). "Out with what, Captain?"

Mai concentrated on petting the kitten in her lap and wouldn't look at me. The kitten had bright crimson fur and icy blue eyes. It stared at me as if I were a five-and-a-half-foot-tall tuna sandwich.

I snapped my fingers. "Out with whatever you two were saying about me before I waltzed in."

"Oh."

"It was nothing," Mai said. "Girl chat."

"So. I'm a girl. Chat me."

"Um." Tiffany twisted and shifted in her seat as if trying to find a place to put her overly large, male-sexual-fantasy breasts. "Nothing. It wasn't anything really. Just. You know. How good you and Jake—I mean Captain Sanders—looked together today."

"Yeah, Captain. You both looked great. I wish I had some hot hunk of man candy running around shielding me." Mai leaned back in the chair and stared at the ceiling. The kitten chewed on her thumb. "Maybe an animal lover with an appreciation for the small and the furry. A veterinarian even. And we'd make love like horny minks on the riverbank at dawn."

Tiffany nodded, and then said in a stage whisper, "He kept looking at your ass today. Captain Sanders, I mean."

"Captain Sanders is more concerned with getting his Mission Accomplished star than my *ass*ets."

Mai favored me with a skeptical look. "What creature of the male persuasion has ever *not* been interested in an ass of some sort?"

Now that she put it that way... "Don't you two have better things to do than sit around and gossip?"

"No," they said in unison.

"Look. Captain Sanders will be on his way to Fort Bragg or wherever soon enough. He's not a Zero Dog. He's not my boyfriend. So cool it."

Mai grinned. "What about a quick...?" She made a hole with one hand and slid the finger of her other hand rapidly in and out. Tiffany giggled, yes, *giggled*, and gave Mai a playful shove.

"If you two are interested, be my guest." I tried on a smile. The smile felt decidedly shark-like.

"He isn't interested in us," Tiffany said, sounding far too cheery. "I don't even think my seduction magic would work on him. He's locked on you like a laser-guided bomb. It's so romantic."

Mai nodded. "*Really* romantic, Captain."

I had to walk away, shaking my head. My skin felt warm, maybe even a bit flushed, from their conspiratorial laughter. Why was my love life anybody's topic of conversation in the first place? I knew they meant well, but the whole giggling-schoolgirl thing had gone straight up my ass like a crowbar turned sideways. I enjoyed attention as much as anybody, hell, I wouldn't be a leader if I didn't, but this kind of scrutiny unnerved me. It seemed as if people and events conspired to funnel me toward Jake, whether I wanted him or not. I didn't like that.

Sarge sat in the kitchen, eating a piece of fried chicken and reading a huge, leather-bound book splayed open on the marble counter. He perched on the stool like a huge purple-skinned gargoyle and glanced up at me. “Hungry, Captain?”

“No. I just came from the laundry room, where Stefan put a zombie head in my ex-laundry basket and killed my appetite.”

“The head could be the key to tracking the necromancer.”

“That's what I came to see you about. Stefan mentioned something about the necromancer's web. You and Jake talked about a silver cord earlier, but I didn't catch it all.” I'd had more important things to do at the time. Like finding a place to feed a bunch of hungry mercenaries.

“It's like the wire guide on a TOW missile. He has to remain connected to keep the zombies under his control. Once a necromancer has an army of zombies it's hard to keep track of threads leading to combat-ineffective zombies, especially after a big battle.”

“So what do we do about it?”

He shifted his bulk and the stool gave a tortured groan. “I'm looking for a spell that'll allow us to trace back along the silver thread. But I might need help.”

“I don't know demon magic.”

He shook his head. “Doesn't matter. I'll manage the spell. I just need you, and maybe Jake, as batteries. Something to tap for extra power.”

Jake again. A girl couldn't escape him, it seemed. Annoying.

"Wait." An idea flashed in my mind and my stomach churned. "If we can track him...can he see us? Through the zombie?"

Sarge took another bite and chewed slowly. "I've heard necromancers can see through their servant's eyes. Don't know if they can use their servants like homing beacons. Might be safest to believe they can."

Shit. "Then fucking terminate the thing. I didn't fucking think it might work against us. What if he attacks here?"

Sarge stayed silent for a long moment, and his gaze dropped to the spell book. "It's a risk. But without that head we have nothing."

Dammit. "What's our exposure on this?"

"He's in retreat. If he attacks here, he'll be operating understrength. I have the head isolated so he can't gain direct intel from it."

I chewed on my lip. Our property had either eight-foot iron fencing or concrete and stone walls around its entirety. The witness who'd seen Jeremiah Hansen flee in the bus had estimated forty or so zombies left with him. Not enough to overrun this compound. If Hansen tried, he'd be signing his own death certificate and hand delivering it to us. Still, I'd feel more comfortable if we had electrified fences or maybe a minefield. "Next time, make sure I know all the risks first. I hate surprises."

"Fair enough." Sarge's look was grim. "I'll take full responsibility."

"Well, I won't have you shot at dawn...this time. I'm sure you did what you thought was right in the middle of all that chaos. Dammit, I just want this done and over with, my people safe and the rest of the money sitting secure in the bank."

Sarge shut the book and pushed it aside. "Something else's bothering you."

I almost didn't answer, but Sarge and I had shared many a commiserating drink in the days before he'd found Shawn. It seemed so long ago now. Where the hell did the time go? Made me sad to think of our lives dripping away like blood from a wound that wouldn't heal. I stared down at the tile floor, wanting to talk, not wanting to talk.

Finally, I gave up. "Bothering me? Nothing. Everything. This job. Jake. I don't know."

"Hmm."

"How pithy. Like a Magic 8-ball, but more succinct."

He smiled. "Even in the face of a brewing zombie apocalypse, lovers shall have their travails. One of the things I love about humanity."

"Don't mock me."

"I'm not." He looked away and touched the book's gold clasp. "All right, maybe I am, a little. Forget it, I'm a bastard." He reached for another piece of chicken.

I frowned. Sarge almost always kept his words to a minimum. When he spoke, I listened. That bit of waxing poetic had caught me off-guard. "So who pissed in your herbal tea? Tell me and I'll singe their pantyhose for you."

That earned me a slow smile. "Shawn and I were supposed to hit the Blazers game tonight, but it got ditched because of this. Then he wanted to come over tonight anyway." Sarge shrugged. "I told him no. Told him I didn't want him here with the zombie head in the house."

The goddamn zombie head again. "One more time. Just how dangerous is that fucking thing?"

"Everything's dangerous. One way or another."

"Save the metaphysical bullshit, please," I said. "Just give me down-to-earth bullshit."

"It's dangerous to humans if it manages to bite one, but only Stefan, Rafe and I have been handling it. Still, I have this...feeling—that storm-coming, bad-moon-rising feeling—that makes the hairs on the back of my arms lift. I don't want Shawn here until this is done."

"Shit."

"Exactly."

He opened the book again and turned through its heavy parchment pages filled with evil-looking drawings, numbers and various spell designs.

I hesitated on the verge of leaving and decided to ask one last, innocent question because God hates a coward. "So. What do you think of Jake? I've been meaning to ask you."

"He'd be good for you."

"That's not what I meant. Why the hell does everyone presume to give me a free evaluation of my love life?"

Sarge grinned. A grinning demon was truly unnerving, like clown porn. "What? You're breaking from the stereotype about the girl who asks the gay friend for insight into the male mind? Gonna try and figure men out on your own?"

"Figure it out? I did that when I was fifteen. It involves tits, beer and either sports or video games. Sometimes all of them together."

Sarge laughed—a sound like a mild avalanche. "Maybe you should look again."

"Fine. So tell me, Mr. Romeo Casanova Cyrano de Bergerac the Third, what is it about Shawn that so pulls in your hellish interest?" I paused. "And if you dare call me a fag hag, I'll send you straight back to Hades."

He paused, idly tracing a glowing design on the marble that began to vanish almost at once. After a long moment he answered. "Why does anybody love anyone? I feel he's another part of me. That he fits against me, and makes me more, makes me *better*. When he laughs, it's as if a weight is lifted from me. When I touch him, it makes me believe there's more out there than death and war and hatred and sorrow. As if there's something greater, more powerful than any of those." He shrugged again and looked me in the eyes. "He gives me hope."

My words came out slightly choked. “You love him.”

“I love him more than anything else under this sun. And more every day.”

“I want that.”

He smiled softly. “Then go get it.”

He stood, picked up his book, kissed me on the top of my head as if I were his daughter, and walked out of the kitchen.

Chapter Nineteen: Saving Captain Walker

Mercenary Wing Rv6-4 "Zero Dogs"
The Zero Dog Compound
NW Hilltop Drive, Portland, Oregon
0602 Hours PST April 17th

I woke early the next morning, before the sun had done anything more than paint the low clouds a dull red and yellow at the horizon. I checked in with Hellfrost and our answering service for any updates on the necromancer manhunt, but there was nothing. Nothing at all.

I kept my morning run to three miles around our track instead of five. The run gave me time to think, but it started to rain as I finished up. Instead of cooling me off, it only made me moist and clammy and frizzed my hair. After a hot shower and some breakfast I made more calls but got the runaround with the police-department gatekeepers and hung up in frustration.

I snagged some more coffee and watched the news, which normally failed to cheer me up, and today was no different. Giant robots fought huge mutated squid creatures in Philadelphia. Any more of this and they'd have to change the name to the City of Tentacle Love. In local news, a low-grade zombie scare had swirled through Portland following our attack on the Bokor Gelzonbi plant. Some guy riding the MAX home from work who had taken too much cold medicine ended up dog piled by concerned citizens mistaking him for a zombie. He suffered three broken ribs, but doctors expected him to recover. Likewise, an old woman had attacked a DMV employee with pepper spray while trying to register her car title—once again, the employee had been mistaken for one of the living dead. Hard to blame her, though.

"People are crazy," Rafe said from the couch. "That's why I don't watch the news."

I grunted. Finished my coffee. Eyed the phone handset as if I wanted to incinerate it (and part of me did indeed), but instead stomped off with it to try once more to find someone in the police department in charge of the manhunt for Jeremiah Hansen.

After twenty minutes of runaround, giving my information and a long explanation to every new place they transferred my call, I finally connected to a detective heading up the necromancer search. He told me there'd been no sighting so far. The man and his magical mystery bus full of zombies had vanished into rainy Oregon air. No charges to his credit cards. The Audi in the Gelzonbi parking lot had turned out to have a bogus registration and zero fingerprints. No eyewitness sightings, despite a sketch artist's rendition on the front page of this morning's paper. The guy had become smoke.

Throughout the conversation I kept getting the *you're-wasting-valuable-police-time* vibe from the detective. "Please keep me apprised."

"Sure thing," he replied, but I could hear the lie in his voice.

Cops.

I stomped back to Rafe, who'd buried himself under couch pillows while he played some video game with a big-chested woman running around shooting guns and blowing stuff up. Nothing ever changed. "Rafe, you seen Jake around?"

His gaze didn't move from the screen. I wished he stayed that focused during mission briefings. "He was looking for you a while ago. Said he was trying to contact government people about finding the zombie king. Said something else but I can't remember it."

"You didn't write it down?"

He glanced at me. "I was fighting a *boss*."

Sigh.

I moved in front of the television and used my most imposing scowl until he made eye contact. "Now that I have your complete attention. I've got an entire legion of Merry Maids coming over in a little while to clean this filth pit, and I don't want you bothering any of them. We clear?"

"Captain, you're killing me. I'm a perfect gentleman."

"Yeah. And no strolling around naked, either. Those people are here to work. Not to be hit on by their clients or emotionally damaged by the sight of your personal equipment swinging in the breeze. Hear me? You behave or there'll be problems."

"Fine. *Fine*. Way to steal all the fun away from Mr. Bo Dangles."

I made a disgusted noise and turned to go.

Sarge appeared in the doorway across the room, filling it from jamb to jamb. "Captain. You have a minute?"

"Of course."

We walked to the bottom of the main staircase where he stopped and faced me. "My research's done. I have nearly all the components for the trace spell. It'll take some time to draw all the spell lines and set up the safeguards."

"How long?"

"Maybe tomorrow night. But I'll need both you and Captain Sanders if we're going to make a go of this."

"I'll let Jake know we need him," I said. "Should we bring weapons?"

"Not necessary if I do it right."

"All right. Give me an update if the status changes."

"Will do."

Nice to have someone sincere about a promise. Sarge headed back up the stairs and I went in search of Jake, musing how I needed to have everyone tagged with some kind of GPS collar. The damn house was just too big to find anyone without a half hour of looking.

I found Jake in the dojo, standing in the gray light filtering in through the windows. He had his cell phone to his ear and his baritone drifted to me across the wide training space. I crossed the wood floor with silent steps, approaching him from behind. Try sneaking up on somebody in a room full of large mirrors. Not as easy as it sounds.

He shut his phone before I crossed half the training floor. When he turned, he caught sight of me in the mirror and snapped his head around to look at me. A smile—no, more of a smirk—crossed his lips. "Preparing to pounce?"

"You seem to enjoy sneaking up on me." I walked the rest of the way over to him, striving to appear nonchalant. "Thought I'd try it out."

"Maybe Hanzo can teach you a thing or two."

"Rub in the salt, will you? So...any word on our guy?"

Jake frowned and shook his head. "Nothing. I've been talking to the DOD and Homeland Security all morning. The NSA's come up blank. No cell-phone traffic. Our guy's gone dark."

"Beautiful. What now? You have a plan? Because I sure as hell don't have anything."

"Not yet. One of my contacts at Homeland mentioned there'd been some internal chatter about what direction to take going forward." He shrugged. "But he didn't have any solid information."

"Shit."

"Exactly."

We stood together and stared out the window at the overcast day. What I wouldn't have paid for some blue skies.

"Close call yesterday with Rafe," Jake said. "A tight situation."

I didn't answer. Didn't look at him.

"You handled yourself well," he continued. "All of you did."

"We didn't get him. End of the day, nothing else matters."

He glanced at me but didn't protest. Didn't try to convince me I was wrong. I always hated when people lied to make me feel better.

After a long moment he spoke again as he stared out at the rain. "I failed a mission once. Few years back."

I tried for flippant. "John Wayne doesn't cry, Mr. Quiet Professional. And neither do I."

A mistake. I regretted the words as soon as they spilled out of my mouth.

He turned to me, his eyes narrowed. "You never shut up and *listen* to me. Life with you is one never-ending stream of words that struck you as far too clever to keep bottled up." He shook his head. "Hate to tell you this, but you're nowhere near as funny as you think you are."

I looked away, shame burning on my cheeks and my throat clenching so tight it felt as if I'd wrapped a hose clamp around my neck. The rain drizzled down, tapping on the brick path across the backyard grass. The silence grew sharper, deepening the cut between us.

I finally turned to face him. "I was out of line. Not even worthy of me. I'd self-immolate on the lawn, but it's raining."

A muscle in his jaw twitched. I watched the intensity of his gaze dial up a few degrees with annoyed anger, but then he burst out with a laugh, more of an involuntary bark, and I relaxed a little.

"You're something else, you know that?"

"So I've been told," I said. "But please, finish telling me your story. I'll keep a tight leash on my tongue. Promise."

He grunted. I'd always admired how men could sum

everything up—the entire range of their emotions—with a grunt. Very efficient if you thought about it.

"We were supposed to take down some group of Winter Elven Separatist Militia Rangers—"

"I hate elves. I ever tell you that?"

"I got the hint when you blew up a bunch of them the first time I saw you."

"That's not fair. How many times do I have to say it? They blew *themselves* up and took the rest of the plant with them. Not my fault."

"Anyway. Those elves were cunning. Used the terrain to their advantage. I was the US advisor to a group of JTF2 assaulters, since the separatists wanted to carve out a kingdom in North Dakota but had fled over the border into Canada. We stalked them through the Yukon for three months straight. Always finding their base camps weeks cold. Always one step behind. We had to call it off when winter made pursuit impossible. JSOC reassigned me to a mission in South America. During the first thaw, the elves attacked a commune of Pointy Hat Gnomes..."

"You were reassigned before you could finish," I said. "Tell me you wouldn't have been right out there in the snow again if your superiors hadn't pulled you off."

"Yeah. I would've been right out there in the snow again."

"We're the same breed, you know. Our team will see this through. This mission isn't over for us, either. Not at all."

He stayed silent, but a shadow seemed to cross his face. I lifted my hand to touch him, but he spoke before I could.

"Your team, not mine," he corrected. "Ten minutes and it's crystal clear your people love you."

I only nodded.

He shook his head. "Do you understand what an honor that is? I get shipped around. Different units. Different people in different countries. I help people with problems, complete a mission, hoping to make life better for them, the world safer, whatever, and then I pack up and head to the next place. A shadow soldier. Little more."

"Don't you...don't you keep in contact with any of them? The people you serve with?"

He shrugged. "Sometimes."

"My people like you, Jake." It felt a bit lame to throw it out there now, as if I were just trying to soothe him, but it was the truth. "They don't take to just anybody. But after yesterday...I'd say things definitely changed in your favor."

He smiled a little, but it wasn't a happy smile. "You were right when you told me this thing would end and I'd be gone—"

"Far as I know we're still on the case, hunting this guy. Unless you've heard something different."

He shook his head, but I saw something uncertain flicker in his eyes and then vanish. Disquieting to see him without all the confidence he'd been shining around since he'd strolled into my conference room.

"Then, hell, we'll see this through," I pressed on, ignoring his uncertainty. "And you can be a reference for us with DHS. There's always some crackpot madman wizard or evil dark lord who needs killing. Come back and work with us. It could get to be a...regular thing."

He looked at me. The quiet deepened, and I fought back a shiver. When had it grown so cold? Cold, but I could feel my heart burning in my chest, though the heat failed to spread through my body.

Jake opened his mouth to reply, but Gavin's voice blared over the PA system and cut him off. The second time we'd been interrupted by that goddamn thing, making me seriously consider having it torn out with the jaws of life and scrapped.

"Paging Captain Walker. Paging Captain Andrea Walker. We're under attack by people with vacuum cleaners, dust mops and household chemicals. Please bring your divine leadership and toasty charisma to the front door and advise. Over and out."

The ceiling-mounted speakers squealed with feedback and a burst of static. Then the elevator-music version of 50 Cent's "In Da Club" started in. God, our PA system sucked hard.

Jake jerked his head in the direction of the door. "Better go direct the troops. Otherwise there's no telling what might happen."

I wanted to say more, but the mood, the *connection* between us, had splintered into fragments I knew I couldn't piece back together. At least not today.

I walked across the dojo. My feet made no sound on the wood flooring. I didn't look back, though I could feel him watching me go.

Nothing else happened that day.

Chapter Twenty: The Fugitive Undead

Mercenary Wing Rv6-4 "Zero Dogs"
Zero Dog Compound
Kitchen
1111 Hours PST April 19th

We got a small hit on the third day after the failed assault on the plant. Two morgues had been emptied of corpses in the middle of the night. A witness reported seeing a school bus in the area. Another crime report mentioned an eyewitness sighting of a bus in relation to a burglary at a local fire department. Also, the Audi the cops had confiscated had gone missing from impound, and nobody knew anything about it.

I'd been on the phone all morning with the police department and our liaison with the Hellfrost Merc Group about the progress of the manhunt. I'd been boiling over with frustration by the end, and had rushed to the dojo to work off some steam. No Jake this time. I hadn't seen him all morning. I worked through an entire range of kata, pushing myself hard through the stylized dance of kicks and strikes. When I finished I was tired and I stank, but I'd achieved a sort of endorphin peace with the universe.

Which lasted all of fifteen minutes.

Jake found me on the way to the kitchen and his expression was all business. "I've been looking for you. We have a problem."

Nothing about our little intimate chat a couple days ago, not even a conspirator glance. If the word *problem* hadn't immediately buzz-killed everything else in my mind, I might've been irked.

"What problem?" The scope of that particular word in my world stretched wider than the Pacific Ocean.

"Best you hear it for yourself." He jerked a thumb over his shoulder. "We have a phone conference with Harker from Homeland Security in ten minutes."

Shit. Not even time to take a shower. "I'm not ready—"

"Andrea, I'm sorry." He turned and walked away, his words echoing in my mind.

I watched his wide back retreat down the hallway. My heart hit hard against my rib cage, like a fist slamming a wall over and over again. A ringing echoed in my ears and my mouth tasted like the inside of a copper pipe.

A thousand problematic possibilities flashed through my mind almost too fast to comprehend. We'd been indicted for war crimes. We'd been sued...again. Rafe had been arrested and the government didn't want negative publicity. Angels had come to murder Sarge. Squeegee was behind on her shots. Tiffany had run away to the Bunny Ranch in Nevada and blamed me for everything. Gavin had actually sold one of his terrible books. Stefan had bitten somebody without permission and would be defanged. The SPCA had shown up about Mai Tanaka's furry army. Foreclosure. Zombie outbreaks. Fire and apocalypse and no internet service.

Jake. Leaving me.

I hurried after him, but the strongest feeling of disconnection rolled through me, as if I were only a passenger along for the ride in a body I'd once controlled. Damn, I was stupid. Why should that last mean more to me than a zombie outbreak? I'd known this would happen. Fucking hormones. The fucking *love me* instinct, always reaching out to another warm body. I'd known my feelings for him, in whatever infantile romantic stage they existed, would interfere with my ability to see with clarity and to stay a decisive leader. I'd lost discernment. I'd failed.

Inside the conference room, Jake stood near one of the large windows with his back to me, staring out at the training grounds. He didn't turn when I entered.

"What is this about?" My voice was little more than a whisper.

"Wait for the call."

I bit back a savage reply and sat. The leather chair felt sticky against my sweaty skin. Heat radiated off me. I stared at the strange tripod-shaped speakerphone in the middle of the desk with its tentacles of microphones and waited.

The phone rang. I put it on speakerphone. "This is Captain Walker."

"Greetings, Captain Walker," Harker said. "I assume Captain Sanders is with you."

"I'm here, sir."

"Good. I have pressing news and not much time to give it. The Department of Homeland Security is altering the contract with the Zero Dogs of Merc Wing Rv6-4."

"Altering? We have a contract. You can't alter it."

"We're the government. We most certainly *can* modify arrangements."

My stomach twisted like a wrung-out dishrag. "What's the change?"

"Effective immediately, Captain Sanders will take over as commanding officer on this mission until the primary objective is achieved. Based upon reviews by our analysts, and based upon recent developments in the theater of war, we've decided it may be more...*efficient* to have the operational unit under direct military control. Merc group Rv6-4 will report to Captain Sanders from here on out."

I made a sound—some kind of strangled gasp. Stabbing me in the heart with an icicle would've been kinder. "You can't be serious. This is some kind of stupid joke."

"Once again, Captain Walker, I assure you, I'm from the government, and we do not joke."

"This makes no sense. We have a line on this necromancer now—"

"Please save your questions and...*disagreements* for the end, Captain Walker. I think this would be best done as a clean severance, don't you?" He continued before I could spit out an answer. "Besides, you and the rest of the unit will still be handsomely paid, as per our contract." Amusement festered beneath his voice. Amusement and a smattering of contempt. The bastard.

"This isn't about the money," I said. "Not anymore. This guy hurt my people. He's a threat to America."

Gentle laughter. "Yes, Hansen's the threat du jour, yet he's just one of many that we must consider when allocating resources and assigning threat levels. I have utmost confidence that, free from other constraints, Special Forces Captain Sanders will prosecute this mission to its successful completion."

I looked at Jake. A muscle twitched in my throat—a spasm that felt like someone had shoved a soldering iron into my neck. "You knew about this?"

He turned away from the window and held my gaze. His face was grim, strained. "Not about me taking over. I got a call on my cell thirty minutes ago from my colonel telling me there'd been new developments and setting up this conference. Nothing more."

I opened my mouth, but nothing came out. I could hear the rush of blood in my ears. Everything had a surreal cast to it.

Harker continued. "We will, of course, give glowing references regarding our work with Rv6-4 and your leadership role to your superiors, Captain Walker. After all, thanks to your efforts, you rendered the gelatin factory inoperable and you saved the American consumer from the threat of tainted food products. No small victory these days."

I stared at the phone. I'd been right from very beginning. Jake *had* been a threat to me. Despite all his words. Despite all his assurances. I'd been a fool to trust him, and a greater fool to let myself fall for him. Because that's what it was—I'd fallen for him, turned my unprotected throat up to him, trusting, despite all my sound and fury to the contrary, and I simply hadn't believed deep down this would ever happen. My hands trembled. I hid them beneath the table so he wouldn't see. My stomach clenched again, and I had to fight the urge to throw up.

A long moment of quiet drew out. The open phone line hummed and buzzed.

"Sir, if I may speak freely." Jake glared down at the conference phone, but he stood very still, as if holding himself in check from smashing the phone until nothing but broken plastic and wires remained.

"If you must."

"Changing the command structure will seriously degrade this unit's operational efficiency." Jake paused and glanced at me, frowning. "This unit's cohesion and overall morale are some of the highest I've ever seen, and that's due to Captain Walker's command. I don't feel this change is the most effective approach to the situation and, in my judgment, it will impede a quick and successful outcome."

I couldn't look at him, couldn't speak. I stared at the tabletop, its surface nicked in places, marked with slashes of black permanent marker in others. I bit down on the inside of my cheek so hard I could taste the blood.

Harker sounded annoyed. "Has the viability of this unit been compromised, Captain? Your report spoke of them in glowing terms. I expected you to be able to lead men and women you describe as consummate professionals."

My mouth dropped open. I realized I had a stupid, amazed look plastered on my face but was helpless to stop it. From the instant I'd met Jake, I'd nursed the lingering suspicion that he didn't respect my people, had looked down on them with a kind of patient, indulgent contempt. The fact that he *did* respect them, and the fact that he hadn't even told me he'd praised us to his superiors, made it all the better. All the sweeter. In that moment I loved him. Fiercely.

"I stand by every one of those statements," Jake said. "But I reiterate—in the strongest terms possible—replacing Captain Walker would have an immediate and severe effect on unit cohesion and morale, to the detriment of the mission."

"I see," Harker said. The silence spun out long enough to be uncomfortable.

My heart had crawled halfway up my trachea. I wanted to run to Jake, to kiss him, and then to kick him for not telling me he thought about us, about *me* in that way. Not feelings I was comfortable with at all—except for the kicking part. I hated myself for the almost childish gratefulness I felt toward him when he'd turned down his chance to steal away my people, the relief that he'd been speaking the truth when he'd said he wasn't a threat—hated myself because *I* should've been the one slinging fire and grandstanding and raising my fist in defiance instead of sitting in a chair, staring at a phone, feeling shocked, weary and weak, feeling as if I'd just spent my summer vacation in the muddy trenches of WWI.

"Well, then," Harker continued when it became clear no one else would speak. "Based on your recommendation, Captain Sanders, it seems it's time for Plan B. I have a Delta Force team who just finished a hunt-and-kill mission on rogue batsquatch. I'll redeploy them to Portland and have them take over the investigation with support from the FBI. You'll end your force multiplier role with Rv6-4, attach yourself to the Delta team, and integrate your knowledge of the necromancer's tactics and current capabilities into the assault and capture phase."

"Sir," Jake said quickly, "switching assets mid operation

isn't—"

"You have your orders, Captain Sanders, and I expect them to be followed. You are reassigned. I'll send transportation to retrieve you."

"Yes, sir," Jake said through clenched teeth.

Harker wasn't finished. "Captain Walker, it seems your men and women must think extremely highly of you if Captain Sanders believes you should remain at the helm. However, since this mission has changed from an assault to a manhunt, and since the Delta teams are better suited and better trained for search and destroy, I'm certain you understand our switching primary operators on this mission doesn't reflect on your leadership or the performance of your people in any way."

"And that's why you revoked my command, right?"

"It was a suggested lateral move. No insult intended. A matter of efficiency only."

I clenched my fists but didn't answer. We needed the money. I had to keep that in mind. I couldn't afford to burn bridges and throw tantrums...but damn it was hard to be adult about it.

"I believe we've covered everything necessary," Harker said. "A car will be coming for you shortly, Captain Sanders." A pause. "Thank you for your service to your country, Captain Walker. Good day."

Dial tone. I reached out and disconnected the phone, and then my hand fell flat to the tabletop and lay there like a dead spider.

"I'm sorry," Jake said. He didn't move toward me.

Such a riot of thoughts and confusion exploded in my mind that I had to close my eyes. My flash of love for him had been swept under by bewildered hurt. Part of me had expected him to stay here with us and not go off after the necromancer without me. I don't know what I'd imagined he'd do—insubordination, retire his command? Stupid and unrealistic. The rational part of me *knew* it. And still...

"It was all for nothing," I said. "And now you're going."

"Yes, I'm going, but it wasn't all for nothing."

"Anything for the mission, right? Even throwing me over."

"I'm a soldier. I have duties—"

"*Fuck* your duties." The words cut me, no doubt far deeper than they cut him. Yet, I'd said them anyway.

He didn't reply.

"Get out."

He didn't move. He watched me with those intense dark green eyes and an expression I couldn't read.

"Get *out*!" I slammed my fist into the table. The phone jumped. The handset fell off and the dial tone began its heedless, unwavering scream.

He walked past me. I stared at my fist, feeling the needles of pain along my knuckles. Enjoying the pain more than I should have, because it hurt less than the pain inside my mind.

He paused at the doorway and looked back. "I'm sorry."

"Don't fucking apologize. If you were part of this team, you wouldn't leave...wouldn't leave us."

"I'm an officer of the US Ar—"

"I know what you are." Then softer, little more than a whisper. "Just go. Please."

Silence...and then the sound of his footsteps, retreating. A door opened and closed. I was alone.

Again.

He was gone by that afternoon. For a moment I'd stood at a hall window, watching him at the end of the driveway, beyond the gate. He'd been waiting for the car Harker promised to send, all his gear in a duffel bag next to him. But I hadn't watched for long.

I endured a parade of comrades all afternoon. Tiffany came in sobbing about it, which both amused and annoyed me. She wanted to take me out drinking, despite what had happened the last time we'd entered a dance club. Rafe gave me a sandwich—steroid and hormone free turkey breast, organic lettuce and alfalfa sprouts. Mai brought me a cup of green tea and asked if I wanted to borrow a kitten or a ferret. I didn't. Hanzo loaned me his entire collection of Bruce Lee and Akira Kurosawa films. Vampire Stefan still slept, so he didn't count. Even Gavin, using his incredible empathy powers, told me if I ever needed a shoulder to cry on, he was there for me, just not between seven and nine p.m. because his online MMORPG guild had a raid scheduled and he couldn't miss it. By then I was ready to start making plans to escape to Lithuania for some alone time.

Another knock rattled the door.

"Go away!" I yelled. "I'm otherwise occupied!"

"It's Sarge." His deep bass rumble also rattled the door.

Oh, for God's sake. I walked over and let him in. He had to turn slightly to fit his massive shoulders through the doorway. He wore black fatigues and an extra-large urban-camo ball cap pulled low over his forehead. I led him into the living room and offered him a seat, but he shook his head and remained standing. "Captain Sanders asked me to hold off destroying the zombie head."

"Why?" The word came out sharper than I intended.

"He still thinks it's the key to finding the necromancer." A pause. "And he's right."

"Then why didn't he take it with him when he shoved off outta here?"

"I don't know."

I stared at the wall. "You have an idea though. I can hear it in your voice."

"I think he wants to come back for it at the right time. Give us the glory."

"Then why the fuck didn't he tell Harker that?"

"Captain Sanders is a soldier. Harker's a bureaucrat."

"So what? I eat bureaucrats for lunch and shit out

paperwork. Surely our resident *quiet professional* could've found the balls to demand more time."

"There was more to it than that."

I narrowed my eyes. "What do you know? Something I don't?"

"Things aren't clear cut. I talked to him before he left. This is political."

"What? Now the dirty mercenaries are a political hot potato? They want Delta Force commandoes to grab the glory? Bullshit."

"I can only tell you what he believed."

"Why didn't he just say that to me?"

"I got the impression you didn't give him a chance."

I didn't answer. What could I say to that? It might even have been true.

"What do you want to do?" he asked. "He wanted to wait on using the zombie head, but I'll have the final preparations for the spell completed tonight."

"We aren't getting paid. Why the hell should we do it?"

He kept silent, merely standing like a purple-mountain majesty of muscle and staring at me. Absolutely fan-fucking-tastic how a *demon* could make me feel guilty without a word, as if I shirked my duty to humanity.

"We don't owe anybody anything," I said. "We don't get paid for charity work. We got overhead. Tons of it. We shank this necromancer guy and Homeland Security will bury it. I bet they won't even bother to pay us the rest of the fee."

Sarge didn't answer.

"Shit, you're worse than my mother, you know that, Sergeant? I fucking swear to Zeus's electric prick."

His lips quirked into a thin smile. "You kiss your mother with that mouth?"

"I kiss lots of things with this mouth," I said. "But I don't kiss asses. You know, it's a sad day indeed when demons have better ethics than the government." I glared at him. "We'll finish the damn job."

"Good."

"Yeah, great. I thought you said you needed both me and Jake to fuel your spell?"

"I think I can use Stefan instead. It'll be tricky. His powers are drawn from the currents of darkness, same as mine. You'll represent the nuclear fusion of the sun. The spell balance will be off a fraction with no Earth grounding. It may fail."

"What are the consequences of failure? We open a rift to another dimension? We create a black hole that sucks in the solar system?"

He paused and considered. "We'll fry the zombie head to the point of uselessness."

"I expected something more dramatic, like inter-dimensional mayhem and Biblical apocalypse. At least a power outage."

"Sometimes life is banal."

"All right then. We'll see what we get. But if this necromancer is a hardened target now, we'll feed the info to Captain Sanders and let him and his GI Joes handle it. I almost lost Rafe last time out. I'm not risking more of my people for nothing." I hesitated and cleared my throat. "Unless it's accelerating the end of the world or something. Then I guess we'd have to do something."

"Zombie apocalypse qualifies."

"Fine." I waved a hand. "Make it happen, Number Two."

"Be at my room at nineteen-hundred hours tonight. We'll get this done." He turned to go, moving with a curious delicacy around my furniture for a creature his size.

"Hey, Sarge," I called, and he glanced back. "Why the hell aren't you a fearless leader somewhere? Why'd you join a bunch of misfits like us? I always wanted to ask you that."

"I'm comfortable where I am."

"That's not really an answer."

"Trust me. You don't want a demon running the show." His lips split in a slow smile. "And I think you sell yourself a little short." He paused. "Though you made the wrong choice on Sanders."

I couldn't help but bristle. "Did I?"

"You did."

"He left me."

"Not by choice. You might want to remember that when he comes back."

My heart beat faster. "He's coming back?"

Sarge turned and walked to the door. I stood but didn't follow. My thoughts and emotions spun and churned inside me, so confused I didn't know what to feel. He opened the door and faced me. "A man in love always comes back."

He shut the door with a gentle click.

Chapter Twenty-One: Reddest Badge of Courage

Mercenary Wing Rv6-4 "Zero Dogs"
The Zero Dog Compound
NW Hilltop Drive, Portland, Oregon
1813 Hours PST April 19th

Nothing to do but wait. I stayed in my room and didn't even go out to supervise the second wave of Merry Maids on their extended campaign through the house waging war on our mess. I'd almost choked on a lung when I'd seen the invoice, but I sure as red hell wasn't going to clean the place myself, so it'd been time to suck it up, grin and bear it.

I spent the rest of the time ghosting through my rooms in my bare feet, making no sound. Music drifted from the speakers. Vivaldi's "Summer". I couldn't get drunk because I'd need reflexes and concentration later. Losing the job had cut the heart out of me. Hell, Jake leaving us, leaving me, had not only cut the heart out of me, it had spiked it on the sidewalk and then punted it over a rusty fence. Worse, I'd managed to convince myself Sarge was wrong about Jake. He'd only said what he had to make me feel better. I knew Jake better than he did, and Jake wouldn't turn away from a mission—not if any hope remained of seeing it through.

Finally, the late-evening sun splashed red on the walls. I sat on the edge of my bed, drinking seltzer from a glass and wishing it were something strong, listening to haunting music and staring at absolutely nothing. Darkness would soon arrive, and then I'd be elbow deep in demon magic, in a room with a still-animated zombie head, trying to use it as a location beacon to track the necromancer. I cared. I really did. It's just that I couldn't seem to work up any excitement. It all seemed unimportant, even more so now, when we wouldn't be paid for our work.

I threw back the rest of the lime seltzer. Gently, I turned the glass in my hands, admiring how the red-orange glow of sunlight frosted its rim like coals frozen in a photograph.

Maybe I'd been thinking about this in the wrong way. Wouldn't it be something to find the necromancer on our own, with no help from anyone? To call up Jake—no, this had to be done in person. To *walk* up to Jake and tell him the Zero Dogs had located Public Enemy Number One and revel as jealousy flared in his eyes.

I hunched forward, forearms on my knees, still turning the glass. A stupid daydream, nothing more, and completely disconnected from reality. I already knew Jake wasn't the jealous type. He'd probably smile and nod in approval, like we were hard chargers and we'd done exactly what he expected.

I missed him.

And missing him annoyed me, big time. He didn't deserve my attention, dammit. Sure, he'd told Harker my team wouldn't follow him, and he'd *seemed* surprised when Harker sprang the command change on us, but all the same, he hadn't fought to stay with us and hadn't fought to keep us on the job, choosing to run off to play with Delta Force boys instead.

My hand clamped around my empty glass, squeezing harder. What the hell was I doing thinking this shit? Being stupid and paranoid, that's all. Jake hadn't tried to usurp my command. From the beginning he'd been all about doing things as a team. He'd been trained that way and trained others that way. I couldn't lay the blame for this at his feet. He'd proven himself when he'd turned down a chance at running the show. Irrational of me to blame him for Harker's actions. Easy. Tempting. But completely unfair.

But it didn't *matter* anymore. Even if I changed, even if I wanted to become more of a team player with him, he was gone and the job had left with him. I eased up my grip before I shattered the empty glass and set it on the comforter beside me. I sighed and leaned back on my hands and stared out the window.

Dammit. Had I been the one to blow this? Been so damn paranoid about somebody infringing on my command I'd failed to take advantage of something...something great and exciting the universe had dropped right into my lap? I stood up and paced. Jake had been right. A very real, very intense heat burned between us. Our rocky start aside, the man had adapted, even admitted when he'd been wrong. In the end, he'd seen me and my people as equals.

Which was a hell of a lot more than I'd ever done for him.

I stopped cold. My hands shook. I crossed my arms and shoved my hands under my armpits so I wouldn't have to see them tremble.

I wouldn't give up on my chance with Jake. No. He'd proven himself to me, and now I'd finish proving myself to him. I'd take the Zero Dogs and find that necromancer. We'd stop him, complete the mission, and after that there'd be no more of this command tension between us. My fears would go away. We'd be free to do whatever we wanted.

Somebody knocked at my apartment door. I sat up and glanced at my watch. The sun had dropped below the mountains, and the shadows had grown long and pregnant with darkness. I'd lost track of time.

That was Jake knocking at my door.

Part of me felt certain of it. It was hard not to run, hell, *sprint* out of my room, leap the couch and wrench open the door. Then I'd either play aloof and hard to get, or I'd throw myself into his arms and cover him with kisses, depending on what seemed right at the time. Probably option two. No, *definitely* option two.

No running after all because my legs wobbled, and I felt none too steady on my feet. The pound of my heart reverberated from my chest all the way down to the tips of my fingers. Finally, I reached the door and opened it.

Sarge stared back at me. He must have seen something on my face, because he got this mild, sympathetic look in his eyes—as if he knew I'd wanted him to be Jake and felt sorry I'd been let down, which must've violated hundreds of demon codes of conduct.

Still, I recovered well. "Oh. Hiya, Sarge. Thought you were Mai." I glanced at my watch again. Oh shit, time for Sarge's ritual. I'd been so busy brooding over Jake I'd almost forgotten. "I can't believe how late it is. Time flies when you're having fun..." I waved a hand at my empty glass, "...drinking and so forth..."

Sarge hesitated. "You okay?"

"I'm a fucking Georgia Peach."

He raised his eyebrows.

"All right, fine," I said. "I miss him a little. The bastard."

"Do you want to go through with this?"

"Of course. I want to show those motarded Delta Force bastards how shit gets done Zero Dog style."

"That's what I wanted to hear." He favored me with a slow smile. "Let's get this over with and go kill some zombies for free."

Kill zombies for free.

A while back I'd said the Zero Dog motto was *The First Bullet is Always Free.* Unfortunately, this would likely take a whole lot of free bullets.

So, despite my burst of enthusiasm, despite my desire to

see the end of this mission, and despite my altruistic urge to save humanity from the hungry undead, the cold-eyed accountant chained to a calculator deep inside my brain was already tapping away at her ten-key pad, desperate to come up with a way I could write it all off on our taxes as a business expense. Charity was one thing, but even charitable contributions were tax deductible. It made me feel slightly skeezy, like a car salesman playing games with interest rates to fleece a customer, but I had a roof to keep over our heads and mouths to feed. Most of them weren't even human mouths with human appetites. If that made me a mercenary bitch...well, that was because I *was* a mercenary bitch. I grinned, feeling better than I had in a while.

Sarge and I arrived at his room. He put his face against an iris scanner and the door clicked. He pushed it open, and I followed him inside. Sarge's rooms were austere in the extreme. Chrome furniture. Glass tables. Antiseptic modern décor in white and steel, black and chrome. Yet colorful signs of life burst here and there, color touches I knew Shawn had added over the years from his good-natured bitching about how Sarge preferred to live in an ultra-modern glass display case. A Rococo painting hung on the opposite wall—somebody dying while other people, including a cherub, stood around holding halberds—a style far too ornate for my taste. My favorite *objet d'art* had always been the quirky mobile dangling in one corner made out of bright brass shell casings, seashells painted yellow and blue and red, and oddly shaped mirror shards.

With the blinds shut, gloom and shadow filled the apartment. He'd moved the coffee table and couch out of the living room, leaving a wide-open space of wood floor. Lines of glittering dust angled out in what seemed random directions. Sarge had drawn a triangle with perfectly symmetrical angles, sketched with a black substance like charcoal. Within the triangle he'd painted a perfect circle with a red liquid long since dried. Not blood, something else I couldn't identify.

"What's all that crap on the floor?" I asked.

"A mixture to open the connection. Fairy snot. Heinz 57 sauce. Mildew scraped from the shower grout of a fashion model living in Norway. Matsutake mushroom paste. Semen from an incubus—"

"Forget I even asked." I felt an almost overpowering urge to go wash my hands and soak them in bleach.

Sarge walked to the edge of the outer triangle and stood staring down at it. A red craftsman toolbox sat against the wall, and a trio of glass beakers sat on top of it, with multi-hued liquids arranged in a row. He moved to the toolbox and bent down, blocking it and half the wall from my view. I heard glassware and metal clinking around as he opened the drawers.

"How's this going to work?" Now that the time was at hand, I found myself a little nervous. Demon magic didn't have anything close to a spotless reputation. Even allowing for all the negative propaganda, it still gave me pause. And incubus semen had me thinking twice already.

He reached into his shirt, pulled out a gold pocket watch on a chain and thumbed open the top with a retractable claw. "Stefan should be here any minute, now that the sun's down. When he gets here I'll arrange everything."

"Beautiful. Demon magic, vampire magic, pyro magic all thrown together. You realize this could be the end of the world."

"Don't be dramatic. Something goes wrong, we'd just blow up the house."

"How perfectly un-reassuring," I said. "Wait a minute. Didn't you say earlier we'd only melt the zombie head? No big deal, you said. Sometimes life's banal, you said. I really think I remember that."

"After I set down the spell grid, I realized I'd underestimated."

A knock sounded at the door before I could express what I thought about *underestimating.* I headed over to answer it. "Must be our lazy vampire dragging himself out of his coffin at last."

Sarge only leaned down and drew glowing runes along the outside edge of the triangle with his finger.

I frowned at him, then pulled open the door and found myself face-to-face with Jake Sanders.

My heart gave a crazy dismayed lurch. I think I tried to say something, but no sound escaped my lips. My hand floated toward him of its own accord, as if to touch his face, to make sure he was real. I stopped it and let it drop back to my side and only stared at him.

Dark stubble shadowed his cheeks, strange since I'd never seen him anything but clean-shaven. His army green T-shirt had wrinkles striping the front, and dust layered his combat boots. He looked like he'd just run the Baja 1000 on foot.

I swallowed and sucked in a breath. A smile started to curve its way up the corners of Jake's lips. His gaze had locked on me as if I were some prize in a grand quest: Excalibur, the Golden Fleece or the Holy Grail. The moment drew out and became almost painful in its silent intensity.

"You forget your socks or something?" I finally managed, but my voice sounded choked even to my own ears.

His smile widened. "Hello, Andrea. Sounds like you missed me."

"I missed you like I miss my pet rat and the bubonic plague."

"At least we have historical precedence. I'll take that."

Easier to keep up the banter than to deal with my riptide of emotions. "Now that I think about it, I missed you like I miss reading Gavin's fiction. Which is somewhere between having my skin flayed off with a potato peeler and buying a used car."

"Thought I told you, keep it up and my ego might suffer."

Damn I'd missed him. "How much longer will that take? Even the Titanic sank when it hit an iceberg."

Sarge's voice rumbled out from behind me. "Would you two mind getting over here? You can wallow in sexual tension later."

I turned and glared at him, feeling heat creep up my cheeks.

Sarge glanced up from drawing the glowing spell lines on the floor and arched an eyebrow at me. "Tell you what. After we finish here you guys can head up to your room and do the dirty deed until you go blind. Until then, I need you both if we're going to make this work."

My mouth dropped open and I started working on my reply—one that would detonate like a fuel-air explosive. Jake set a hand on my shoulder and I almost leapt out of my skin.

"Come on, soldier," he whispered. His breath on my neck sent a shiver through me. "Let's get this done."

For a moment—a very brief moment—I considered grabbing the hand on my shoulder and trying to flip him. Old reflexes die hard. But in the end I let him touch me. Because I liked it, and I wasn't afraid to admit it anymore. "Aren't you supposed to be somewhere? With Delta Force guys or something?"

"Yeah."

"So what the hell are you doing here, Jake? You AWOL?"

"Not at all. I'm following up a significant lead on the target." He smiled, but the smile had little humor. In fact, the smile bore a passing resemblance to a barracuda-wolf hybrid. "I pulled some strings, managed to get my reassignment paperwork delayed. The commander of the Delta team's a buddy of mine from way back. Besides, we're allowed some latitude on decision-making in the field."

"Somehow I doubt it's as easy as that. And I notice you didn't say you had clearance."

"I don't." He leaned toward me. "But this is important. You guys earned the right to see it through."

I nodded while my stomach did a slow somersault. Part of me hadn't wanted to believe Jake was back, even when I opened the door on him. He was something I'd wanted, yearned for and barely had the guts to articulate, even to myself. A dark part of me remained certain he'd be snatched away from me again. The same dark part in my mind always whispering that if I chose to take hold of what I wanted, it would slip away again in a haze of regretful words about duty and sacrifice and I'd be alone. Not now. I could see it in his eyes that he meant to see this through, no matter the cost. Stupid or brave, I didn't know and didn't care. Even if he were here only for the end of this mission, I'd take that, and I'd leave another day for another day and live the moment.

His hand slipped over mine. He lifted it up to his lips and kissed it softly, a gesture I found strangely touching. "I didn't want to leave you. I had nothing to do with their decisions."

"I know." And I did. When Harker had tried to give him command of my people, Jake could've descended from heaven with a twenty-four carat halo and mother-of-pearl wings and I'd still have lit into him.

"I know how much your people mean to you," he continued. "I'd never come between that."

"Jake, I shouldn't have—"

He shook his head and held up his hand. "Doesn't matter. You were straight from the first. I saw the position you were in, so how could I blame you? But riding in that car, leaving here, I realized I'd made a huge mistake. I knew I couldn't leave you."

I swallowed. My mouth had gone dry and a painful knot lodged in my throat.

He slowly leaned in toward me. "And what I said about not being a threat to you?"

"Yes?"

"I lied." He kissed me hard. I melted against him. Part of my mind suspected things were about to get X-rated.

Sarge cleared his throat. We drew apart like teenagers caught necking on the porch. Jake and I looked at each other. We both burst out laughing at the same time, and together we walked the rest of the way over to Sarge, who regarded us with strained amusement. "Too cute. And it's about fucking time."

"Sarge," I said, keeping my voice calm. "Have I told you how much your recent behavior reminds me of Gavin? Just thought you'd like to know."

Sarge grunted. He looked at Jake, and I sensed something flash between them. Out of the corner of my eye I saw Jake give a slight nod, and Sarge returned to his work. I took a deep breath and concentrated on ignoring male posturing. I didn't want my good mood to sour.

Jake and I gave him plenty of space to work. He sketched complex designs along the interior of the circle, angular shapes surrounded by flowing patterns that reminded me of water. He drew along the floor with his finger, and everywhere he traced, a blue glow lingered like a propane flame.

After a short while, he sat back and inspected his work. "All right. Each of us will sit at one point of the triangle. I'll direct the flow of power from the northern tip. Don't touch the lines."

We split up, me to the western point, and Jake to the east. I sat down, careful not to mess up the lines. I didn't want my face seared off or my hair bleached white or anything.

"We're not going to do something really evil, are we?" I asked. "Because I draw the line at sacrificing small animals and ritual defilement."

Sarge cocked an eyebrow at me, and then glanced at Jake. "You see what a demon has to put up with?"

Jake grinned. "I thought these kinds of things always ended with an orgy."

Both of Sarge's eyebrows shot up, and I giggled. Yes. Giggled exactly like Tiffany. I slapped a hand over my mouth to kill the sound, praying Sarge hadn't noticed.

"I'm going to ignore that quip," Sarge said. "And I'd appreciate some silence while I work. Hold on. Let me get that severed head."

"There's something you don't hear every day," Jake said.

"He's a demon. I bet he says that more often than I care to think about."

Sarge returned with the severed zombie head still in my laundry basket. I didn't believe either irradiation or autoclaving could save my basket now. He set it down and lifted the zombie out by the hair. The zombie appeared less than pleased, biting at the air and staring at me with flat dead eyes that held the classic *I want to eat your face* expression, and not in a good way.

"I'm going to play polo with you when we're done," I told the zombie. The zombie didn't seem impressed. That was the problem with zombies. They sported a whole *fuck you, I'm dead* attitude I hated.

"So what do we have to do?" Jake asked.

"Simple. I'll do the hard part directing the energy through the lines. You both are here to amp up the power I can draw and to serve as grounds."

"Do we have to *plug* ourselves in?" I asked, and Jake snorted.

Sarge gave me a look. "The sexual innuendos must stop. Now."

Geez. Nobody had a sense of humor anymore. Though it *did* feel good to be dishing out the obnoxious behavior for once instead of being its victim. Having Jake back made me feel almost giddy. Stupid, but I couldn't help it.

Sarge placed the head in the center of the circle, careful not to disturb his lines. Multicolored glowy lights flickered to life in rows on the floor, radiating out from the head like a Pink Floyd laser-light show, and me without my illegal substances. Sarge sat back down at the northern tip of the triangle and arranged his mass into the lotus position. Jake and I copied his pose.

"This will feel like you're about to work magic," Sarge continued, "but you won't be able to complete any spell."

"Spellus-interruptus, right?" Jake said.

Laughter barked out of my mouth, sounding like an angry otter. Not dignified, but what the hell.

Sarge frowned at Jake. "I'm beginning to think having you

return was a mistake. Clearly, the captain is a corrupting influence."

"We'll behave," I assured him. Time to be serious. Make lists. Kick asses. Talk shit about it on the internet. "Let's just get this done."

Sarge began to chant in a soft monotone. Strange shimmering vapor rose from the spell lines. A high-pitched whine began in my ear, like a mosquito. I scowled in annoyance, wondering if the whine was supposed to happen. Sarge closed his red and black eyes and let his massive head fall back. I glanced at Jake, who shrugged. I closed my own eyes and let my head tilt back. So far I'd sensed nothing.

It hit all at once. Zero to sixty in half a second. Power flooded through me as if some invisible gate had been thrown wide open. My spine arched. All the fine hairs on my arms and the back of my neck lifted. My eyelids snapped wide open and I gritted my teeth against a scream of surprise.

The power moved through me and down into the lines on the ground. Their glow brightened, kaleidoscoping along the ceiling. Jake still had his eyes closed, but he'd tensed, and all his muscles stood out against his shirt, while the veins bulged in his forearms. A black nimbus had encircled Sarge. His chanting grew louder. I couldn't sense any evil, unless it came from the zombie head, but that was only stupid evil, the way a garden slug will eat your best strawberries just because it can. Instead, a sensation of barely controlled power crushed down on me. The zombie's eyes were open wide, its mouth slack, and that black nimbus, like a shadow defying the direction of the light, reached out and encircled it.

Images flashed through my brain, so vibrant and real they eclipsed the view of Sarge's room. The images blurred at first, but then they focused and I saw through the eyes of someone else—a vertigo-inducing sensation which had both my mind and stomach reeling. I immediately knew I looked through someone else's eyes because I could see the blurry outline of the nose dead center of my view.

It only took me a moment to realize what it was I looked at—or what the eyes I ghosted behind looked at. Fear ripped through me like a jigsaw through rotted pine, leaving me weak and disconnected from my body.

Night. A windshield, but a strange one, with wide, flat glass. The top arc of a huge steering wheel. A bus? A man's hands gripped the wheel. The view turned, glancing through a side window. Outside the bus, hundreds and hundreds of dark shapes shambled up an incline toward a fence. Beyond the fence sat a huge house with lights in many of its windows and security lamps creating wide pools of brightness. I recognized it at once. The Zero Dog Compound. *Our* house. The zombies surged toward it in a dark tide.

The view swiveled back to center. The bus moved forward, gaining speed. No sound, but I could imagine the roar of the engine...or did I hear it, faintly, from beyond the window? Things began to overlap and nausea turned my stomach again.

The bus passed the zombie front line, pulling ahead, and raced up our driveway toward the iron gate. The driver roared past the intercom and keypad without a glance and rammed the bus into the gate. The front grill smashed it aside with a loud clang and a dismayed screech of metal. The bus veered toward our garages where we stored the Bradley and a good chunk of our parts and ammo.

My heart felt as if it steadily dissolved as the bus shuddered to a stop outside the closed bay doors. The view swiveled and changed—a man's hand reached out and pulled the handle, opening the doors. Zombies began to stumble and fall down the steps onto the asphalt.

The man's hand came up into view. He turned his hand over and focused on it. Then it clenched into a fist and the view vanished as if we'd lost a satellite feed. Power dispersed and I felt it buffet me like a shock wave before my mind's eye slammed back into my body in Sarge's apartment again, and I was seeing with my own eyes once more.

"Holy shit." My heart hammered like the double bass drums in a heavy metal band. I staggered to my feet. "He's *here*."

I fought against the fear and the adrenaline shock spiking through my body. They made my thoughts scattered and disconnected—too bright and too fast to concentrate on. My fists tightened, crushing my fingers into my palms. We'd been outmaneuvered.

Jake looked at me, and I could read the same thoughts in his eyes. Without a word, he pulled his Beretta from the holster in one smooth motion, drew back the slide and thumbed off the safety. The gunshot sounded flat and loud. The zombie head toppled over with a bullet dead center in its forehead.

Sarge pushed himself to a squat and kicked the lines of dust apart with his boot. I stood up, already calling my magic. Heat shimmered around my hands like an Arizona highway at high noon. Jake had his M9 Beretta out and pointed at the floor. Sarge hurried from the room and came back with a rifle in his hands, one of the SCAR-16S carbines I'd shot with him a few times on the range. A belt strung with ammo pouches hung over one huge shoulder. He pulled back the bolt. I felt rather left out without dramatic round chambering for Hollywood effect. Who would've guessed throwing fire could have any drawbacks?

"At least he won't be hard to find," Jake said, just as the alarms began to wail.

Chapter Twenty-Two: Hell in a Very Clean Place

Mercenary Wing Rv6-4 "Zero Dogs"
The Zero Dog Compound
Main Stairs
1911 Hours PST April 19th

I didn't remember much about the time between hearing the perimeter alarms and sprinting down the hall. It was only a blur of motion and stark anger interlaced with fear as Jake, Sarge and I pounded down the stairs. Jake took the lead, me in the middle, and Sarge brought up the rear with his SCAR-16—and I was so upset my usual gutter-inclined mind didn't even make a quip about being in the middle of a Green Beret and demon sandwich.

The alarms continued to bray their mindless warning cry. Gavin almost crashed into us on the second-floor landing. "Captain, it's the fucking zombie apocalypse!"

I grabbed him and dragged him with me. "I know, come on. We've got to get everybody together."

"So why don't you use the intercom?"

Shit, why hadn't I thought of that? I had to hurry up and pull my head out of my ass if I planned to lead us out of this alive. I veered off at a full sprint toward my office.

Jake ran after me. "Andrea—what the hell?"

I slid to a stop at my office door and ran inside, nearly knocking over my cactus in my dash for the intercom. First I killed the alarm so I could hear myself think. Then I slapped my hand down on the broadcast button, fighting off the panic trying to break my voice as my words echoed through the house. "Attention all Zero Dogs, we're under attack. Defense condition one. Grab weapons and get to the living room immediately."

Gathering everybody in one place had its disadvantages, limiting fields of fire and ability to respond to scattered threats, but without a planned defense we were toast. If we regrouped fast enough, there remained a good chance we wouldn't end up trapped inside the house.

Jake pulled me away from the intercom. "Come on. There's no time."

I must have hit the wrong switch as he yanked my arm because the melodic strains of Santana and the song "No One to Depend On" started coming through the ceiling speakers. No time to fix it now. We were already off and running again.

"Great soundtrack, Captain," Gavin wheezed from behind me, winded from running. If we survived this uneaten, I vowed he'd get mandatory physical training, whether his job was to sit on his ass and drive stuff or not.

Moments later, we thundered down the short hall leading to the great room. Rafe crouched on the back of the sofa in werewolf form. He gripped a golf club, his titanium driver by the look of it, in one massive pawish hand. I blinked at the sight of a horror-movie-esque werewolf appearing ready to spend some quality time on the green. Squeegee the mutant housecat paced near the big window, hackles raised and a low rumbling growl coming from her throat. Stefan lounged against the wall inspecting his manicure as if this were just another night at the office. But there was no sign of Mai, Hanzo or Tiffany anywhere. *Shit.* "Where's everybody else?"

Stefan shook his head. "We have yet to see them."

Jake and Sarge hurried to the plate-glass window and stared out into the darkness.

"Zombies inside the gate," Sarge said. "A helluva lot of 'em. Coming up the hill toward the house."

My thoughts spun in frantic circles, tumbling all over each other so rapidly I couldn't grab one to hold it and focus. Things kept happening so damn fast. Sure we had a fire-escape plan, but we'd never prepared a zombie-assault-escape plan. We'd always been the aggressors, doing jobs in other people's backyards. This house was no fortress. And how had the necromancer created all those zombies in so short a time? Sarge and I had briefly discussed the possibility of the necromancer tracking us back here through the zombie head we'd stolen, and I'd just put in an order for claymore mines and barbed wire, but we'd both agreed the probability of attack had been low, and nothing to fear in the short term.

We'd been very wrong.

The panic twisted tighter. My lungs felt like a hundred-foot python crushed my chest, and the muscles in my legs burned. *Get it together.* I clamped down without mercy, gritting my teeth and clenching my fists until I had myself under control.

"All right, people, listen up." My voice whip-cracked with command, and that made me pretty damn proud of myself. "Somebody's fucking with us, and the Zero Dogs don't take that shit."

"That's right," Rafe growled. "I do the fucking around here."

"And I do the fucking around, around here," Gavin added.

Holy goddamned Glorious Reformed Church of Cthulhu, somebody kill me now. The localized zombie apocalypse upon us and I had to deal with *this.* I should've gone to law school like Mother wanted.

Too late for that now, so I started barking orders. "Sarge, Rafe, Stefan, get Gavin to the Bradley so he can bring it around front. Keep a path clear so we can get everybody the hell outta here."

Sarge nodded, pulled a 9mm from somewhere and tossed it to Gavin, who fumbled and dropped it on the carpet. I tried not to weep.

"There's a crapload of zombies out there," I continued. "Keep tight. Don't get surrounded. If you can't get to the garage, get your asses back inside." I *didn't* say that if we couldn't get to the Bradley we were up shit river without Mickey Mouse and a steamboat because that meant we'd been trapped. Trapped meant we had to hunker down, barricade up and hope we didn't run out of ammo. Bloody business, any way I cut it. "Me and Jake will find Tiffany, Hanzo and Mai and meet you at the front door. Now move, move, *move*!"

Sarge had the assault rifle up and at his shoulder, already moving in a slight crouch toward the kitchen and the patio doors, followed by Rafe and his golf club, Stefan with his claws and fangs, and Gavin, who seemed uncomfortable with the 9mm, even though we'd all had plenty of pistol training. I watched them go, part of me wanting to call them back. Fighting zombies in the dark would be even more dangerous than tangling with them in daylight.

They disappeared through the doorway while my heart pounded hard as a rain of cluster bombs. Something crashed outside with enough force to make me flinch. Jake moved beside me, setting his hand on my shoulder. I was grateful for the contact, though my guts still felt like they twisted inside me like snakes.

"They're professionals," Jake said. "They'll be all right."

He told me what I wanted to hear, but a cold voice inside me whispered I only deluded myself. None of us were safe. None of us would escape. Gunfire ripped through the night. I took a step toward the sound and then caught myself and clenched my fists.

"Come on," I said to Jake. "Let's go find the rest of my people and get the hell out of here."

Chapter Twenty-Three: Full Metal Reanimator

Undead Army of the Unrighteous Order of the Falling Dark
The Zero Dog Compound
Garage
7:21 p.m. PST April 19th

Necromancer Overlord Jeremiah Hansen might as well have been Napoleon at the Battle of Austerlitz, such was his brilliance. He'd already sent the bulk of his zombie forces against the main house. They'd advanced toward the ground floor in a dark, shuffling mass and piled up against the windows and doors. They smashed at the glass with rocks, patio chairs and decorative lawn gnomes. The heavy chatter of gunfire roared somewhere to the north. He directed another zombie wave off toward the gunfire, hoping to catch the mercenaries in the open where he could surround and destroy them.

Jeremiah kept back an honor guard with him at the garage. The honor guard consisted of the fifty zombies who'd survived the attack at his gelatin plant, zombies he'd come to think of as his core veterans. He'd decked these battle-tested undead out in firefighter gear—a little trick he hoped took the fire out of that mercenary woman's Bunsen burner. He'd already used his honor guard to break into the garage, where he'd found a ton of really great stuff, including the mercenaries' black tank vehicle that had caused him such grief. Hard for his undead army to do much against armor like that. So, as Blake would say, he'd just have to remove the asset from the balance books.

A quick search turned up some weapons among the stores of ammunition. He grabbed some cylindrical grenade-looking things. Perfect for what he had planned. He looked at the closest zombie, a twenty-something woman, her once-flawless skin now not so flawless—rather gray, truth be told—blonde hair the color of straw on the ground at the county fair, and painted into some kind of designer dress that looked as if it'd been expensive before she'd died in it. She wore narrow, spike-heeled shoes, also expensive-looking, ruined now by mud and grass. A conspicuous Gucci handbag hung from one slumped shoulder. She'd been beautiful once, yet with one of those spoiled rich, bitchy faces that had given him nightmares in high school.

"This is going to hurt you more than it's going to hurt me," he assured her. "But your sacrifice will never be forgotten...um...whatever your name is."

She moaned an interrogative. Something that sounded like, "Guuhuann?"

He couldn't help staring at her lips when she moaned. Most of her shiny lip gloss had smeared off and now some kind of fungus grew there. Kind of disturbing, actually. He might've thrown up in his mouth a little.

He put one of the grenade canisters in her hand, concentrating on guiding her actions through their silver cord connection as she climbed up on the back of the tank using boxes and an empty 55-gallon drum. The entire time she filled the air with a constant stream of moaning and groaning as if she were bitching at him about the hard work. She fell twice, thanks to those stupid-ass, ridiculous shoes. He nearly yanked out all his facial hair in frustration. The gunshots grew steadily closer, distracting him, filling him with the frenetic, unrelenting urge to *hurry*.

He closed his eyes, concentrated and looked through the distant dead eyes of one of his zombies. He caught a bleary glimpse of a huge, dark shape. The demon, Jeremiah recognized an instant later, when muzzle flashes from the gun it held lit its terrible face in bursts like lightning. He saw some pale creature—a vampire—fighting alongside a werewolf swinging a golf club around like a war hammer, both of them bashing and breaking and slicing their way through his zombie front line. To his left, a gigantic housecat pounced on his undead minions and tore them to shreds. What next? Chimpanzees with rocket launchers? God, what a headache these people were. A freak-show circus with claws and guns. He shifted more reinforcements in that direction, trying to swamp them beneath the undead tide.

Back inside the garage, his chosen zombie fashionista finally made it to the top of the tank. The hatch gaped open. She stood there swaying, looking down into the hatch, toying with her designer Gucci handbag with one hand while the other clutched the grenade.

Blake ghosted up beside Jeremiah, apparently finished hiding his Audi as per their Assault Plan Action Item Number Three. Somehow the man had freed the car from police impound without complications. His abilities struck Jeremiah as a trifle disquieting.

"A detachment of mercenaries is trying to fight its way here," Blake said.

"Tell me something I don't know."

"If they reach this vehicle…"

"Don't get your undies wet. I'm all over this. Watch." He saluted the girl zombie and she stepped forward and fell into the turret with a thud. A pained groan echoed out of the hatch.

"Impressive." Blake stroked his chin. "What exactly did that accomplish?"

"Follow me and see." He hurried outside, moving the rest of his zombie flame-resistant commandoes out with him. Blake followed close behind. No moon tonight, just starlight, and the darkness lay deep and thick, while the night air sang with a chorus of gunfire, zombie moans and the dull, arrhythmic thud of feet on the grass. Jeremiah and Blake took shelter behind some trees, and Jeremiah closed his eyes and concentrated on directing the fashionista zombie inside the tank to reach over and pull the ring pin on the grenade.

"Watch this," Jeremiah said. "Say fucking *hasta lombardo* to their wheels."

They waited. There was no explosion. His zombies shifted, now both restless and hungry. One of them moaned like a Swiss yodeler with a sore throat.

"What the fuck?" Jeremiah felt his face flush.

"I take it you expected something more dramatic?"

Jeremiah ran to the garage door and risked a look inside. Violet smoke billowed from the top hatch in a thick cloud. The air stank with a sharp, foul odor.

Blake stalked up beside him again. "A smokescreen. *Excellent.*"

"You're not helping me. And people who aren't helping me get eaten."

Blake gave him a slim smile and set his briefcase on the top of a workbench. He popped the clasps, revealing a collection of folders, his PDA, a wicked-looking handgun and a gray cylindrical canister. "I procured this in case it proved useful. A thermate incendiary grenade. Extremely handy to have at business meetings and working lunches."

"Blake, you are a very useful *hombre.*"

"I do my best." He walked to the vehicle, pulled the pin on the grenade and tossed it into the hatch. A confused, high-pitched "Garuunh?" echoed out of the hatch, which still belched violet smoke, and everything had been obscured by purple haze. Any moment now Jeremiah expected Jimi Hendrix to come out and light his guitar on fire.

Blake wiped his hand on his trousers. "I suggest we beat a

hasty retreat, since we're surrounded by a great deal of explosive and flammable materials."

They made it across the driveway and took cover behind a Douglas-fir. A stray branch smacked Jeremiah in the face and he ended up with the taste of pine in his mouth and sap on his cheek.

A deep bass rumble shattered the garage windows and rattled all the glass in the house, followed by a rapid series of small explosions—ammo cooking off. Another, larger explosion blew out the back of the garage in a huge ball of swirling fire flecked with debris. A smoking spike-heeled shoe went spinning through the air and impaled itself in the lawn. He thought there might still be a foot in it, but he didn't look too closely. He'd always remember the sacrifice of what's-her-face, the zombie with the chic purse.

The garage burned like a toy house built of kerosene-soaked popsicle sticks. The fire spread to the roof as more explosions ripped through the inside, making him flinch with every thunderclap boom.

"I think things are breaking our way this time," Jeremiah said.

Blake smiled. "I believe you are correct, sir."

Chapter Twenty-Something: Bridge on the River Styx

Mercenary Wing Rv6-4 "Zero Dogs"
The Zero Dog Compound
Great Room
1922 Hours PST April 19th

Jake moved to take point. He had his M9 out and a force barrier shimmered to life in front of him. I fell in behind to cover our six o'clock. We hadn't taken more than a half dozen steps when glass shattered somewhere behind us. Gunshots rang out from the patio, single shot groupings—the rapid *crack, crack, crack* of rifle rounds.

Shit. I again had to force myself not to run toward the sound of gunfire and join the fray. I looked toward the plate-glass window. Dark forms stumbled toward the house in an uneven line, too many to count. We were going to need backup.

I set a hand on Jake's shoulder and he glanced at me. "Can you get Delta Force guys here?"

"They're in transit, not even in Oregon yet. No way they'll get here in time." He shook his head. His mouth slashed across his face in a grim, jagged line. "But I'll send out a distress signal to the DOD and see what I can get."

"Do it. I'll call 911, see if I can get SWAT here, give us some support." Besides, it'd give Tiffany, Mai and Hanzo some more time to reach us. Maybe we'd get lucky and wouldn't have to go searching through a dark house under zombie assault.

Jake nodded, pulled out his cell phone and dialed.

More gunshots. A long wolf howl echoed outside, lifting in pitch until it suddenly dropped into a snarl that sounded more like a blender full of gravel. Again, I took a step toward the door to the kitchen, wanting to be out there with my people in the thick of things, before I stopped myself. I shoved my hand into my jeans and pulled out my cell phone and hit 911, keeping my eyes on the window and those dark shapes lurching across the lawn. One of them fell into the bomb crater.

It took bloody forever for my phone to connect. The ceiling-mounted intercom speakers started playing something by Yanni. Next up, Zamfir, Master of the Pan Flute. Fitting music by which to die.

"911. What's your emergency?" The operator sounded bored.

"I have zombies overrunning my house. They're through the wire and in the goddamn flowerbeds."

"Did you say zombies, ma'am?" A little more interest now, but not much. From the sound of it, a person worked the emergency phones for two months and had seen it all, ranging from cannibal corpses to anal-probe-obsessed aliens.

"Zombies, as in walking dead people who want to eat you." A flurry of gunshots cracked outside.

"Is that gunfire?" Definite interest now and a bit of alarm. About goddamn time.

"We're shooting zombies. What do you fucking think?"

"Please remain calm, ma'am. I have a unit on the way. You need to make sure all those weapons are on the ground when the officer arrives."

"Yeah, that ain't gonna happen. Wait—are you sending *one* officer?"

"We're sending a unit now—"

"Send *all* of them. Now!"

An explosion tore apart the night, as loud as ten thunderclaps at least and a couple of low-rider stereos thrown in for the hell of it. The windows rattled in their frames. Glass shattered on the side of the house nearest the garage. That definitely couldn't be good.

"Ma'am? Can you hear me?" A gratifying note of panic echoed over the phone for the first time. "Is everyone okay?"

"No!" I screamed into the phone. "We have zombie infestation out the ass and half the house just blew up! Now get us some fucking help!"

I snapped the phone shut. Jake had already finished his call. I could tell from the look on his face he didn't have an answer I wanted to hear.

"The DOD's in contact with the governor about rolling out National Guard units."

The good news surprised me. "How long?"

"At least an hour. More like two. They're thinking containment, not rescue."

"Shit." Containment, not rescue. I should've guessed the universe would continue its long history of taking a crap on my head.

A shape thumped off the window so hard the glass shook. I whipped my head around and recoiled in horror. A zombie mime slapped his white-gloved hands against the glass. His white makeup caked and smeared over his gray flesh, his beret sat askew on his head and one of his suspenders dangled at his side. A track of dried blood ran down from the mime's right eye socket, where there gaped an empty hole bisected by black makeup lines. The undead mime pressed his face against the glass, biting at it, smearing greasepaint and flicking a black tongue between painted black lips. I might've screamed, but I couldn't tell because I had already called my magic and the power began to arc through me. Heat started to radiate off my skin.

Jake had his pistol up and aimed at the zombie mime. Another zombie, this one a middle-aged woman in a mud-caked dress, stumbled up to the window and began to bang on it. More Reanimated Corpse Threats swarmed up against the house. They stared at us with dead eyes.

If we attacked, we'd just break the window, and that would be only slightly less counterproductive than dousing ourselves with butter and chives and rolling out the red carpet for a zombie luncheon.

"Forget them," I said. "We have to keep looking for the others."

Jake turned back to me. I took off toward the hall to the north wing at a run. Jake cursed under his breath and ran after me, but I didn't slow. I had to fight to keep my worry from distracting my focus. If Mai, Hanzo and Tiffany weren't in their rooms, we planned to sweep the entire ground floor and finish at the front door. If all went right, we'd pick up my missing people and escape in the Bradley. If we couldn't meet up...well, I sure as hell wouldn't leave anyone behind, even if I had to burn the house down around me to reach them.

I ran under the arch into a hallway filled with darkness. A tall zombie stood swaying at the end of the hall. It sniffed the air and moaned. A surge of fear rushed through me as I stumbled to a halt. The zombie dragged its hand along the wall as it stumbled toward me, a dark shape reeking of decay and giving piteous moans.

I threw out my hand and loosed a stream of fire that knocked it backward. The zombie thrashed and burned. Jake ran over and put it out of its misery with a headshot, and we spent the next thirty seconds jumping on it, trying to put out the flames. Smoke curled along the ceiling and a smoke detector began to screech. The sound stabbed through my brain like an ice pick.

Jake shot the smoke detector, and it died with a warble and a sad beep. Best wasted bullet ever, in my humble opinion.

"Let's go." I started forward, but Jake grabbed me and pulled me back. Fury sparked inside me. "What the hell, Jake?"

"I go first," he said. I opened my mouth to tell him to shove it sideways and do a hula dance but he held up a hand. "Don't breathe fire at me. I have the gun and the barrier magic. You can cover my ass."

I nodded—maybe a little ungraciously, but I had no time for getting panties in a bunch. Good tactics had to rank ahead of pride. If I had to avoid using fire, I'd be less effective until I armed myself.

We moved out and turned down a connecting hallway. Lights might give our position away, so we stalked through the darkness. I could hear faint, trailing moans and an almost continual muffled banging, but when I glanced behind me I saw nothing but dark hallway and beyond it, shadowy shapes of furniture and random décor.

The laundry-room door gaped open like a wound. Jake cleared it as I covered him. Nothing inside but drifts of unfolded clothes in laundry baskets. We pressed on. I set my hand on Jake's shoulder and when he glanced at me I signaled, indicating our objective just ahead.

Tiffany's door was closed. We stacked up against the wall. Jake glanced at me for confirmation. I nodded. He swung out in front of the door—

Something moved in the darkness.

"Look out!" I yelled.

Another zombie careened around the corner, hands out, and grabbed for Jake. He pivoted and with one fast, deceptively smooth motion he put a bullet in its forehead and dropped it. Then he spun back and kicked in the door. The frame splintered and the knob punched a hole in the drywall when it banged open.

He glanced at me. "Check inside. I'll hold them off."

I started forward, but he stepped in my way. When I looked up at him, he pulled me into a fierce kiss. "Be careful," he said when we moved apart. I bit down on a quip about how sucking face while being attacked by zombies couldn't be recommended by the Surgeon General and brushed past him into Tiffany's rooms, yelling her name. No answer. I ran through the apartment, sick at heart with dread, but the place was empty. More gunshots came from the hallway, making me flinch.

I ran back into the living room, summoning my magic, feeling the heat waves radiating off my skin. "Jake, you okay?"

"Peachy," he called from the hallway. "She in there?"

"No..."

A cup of tea sat on an end table, still steaming. A romance paperback lay open and text down near the lamp. Tiffany had been here and not long ago. I hurried back out into the hallway. Jake stood against the wall, scanning up and down the hall. Several zombie bodies lay crumpled on the floor, their dead eyes now completely sightless.

The power cut out. John Tesh's orgasmic synthesizer crescendo died an instant death. The hum of the house—something I was never consciously aware of until everything electronic suddenly went dark—lapsed into silence. Even though we'd had no lights on to avoid attention, the house seemed to swim in gloom now that I knew the lights *wouldn't* come on, even if I wanted them. Bad time to regret not buying that automatic generator six months ago.

My breath rasped in and out of my mouth. "Not good."

"No." He ejected the Beretta's clip, squinted at the remaining rounds and slapped it home again.

Moans echoed down the hallways and stairwells. More glass shattered—damn all those windows. Sure, I'd loved the view, but they were a complete liability in a zombie attack. It seemed ludicrous to the point of criminal negligence that I'd never planned for the zombie apocalypse before. If we survived, I'd move us into an underground bunker hidden in the Rocky Mountains.

My cell phone rang, startling me. I pulled it out and stared at it lying in the palm of my hand. I flipped it open. "Yeah?" If it were a telemarketer, I'd shove the phone up some zombie's ass and leave it there forever.

"This is 911 Emergency." The same woman dispatcher I'd talked to earlier. "Has the police officer arrived?"

"Hell if I know. Look, I'm fucking *busy*."

"Did you see any police lights? We haven't heard from him since he headed to your location."

"Maybe that's because he was *eaten* by all the *zombies*." I snapped the phone shut, thought hard about flinging it into the wall, but restrained myself. I didn't have any phone insurance. I glanced at Jake. "I've got a bad feeling about this one."

He gave me a tired grin. "We still have bullets. And if you still have bullets, you're still kickin'."

"Three of my people are out there without any support, without any armor," I said, and cursed. "And here I am flailing around trying to find them, not helping anybody. We need to step back, think this through. I need a view of the battlefield."

As afraid as I might be for Tiffany, Mai and Hanzo, I had to get a handle on the situation. I hadn't heard the Bradley, though I could still hear small arms fire somewhere, but did it come from outside or inside? My people needed me to lead. And to lead I had to know what was going on. Without any battlefield intelligence we had no hope of coming up with effective strategy.

"If we head upstairs, we might get cut off," Jake warned.

"We're already cut off. I don't know where the hell he got so many damn zombies. Did a circus troupe come down with the plague or something?"

Jake didn't answer. Another explosion rumbled outside, this one much smaller. A grenade, it sounded like. I fought off the panic and the frantic *need to do something now* thoughts crashing through my brain.

"All right." I took a deep breath. "I haven't heard the Bradley or the chain gun." I swallowed and my throat clicked.

"We get a look-down view and start fighting from the balconies and the roof if we can't get to the Bradley. With no intercom and no headsets we can't communicate a rally point."

He nodded. "Then we get to the armory first, then get our look down and plan from there."

When we ran down another hall, glass crashed—a sound I'd come to dread. The sunroom at the end of the hall began to fill with zombies spilling in through the windows and clambering over furniture. They came right for us.

Chapter Twenty-Four: Cheeseburger Hill

Undead Army of the Unrighteous Order of the Falling Dark
The Zero Dog Compound
Lawn
7:34 p.m. PST April 19th

Necromancer Jeremiah Hansen watched as his undead hordes laid siege to the huge house. A hundred or so feet away, the garage burned with a ferocity he found slightly unnerving. The structure was little more than a flaming skeleton with skin that shifted and danced, shedding angry red-orange light, breathing out smoke with dark, scorched shapes in its bowels. Mostly it resembled a waiting room in Hell, or perhaps the dentist office after a firebomb. Random ammunition cooked off with pops and bangs, and chunks of twisted, smoking wreckage and debris lay everywhere. Even sections of the lawn had started to catch fire.

Ever since the gelatin-plant inferno, he'd discovered a newfound appreciation and respect for the concept of fire. It wasn't just for hotdogs and s'mores.

His zombie troops stayed well away from the flames, and he could feel their fear of it. That was fine, since he'd sent them away from the fire to assault the house from all sides. The group of mercenaries trying to reach their tank had been driven back into the house when his zombies almost overwhelmed them. The big demon with the fiery eyes had been a nasty shot, and that werewolf thing had been rather vicious with his golf club. Those two had thinned his undead ranks quite a bit, but after Jeremiah had blown up the garage, the fight had seemed to go out of them and they'd fled back to their mansion.

He stared at the big house. So many windows to break, so little time. And damned if the front door hadn't been *unlocked*—though getting a zombie to open a doorknob remained a tricky bit of business. In the end, it had only taken minutes to begin pouring his undead minions inside.

Blake set his briefcase between his knees and fiddled with his PDA. "It seems more police are en route."

Without a word, Jeremiah sectioned off a group of zombies from the horde and sent them toward the road to await the cops. A stalling tactic. He needed more time to storm the house and collect his new and improved paranormal zombies.

Gunshots rang out from time to time, sometimes in single shots, sometimes in bursts. A woman shrieked inside the house, and then a zombie crashed out a third-story window missing its head. Oops. Spoke too soon. The head followed a second later, tumbling through the air and moaning in frustration.

"I think it's time I invited myself inside," Jeremiah said.

"Superb." Blake brushed ashes off the shoulder of his suit. "Enjoy yourself. I shall observe the festivities from here. I have an early morning conference call with *TIME* magazine to arrange the details of your interview."

Jeremiah smiled. An interview with *TIME* magazine. Despite being a business-speak-spewing executive prick, Blake was worth every penny. Let's be honest, who else carried a shockingly convenient incendiary grenade in his briefcase? Jeremiah's mother had carried a bottomless purse the size of a pillowcase and even that elephantine handbag had never contained one of *those*.

Blake stooped down—like a chicken hawk swooping upon

an unsuspecting fowl—and opened his briefcase. He withdrew the automatic pistol from beneath a sheaf of papers and handed it to Jeremiah. "This may prove useful in a contentious meeting."

Jeremiah took the gun, liking the way the pebbled stock felt rough against his palm. He would bring his zombie honor guard, but hey, pimping a phat gat wouldn't exactly hurt his street cred.

He put the pistol in his waistband and held his hand out to Blake. "You've been impeccable, Blake. Really. Good to have you on board."

Blake stared at his hand for a moment, and then shook with him. His skin felt cool, almost cold. He favored Jeremiah with a slash of a smile. "Of course. I strive to excel."

Jeremiah turned away, rounded up the zombie honor guard decked out in firefighter helmets, jackets and boots and used his magic to prod them all toward the house. They started toward it with a resounding moan—not quite the most inspiring battle cry, but one took what one could get.

He had a date with a certain pretty female mercenary leader who shot fire out of her hands and had incinerated his place of business when they'd first met. Oh yes, he did indeed have an offer she couldn't refuse.

Around him, the zombies marched and moaned. Marched and moaned. Sounding exactly like a geriatric banzai charge.

Running.

Zombies everywhere now. Their plaintive moans echoed down the hallways and drifted out of open doorways. A few zombies even spider-crawled toward us across the hardwood and grabbed at our ankles as we sprinted past.

Toppled furniture, broken glass, wreckage and debris lay scattered everywhere. I had no time to mourn the money I'd wasted on the housecleaning service. I wove in and out of the wreckage with Jake running a half step behind me. He knocked zombies down with his barriers, pinned them against the walls, sealed off doorways and pushed us a clear path through their gnashing teeth.

We'd been forced away from the main stairwell by the flood of zombies and almost trapped by more zombies coming up the main hall from the southern end of the house. We'd had to circle around through several rooms to try and reach the main stairs again, but the wreckage and darkness slowed us.

I jumped over a toppled credenza, skidded a little on glass shards, but kept my balance. I had to slow to keep from falling. Dark shapes moved outside the windows, barely visible through the thin curtains. Jake vaulted the credenza and came down on the other side of me. I started to run again—

Glass shattered near my face, and I flinched away. A zombie arm shoved through the broken pane, grabbed my shirt and yanked me toward the window. I caught a glimpse of gnashing teeth and flat, dead eyes. Something moaned in triumph.

"Hands off, pus bag!" I screamed, wrenching the hand back, twisting and shoving hard at an unnatural angle until I heard the bone snap and saw the teeth of glass still in the frame bite deep into its flesh. By pure reflex I let loose the flames and sent a runner of fire up the stained jacket to light the zombie up like a tiki torch.

"Come on," Jake yelled, pulling me away from the window. We ran again. A zombie loomed in an adjoining doorway, but Jake smashed his barrier into it, slamming it backward and leaving a huge, splintered dent in the doorframe.

We finally reached the stairs. No zombies on the steps, but plenty of them staggered toward us from all directions. Jake raced up the stairs first, barrier out and pistol aimed. I kept one hand on his back and watched, heart hammering, the mass of zombies gathering below us and pushing their way to the bottom step.

The second-floor landing was empty. I grabbed the banister post and swung myself around to the next flight, but Jake had stopped on the second stair and I bumped into him. He stood absolutely still, staring upward. I followed his gaze.

A zombie head tumbled down the stairs, thudding down step by step like a bowling ball. Hanzo stood at the top of the third-floor landing, ninja sword in hand and half-congealed zombie blood along its blade. Behind him stood Mai supporting Tiffany with an arm around her shoulder. Blood stained Tiffany's arms up to her elbows, and lines of strain turned her beautiful face weary and older than it had looked the last time I'd seen her.

My heart clenched. I started to run up the stairs toward her, calling her name, but something grabbed me, a huge shape lurching out of one of the rooms and clamping a cold hand on my arm. I spun toward it. More shapes, dozens, stumbled out of the shadows and connecting halls onto the landing.

A flurry of gunshots sang out, so loud and so close my ears rang and I must have had cordite striping all over my face. Zombies swarmed all over me, clutching at me, pulling me away from Jake and darting their heads forward to bite. I slammed a fist into one gray, moon-shaped face and elbow crushed another head. Jake yelled my name. A flood of small creatures scurried down the stairs and threw themselves at the zombies. I saw one of them latch itself onto a zombie face and start tearing away. It was a little creature that looked like a sunshine-yellow platypus with wolverine claws, studded with spikes and a razor-sharp bill.

A zombie almost sank its filthy teeth into my neck. I jerked backward, kicking it in the chest. Another zombie pulled me off balance, and I shoved it away with a grunt of disgust. Too hard. I stumbled back, losing my balance. A fat old-man zombie tried to push me down, but I hit the banister and threw my weight to the side to avoid going over. I stood too close to the lower flight of stairs. The world spun as I bounced off the wall, hit the rail and toppled down the rest of the stairs to the ground floor. I slammed into several zombies working their way up the stairs like a wrecking ball. The stench of decay choked me and I struggled to breathe.

"*Andrea*!" Jake screamed.

I looked toward his voice, but my head spun and it was hard to find him. I pushed myself to my feet, blood rushing in my ears. The male zombie I'd partially landed on sat up and reached for me. I kicked it in the face. Eager, hungry moaning sounded all around me. I caught a glimpse of Jake as he flung out his hand. A zombie about to clamp down on my arm staggered back as a shimmering barrier opened between us.

"Watch out!" I yelled.

On the second-floor landing, Jake turned just in time to dodge a zombie lunge. He put a bullet in the top of its head from close range, spackling the wall with chunks our interior decorator would hate. More zombies pressed in on the second-floor landing, coming from every adjoining hallway and room. Too many for me to fight through. If I cut loose with flames, I might accidentally burn my own people—and I couldn't risk that ever again.

Some of the zombies on the second-floor landing diverted toward me, half-falling down the stairs. The zombies I'd knocked over on my way down were already trying to stand up again. Behind me, on the ground floor, zombies pushed and shoved against each other, fighting to get to me at the narrow mouth of the stairs. I was completely cut off.

Jake backed up a couple steps as the zombies closed on him and then he wheeled back to me. "Run! I'll cover you!"

"But—"

"I'll find you! *Go*!"

I had one last glimpse of Jake, Mai, Hanzo and Tiffany fighting, driving their way down into the horde, but now the zombies coming down the stairs were halfway to me and more swarmed all around me, grabbing and tearing.

I back-fisted one zombie head and front-kicked another,

sending the zombie flying back into its moaning comrades. I wouldn't abandon my people. No way in hell I'd run off and leave them.

I called my magic to life and my next punch transformed into a flaming fist of death, straight into the face of a zombie. Its nose shattered and its head rocked back, but the real effect came when I pumped more energy into the spell and the zombie's head burst into flames. I leaned back, pivoted and kicked the damn thing back into its shuffling friends, who stumbled away from the fire.

Another gunshot cracked through the air and a zombie near me went down. Then another. Jake still stood on the second-floor landing, his empty hand out, a barrier holding back dozens of zombies trying to get to him. His other hand held the smoking 9mm, but the slide was back, and the gun was empty. A zombie who had no legs from the knees down grabbed his ankle and dragged itself forward, mouth gaping, straight for his calf. Jake cursed and stumbled. He yanked his leg free, but hit the wall and fell back on the stair incline.

Somebody screamed. An instant later I realized the scream came from me. Crazy shifting firelight lit the stairwell and the halls as the head-punched zombie burned. In that light I saw a pack of Mai's weird platypus creatures hopping down the stairs, past Jake, to swarm all over the legless zombie, tearing it to pieces.

Jake clambered to his feet again. He couldn't lower his barrier to reload the pistol or all those zombies would fall on him. Hanzo hacked away at grasping zombie limbs that managed to get around the barrier. Jake stared down at me. I could see the terror etched on his face—terror for me. His eyes widened.

"Look out!" He pointed behind me with the empty gun.

I threw myself to the side without even looking. A woman zombie fell forward where I'd been an instant before. She would've pulled me down with her. More zombies came up from behind me, and the others from the stairwell had already begun inching around the burning remains of the zombie whose head I'd melted. Jesus, they were everywhere.

No time. I slammed down a spell into the carpet and a wall of fire flared up with a roar. The zombies staggered away from the heat. For a moment, the zombie line faltered and I caught a glimpse of a man standing at the far end of the hall dressed all in black with a Vandyke beard and watching me with an intensity that bordered on admiration. I recognized his face right away. Necromancer Jeremiah Hansen, the man I'd last seen in the office of his gelatin-manufacturing plant, right before Hell was born again on earth with me as its mother. The zombies closed in again, and some of them pushed their way through the fire, driven onward by the necromancer despite their hatred of flames.

I jumped over the woman zombie who'd almost had me. She pawed at my legs but couldn't hold on. I leapt through my own wall of flames, feeling the heat scorch against me. I landed, threw myself into a roll and came up smoking but not on fire. The zombies had cut me off from the stairs. No chance to get back to Jake. Surrounded like this, I'd end up trapped in my own inferno.

I escaped through the anteroom off the stairwell and shoved open the door. The zombies chased me. I didn't even have a chance to catch a last glimpse of Jake before I rushed through the archway, through a short hall and into the weight-training room, with the undead on my tail, dead and hungry and me their meal on heels.

Chapter Twenty-Five: The End is Nigh…Thank God

Mercenary Wing Rv6-4 "Zero Dogs"
The Zero Dog Compound
Weight Training Room
1951 Hours PST April 19th

I leapt over the bench-press machine and dodged a rack of dumbbells, sprinting toward the far door that led to our dojo. The door stood less than twenty feet away. A chorus of piteous moans filled the air behind me. I didn't dare look back.

I moved so fast I almost bounced off the door when I reached it. The dojo training floor appeared empty through the blinds. My hand slid on the doorknob, too slick with sweat to find purchase. *Shit.* A loud clanging and crashing rang out behind me—free weights tumbling to the floor—and a surprised moan filled the air. I glanced back. The zombies had crossed half the room already, lurching their way around and through the weight-lifting machines and barbells. They sniffed the air and groaned like starving men sitting down to a feast.

My heart pounded so hard my hands trembled. The strength faded from my legs, as if my muscles ghosted into transparency. I gritted my teeth and grabbed the doorknob with both hands. It wouldn't turn. Locked from the other side. Shit. Shit. *Shit!*

A hand slapped hard against the glass on the other side of

the door, rattling it in the frame. A rotting, scarred head appeared right in front of me, with dead eyes and flayed cheeks. The zombie's teeth clacked off the glass as it tried to bite off my face and left a dark smear of clotted blood and saliva behind instead. More zombies staggered into view in the dojo, teenagers with sagging jeans, a gray-skinned old man in a pith helmet, some Asian guy wearing one bunny slipper. They began to pile up against the door, beating on it.

I wheeled back to face the undead already in the room with me, sucking in a deep, steadying breath and sparking my magic to life. If I had to die, I'd go down in flames and take as many with me as I could. Flames began to burn in an arc around my hands as my power gathered. I lifted them...

...and the zombies stopped moving. These zombies were different from the others. They wore firefighter gear haphazardly thrown on their bodies, heavy jackets and helmets, but nothing over their faces or blocking their gnashing teeth. The theft at the fire station finally made a twisted sense. The necromancer wanted fireproof undead.

The zombies stood absolutely still, watching me with flat, hungry stares. The zombies on the other side of the door fell into an ominous quiet. I glanced back and saw them clustered at the window, staring through the blinds at me like dogs watching food about to fall from the table.

"Hi. I'm Jeremiah."

I whipped my head around to see a man climb up on an inverted weight bench and sit on the top. All hail the necromancer Jeremiah Hansen, who pointed an automatic pistol at me and smiled almost shyly. I froze, but kept the fires burning and my magic hot, not sure if I could get off a spell in time before a bullet buried itself in some section of my body of which I felt particularly fond.

We stared at each other for a long moment. Nothing moved.

"Your buddies are tracking mud on my carpet," I said at last.

He laughed. "They're tracking all kinds of bodily fluids everywhere. They're zombies."

Well, that scored an ick factor in the high nineties. If I survived this, I vowed to live in a bubble for the rest of my life. "So...Jeremiah. What do you want exactly?"

"Exactly? You ruined my little foray into the free market, you realize that? You pretty much killed a local small business, and that's goddamn un-American."

"Dead people who wander around eating live people sounds goddamn un-American to me."

He ignored my riposte. "I saw you in my office. When you mercenaries attacked me."

"Why are you wasting my time with this?" I demanded. "Either sic your zombies on me or get the hell out of my house."

"I want something from you. What's your name?"

"Kiss my ass."

He gestured with the pistol. "I could just shoot you."

"Captain Andrea Walker." I would've sounded off with my serial number too, but I could never remember it, especially not with a gun barrel pointed at my head.

"There's no way out of this, Andrea. Let me float a little scenario past you." He paused, and then smiled and shrugged. "Actually, Blake, my second-in-command, frowned upon this meeting, but *I'm* the leader here, so that's that. Anyway, I'm really looking for two things, and they're kind of on opposite sides of the pole. One, I'm looking for a significant other."

I stared at him. He stared back.

"Place an ad in the personals," I suggested, trying not to notice my arms had gooseflesh at his creepy insinuation.

"Hmm. Done that already. No dice. Now, the second thing I'm looking for is a zombie who can shoot fire. That would be a very handy zombie to have around. So, I'm wondering. Are you interested in a little joint venture? A little rebuilding of the budding business empire you ruined? Or should I just turn you into my zombie Zippo lighter and have done with it?"

"You don't know me," I said, incredulous. "What's to stop me from lying, becoming your girlfriend and killing you later?"

"Zombies. Lots of them. Who will suddenly be devoid of a master and very hungry. But I'm hoping you, as a soldier of fortune, have a mercenary side—or let's just say a *pro-business* side. Honestly, it's fun being evil. I saw how you blew up my factory." He shrugged. "I think you'll enjoy being bad if you give it a chance."

"Are you fucking *insane*?"

"I don't know." He paused, considering. "Is that a rhetorical question?"

"I can't believe this shit."

He didn't answer—content to watch me from his perch on the bench while his zombies stood dead still, and I almost laughed crazily at my stupid pun, worth its weight in post-bailout US dollars. The very last thing I'd expected was a recruitment offer, much less some kind of half-assed attempt to ask me out. "I…have a thing for somebody else."

"Ah." He rubbed his cheek. "Hmm. Too bad. So how long have you known him?"

"I don't know…a week."

"Not to be a dick, but that's not very long. Seems to me you could transition over to my team. True love is for bedtime stories and anniversary cards."

"That's really cynical."

He cocked his head and regarded me with something like pity—surreal, since he'd just asked *me* out and been shot down. "This is a world where creatures eat each other to survive. It's an incubator for the cynical. Besides, I already said I was evil. Evil is a big tent."

"Yeah? Well, my answer's no."

"Is that your final answer?"

"Why the hell would I change my mind *two seconds* later?"

"Oh, I don't know. Maybe you suddenly decided true love, or true lust, or true infatuation isn't worth being eaten alive. I'm just sayin'."

I lifted my chin and gave him my coldest glare. "Some love is worth dying for."

He shrugged. "Well, that could be a problem, but not a huge hurdle. I think it's best to be optimistic." He laughed. "Cynically optimistic, that is. What's love, anyway? I think the best love involves people who might even be indifferent to one another at first, but then grow closer as they build common ground between them. Like arranged marriages, but with zombies for chaperones. Let's face it. Evil people need love too."

"I can't believe I'm hearing this."

"I hoped you'd say yes, maybe help with the day-to-day running of the empire. Most people don't believe this, but I'm kind of shy asking women out." He waved his free hand at the zombies. "It helps to have a lot of wingmen to back me up. But I'd prefer it if you agreed, because, if I turn you into a zombie, there are some downsides. You won't be warm anymore. You'll lose that winter-fresh breath, and your vocabulary will suffer."

"You *are* insane."

"You said something like that already." He shook his head. "Evil and insane are two completely different things. I have evil tendencies. It's a disorder."

Gunshots sounded somewhere in the house—too far off to give me hope.

"You want my final answer?" I said. "I'll give it to you. I wouldn't trade Jake for you if you came with a layer of chocolate mousse, a ten-inch ever-ready vibrating dick, a personal Italian chef and half a billion dollars."

Jeremiah sighed and closed his eyes. "So be it. I guess I'll let you have your true love for dinner." He flicked his hand at me, and the zombies surged forward, their chorus of moaning filling the air like the Mormon Tabernacle Choir after binging on habañeros caviar and stale crackers. "Let her eat Jake!"

I loosed the spell I'd been holding back and sent daggers of fire spitting toward the necromancer. He was too quick, half-rolling, half-falling off the bench out of sight behind his advancing wall of zombies. The fire scorched black marks all along the wall and ceiling but didn't catch.

I stumbled backward until I pressed up against the wall. The closest zombie was less than two meters away, clacking his teeth together with a sound that made me think of billiards and pool halls. I pulled in all the energy I could for my last spell. I planned to do the phoenix thing, sans rebirth. Sorry about the house everybody, but the armory was far enough away that my people would have time to get away before the place exploded.

Gunshots cracked behind me in the dojo. I spun around, my heart suddenly lifting. The door to the dojo slammed open so hard it left a dent on the wall, and I was glad I hadn't been standing in front of it. Jake ran into the room with his pistol in hand, up and ready for business.

"Andrea!" he yelled, and drew up short when he saw the wall of advancing zombies.

"Here!"

He turned toward my voice. I saw the intensity of the relief in his eyes and it made me flash hotter than any fire coming from my hands.

I ran toward him. A zombie hand clamped down on my arm and jerked me backward. Jake swung the gun with one fast, smooth motion and shot again. The zombie hand clenched tighter, making me cry out before it fell away. Another zombie groped for me, but I grabbed its arm and twisted it back at a sharp angle, a move that would force any normal opponent to flip himself to avoid having his arm broken. No luck here. The zombie's half-rotted arm came off in my hand. I stumbled off balance. The zombie gnashed its teeth at me. I reared back and smashed it in the head with its own arm, sending it falling into its comrades.

A shimmering barrier slammed down between the zombies

and me. They pressed up against it, groaning and beating their fists while trying to chew through to get at me. I turned on my heel and darted back to Jake. He pushed me through the door into the dojo. I risked one last glance over my shoulder and saw Jeremiah through a break in the zombie horde, watching me go, his face haggard and tired. Then I lost sight of him.

More gunshots rang out behind me, but I couldn't glance back because zombies staggered in from the main dojo entrance, four at least, right in my way. One of them fell toward me with its arms outstretched. I dodged aside and drove my flaming fist into its head, which had the added bonus of lighting its hair on fire. I swept a hand toward a woman zombie and tossed daggers of flame. The woman zombie careened into the wall, burning the way a marshmallow soaked in ethanol and coated with pitch will burn, but then she bounced back and came for me again, frantic moans spilling from her twisted mouth. I shot my foot out in a vicious sidekick and the zombie slammed into the wall.

Something clutched at my ankles. Zombie hands. I looked down at the zombie I'd punched. A nimbus of flames burned around his head. His mouth gaped open as he tried to sink his teeth into my calf. I lifted my combat boot and brought it down with all the force I could muster, screaming "*Keeyah!*" so loud something tore in my throat. My boot heel crushed through the zombie's temple, breaking skull, sending brains out its ears as if I'd squashed a Twinkie with an anvil. I didn't think I'd ever look at homemade oatmeal the same way again.

More 9mm shots popped in rapid succession, followed by the sound of a magazine ejecting. I turned back in time to see Jake slam the weight-room door shut and lock it. He glanced at me, and then down at the mess near my feet. "Remind me not to piss you off when you're wearing boots."

I gave a hoarse, coughing laugh. Then I grabbed him and pulled him into a kiss so fast his teeth cut my lip a little, though I couldn't have cared less. We broke apart when we heard the rapid stutter of a belt-fed weapon followed by an explosion that shook the wood flooring.

"I know that shooting," I said. "Sarge!"

Jake took my arm. "We got cut off and driven back, so Tiffany, Mai and Hanzo retreated to make a stand at the armory while I came after you."

"You won't hear me complaining. Let's get bigger guns and finish this. I can't keep risking fire magic or I'll end up burning the house down no matter how careful I am."

A resounding *boom* made me flinch. The door to the weight room shuddered as if somebody rammed barbells into the panel. The glass cracked, and then broke completely. A zombie arm shoved through the jagged pieces, waving about in the air.

We escaped out of the dojo. Zombies filled the access way to the west wing, so we raced toward the stairwell at the east wing tower, trying to make it to the third floor and the rest of the Zero Dogs.

A few zombies loitered in the stairwell landings, but Jake and I dispatched them quickly. By the time we reached the top, the zombie horde was on our heels again, flooding into the stairwell from the first floor. These bastards just never gave up. The armory was at the other end of the house in the south wing, and we had to cross a lot of dangerous ground to get there.

"Come on." I dragged Jake back from the stairwell toward the exit.

"Only seven rounds left," Jake said. "Better hope we're in the clear or this could get dicey."

I pushed open the door to the third floor. The zombies packed the hallway from wall to wall, so many of them I couldn't even see the far end of the house. Below us, down the stairs, the ground-floor zombies had already begun to lurch up the steps after us. I could hear the *thump, drag, thump* as they climbed.

"It just got dicey." I took one long look at the advancing horde and wished I'd finished that bottle of scotch and screwed

Jake when I'd had the chance.

Jeremiah Hansen, Napoleon of the Dead, watched his zombie legions file through the door between the weight room and the dojo. Really, who built a *dojo* in their house? That just might be one of the coolest things he'd ever seen. When he was filthy rich and building his own mega mansion down in Florida, he'd make certain he had his own dojo, and bigger than this one.

Captain Andrea Walker might've escaped thanks to her commando boyfriend, but she wouldn't get away for long. He knew they'd been trapped on the third floor, cut off from their friends. Only a matter of time until a zombie bit them. She'd scorned his offer of a romantic liaison, not that he'd been surprised. He was taken with her, but he didn't stack up well against her Rambo-style lover boy—though for all of the guy's muscle, Jeremiah suspected his own pistol had been bigger. Losing vital and human Andrea sucked, but what were you gonna do? She didn't seem turned on by evil, and since she'd actually *burned down* his place of business, he wasn't going to have the cash, the sports car and the shiny bling to impress her. Still, their conversation had been rather cordial, except for her actual turn-down comment, and overall she'd been almost pleasant until she'd tried to shoot him with fire daggers. In truth, it was almost as if they were already married, and he found that amusing in a really twisted way.

His cell phone went off, playing Rob Zombie's "Living Dead Girl" for a ringtone. God, he rocked the clever sometimes. "Yeah?"

"Blake here." The man sounded calm enough to be sitting on the beach with an umbrella drink. "I thought I should inform you the police have begun to gather in a location several streets south of us. They will be using SWAT teams when they commence operations. Also, National Guard units have begun mobilizing. The 41st Infantry Brigade, I believe. Their presence is expected within the hour."

Ah, *crap*. So difficult to put in a focused workday anymore with all these outside distractions. He'd taken too much time getting this done, but the ferocity of the resistance had been something of an unpleasant surprise. Of course, the situation had never been ideal from his point of view. He fought a hardened foe and he didn't have infinite zombie reserves. Already he could sense a huge amount of severed controlling cords. He estimated well over sixty percent losses of his undead army so far. He had nothing to show for it yet—not one infected or eaten mercenary, although they *were* trapped, and he had Captain Walker and her personal military pistol boy holed up in a room on the third floor.

"Thank you for letting me know," Jeremiah said. "Bring the car. I think the bus is a lost cause."

"I agree. That asset must be written off. So, we will be leaving then?"

"We'll be leaving with two zombies. The pyromancer and the commando." He'd regret Andrea losing her bonfire of personality when she became a zombie, but Mr. Tall Dark and Rambo would bring him his coffee every morning. And maybe Jeremiah would use him for a dartboard too, just to rub it in. "I'll send the rest of the undead at the cops to buy us some time to get clear. Give me five minutes to wrap this up."

He shut the phone and put it back in his pocket. Another chattering roar sounded from somewhere upstairs—some kind of machine-gun noise. He closed his eyes and sorted through the cords until he found the one he wanted and dropped into the zombie's head, seeing what it saw. The zombie stood packed tight with other zombies near a sunroom. The head of a preppy zombie in front of him exploded, and another zombie began to jerk and flail as bullets ripped through its upper torso and head.

Jeremiah caught a glimpse of an angry demon in full body

armor holding a really big machine gun. Blood, a shade darker than his purple skin, had splashed across his bulletproof vest as if a psychotic Jackson Pollock had been at work. Another zombie fell under the weight of dozens of yellow things resembling mutated platypus. Platypi? The werewolf bashed skulls with his bent golf club. The last thing he saw before the cord was severed and he was kicked back into his own head was the beautiful, sexy, alluring face of a woman with slit pupils and black hair wearing what looked like chain-mail armor. He was certain she would've been lithe and voluptuous, if not for the heavy armor and the dual machine pistols in her feminine hands. She piqued his interest. If Captain Walker wasn't interested in a necromancer, then maybe this cute chippie would be. But then she yelled, "Die zombie goat-fuckers!" and shot his zombie in the face. With both machine pistols.

Kind of a hard-on killer, that.

He snapped back into his body and hurried (as fast as he could with his shuffling zombie honor guard) up the stairs to the third floor. If nothing else, he had to come away with a sexy flamethrower zombie and that damned army grunt or this venture would be a complete loss of materiel, personnel, capital and time.

Not to mention his ass was personally on the line.

Zombies burned.

Perhaps they burned a little too well, I decided, but without a gun, I was forced to rely on my pyromancy. Not a problem in most situations, except that I couldn't remember how up-to-date our insurance policy might be or if I'd paid the last premium. If the house burned down and we weren't fully covered, that would be a Very Bad Thing.

Of course, being eaten and/or turned into a zombie also scored high on the list of Very Bad Things, rating higher than burning down my own house by accident. So I charbroiled zombies. Over and over again.

Jake stood beside and a little in front of me, but clear of my line of fire. We'd been depending on his barrier magic to survive. He slammed the invisible wall into the zombies and pushed back the undead horde while I fried any that managed to get past him. I could see from the sweat streaming down his face he was near exhaustion. Weariness clutched at me too—adrenaline burnout, casting fatigue, caffeine withdrawal, you name it, I felt it.

We'd holed up in a suite of rooms—Mai's from the look of it—filled with a chaotic smorgasbord of exotic-looking knickknacks, pet trees and litter boxes, wicker furniture and beanbags. We tried to hold the doorway, but Jake's barriers sometimes interfered with my fire spells, and as his strength started to give out, his barrier flickered and seemed to diminish. Zombies tried to crawl beneath the invisible wall. Piles of charred zombies littered both sides of the doorway. The doorjamb, ceiling and hallway walls were scorched black and burning in places. Flames threw erratic shadows throughout the room, while dark smoke curled along the ceiling. I could taste bitter ashes in my mouth. The burning zombie corpses filled the air with the smell of cooking sausage and an odor that reminded me of sauerkraut, which I also added to my list of things I'd never eat again if I survived.

Movement—I caught a flash out of the corner of my eye. "On your right!"

Jake turned and hammered his barrier into a half-decayed zombie crawling over the couch. He knocked it backward into the air, where I scorched it with a column of fire. Flames kissed the ceiling but didn't die out. The room began to fill with more smoke. Another very large zombie woman threw one of the wicker chairs and forced us to scatter out of the way.

"We can't hold here." Jake punctuated his sentence by putting a bullet hole in the chair-thrower's forehead. More zombies streamed through the now-unprotected doorway. From somewhere in the house came the deep ripping sound of an M249 Squad Automatic Weapon burning off rounds, and hope surged through me. My hope deepened when the walls echoed with a triumphant werewolf howl.

But too many zombies stood between us and the rest of the Zero Dogs. Neither of us had armor. All it would take was one bite of their filthy mouths and yellow, scum-covered, stinking teeth to end our distinguished careers. I sent another slash of fire against the zombies, igniting their front line, which fell to the ground and began to shake and flail like converted sinners at a tent revival. Another wave of zombies walked right over the top of them—the necromancer driving them forward, regardless of their inbred fear and hatred of fire.

A huge yellow arm swung toward my head, and long fingers grabbed at my throat. Jake yanked me out of range and pumped two bullets into the head of a flabby male zombie wearing what looked like women's garters and a sheer muumuu. For the first time since I took command of the Zero Dogs, I almost hurled my lunch in a combat situation. That image would never go away, no matter how many kittens I adopted or how much alcohol I drank.

"Get to the balcony." Jake half-guided, half-shoved me toward the French doors off the dining room. "We'll climb down from the roof."

The balcony door deadbolt was locked. I fumbled with the switch, cursing like a driver on I-5 at rush hour.

"Hurry up," Jake advised, the utter calm in his voice making me more nervous than ever.

"You're not helping."

He fired off three rounds in rapid procession. "Andrea, a little faster, please."

Finally, I flipped the lock and shoved the door open. A cool breeze brushed against my face, and it stank of smoke and gunpowder and white phosphorus but was also laced with the delicate scent of the gardenias Mai had planted. I ran out onto the balcony, feeling my facial muscles twist into something, a grimace, a smile, I didn't know. The night's symphony had reached a crescendo of gunfire and explosions and the furious, needy roar of fire.

"Hello," Necromancer Jeremiah Hansen said in a low voice. "I think I'm contractually obligated to say, *So we meet again.*"

Jeremiah sat on the corner of the iron balcony railing with two guard zombies flanking him on either side. The business end of his pistol pointed right at my chest, and for only being a 9mm, the damn barrel looked cavernous from this angle. Dim firelight painted his face a soft yellow and red, highlighting his hair. The glow from the burning garage even made the zombies appear halfway alive.

I opened my mouth to reply, but someone pushed me and I lost my balance. The tiles rushed up to greet me. I barely had time to twist and save my head from smacking the ground.

Jake cursed. I rolled over and looked back, my heart hammering away, and saw him pinned up against the wall by two more zombies. One was the mime zombie I'd seen earlier through the glass. Ash dusted the mime's black beret, and its white greasepaint had begun to run in the heat. His stripes and suspenders and pristine white gloves appeared strangely surreal and horrible in the darkness. The other zombie was huge—a dusky-skinned Samoan of epic proportions. Jake's arms were crushed against the wall and his gun had fallen to the tiles. The zombies halted just inches from tearing into his neck with their yellow teeth.

I lifted my hand to burn them down. I'd have to be precise to avoid catching Jake in the flames. Before I could release my magic, one of the zombies next to Jeremiah shuffled toward me, staring at me with hollow eyes. This zombie looked as if he'd been a mechanic when he'd been alive, judging from the stained coveralls and the ED name patch. Now, half the skin on Ed's face was gone and I thought I saw something white—a maggot maybe—squirming in his right ear. Ed moaned, sounding like a man laughing through deep pain.

I wheeled to face him and prepared to sear Ed's face off.

"Don't," Jeremiah said.

I hesitated. Zombie Ed stopped and stared at me. The two zombies holding Jake didn't move, though I could see they didn't like it. The necromancer held them all in check.

More cacophony from the house—heavy gunfire and explosions shook the frame and rattled the few windows which hadn't already been smashed or blown out. Jeremiah glanced through the door and the zombies inside the room turned en masse and began to file into the hall, no doubt to attack Sarge and the rest of my people.

I shifted my attention back to Jeremiah, lifted both hands and prepared myself to go all out, to burn like a jet engine, so hot I'd melt the railing.

"Ever been cremated?" I gave him my most evil smile.

"Is that a trick question?" He gestured with the pistol. "You can't kill me and save your precious sweetcheeks grunt over there. The moment I die, the zombies go rogue and eat everything within a ten-mile radius, including him."

I didn't lower my hands. "What do you want?"

"I'd still like you both to come with me. I even have snazzy transportation."

"Like hell."

"Not *that* bad, I don't think." He smiled. "It's just a bite...and then no worries."

"Fuck you. They always sound hungry and they reek. You're a shitty salesman."

Jake laughed. The zombies shifted and the Samoan moaned as if he tried to protest. The mime, however, stayed silent.

"You're hurting the feelings of certain undead people," Jeremiah warned.

"Let's make a deal," Jake offered. "You let her go. I'll come along with you."

My heart took a nasty lurch. "Jake—no, dammit!"

"I want her," Jeremiah said, sounding unimpressed by his offer. "A zombie who can shoot fire would be very useful."

"I'm a barrier mage. I'd be your own personal invisible bulletproof vest."

Jeremiah paused. "Hmm. Yeah. Sounds great." He tapped a finger against his chin. "I'll take both, then."

Jake looked at me, turning the intensity of his gaze up to redline. "Andrea, did I tell you I think I love you?"

My breath caught in my throat. "I love you t—wait...*think*? What? You have some kind of sliding scale? You have to run it by committee or something?"

He shrugged and flashed me that troublemaker grin. If I lived through this, I'd make him pay.

"That's sweet," Jeremiah said. "Touching, like the Lifetime channel or baby seals. Now you can rot together as the undead, working for me. Goodbye."

I readied myself for one last play, even if it meant I had to blow apart the entire balcony in one final defiant supernova.

Ed the zombie mechanic shuffled toward me. Mime zombie and Samoan zombie leaned toward Jake's throat, moaning happily. I drew in breath to shout, to scream, to set loose an inferno.

Jake stared right at me with that same intensity I'd seen that day on the street, the first time I'd noticed him beyond the police barricades. His voice sounded low and perfectly calm. "Light me on fire, Andrea."

For an instant I was sure I'd heard him wrong, so insane was his request. I readied myself to light up the two zombies, hoping to free him, even as Dead Ed put his hand on my shoulder and tightened his cold fingers in my shirt. I couldn't kill all these targets at once without burning us all up. One of us would get bitten, no matter what I did. I couldn't breathe. Despair choked me. I wanted to scream, wanted to cry, wanted to sear the world for its cruelty—giving me Jake and then taking him from me just when we finally realized what we meant to each other.

Jake never blinked. "Trust me."

And I did.

My stream of fire flared so hot it burned blue-white. It shot out toward him, three feet at its core, tongues of flame spitting off its sides. It streaked right for his chest...and hit his barrier and deflected directly into the mime and the Samoan, throwing them backward with searing force. The burning Samoan toppled over the railing. The mime whirled around in circles, slapping at his flaming beret, his greasepaint bubbling as his face melted. Jake dropped down, so fast I barely saw it, snatched up his Beretta and fired.

Ed the zombie, whose stinking carrion breath had been wafting in my face with his crooked teeth just inches from my flesh, fell with part of his skull missing. The slide on the Beretta came back, the pistol now empty.

I spun back toward Necromancer Jeremiah, determined to end this forever. His face twisted with shock and outrage. He lifted his pistol, and before I could loose my spell, he pulled the trigger. The muzzle flashed like a picture bulb.

The bullet ricocheted off the barrier that shimmered in front of me just in time, and the last zombie bodyguard dropped to its knees, a neat hole in its forehead. The necromancer's eyes widened. I couldn't send fire at him because Jake's barrier blocked my line of attack. The pistol muzzle moved toward Jake, but Jake swung his arm, whipping the barrier around and into the necromancer first, knocking him off the edge.

I heard a scream and crashing branches and a thud. Jake and I ran to the edge of the balcony and looked down, but I couldn't see anything in the thick foliage of shrubs and trees and hedges.

The gunfire had grown louder and almost constant, punctuated with thunderclap explosions. It sounded like the Battle of Moscow raged out in the hall. Jake dragged me back from the railing. Before I could speak he folded me in his arms and kissed me. Kissed my lips, then my face, and my lips again, holding me in a fierce, strong grip as if he never wanted to let me go again.

I finally broke the kiss, breathless. “Come on, we have to find my people.”

Three zombies had wandered back inside the room from the hall. They staggered toward us. I stepped forward and gathered my power—but again, before I could cut loose, gunfire roared and one zombie head exploded like a cantaloupe filled with plastic explosives. When the zombie collapsed, I saw Sarge standing behind it, dark blood all over his combat gear and armor, the M249 SAW braced up against his shoulder, its barrel smoking. One of the zombies turned toward him. A golf club hissed down and crushed its skull, and Rafe stood there with his wolfish leer. Stefan grabbed the last zombie and bashed its head against the wall, leaving a huge dent in the wallpaper and a bigger dent in the zombie’s forehead. He dusted his hands off and shoved them into the pockets of his tuxedo slacks, rocked on his heels and managed to look inordinately pleased with himself.

A moment later Mai and Hanzo rushed in. Gavin followed them, dragging an empty rocket-propelled grenade launcher on the ground behind him, looking tired and disheveled. Squeegee came next, fur still all fluffed out, hair standing up Halloween-cat style. Last came Tiffany, a TEC-9 in each hand, her wings spread like a hawk, streaked with soot and blood, looking like some video-gamer geek’s secret fantasy.

I ran to them, unable to stop grinning. They rushed toward me and surrounded me. Everybody talked at once, and Mai was crying, and I think Gavin cried too. I swiped at my cheeks and found them wet, crying and I didn’t care. Jake’s arms slipped around me, and everybody was close, smelling of war and violence, but we were still here.

Still here. Together. We’d all pulled through, and with Jake, that was the only thing in the world that mattered to me.

Chapter Twenty-Six: A Long Road Home

Defeated Undead Army of the Unrighteous Order of the Falling Dark

Passenger Seat Audi S6 Sedan

NW Pittock Drive, Portland, Oregon

8:48 p.m. PST April 19th

The world came back slowly for Jeremiah Hansen, transitioning from a black morass of nothingness to a gray one. His head thudded with pain. He opened his eyes and realized he sat in a car. A really nice car. Blake's car.

"What happened?" His words came out as a groan.

"You were knocked off the balcony during the final battle and lost consciousness upon impact," Blake answered. "I took the initiative of removing you from the shrubs and leaving the area."

He raised his hand to his forehead, rubbing his temple. Dozens of scrapes and cuts lashed his forearms. He stank of smoke and evergreen shrubs worse than a hanging air freshener pine tree that had dangled in a barroom its entire life. "Did we win?"

"Unfortunately not."

Well, that sucked. "Where are we now?"

"I took the precaution of decamping to our staging area

when momentum turned against us." Blake pointed up the hill at the mercenary compound, though trees blocked much of the view. Part of the house and grounds had caught on fire. Single gunshots rang out from time to time. The red and blue strobe of emergency lights bathed the front of the house. He could see tiny figures running around in some of the spotlights.

"Shit," he said. "That didn't exactly turn out like I wanted."

"Indeed. Do you retain control over any of our undead assets?"

Jeremiah closed his eyes and checked his silver web. All the cords had been severed and lay in a nasty ethereal tangle in his mind. Hundreds of zombies. Gone.

Again.

"No," Jeremiah said.

"Unfortunate."

"At least we got away."

Blake turned and looked at him. The man's eyes were colder than a dead mackerel. "I believe the time has come for some significant...readjustments...to the operating hierarchy."

Jeremiah froze as fear iced through his veins. That was the shit bad guys said right before they killed somebody off. He had no weapons and no zombies to defend him. He glanced at Blake's hands. Thank God they were empty. But did that mean Blake had something else up his sleeve? Was the passenger seat Jeremiah sat in secretly constructed to channel 50,000 volts and eject his electrocuted corpse into the night? And if he got hit with 50,000 volts, would his hair catch on fire? That seemed particularly distasteful, especially after his run-in with the lady fire slinger from the warmest pits of Hell.

Blake seemed to read his thoughts and a smile quirked the corner of his lips. The smile did nothing to quell Jeremiah's fears. He started to reach for the door handle and realized he was buckled in.

"No need for dismay, Mr. Hansen. I intend you no harm. You have certain talents hard to come by in this world. I do not waste resources with impunity."

"So you're not going to kill me?"

"On the contrary. Rest assured you have nothing to fear from me." He smiled again—a sharkish grin showing off very white teeth. "Yet, things have indeed changed. Your corporation is being...absorbed into mine. A takeover, if you will. Though I would hope it isn't altogether hostile."

"What are you talking about?"

"You will work for me now. Oh, you'll be paid very well for your services. But I think the time has come to embrace a wider, more dynamic vision for our, or should I say, *my* company. You followed the time-honored, but pedestrian philosophy of first attaining wealth, and then using it to attain power. I know a few...shortcuts, and I have larger dreams than a gelatin-manufacturing industry, I must admit. I believe my hour has come at last."

"All right." Jeremiah sighed out the breath he'd been holding. So he wouldn't be top dog any longer. So what? It had been nothing but a constant pain in the ass anyway. His operation had been all teeth and no tail and he'd been forced to focus too much on the day-to-day minutiae. He had a sneaking and grudging suspicion that Blake might be able to do things better. "I have a few conditions though."

Blake chuckled. It was a dry, whispery sound, like wind rattling rotting reeds. "Name them."

"A good health-care plan. Full coverage, and I don't want my premiums going up every other month. With dental and prescription coverage, mind you. Six week's vacation. Performance bonuses, including a healthy severance package. And...sex ninjas."

"Most of those can be met easily enough. However, the last condition...we shall see."

"Great." Better than he'd hoped for actually. "What now?"

"Now we prepare," Blake said. "We make some acquisitions. Network. Seed the public consciousness and test the market of the zeitgeist. World domination is attained with great care, one day at a time, minute upon minute, a mountain built of countless grains of sand."

Blake shifted the Audi into reverse, gracefully backed out, and they drove down the road into the night.

Chapter Twenty-Seven: All Quiet on the Urban Front

Mercenary Wing Rv6-4 "Zero Dogs"
Mandalay Bay, Poolside
Las Vegas Boulevard, Las Vegas, Nevada
1118 Hours PST April 28th

I was pretty happy.

Check that. I was *really* happy. At this exact moment I sprawled on a lounge chair near the pool and baked in the sun. Jake and I had escaped the Portland rain and fled to the Mandalay Bay hotel in Las Vegas for the rest of his leave. The ice in my glass clinked and rattled as it melted. Palm fronds rustled in the breeze. I squinted up at the vibrant blue sky through my sunglasses and thought about nothing at all.

"I knew I was pressing my luck," Jake said from the lounge chair beside me. "Up six hundred, all my chips bet the hard way, and the dice come up seven. That shooter stank of bad luck, and I knew it from the beginning."

I lifted my head and glared at him over the top of my sunglasses. "Excuse me? *I* was throwing the dice, if you'll remember. And I do *not* stink of bad luck."

He grinned and sniffed the air. "Yep. Suntan lotion and bad luck."

I leaned back and closed my eyes again. "Well, I didn't have any problem winning. Besides, your whining has disturbed my sun-inspired meditation."

"Evil of me."

"Yep."

The rest of Merc Wing Rv6-4 Zero Dogs were scattered across Las Vegas and staying in various hotel-casinos until the repairs to our house were finished. Well, not that long. I'd splurge for a week in Sin City using a chunk of our government funds, and then we'd be back to staying at some cheap national chain motel in Portland until the contractors fixed all the fire, bullet and explosives damage. Most of the repair costs had to come out of our bank account since our homeowner's insurance policy didn't cover banzai zombie attacks. An egregious oversight, I now realized. The loss of our Bradley Fighting Vehicle hurt. Hurt bad.

Special Forces Captain Jake Sanders had pulled some strings with the big dogs and we'd ended up getting two-thirds of the contract payment on Necromancer Jeremiah Hansen, although none of the charred bodies had been identified as his. It was entirely possible to survive that fall with a bit of luck, and there'd been no dead body below that balcony. I knew because I'd checked.

That's pretty much how the story ended. Zero Dogs victorious again, story at eleven.

Oh, and I never wanted to see another zombie for as long as I lived, maybe even longer.

Speaking of stories, before we'd left for Vegas, Gavin had told me he wanted to write a new book based on our adventures. In it, he planned to change me into a horny, yet depressed, female centaur and Jake into a demon with three penises—a tri-cock monstrosity, if you will—with magical sperm that cured mental illness. I told him if he wrote that book he'd discover, to his vast grief, *exactly* how it felt to be set on fire from the inside out. So he'd decided to stay across town at the Circus Circus, as far from me as possible. Wise choice. *Very* wise choice, indeed.

"I wonder what everyone else's up to," Jake said.

"I don't. Most of them have probably been arrested by now. Not my problem because I'm on vacation. And so are you." I exaggerated a little on the *not my problem* part, but I'd brought along some bail money. Just in case.

"Yeah." Jake stretched and grabbed his Corona. "Seven days R&R."

"And then back to Fort Bragg."

He stayed quiet for a long moment. "Only for a short while. Then I'll be back on the West Coast again."

"I wish you could stay. Closer, I mean."

"So do I. But there are always airplanes." He reached out and traced a finger down my cheek. "I'm not going anywhere, Captain Walker. And neither are you."

We didn't say anything for a while, both of us content to bask in sunrays, not wanting to think any further into the future than to decide where we wanted to eat dinner.

I finished my drink and rattled the ice at Jake. "I'm empty. How about a refill?"

"What am I? Your cabana boy?"

"Exactly. Why do you think I rented a cabana? I expect you to wait on me. I'm a princess. No, a fire goddess. You'd do well to remember that, soldier boy."

"And what the hell do I get out of this arrangement?"

I smiled but kept my eyes closed. "I'll warm you up tonight."

"Do I have to wait that long? Because that bikini looks as if it's begging to come off."

"Ahem." I rattled my glass again. "Drink first."

"Yeah. Let me get right on it." He leaned in and kissed me on the lips, then began to trace kisses along my jaw, down my neck...

Jake's cell phone rang and shattered the mood, leaving our

peace and quiet in jagged shards on the pool decking.

"I thought I advised you to throw that thing in the pool?" I said.

He grumbled something disagreeable while he tossed towels left and right, digging for the phone. I started to hum "Cheeseburger in Paradise" along with the ringtone, just to be obnoxious. I'd changed his ringtone on the plane as a surprise. He didn't seem to appreciate the joke, though. He finally found the phone and favored me with a raised eyebrow as he brought it to his ear.

"Captain Sanders." He listened for a moment and then glanced at me. The look on his face made me sit up in alarm. He stared off at the bright blue pool water, and his scowl deepened as he listened. I could hear a deep voice from the cell. It sounded like Sarge...

"No," Jake after a pause. "No, don't do anything yet. I'll let her know. Thanks, Sarge. How's Shawn? Yeah?" Jake laughed, and I relaxed a little. Laughter meant the world wouldn't end in the next ten minutes. "Tell him he needs better taste in men." A pause. "All right, yeah, we'll sort it out. She'll call you back. Take care, man." He snapped his phone shut, put it back on the table and sat back down on the lounge chair. Sunlight flashed off his sunglass lenses.

I waited for him to speak. And waited. The silence grew unbearable.

"You going to tell me what the hell that was about? Or would you rather sleep in the lobby tonight?"

Jake shrugged with an irritating amount of nonchalance. "I didn't want to bother you with a lot of distractions. That was Sarge."

"Why'd he call *you*? Why didn't he just call *me*?"

"Probably because you threw your cell phone into the pool already."

Oh yeah. "Is there trouble?"

"Calm down, Batgirl. Nothing to get excited about. Let's

see...a bunch of the contractors all quit because they say your house is haunted. It seems a ghost jellyfish has been seen floating around the worksite—"

"A ghost jellyfish? Our house is haunted by a *jellyfish*?"

"And Sarge wanted me to let you know another job's come up. A gigantic Japanese fire-breathing chicken called a Basan is running around attacking Crispy Chicken to Go franchises in Beaverton and Gresham. Now their corporate representatives want the giant chicken fried."

"How much are they paying?" I hesitated, and then shook my head. "No. *Nope.* I'm on vacation. With you. Giant chickens can wait. And I don't even want to know about the ghost jellyfish."

Jake leaned in close and tried out his terrible French accent. "You say the most romantic things, *mon cheri.* I cannot resist talk of giant fowl and ectoplasm-based invertebrates."

"Then carry me to my room, cabana boy." I strove for imperious, but found it a challenge not to laugh. "Your fire goddess is exhausted from fighting zombies."

He flashed me the grin I'd come to love and scooped me off my lounge chair into his arms. He carried me along the deck, past the sun-dappled water of the pool. I loved the feel of his skin and muscles. I snuggled closer to him as the warm breeze traced along my skin. It didn't take much effort to ignore the stares of the other hotel guests.

I lifted my head toward his, lips parted, eyes half-closed.

He paused on the deck and kissed me deeply again...

...and then threw me in the pool.

Son. Of. A. Bitch.

About the Author

Keith Melton has written two other completely unfunny books, *Blood Vice* and *Run, Wolf*. He has the annoying tendency of referring to his friends as minions and dislikes gelatin desserts. He is currently plotting his return to power from a reeducation camp in the desolation of Eastern Oregon. *The Zero Dog War* is Keith Melton's third published title.

To learn more about Keith, please visit www.keithmelton.net.

CPSIA information can be obtained at www.ICGtesting.com
Printed in the USA
LVOW091651191211

260159LV00003B/81/P